ALSO BY JOSEPH FLYNN

The Concrete Inquisition
Digger
The Next President
Hot Type
Farewell Performance
Gasoline, Texas
The President's Henchman
The Hangman's Companion
Pointy Teeth
Blood Street Punx
Nailed
One False Step
Still Coming
Still Coming Expanded Edition
(with Committing Fiction blog,
List of Characters, Biographies of
Major Characters, Sample Scene Breaks)

Coming Fall 2011
The third Jim McGill novel

Round Robin

by

Joseph Flynn

Stray Dog Press, Inc.
Springfield, IL
2011

Published by Stray Dog Press, Inc.
Springfield, IL 62704, U.S.A.

Originally published as an eBook, May 2011
First Stray Dog Press, Inc. Printing, September, 2011
Copyright © Stray Dog Press, Inc., 2011
All rights reserved

Visit the author's web site: *www.josephflynn.com*

Flynn, Joseph
    Round Robin / Joseph Flynn
    339 p.
    ISBN 978-0-9830312-4-6

Printed in the United States of America

PUBLISHER'S NOTE
This is a work of fiction. Names, characters, places, and incidents are either the product of the author's imagination or are used fictitiously; any resemblance to actual persons, living or dead, events, or locales is entirely coincidental.

Book design by Aha! Designs

DEDICATION

For my Godparents,
William and Virginia Flynn,
and for my aunt Ruth Leroux and
in memory of Chef Paul Leroux

ACKNOWLEDGEMENTS

My thanks to Caitie and Catherine
for the words and the pictures.

Round
Robin

PROLOGUE

On the night of November 9, 1989, Manfred Welk lay in his East Berlin Stasi prison cell singing *The Police State Blues,* a personal composition.

Lord, here I am in jail,
Yet another day,
These walls 'n' bars that hold me,
Ain't never goin' away.

Manfred sang in English, doing his best to twist his pretzel-thick German accent into a Mississippi Delta growl.

They put me here five years ago…
Sent me away for life,
All 'cause of an evil woman,
That witch I called my wife.
Gave that woman ev'rything,
Ev'rything that money could buy,
And how the hell does she thank me?
She turns me in for bein' a spy!

Manfred was accompanied on harmonica by his cellmate, Billy Tuxton, late of Manchester, England. Billy stood on his cot and looked out the cell window as he played. On the other side of the Wall, he could see the bright lights of West Berlin. Freedom, fraüleins, fornication and foaming beer, all but close enough to reach out and touch. And tonight it looked like the whole damn town was having a party. The sight made Billy's heart break.

He wailed on his mouth harp as Manfred moved on to the next verse.

> *You know you can't trust women,*
> *They'll always turn you out,*
> *And, damn sure, stay away from mine,*
> *'Cause she's one real sour Kraut!*

Manfred smiled as Billy's playing faltered momentarily. That last line always made the little Engländer laugh. Then both men revved it up for their big finale.

> *But one thing I got to tell you,*
> *One thing I gotta say,*
> *Won't always sing*
> *These police state blues,*
> *I'll get outta here some way...*
> *If they lock me up forever,*
> *I'll live forever and a day,*
> *Yeah, they can lock me up forever,*
> *I'll live forever and a day!*

Manfred and Billy belted out a reprise, giving it their all.

This was invariably the point at which the guards banged on their door and shouted at them to shut the hell up — just to let them know how long forever really could be — but tonight there was no interruption. Confronted by the unexpected quiet, Manfred and Billy fell silent of their own accord. They looked at each other and then at the cell door ... waiting ... wondering.

Had the guards developed a taste for the blues? Would Manfred and Billy hear polite applause for their performance? *Had the guards deserted their posts?*

Not knowing what to expect, Billy glanced back out the window, and he started to tremble.

"Bloody hell, bloody hell!" he shouted. "Would you look at this?"

"What?" Manfred asked, bounding to his feet.

Billy turned a stunned face to his cellmate.

"The Wall ... it's bleedin' open!"

Manfred leaped up onto the cot next to Billy. He braced himself on the cell walls, his arms around Billy, so his great weight wouldn't collapse the cot. The two of them watched as a huge throng of people flooded out of the East and into the West.

Where were the border police? Where were the dogs? Where was the gunfire?

Even more amazingly, people flocked the other way, too, heading to the East. As the groups merged, people embraced, danced, drank. By the hundreds, by the thousands. Right out in the street. In East Berlin. What would Marx and Lenin think?

Billy looked at Manfred, anxiously.

"Tell me you see it, too. That it isn't some bloody hallucination."

Manfred smiled and nodded. He draped one massive arm around the little Brit.

"It's real, Billy ... the Wall's open. We've outlasted the bastards. We've won. "

Billy smiled back, hugged Manfred and then turned his gaze back to the window, tears running down his cheeks. Manfred took another look at the glorious spectacle, too. He was sure that he and Billy would be free soon.

He returned to his cot, lay down again and resumed singing.

Not the blues in English this time, but a lullaby in German.

As if there were a small child nearby.

CHAPTER 1

Chicago, October, 1990

Round Robin Phinney presided over the main counter at Screaming Mimi's Deli with a carving knife in one hand and a serving fork in the other. At five-eight and pushing two hundred and ten pounds, Robin didn't look like someone you messed with at the best of times, and especially not when she was holding sharp-edged steel. But at Screaming Mimi's, everybody went after everybody. It was expected. It was how the place got its name.

In the thick of the lunch crowd, Tone Morello was going after Robin right now.

"You ever gonna get it through your fat head, what my name is?" Tone asked.

Robin gave him a brief look while continuing to carve paper-thin slices of rare roast beef with a precision a brain surgeon would envy.

"Now, Ant–knee, don't be that way. Be nice. I might give you a little something extra."

Robin batted her eyelashes and made a kissy face at Tone.

Tone stuck an index finger down his throat.

"You know what your problem is, Robin?" he said. "You're terminally hard up. You couldn't get a date if the dog–catchers' convention came to town. "

Tone had spent the better part of a week thinking that one up.

It got a chorus of *oooohs* and *aaaahs* and *uh–ohs* from the lunch crowd. They knew this was going to be a good one. Robin replied without bothering to look at Tone.

"Yeah, that's my problem, all right. Yours is you're thirty–seven years old and you still wear a training condom on little Peter. That's your problem, Ant–Knee."

Several of the male customers groaned in sympathy for Tone. The women hooted and howled. Which wasn't music to Tone's ears. He considered himself quite the ladies' man.

Robin served Tone his sandwich with a smile.

He didn't have time to think of a new line, so he fell back on a reliable old one.

"How would you know how big I am? You ain't seen it, and you never will."

"Don't have to," Robin said. "It's those dainty little hands and feet of yours. They give you away."

Tone was not a small guy at six–one and one eighty–five. He was darkly handsome, too, even if it did look like he had his hair done at Jiffy Lube. And he actually was a big hit with a lot of the ladies. But he did have unusually delicate hands and feet, and he was sensitive about them.

Robin knew it like she could read his mind.

She said with glee, "Small here, small there ... gotta be small everywhere."

"It's the nose that tells the size," Tone said, hoping to salvage some pride.

Tone had an emphatic Roman nose.

"Well," Robin conceded, "I have heard that you give good nose, Ant-knee."

This time even the men joined in the laughter. It was too much for Tone to bear. It also brought him back to his original point.

Red faced and tight lipped, he said, "My name's not Ant'ny, it's not Anth-o-ny, it's not even Tony. I'm Tone. Tone Morello. I had my named changed legal. You could look it up in the TV Guide, or wherever they keep the list of official names. Or you could just let it finally sink into that fat head a yours, you know."

Tone wanted to deck her.

Except Robin still had an eight-inch knife in her mitt.

He knew she'd use it, too.

As it was, she slapped her forehead with her free hand and said, "Yeah, what a fathead I am. How could I forget a name like Tone Deaf? No, wait, that's not it." Robin made a show of thinking hard. "Tone Arm? Dial Tone? No, I know, it's Tone Mo-ron-o ... Aw, heck, it's just Ant-knee."

Tone wasn't as dumb as Robin made out. He knew when he'd had enough. He took his sandwich over to Mimi at the cash register and asked for a bag so he could have it to go.

Robin turned to the crowd of people still waiting to order lunch.

"All right," she said, "who's next?"

Screaming Mimi's Deli, just west of North Michigan Avenue, just north of the Chicago River, occupying a long, narrow, street-level space at the corner of a building with landmark status, in the 38th year of a 99-year lease, served a purpose above and beyond offering highly spiced, fairly priced food to hordes of office workers, bicycle couriers, meter maids, retail clerks and cops. It gave everybody a chance to blow off steam. You could come into Mimi's and say anything you wanted to anybody else who was there. At the top of your voice if you liked.

Patrons at Mimi's were served by three counter people. Manny Tavares, an unrepentant '60s leftist, handled political arguments. Judy Kuykendahl held forth on women's liberation and sexual polemics. Round Robin Phinney, at center stage, took on all comers. On any subject.

Each counter person could hand the customer his order over the top of the counter, or could step forward into nooks between the display cases, and plunk down the plate of food on a chest high shelf no more than a foot from the idiot he or she was shouting at. It was, however, considered bad form for any employee to spray saliva on the order. Unless the customer had done so first. These nooks were known as the in–your–face spaces.

In the interest of preventing actual mayhem and total anarchy, there were some house rules. Mimi posted them on the back of the cash register just inside the entrance. They were:

— Money talks, all else walks.
(Mimi didn't believe in sharing her income with American Express, Visa or Mastercard. And don't even think about personal checks. Hers was strictly a cash business.)

— No fighting: fists, food or otherwise.
(Altercations were limited to battles of wits; words were the weapon of choice.)

— No four-letter words, foreign or domestic.
(Mimi was a great fan of the late Bill Veeck, who had believed that common vulgarisms are a sure sign of a limited intellect and an even more stunted vocabulary.)

— No obscene gestures, especially Italian.
(Mimi called these "four-finger" words, even if you needed only one finger.)

— No Travis Bickle evil eyes.
(Mimi had seen "Taxi Driver" and had decided that anybody with a lunatic stare or who even said "You talking to me?" funny would get the heave-ho.)

— No producing offensive body odors.
(Only because a couple of clowns had made this rule necessary, going after one another with a series of noxious emissions and exhalations. Mimi had never imagined people could pass gas and belch at will. At a place where people ate, for God's sake.)

— No ...
(The last rule was deliberately left incomplete to indicate Mimi's freedom to impose further rules as she saw fit.)

All of these edicts were upheld by Mimi's enforcer of the week, one of the cop regulars at the deli. The job rotated every Monday, with the cop getting free lunches for his trouble.

If you broke one of Mimi's rules, you were gone for good. There were no appeals. She'd even put your name on her no-carryout list, so you couldn't have your lunch delivered, either.

Within those limits, everyone and everything was fair game. Customers would jump on the deli staff. Employees would slash right back. Each group could and would do battle within its own ranks. Alliances between cliques of customers and staff formed in one instant and were betrayed the next. Demonstrations of quick, scalding wit were rewarded with laughter and applause. The slow, the dull, the meek and the weak were eaten alive. Which always made everyone else feel good as they headed back to work.

Mimi Greenblatt was the ringmaster.

Round Robin Phinney was the undisputed heavyweight champ.

This, of course, made Robin the target for every wise guy, young and old, who walked through the door. Her current opponent was David Solomonovich. At age 14, he was some kind of a genius. He spent his mornings at the University of Chicago and his afternoons at his father's nearby lab doing some kind of consulting. He stopped into Mimi's every day well after the lunch hour rush for a carryout sandwich. He said he timed his arrivals so he could go *mano a mano* with Robin and not face any distractions. The truth was, David was small for his age and tended to get stepped on in a crowd.

David kept bragging to Robin about what it was he studied and what kind of work he did, and she kept forgetting. Intentionally. Which drove David crazy. Robin knew this of course; it was her way of keeping an edge on him. David might be smarter than Einstein, but Robin was as wily as Machiavelli. It would be a while yet before he'd be a real challenge.

There was one problem David presented for Robin, however.

In the time honored tradition of eccentric geniuses, he could behave erratically. As proof, he seemed to be developing a crush on Robin.

Today, he greeted her with, "Hey, Robin, how's my main bad mama?"

"Your nanny letting you wander off campus again, David?" Robin asked. The neighborhood around the U. of C. was predominantly African-American. "Or are you watching *Mod Squad* reruns after school?"

"I work after school, as you very well know," he said stiffly, his pride wounded, "and I've been self-sufficient since I was two."

"Great, I'll get you a plaque for your office. What'll it be, kiddo?"

David looked at Robin slyly.

"I'd like some tongue."

Robin shrugged and nonchalantly stuck hers out at him.

"You know that's not what I meant," David said, turning red.

Manny grinned at David's discomfort; Judy gave a frown of feminist disapproval; Mimi laughed out loud. The deli owner thought David was precious. She often put a free cookie into his carryout bag. That drove David crazy, too. He glared at Mimi. She put a hand over her face, but kept laughing.

Robin decided to indulge in a rare display of mercy. After all, David was young, and he was brilliant. She didn't want him to grow up and become a mad scientist or something.

"You want calf tongue, David?" she asked. "On rye? With the usual stuff on it? I have to think that's what you were talking about. Not that a handsome young guy like you, someone with a lot of class, would use some slimy lounge lizard line on an old battle-axe like me."

Robin was thirty-nine.

The boy looked at her and said, "You're not so bad ... or so old."

He meant it, too, Robin knew. He was paying her as sincere a compliment as his shaky young ego dared. That was what troubled her. She could handle all the hostility in the world without batting an eye. Simple affection, even when it came totally misplaced from a young boy, scared her.

"You want that sandwich, David?"

"Yeah," he said. As she bent to work on it, he started to tell her about what he was doing these days at school and on the job.

Robin cut him off without bothering to look up. "Boring."

"It is not. Superconductivity is utterly fascinating. Our new composite materials are getting closer to working at room temperature."

"So's the fish I'm thawing for dinner."

"The work I'm doing is going to affect every facet of your life someday."

"David, my life is boring, and so is your work."

He continued to argue with Robin until Mimi reminded him of the time and sent him packing with a free cookie. Which he may have resented, but was smart enough to take.

"I think you've got a new young beau," Mimi said to Robin.

"Great. As soon as I develop a taste for child molestation, I'll whisk him off to my boudoir," she replied.

The two women sat in Mimi's office at the back of the kitchen. It was 2:30, the time at which the deli closed; it opened at 7:30. The staff started at 7:00, and cleanup lasted until 3:00. Mimi had decided long ago that eight hours a day were long enough for anyone to work. But she and Robin worked only seven and a half. They left the cleanup to the rest of the staff. After all, Mimi was the owner and Robin was buying her out.

The plan was that Robin would complete the purchase over the next two years, making the final payment when Mimi turned sixty-five and retired. Mimi finished tallying the day's take. She banded and stacked the bills by denominations and put them in a bank deposit bag. She sealed the bag and put it on the floor next to her desk.

"Another good day," she said. "Thank God people always get hungry."

"Yeah," Robin answered without enthusiasm.

"What?" Mimi asked. "You're letting a little boy's puppy love bother you?"

Robin rolled her eyes. "It's not David. I can handle him like anyone else. It's my house."

"What about it?"

"Just about everything about it. I've got to go home and wait for a plumber because the garbage disposal's all gummed up. It happened this morning just before I left for work, and I can just imagine what my kitchen's going to smell like. Last week it was the plumber again when a pipe burst, and while the guy was down in the basement he said he wasn't an expert but thought it looked like I should have my wiring checked."

"I thought you had all that stuff done when you bought the place," Mimi said.

"I had most of it done when I bought the place," Robin corrected, " and that was seventeen years ago. Two years after I started here."

"It's been that long that we've been together?"

"Yeah."

"My, how time flies. I'll be gone before you know it."

It wasn't clear to Robin whether Mimi meant retired or dead. She didn't seem too happy about either prospect.

"The problem is," Robin said, "if I keep having a lot of expenses with my building, I'm going to have to dip into the money I'm putting aside for the buyout."

That returned Mimi's focus to the present.

"Oh ... that's not good."

"Tell me about it. I might have to take a second job."

That was definitely not good. Not for Mimi. She couldn't have Robin, her star, working in somebody else's deli. That would be like a gourmet place having its chef moonlight. No, that wouldn't do at all. And it wasn't like Robin could pick up some other kind of part-time job, not with her personality. Mimi didn't see her selling shoes or doing telemarketing.

At the same time, Mimi was counting on having Robin buy her out, counting on the money. It would be a pain to find another buyer now, and she couldn't see Robin working for a new owner. She really couldn't see selling her deli to anyone but Robin, for that matter. There was a tradition to carry on.

"Don't worry," Mimi told Robin, "we'll work something out."

"Of course, we will," came a male voice.

"You bet," said another.

The second voice belonged to Sergeant Stanley Prozanski, the cop who escorted Mimi to the bank everyday to deposit her receipts. He was under strict shoot-to-kill orders in the event anyone ever tried to grab's Mimi loot.

Though she'd never admit it, Mimi considered Stan her fella. He was due to retire soon, too, and everyone was sure that when the time came he and Mimi would go off somewhere warm together. Mimi patted her hair and smiled at Stan when she saw him.

Mimi's hair was pink, an unusual shade to be sure, but it was even in tone and her roots never showed thanks to a weekly trip to the beauty parlor. She, herself, liked the color of her hair, saying it set off her emerald green, contact-lens-enhanced, eyes. Mimi believed in doing everything she could to look young. Everything that didn't involve exercise, dieting or surgery. She believed greatly in the powers of cosmetics and clothing with a high elastic content. Her approach to youth pleased her. She said that in the right light she could pass for forty.

To which a wise-guy in the deli had once replied, "Yeah, the right light. A firefly at five hundred yards."

The wise-guy had been banned within a week after Robin, having seen that Mimi actually had been hurt by the crack, had provoked the joker into calling her a woman's least favorite four-letter name ... the one that rhymes with punt.

Stan had said that if he'd heard the guy make either slur he would have shot him. Robin privately doubted that, but Mimi didn't. Stan's lunch was always on the house.

The other man who'd entered the office was the only man in Robin's life. The only man she truly loved, her father, Dan Phinney.

"Hi, Daddy," she said.

And for the first time all day Robin smiled.

CHAPTER 2

Robin knew it was ridiculous, but she couldn't help it. Every time she saw her father she felt like a little girl again. She almost expected him to sweep her up into his arms and take her out for an ice cream cone. Robin also suspected that her father still saw her the way she was when she was a child. Happy and pretty and slim.

He had never spoken one critical word to her in his life. Even after her dark, shining hair had been chopped to a dull no-style style, her sparkling blue eyes had turned dark and cold, her long slender shape had been armored under eighty pounds of hard fat, her father's love for her had remained constant, unquestioning and complete.

Robin felt she would die when her father did.

Which he recently almost had.

Which was why she couldn't let him help her with her problem.

"I'm still pretty handy, you know," Dan Phinney said as he drove his daughter home. "And I'm not an invalid."

"You had a major heart attack, Daddy. Less than a year ago."

"So does that mean I can't do a little plumbing and wiring for my girl?"

Dan Phinney had been a building inspector for the City of

Chicago. An honest one. He didn't have to spend his retirement looking over his shoulder and worrying that some vengeful prosecutor might be about to indict him for past sins. In fact, he'd taken his job so seriously that he'd taught himself all of the building trades he'd once inspected. He both knew good work when he saw it and he could do it himself.

"Daddy, you know what the doctor said. You're lucky to be alive."

Dan turned to Robin and said, "Aren't we all?"

Robin looked at her father. His question was more than rhetorical. Robin stifled a response with razor wire on it. She was a different person with her father.

She said, "Yes, Daddy, we are. But I'm still not going to let you crawl around my building, busting a gut and killing yourself."

"I found that building for you, you know."

"I know. I'll always be grateful. And guilt won't work, either."

Dan Phinney laughed.

"Okay, okay, I give up. How about I just front you the money you need?"

"No."

"Why not? I'm going to leave most of what I have to you anyway."

"Daddy, I want you to live long enough to spend every penny you have."

Dan Phinney sighed and put a hand on his daughter's leg.

"You mind if we pick up your sister before I drop you off? She needs a ride today, too."

Robin said that was fine, and then she smiled wickedly.

"What?" her father asked, seeing Robin's expression.

"I was just thinking. You want to help me? Persuade Nancy to come over and muck out my garbage disposal."

Robin and her father both laughed at the idea.

Robin's sister, Nancy Cassidy, was everything Robin was not. She was petite, blonde, married and the mother of two grown boys. She was three years older than Robin but looked five years younger. Unlike Mimi, Nancy's formula for staying young consisted of granola, tofu, eight glasses of water and vigorous exercise daily. Not that Nancy didn't help her natural hair color along with a few bottled highlights. But most of her good looks came from a fortunate gene pool and the fact that Nancy was *in control of her life.*

She did a pretty good job of controlling her husband, Charlie, and their two sons, Johnny and Michael, too. Charlie had been Nancy's high school sweetheart, and the starting fullback on the football team. Unlike a lot of former teenage jocks, Charlie hadn't gone to fat. Nancy had seen to that. Robin also thought Nancy had somehow made sure that Charlie had kept all his hair, too, without a strand of it going gray. At any rate, they were still a handsome couple, and Robin was sure they still had frequent sex.

Yet another difference with Nancy.

Robin and her father picked up Nancy at the real estate office where she worked part time with Patty Phinney, Robin and Nancy's mother, and Dan's estranged wife. Patty sold condos, lots of them. Nancy managed the office. Nancy's job was supposed to be a full-time position, but she never needed more than four hours a day to do it. The abbreviated schedule was made possible by the fact that nobody would dare cross Nancy or compromise any of the efficiency measures she'd put in place.

Nancy slid easily into Dan's car, a new Chevy Camaro that he'd treated himself to when he'd found out he was going to live. She was so trim that she could glide through the narrow opening and perch comfortably on the minuscule backseat without Robin having to scoot forward.

Nancy kissed her father's cheek and squeezed her sister's shoulder by way of greeting.

"How are you today, Dad?" Nancy asked, buckling her seatbelt.

"Peachy," he said, entering traffic. "Your mother ready for a divorce yet?"

Dan and Patty Phinney had been separated for nineteen years.

"Just as soon as the pope okays it," Nancy replied.

"You know, I think I've been pretty patient with your mother. I've let this separation thing go on almost as long as the time we lived under one roof. I think maybe it's time for a change."

Robin and Nancy glanced at each other.

"How come, Dad?" Nancy asked.

"Well, you know, a good-looking guy like me, driving a fancy car like this, I've been getting a lot of looks from the ladies. Come hither looks."

"Daddy," Robin said, "you're not going to give all your money to some little gold-digger instead of me."

Robin was twitting her sister who already knew that Dan Phinney intended to leave the bulk of his estate to Robin, and professed indifference. That didn't mean, however, that she was going to let Robin's jibe pass unchallenged.

"Maybe you're right, Dad. There's no reason why you shouldn't have a girlfriend, or even a new wife. I'll talk to my pastor about what you and Mom would need for an annulment."

Robin's face fell. She honestly didn't care about her father's money, even though she could have used it at the moment. She'd always felt it was important to make her own way in life ... but the idea of sharing her father's attention with another woman made her heart constrict.

"Yeah, Dad," Nancy continued, twisting the knife, "you could get back into circulation, and maybe you could find someone for Robin and double date."

Robin stared death rays at her sister. She wanted to lash back, but she couldn't. Not in front of her father. Not with his heart condition.

So she said, "You know, Nancy, it's been a long time since you've dropped by Mimi's. Why don't you stop in for lunch tomorrow? On me."

Robin's smile would have chilled a Sicilian hitman.

But it didn't make Nancy blink.

"Thanks, but I couldn't. All that fatty meat, all those empty calories. Not for me, thanks."

Oooh, Robin wanted to — well, what she'd like to do was sit on Nancy. Squish her like a bug. Leave nothing but hands and feet and Summer Blonde hair sticking out. Dan Phinney interrupted this pleasant thought.

"Actually, I am thinking of finding someone for Robin," he said.

"What?" both daughters asked at once, shocked.

"Relax, honey," he said to Robin. "I mean, I'm trying to think of someone who owes me a few favors who could help you with your building."

"Oh," both girls said. When she heard what the problem was, Nancy added, "I'll just have Charlie stop by."

Nancy's husband was the half owner of a heating-and-cooling business, and was almost as handy around a house as Dan Phinney. Plus, he had a healthy heart since Nancy made him eat as sensibly as she did. On top of that, Charlie was an honestly nice guy who wouldn't mind extending himself for his sister-in-law.

It made perfect sense to let Charlie help her, except Robin didn't want to accept any help from Nancy. Especially after the crack she'd made about Daddy finding a girlfriend.

"Charlie's got enough to do already," Robin said. "You push him too hard as it is, Nancy." There, she'd got her dig in, and from the way Nancy's eyes had narrowed Robin could tell she'd hit a tender spot. Better yet, Dad hadn't noticed or pretended he hadn't.

"Have it your way," Nancy said blandly, having given Robin all the satisfaction she intended to.

Dan Phinney pulled the car over to the curb in front of Robin's Near North house.

"If you don't want Charlie to help," he said, "I'll keep thinking to see if there's someone I know."

"Daddy, I've already got a plumber coming," Robin said, stepping out of the car.

"Plumbers cost money. If I think of someone, he'll work for

free."

While Robin tried to think of an objection, Nancy slid into the front seat and pulled the door closed. Her father waved goodbye and Nancy smirked.

Robin was left standing there, not knowing what Nancy might say to her father now that she had him alone. Not liking what might be coming her way. Whatever it was.

Robin's building was a two-flat with a basement on tree-lined Menominee Street, not far from her work, not far from Lincoln Park, not far from Lake Michigan, smack in the middle of the gentrified, yuppified Near North Side. It sat on a lot-and-a-half. Two months earlier, while she'd been weeding the flower beds out front, a guy had pulled up to the curb in a two-seat Mercedes convertible, given the place the once over, asked her if she was the owner and then offered her $750,000 on the spot for the building.

She'd told him to suck on his dual exhaust.

He'd chuckled good-naturedly, gave her a little wave to show there were no hard feelings and idled off, rubbernecking. She'd heard him call out to a neighbor down the block, and got up from her weeding in time to see the neighbor invite the Mercedes man into his building. Now, the neighbor was gone and so was his house. The yuppie had bought it and torn it down to make way for a new vertical urban palace he was having built. Robin looked at the construction site and thought a neighborhood didn't have to go downhill to change for the worse.

Nineteen years earlier, she'd paid exactly one-tenth of what the Mercedes man had offered for her building. Even then the area had been highly regarded, but yuppies had yet to come into their own and run amok on the real estate market, and the building had been sold at a tax-delinquency auction. The bidding hadn't been terribly competitive because the previous owner had been as negligent in his maintenance as in his tax payments. Back then, Robin had let her father repair all of her home's most egregious faults. In fact, she'd labored right along with him, as far as he'd let her, as far as willing hands and a strong back could compensate for a complete lack of mechanical skills.

What she couldn't accomplish inside, she made up for outside. She'd had the dead tree out front cut down. Then she broke up and dug out the stump herself and planted a wonderful little dogwood that made her heart burst with joy when it blossomed each spring. She'd rented a roto-tiller, turned over the soil, planted seed and grown a lawn green enough to make the Irish sing. She'd put in perennial beds of black–eyed Susans, daisies, golden yarrow, delphiniums and coreopsis, all under planted with early blooming bulbs. And as soon as she was sure the last frost had passed each April, she filled in the beds with a riot of colorful annuals.

After her father had brought the building's life support systems back to working condition, she'd thanked him with all her heart and then absolutely refused to let him do a bit of the plain old scut work. By herself, Robin had chipped away old paint, peeled old wallpaper, pulled up old linoleum, scoured all the fixtures, scrubbed every square inch, and then repainted the place top-to-bottom.

Robin lived in the apartment on the second floor, and there was a small apartment space at the front of the basement, left over from the previous owner. On the first floor, Robin created her park.

The park was Robin's retreat. Retreat from the world, from the past, from herself. She'd started by having every non-supporting wall on the first floor knocked out. The resulting space was loft-like. Robin painted it bright white and refinished the hardwood floors from front to back. In the middle third of the floorspace, to the left as you looked at the rear of the building, Robin had a kidney-shaped piece of moss green carpeting laid. In counterpoint to this, she positioned two large plastic ovals and filled them with tan gravel. Directly in front of the living room windows she had a bi-level pond installed. The lower level was an aquarium; the upper level was a wishing-well into which she dropped a coin daily, collecting and donating the proceeds to charity quarterly.

After the "grass" and "soil" and "water" areas were laid out,

Robin started buying potted plants and trees. She picked carefully, having done her homework. She wanted flora that would do well indoors, that would thrive without running wild, that would provide a lush, green screen against the outside world. She planted tubs of hardy dracaena, rubber trees, jade plants and palms; she bought potted Norfolk Island Pines, ficus, schefflera, coffee plant, citrus, bamboo and Chinese evergreen. She hung baskets of spider plants, trailing jasmine, grape ivy and philodendron. Adjacent to the pond she planted Baby's Tears and English ivy. She nursed containers of New Guinea impatiens, begonias and hibiscus to bloom through the winter.

With the greening of her garden came the accoutrements. Grow lights, watering cans, pruning shears and two honest-to-God park benches bought surplus from the Chicago Park District. Robin spent at least an hour a day in her park and often quite longer. Sometimes she read. Other times she sat and thought. Not infrequently, she cried.

She wouldn't sell her house for all the money in the world.

The problem was, it looked like she'd soon need more money than she had to keep it, and to keep it up.

Robin made $50,000 per year working for Mimi. Which sounded like a lot. Until you got done lopping off all the payroll deductions and health insurance costs. Her house payments were chickenfeed by now, but her property taxes were stupefying. And the premiums for her homeowner's insurance were over the moon. When millionaires moved into the neighborhood the miserable cruds raised your cost of living. They drove up property values and real estate taxes soared. Everybody had to pay the added freight when a neighborhood turned chic. So Robin did. She was not going to lose her house by being late paying her taxes.

She lived simply, which didn't bother her. She paid her bills each month and had just enough left over to make a payment to Mimi Except now she was facing added expenses that she couldn't afford and she wasn't sure what she was going to do about it.

"Robin Phinney?" a man's voice asked.

She snapped out of her reverie and saw a portly older guy in coveralls holding a toolbox. The plumber had arrived.

"Getting to be a real nip in the air, huh?"

Robin hadn't consciously noticed how cold the fall day had grown, but now that the guy had brought it up she realized she was shivering.

"What do you say we go inside and see what I can do for you and how much money you're going to owe me?"

The plumber grinned.

Robin didn't.

That night the nine o'clock news on the TV in Robin's bedroom told her that the city could be in for a hard frost by early morning and showed her half a dozen animated maps explaining just where the cold weather was coming from and how bad it would be. The weatherman seemed gleeful about the prospect of frigid air arriving not two weeks after the official end of summer. Robin killed his inane image with her remote control.

She got out of bed just long enough to turn the heat up to 76 degrees, warmer than she needed but comfortable for all her plants downstairs.

Having to get up for work at 5:30 a.m., Robin usually went to bed early. Tonight she'd barely done the dinner dishes before crawling under the covers. After the plumber had cleared the garbage disposal at a cost of $60, and had advised her either to get a new one at a cost of $249 or start throwing her food waste in the trash, she'd hit bottom, unable to see any solution to her money woes.

Now, facing an assault of cold weather on her morning trip to work, she turned out the lights at 9:35…

… And woke up shaking from the cold. Even under two wool blankets and a goose-down comforter. The sky outside her window was as black as the devil's sense of humor. Three-thirty a.m. Robin slid her feet into her slippers and pulled her robe around her. She crossed the room and put her hand in front of the heat vent.

Cold air poured out. The fan was still on, but the furnace wasn't.

Robin took stock of herself. No headache, no nausea, no blurred vision. So there probably wasn't a gas leak. She was cold, but she was safe.

Then a thought hit her like a slap across the face. The park wasn't safe. All of her plants — and maybe her fish — had to be dying!

Robin started to panic, not knowing how long she'd managed to sleep with the heat being off. Certainly, under the covers, she hadn't felt the cold as immediately as everything downstairs would have. Through pure grit, she got a grip on herself.

She raced to her bedroom closet and pulled out a huge armload of clothes. She ran downstairs to the park. She turned on the lights and her heart sank. All of her plants were turning in on themselves, shrinking from the cold. Robin threw the pile of clothes on the nearest bench. One by one, she started dressing the plants in her garments. Trying to provide them with warmth.

Praying she could save them.

CHAPTER 3

At first light, Robin made a phone call, fervently hoping she would reach a human being and not an answering machine. All around her in the park a bizarre fashion show had been staged. A ficus wore a housedress. A rubber tree was decked out in a ski parka. Four pots of begonias shared the warmth of a woolen muffler.

"Easy Living Heating and Cooling," a voice on the phone spat out .

"It's me, Charlie" Robin said.

"That you, Rob?" Charlie asked, losing some of his abruptness. Instead, there was almost a note of surprise in his voice.

"Yeah. Charlie, are you busy?"

"Out the wah-zoo. You think I'm here this early everyday? A cold snap like this, every jerk who let his furnace go without maintenance is yelling for help. You wouldn't believe it."

"Yes, Charlie, I would."

There was a short pause on the line.

"Your furnace went out, Rob?"

"Middle of the night. I had to run downstairs and put long-johns on all my plants."

Charlie laughed.

"It's not funny, Charlie. Some of them died."

"Sorry, Rob. I'll be right over."

Robin hated the way her brother-in-law shortened her name, but she loved his generous heart. She wondered how he put up with Nancy. Had to be the sex.

"What about being so busy?"

"You're family. Everybody else just got bumped down a notch."

"Can I ask you one more little favor?"

"What?"

"Can we keep this just between us? Not tell Nancy?"

This time there was a long pause.

Finally, Charlie said, "I can't lie to you, Rob. I'd have to tell Nancy. That's just the way our marriage works."

Robin gritted her teeth. Boy, if this guy couldn't keep a furnace repair from Nancy, she was never going to have a worry about him cheating on her. But then the very thought was laughable. Cheat on Nancy and she'd make Lizzie Borden look like Miss Congeniality.

"Let's skip the whole thing then. I never called, okay?"

"That I can manage."

"Can you recommend somebody else I can call?"

"Rob, a cold snap like this, it's God's way of having heating contractors work around the clock. Everybody's gonna be booked."

"Damnit, Charlie," Robin said, "I can't let my park die."

"Rob, all I can tell you is you got a little breathing space. The forecast I heard on my way to work this morning said it's going to warm up again this afternoon and stay seasonable for a few days — before the next cold snap."

"So you think I'll be all right?"

"As long as you find somebody to fix your furnace in the next few days," Charlie said.

Robin got into work late, after the breakfast crowd had come and gone.

Mimi said to her, "In my office."

Robin apologized. "I'm sorry. My heat went out last night and—"

Mimi crooked her finger at Robin, not wanting to hear the details. When her door was closed, Mimi sat behind her desk and looked at Robin.

"I spoke to your father last night," she said.

"What?"

Robin suddenly felt as if she was back in grade school and had been summoned to the principal's office. Her face turned red.

"Don't get upset. I knew him a long time before I ever met you. I wanted to get his opinion of an idea I had last night."

"What idea?" Robin asked uneasily.

"This idea."

Mimi tossed a copy of that day's classified section from the *Trib* on her desk. One ad was circled in red. Robin gave Mimi a look, then picked up the paper and read the ad aloud.

"Wanted. Handy person. Must be able to repair and maintain all mechanical, electrical and plumbing systems in fashionable Near North two-flat." Robin gave Mimi a look before continuing. "In exchange will receive charming garden apartment rent free."

The ad listed Robin's name and phone number, but not her address.

"I got it inserted special, after deadline, because I got a friend over at the paper," Mimi said. "It'll run the next three days."

Robin's face was a mask, an unsmiling mask.

"You had no right to do this. Call your friend and pull the ad."

"You're sure?" Mimi asked quietly.

"Yes."

"Okay. Then I'll have to give you this."

For one dizzying moment, Robin thought Mimi had handed her a severance check, but then she saw the amount was far too large for that. It was several thousand dollars. The amount clicked jarringly into place for Robin a second later.

"This is all the money I've given you so far for the buyout," Robin said.

Mimi nodded.

"Deal's off," she said.

"Just because I was late one day?" Robin couldn't comprehend it. "This is a joke, right?"

Mimi shook her head.

"Robin, sweetheart, if I could afford it, I'd give you this place when I go. But I can't afford it. I've got to have a buyer. If you need to fix up your house, and you won't take help from your father, you won't take help from your sister, you won't take help from me, then you need that money."

Mimi inclined her pink-haired head toward the check in Robin's hands.

"What else are you going to do? I'd still like you to work here, of course. But if you can't, I'll have to understand."

Mimi looked like she might cry.

Robin didn't know whether to cry or rage.

"You cooked this up with my dad," she hissed.

"We talked, honey. I told him what I had in mind. He said he didn't think it would work, that you'd already turned down help from him and Nancy, but I should take my shot."

"I won't have a man in my house," Robin said flatly.

"It could be a woman. Someone good with her hands. The ad says handy *person*."

Robin glowered.

"It might do you some good to have company for a change."

"I don't want company."

Mimi shrugged, looking like she'd lost the battle and it was breaking her heart.

"Goddamnit, Mimi, I'm tempted to hire a lawyer."

"You can't afford one."

Robin looked like she might have a stroke ... and then she put her face into her hands and wept. Mimi gave her a minute before handing her a tissue. Robin blew her nose and backhanded away her tears. She looked straight at Mimi and said, "I'm going to buy this place. I am."

She dropped the check on Mimi's desk.

"Give the ad a chance," Mimi said.

Robin squeegeed one last tear off her cheek.

"I won't have a man in my house."

"Of course not, sweetie. Just see what turns up."

Robin thought back over the course of her morning. She'd tried finding another heating contractor to fix her furnace but, as Charlie had said, they were booked solid for the next week. The weather forecast had predicted that the cold would be back in three days, four at the outside. Maybe Mimi's idea would be her salvation.

"I've got to get ready for the lunch crowd," Robin said, standing up.

"Sure," Mimi said. When Robin got to the door, Mimi stopped her.

"Sweetie."

Robin turned to face her.

"I want you to know it was very hard for me to face the thought of losing you."

Robin barely nodded and left.

Mimi slumped behind her desk.

Oy! That was the hardest thing she'd ever done. Including her divorce.

There was no way in the world she'd really have let Robin go. She'd have jumped over her desk to grab that check back if Robin had headed for the door. But Dan Phinney had told her it would take something drastic to get Robin to go along with her plan.

Well, today she'd been as *meshugge* as she ever planned to be.

If Robin's ad didn't find somebody for her, Mimi would just give her the deli and finally accept Stanley Prozanski's standing proposal of marriage. That wouldn't be exactly the retirement she had planned, but it would have to do.

Be a crying shame though, if she went out known as a soft touch.

CHAPTER 4

When Robin got home her phone was ringing. She was sure who was calling. Some pot-bellied, tattooed simian with dandruff, tufts of hair growing out of his nose and body odor that would gag an alley-cat, somebody who'd had the ad read to him and was eager to knuckle-walk right over and see if he might find a new lair. Well, no thank you. Robin would just let the phone machine handle that little chore.

Except it didn't. The tape was full.

Robin had to wait until the phone stopped ringing.

It started again thirty seconds later.

"What?" she asked harshly, picking up the phone.

"You the one with the ad in the paper for the handyman?" a male voice asked.

"Handy person," Robin corrected.

The guy laughed. "Yeah, right. Well, I'm a man and I'm a person and I'm handy. What I want to know, is it you I'd be workin' for?"

"I'd be very surprised if it was."

"Yeah, me too. 'Cause I got one ball-buster at home already. I don't need another."

The guy called Robin a dike and hung up.

It made her pause and think. She was a master at face-to-face confrontation, but the telephone was a different medium. On the phone, she was either familiar with family or businesslike with business calls. With phone solicitors, she didn't waste her breath and simply hung up on them. If she was going to make this interview thing work, she'd have to see these people in person.

But not at her house.

Nobody was getting that close until she'd had a chance to screen them. What she'd do was listen to the tape. If there was anyone who sounded remotely acceptable she'd invite them down to Mimi's early, before the morning rush got going, buy them a cup of coffee and look them over.

That seemed a safe way to do it.

Robin listened to twenty-two messages. Seventeen callers were male, five were female. Six of the calls were obscene, including four in which the creeps were dumb enough to leave their phone numbers, and who'd be hearing soon from Stan Prozanski. Of the remaining calls, Robin picked the two men and two women who most closely sounded as if they'd been raised indoors by actual human beings.

The two men, however, were chosen strictly to provide legal cover. Mimi had told her that the term "handy person" had been mandated by the newspaper to avoid charges of sex discrimination. So, Mimi had said, while Robin might be excluding half the world's population in her own mind, it wouldn't be a bad idea if she gave herself a fig leaf to hide behind publicly.

Robin made her four calls and set up two meetings, one man and one woman, on each of the next two mornings. Who could argue with such an equitable arrangement? Over the phone, one of the men had sounded African-American, and one of the women had a Hispanic surname. More politically correct cover. She only hoped that one of these two broads knew her stuff, was quiet, clean and generally invisible any time Robin was at home.

That night, the cheery TV meteorologist said the cold weather would be back in three days.

Lupe Ayala showed up right on time the next morning and Robin almost hired her on the spot. She was tiny, soft spoken and, from the way she talked, could really do the job. She'd apprenticed in plant maintenance at Procter & Gamble, had been there four years, showed glowing letters of recommendation from all of her superiors, everyone from her immediate supervisor on up to the plant superintendent. She was looking for a new situation because the plant where she worked would be closing.

To each question Robin asked about heating, plumbing and wiring, Lupe shrugged nonchalantly and said, "Oh, suuure. I can do that."

There was no boastfulness in her manner, just a calm certainty, indeed a sense of polite forbearance, as if Robin had asked if she could tie her shoelaces by herself. Feeling a bit surprised, Robin thought that she might actually like having this little pixie in her basement. Lupe would work her magic, solve Robin's problems, and she was so small and quiet she probably slept in a matchbox. Just what Robin wanted.

Robin was about to offer her the job when Lupe mentioned Chuey.

"Chuey?" Robin asked. "Is that your boyfriend?"

Lupe giggled.

"He's my frien', but no is a boy. Is a pet."

Not a dog, please, Robin thought. She couldn't handle barking.

"Chuey's not a dog, is he? A chihuahua, or something."

Lupe laughed.

"Oh, no, not a chihuahua. Chuey, he'd eat chihuahuas."

"What?"

"Chuey a python."

"A snake?" Robin asked incredulously.

"Only little one," Lupe said. "Twelve feet. Supposed to be eighteen, but I think Chee-cago too cold for him, stunt his growth."

Twelve feet seemed plenty big to Robin; she'd heard more than one horror story about exotic snakes that had slithered away from their owners. She imagined going into her park and lurking there in the foliage ... Well, no, that definitely wouldn't do.

Still, she asked, "Do you keep him in some sort of glass cage, or something?"

Lupe dismissed that notion with a wave of her hand.

"Oh, no. Chuey, he sleep with me."

Robin tried hard not to cringe.

"Very good for security," Lupe confided. "Nobody break in, nobody sneak into my bed, they know I got Chuey there."

Robin didn't doubt it for a minute.

"Tell you something else, too." Lupe looked around, leaned forward and dropped her quiet voice to an even more intimate level. "You got boyfrien'? He come on all macho. Say, '*Mira, Mami,* look what I got for you,' and whip out his thing. I show him Chuey, say, 'Lookit what I got already.' Boyfrien', unless he hung twelve feet, know he have his work cut out for him."

Lupe giggled and nodded at the undoubtedly fond memories running through her head. Then she added philosophically, "Ones who run away not real men anyway."

She said she was going to take her severance pay and open a snake shop. She thought there'd be a big market among the women in town. She also said Chuey was getting lonely with her away all day and could use another snake for company.

Robin thanked Lupe for coming in and said she'd let her know what she'd decided in a few days.

Roger M'Beneka Kikume came into Mimi's two minutes later. He looked like a smiling ebony god. Six-four and solid muscle, his face chiseled into planes that Rodin would have admired. He would have been an intimidating figure except for the smile, the sparkle in his eyes and the darling little boy he held in his arms.

He politely asked if he might have tea instead of the coffee that Robin offered. He also declined the offer of milk for his son, accepting instead a small glass of ginger ale.

"A lot of people, other than Northern Europeans, are lactose intolerant," he explained sitting across a table from Robin.

He went on to explain that he'd earned both his bachelor's and master's degrees from the University of California.

"UCLA?" Robin asked.

Roger smiled indulgently. "Berkeley."

"The place where that guy goes to school naked?"

"Yeah, that's the place," Roger smiled, gently tilting the glass of soda so his son could drink. "Home of the free speech movement, political correctness and some of the smartest people you'll ever find anywhere."

Roger showed Robin several snapshots.

"These are buildings I've bought since I returned to Chicago. I was born here, and I want to make my mark here."

The pictures were of three buildings. Each was immaculately kept inside and out. Roger explained that he and his family did all the work on the properties and while he was self taught he knew everything there was to know about maintaining a building.

Robin was impressed, but the pictures Roger had shown her and the stories he'd related raised an obvious question in her mind.

"If you have all these nice places," she asked, "and all that education, why would you want a little basement apartment?"

Roger looked her in the eye.

"Right here's where I need to ask you a delicate question," he said. "I need to know if you're prejudiced."

Robin bristled, and her body language was enough to make Roger raise a hand.

"I don't mean about the color thing."

"Then what?"

Roger held up his son. He said, "I never introduced you. This is Patrick Three-Two Kikume."

Robin sighed. She knew when she was supposed to pick up on a cue.

"Okay, what's the middle name mean?"

"Wife number three, child number two."

"You've been married three times, and this is the way you keep track?"

"I have three wives, and I'm engaged to number four. That's who I want the apartment for. I'll do the work, but she'll live there."

"You have three wives ... and you're about to make it four?" Robin repeated, making sure she had it right.

"Yeah, that's why I need a fourth home. You keep them under one roof, they start to cycle together, and let me tell you that ain't pretty. So, Miriam, my fiancé, she'll stay in your apartment until her second pregnancy and by then I should have another building of my own ready for her."

"Sure," Robin nodded, "makes perfect sense."

Roger smiled, happy that she understood.

"Except polygamy's illegal!" Robin hissed venomously.

She would have shouted it at the guy if he hadn't had a little kid in his arms. As it was, Patrick Three-Two suddenly viewed her with alarm. Roger tried explaining he was already suing in federal court, claiming that laws mandating monogamy violated his Constitutional right to practice his ancestral religion. He was sure he would win. In fact, a landlord who denied him occupancy based on cultural bias might herself be subject to legal —

Roger bit his tongue because, at that moment, he looked into Robin's eyes and recognized what his two-year-old boy had already perceived. This woman was dangerous. Furthermore, they were in her habitat. Best to leave while leave-taking was possible.

Roger M'Beneka Kikume got up, thanked Robin for the tea and ginger ale and quickly carried his second son by his third wife away to safety.

Robin shook her head and got ready for a day of work.

After that start to her morning, Robin was extra snappish with the breakfast crowd, and having heard a weather forecast on the radio that the cold might be back sooner than expected, she was feeling borderline vicious by lunchtime.

Matters weren't helped when Tone Morello showed up that day with reinforcements. Of the ego variety.

Actually able to read several simple sentences aloud, Tone was a sportscaster for a local network affiliate. His specialty was punctuating his news scripts with appropriate grunts and groans. Whenever any jock in the highlights he narrated suffered a blunt trauma, Tone was on the money with just the right empathetic *aaaargh* or *ooooh*. Blows to the groin were his specialty. He made his viewers feel the pain. For this, Tone was handsomely paid, and, of course, enjoyed numerous fringe benefits. Such as all the cheerleaders — strictly over eighteen years of age, mind you — he could eat.

Of course, being a sports guy, Tone was also highly competitive. He couldn't let Robin get away with her slander of him. Otherwise, word would get around fast that she'd called him a dinky-dick and he'd never be able to show his face in another locker room or to another camera.

So, today Tone showed up at Mimi's with two cheerleaders from Chicago's pro basketball team, a blonde and a redhead, each dressed in skimpy black spandex and featuring T&A from here to there. Given the brevity of their costumes and the relative chill in the air, they displayed endless goose bumps and other points of interest. They clung to Tone's arms like they'd been sutured there.

Predictably, all the men in the deli enjoyed the spectacle while all the women did not. Feminist Judy Kuykendahl sneered openly. Everybody, however, expected a good show when Tone and friends stepped up to the counter in front of Robin.

Robin regarded the threesome bleakly.

"Look," she said, "five boobs out for a stroll."

Tone's face flushed but he restrained himself.

"Five?" said the redhead, puzzled. "I don't get it."

Tone gave her a look, and the blonde shushed her. They were working from a script today, like the San Francisco 49er's offense, and they couldn't let themselves be distracted.

Tone asked, "What would you ladies like to eat ... anything at all."

The cheerleaders went into their routine.

"I know what I'd like," said the blonde with a nasty little grin.

"Me, too," replied the redhead.

They both licked their lips with pointy pink tongues.

Hardly subtle, but it got all the male patrons giggling like sophomores.

"You think they got foot longs here?" asked the blonde. "Those all-beef wieners."

"If they don't, I know where we can get one," said the redhead.

All the female customers jeered and booed. Manny Tavares had to wrest the knife out of Judy Kuykendahl's hand.

Robin said, "You here to revive Vaudeville or you want something to eat, Ant-knee?"

The girls had been prepared for this slur on Tone's name.

"Ant-knee?" said the blonde to the redhead. "You know any Ant-knee?"

The redhead shook her tresses.

"No, you know who I know?"

Together they let go of Tone, whirled around to face the crowd of customers and launched into a cheer routine as if they were leading a pep rally.

"Tone, Tone, he's our man! If you can't say it, we sure can!"

They spun Tone around to face his public, each did a cartwheel, high-kicked, bounced up and down and set up such a show of jiggling flesh that the men in the deli were left drooling and the women were agog.

"Yaaaaaaay, Tone!"

The cheerleaders jumped high into the air, came down to do full splits in front of Tone and bounced right back up to their feet, their faces flushed, the smiles wide and their bosoms heaving.

Every man in the place broke into applause.

At the cash register, Mimi urgently scribbled down a new rule: No indecent exposure. She didn't like the way her Stanley was smiling at these bimbos.

Tone and the girls turned back to face Robin.

She ignored him and looked at each of his accomplices.

"He's pretty big, huh?"

They knew what she meant.

"The biggest," said Red.

"Even bigger than that," added Blondie.

"You know this from personal experience?"

The two girls giggled and nodded.

Tone beamed.

Until he saw Robin nod, too, as if she'd come to some serious conclusion. Tone didn't know what she was up to but his smile vanished under a wave of anxiety.

Robin reached into the display case. She brought out a hot dog. It was a fair-sized wiener, long and plump, but on one side of it Robin placed an uncut hard salami and on the other a full roll of bologna. Each of which made the hot dog look Lilliputian.

"Now, ladies," Robin said, "in the interest of informing the public, without being totally indelicate, point to the item you'd say best represents your good friend here."

Tone started smiling again.

The redhead looked at Tone for a hint. Would he prefer the salami or the bologna?

"Now, now. No cheating," Robin said.

"That's right," Tone added. "Just be honest. Whatever you say is okay with me."

"Of course," Robin informed the cheerleaders, "I should warn you ladies before you indicate your choices that you'll not only be revealing intimate details about the dimensions of Ant-knee's anatomy ... but also about your own."

Snap!

Everyone in the place heard the trap spring shut.

Even Red got it. Sure, she and Blondie could say Tone was hung like a Clydesdale, but then they'd be telling the world they were loose women in more ways than one. The bigger they made Tone, the more cavernous they made themselves. The two cheerleaders looked at each other with sick expressions.

All the customers and staff grinned like hyenas. Judy gave Robin a thumb's–up.

Tone looked like he was about to blow a blood vessel. He

grabbed the Boobsey Twins' arms and squeezed, silently demanding that they sacrifice their own egos for the sake of his. But they shook him off, came to the same swift decision and pointed to the hot dog. The teeny-weeny hot dog. They ran jiggling from the deli, hoots and howls of laughter chasing them.

Robin looked at Tone and asked, "Something I can get you? To go with your humble pie. Ant-knee."

Robin's victory over Tone was forgotten by the time she got home that day. She went down to the basement and looked for something that was obviously wrong with her furnace: a plug that had been knocked loose, a broken wire that she could tape together, something. No luck. Being as bold as she could, she removed the metal panel that concealed the inner-workings of the beast. It looked like so much blackened, curved metal tubing to her, a colander of industrial spaghetti. She had no more understanding of how this thing was supposed to heat her house than if someone had told her it all worked by magic.

She was so angry and frustrated she wanted to kick the damn thing, but she thought better of it when she remembered it was a gas furnace. Kicking it might cause a leak that would result in the house blowing up or her being asphyxiated. Having no alternative, Robin screamed.

Then she went up to her park to look at her plants, hoping, praying that they wouldn't all be dead soon. She took small comfort in remembering that at least the aquarium was heated electrically. Her fish should survive. Later, Robin went up to her apartment and didn't eat the dinner she fixed.

Lying in bed, under the covers, she watched the weather forecast, hoping for a reprieve, a change in conditions that would give her more time to work something out.

But with even more glee than usual, the weatherman said the cold was now due to return tomorrow night.

There might even be snow.

Robin clicked off the set and pulled the covers over her head.

CHAPTER 5

Robin's interviews the following morning were less unusual but no more productive than the previous day. The woman was technically competent. She was also a lesbian. Don't worry about that, she'd said, because Robin wasn't at all her type. She would have to hurt Robin, however, if Robin ever made a play for any of her girlfriends. The man didn't want to harm Robin, he wanted to save her. He was a part-time minister, and he wanted to know if he took the job, could he use Robin's laundry room for baptisms? He'd be honored to wash her sins away first thing. Right there in her laundry sink.

Robin was so depressed she couldn't muster the energy even to defend herself. People would take shots at her and all she could do was take their orders and serve them their food. Everybody figured that Robin was setting some sort of trap for them, sucking them in by allowing them to take their little digs before she tore their heads off. So nobody pushed it too hard with her.

Still, Robin was glad Tone had decided to stay away that day.

David Solomonovich, however, showed up after the lunch rush.

"Hey, mama," he said, "you sure are lookin' —"

Then David got a good look at her.

"Awful," he finished. "Just terrible."

"How nice of you to notice," Robin said dully.

The realization that maybe he'd actually hurt Robin stunned David, made him feel worse than any insult he'd ever received at Mimi's.

"I'm sorry," he said, his fourteen-year-old voice small and hollow.

"What do you want, David?"

"Pastrami."

"On rye?"

"What else," he said. "Wonder Bread?"

He hoped Robin would rise to the bait, but she didn't. David watched her work. She plodded through the motions and didn't say a word to him. He thought what he was seeing was terrible. Robin was too young and vital to abandon her gift for vitriol. The world was losing something important here. It would be like ... like Michael Jordan retiring at thirty.

Robin gave David his sandwich silently, accompanied by nothing more than a dull stare.

David took one deep breath, another and then a third.

"Are you hyperventilating?" Robin asked.

David was just building up steam for what he had to say.

"I just want you to know," he said, "that whatever's wrong, I'll do anything I can to help you. And I may be just fourteen, but you'd be surprised what I can accomplish."

David's pledge of help, friendship and, implicitly, love reduced Robin to tears.

Not that she let anybody see her cry. She couldn't afford that. She turned, walked through the kitchen door and left work early. On the way home, she cried.

When Robin got home she found a man looking around her building. She'd first spotted him from up the block. He was bent over peering into the basement windows. He duck-walked from one to another. In that compressed posture, he made her think of an anvil, massive and dense, and his huge crew-cut head seemed a fitting platform on which to beat red-hot iron into horseshoes with a hammer and tongs.

As she came closer, the man stood up and Robin saw he was really huge, well over six feet tall and wide enough to cause an eclipse if he ever got airborne. The giant saw Robin approach, gave her a momentary stoic glance, then turned away and started walking toward the back of Robin's house.

She figured him for a burglar.

It was a measure of her mental state that she decided to stop this guy by herself. She knew better than to call out. She'd need surprise on her side. She'd jump on the bastard from behind. He was big, but she wasn't exactly Twiggy herself. Her weight would knock him down and she'd beat his head into the sidewalk with her bare hands.

Of course, it would have been better if he'd had some long hair to grab onto, but she'd manage somehow. Maybe grab his ears. Use them to get him kissing concrete.

Robin started to run on tiptoe, making the best time as quietly as she could. She got to within ten feet of the guy without him knowing it. She had to get to him before he got into the backyard where they'd be out of sight of the street. She had to take him down where one of the neighbors could see what was happening and call the cops. If she tackled him in the backyard, out of public view, and something went wrong ...

Robin picked up her speed. She was close now, only six feet to go, when her right ankle turned under. She shrieked in pain and stumbled forward out of control. The behemoth turned and saw her. She screamed again, raising both fists to pummel him before she fell flat on her face.

He caught her with no more difficulty than if he'd been playing oopsy-daisy with a toddler. His strength was beyond anything Robin had ever imagined. She must've been mad to attack this man. Why, he could drag her behind her house and do anything he wanted with her.

She was filling her lungs for one last yell — for help this time — when he stood her up, steadied her and asked if she was all right. He had a German accent.

"What do you want?" Robin asked, shaken.

He gave her a small bow. The guy was a real foreigner. Americans didn't bow.

"I am here about the handy person job."

With that, he bowed again, turned and continued on his way to the back of the building.

"What?" Robin asked in disbelief.

The behemoth didn't answer. Robin had to hobble after him.

He had gone up the back stairs to the first floor landing. He was looking in the rear window at her park. She couldn't believe the nerve of this guy.

"Hey, what the heck do you think you're doing?" Robin asked, looking up at him. She wasn't going to go charging up the steps after him, not the way her ankle was throbbing.

He saw how she was favoring it.

He said, "Rice."

"What?" Robin asked, more confused than ever.

"Rest, ice, compression and elevation. That's what your ankle needs, and quickly."

"Thank you, doctor."

He missed the sarcasm. Or ignored it.

"Would you like me to carry you to your apartment?"

Suddenly the fear was back, and it must have shown on her face. The tiniest hint of a smile played on the giant's lips.

"I do not bite ... unless requested. I am here about the job."

Robin had good reason not to yield all of her suspicions.

"How did you know where to come? The address wasn't listed."

The guy shrugged. "It isn't hard if you know how. I wanted to look at the building. Check the apartment. See if it is a fair trade."

She couldn't believe this man's gall. Intruding on her privacy. She wanted to tell him off so bad it hurt. Worse than her ankle. Which was killing her. And that was his fault, too. But looking at him, one flight up, so massive, with that deadpan mug, it'd be like insulting the side of a mountain.

Robin was about to find her voice when he beat her to the punch.

"You have a very nice space in there." He nodded over his shoulder to the park. "The plantings are lovely. But they look like they're withering. Are you having problems with your heating?"

The guy stabbed her in the heart with that one.

He walked down the stairs to stand next to Robin.

"You will show me the garden apartment?"

Phrased as a command—in that damn German accent—with just a hint of intonation to make it a question. Robin gnashed her teeth and hobbled down the outside stairs to the basement. The guy blotted out the sun behind her.

She opened the door and they stepped into the back of the basement, the working area with the furnace, the circuit breakers for the electricity, the water main, and the laundry facilities.

The giant noticed that the face-plate of the furnace had been removed.

Robin saw him looking at it.

"May I see the apartment please?"

"Can you fix that furnace?" Robin countered.

Ja.

"Can you do wiring?"

Ja.

"Plumbing?"

Ja, he could do that, too.

Robin stared at him hard, trying to make him crack if he was BS-ing her. All she got for her trouble was that infuriating little smile again. She turned gingerly and opened the rear door to the basement apartment.

There were only half the rooms of her own apartment, but they weren't tiny spaces. Still, with the two of them there, with their combined sizes, she thought there was hardly room to breathe. And Robin realized she hadn't been this physically close to a man in a private setting for a very long time. Her face turned a bright red.

He saw her discomfort, of course, probably guessed what she was thinking, but Robin had to give him credit for not saying anything or even smirking. Which made her even angrier, because she didn't want to give him credit for anything.

Robin said, "As you can see, there's a living room, a bedroom ..." She opened the door so he could look in. "... a dining-L and kitchenette and a bathroom." He looked at this, too.

Robin had furnished the apartment over the years with her castoffs. She hadn't ever expected to rent the space. She just used it as a place to crash when she was doing yard work or had several loads of laundry to do. Now, she watched this monstrous schnitzel sit on the sofa, click the TV on and off, check the bed's firmness with his hand.

She felt as if she was losing control of her home.

"I will take the job," the giant announced.

"I don't think so," Robin replied, shaking her head. "I don't think I can do this."

The guy looked at her, not trying to be intimidating in any way. Just looking to see what he could see. He shrugged and walked toward the open door at the rear of the building. He stopped in the doorway and looked back at her.

"So, tonight the cold will come and all your plants will die."

"Damn," Robin said.

He was right and she was right back where she'd started.

"A pity," the giant agreed and started up the stairs.

"Wait!"

He turned and waited for Robin to hobble over to him. This time she did her best to see what was inside of him.

"You married?"

Nein.

"Girlfriend?"

Nein.

"Boyfriend?"

The giant just gave her a look.

"Pets?"

Nein.

"No drugs."

Nein. No drugs. This time with the smile.

"Noise?"

He said, "I'm told I snore."

"Thanks for sharing, but down here, I don't think I'd notice."

The giant shrugged.

"You're not an illegal alien?"

"I'm a resident alien."

He showed her a green card.

Just when Robin thought it might work, at least for a little while, he added, "I was sponsored by the CIA."

"What?"

"I was a political prisoner in East Germany."

"Are you kidding me?"

He shook his head.

"I was a spy."

"That does it," Robin said. "Get out of here."

Instead of leaving, he stepped over to the furnace, reached in and did something Robin couldn't see. Then there was a click, a thump and the furnace came on. The giant turned toward Robin like a magician waiting to see how his trick had been received.

Robin beamed with joy.

Until he turned and shut the furnace off.

"I'll leave now," he said.

"That CIA stuff was real? You're not just some crazy?"

"My wife denounced me to the state. While I was in prison, she divorced me and took my daughter from me. My daughter was a baby at the time. Would you like to see her picture?"

Robin shook her head.

"What's your name?" she asked.

"Manfred Welk." He pronounced his last name Velk.

Robin sighed. Cursed under her breath. Then gave in.

"You're hired, Manfred. Don't let my plants die tonight."
Manfred clicked his heels.
Gave her his little smile.
And turned on the furnace.

CHAPTER 6

Robin woke the next morning feeling as warm as oven-fresh bread: the heat was on. Her park had been saved. The glow of physical comfort and psychological relief lasted only until she remembered the price at which they had been purchased. Had the giant already moved in?

She'd given him the keys he'd need before he'd left yesterday.

She started to swing her feet out of bed to go find out, but she stopped. She flipped back the covers and looked at her injured ankle. It was tightly wrapped in an elastic bandage. The giant — then she remembered his name — Manfred had done it for her. He'd gotten the bandage from his car, an ancient but well kept diesel Mercedes. He'd again offered to carry her to her apartment, but as far as Robin was concerned Manfred was her moat monster, never to be allowed into the upper reaches of her castle. Robin let him wrap her foot and ankle outside on the front step.

He'd been deft and impersonal about it, as if this were something he'd done a million times. Even so, having a man touch her in any way at all had been enough that she'd had to fight to keep from trembling. Manfred had pretended not to notice. He'd just looked at the job he'd done and told her to keep her weight off the ankle as much as possible. Then he'd bowed and said he'd be back with his belongings tomorrow.

Today.

Robin got out of bed carefully, testing the ankle. Not bad. Tender but not painful. She'd remembered what Manfred had said about icing the injury, but she hadn't wanted to undo the tight, clean wrapping job he'd done with the bandage and had skipped the ice. She still didn't want to unwrap it. She'd just take a sponge bath this morning and leave it on. This afternoon, after work, she'd come home and ice it.

As she hip-hopped through her ablutions, tip-toed into her clothes and ate breakfast with her foot up on a chair, Robin kept wondering: *Was he down there?* Was this going to work? And how in God's name could a guy that big ever have been a spy? What kind of crowd could he possibly blend into?

The phone rang and Robin jumped.

It was him, Manfred.

Had he known she'd been thinking about him? Did the CIA teach mindreading?

He said, "You have a two-car garage in back. Does our agreement permit me to use one-half of it?"

Robin had to think. This whole deal had been Mimi's idea. She hadn't even thought about the garage. She, herself, had no car. She walked, took the CTA or got a ride from her dad when she wanted to go someplace. Other than housing a few garden tools, the garage was empty. And Manfred had his nice old car. Still...

Robin said, "I suppose. If you do enough around here to justify it."

Without pause, he replied, "I am sure you would let me do no less."

Not even moved in yet, and he was busting her chops. She had a good mind to ... No, she didn't. Not yet. The furnace might be only temporarily fixed. She wanted her house to be in perfect running order before she dumped Herr Manfred Welk.

So she said, "You bet I won't."

Robin treated herself to a taxi that morning to get to work. She didn't know how this situation was going to work out long term, but for the moment she felt as if a tremendous financial burden had been lifted from her so she decided to splurge. And since the cabbie was silent, drove safely and took the most direct route, she even gave him a good tip.

Mimi noticed her injury as soon as Robin hobbled through the door.

"What happened?"

"I hurt myself chasing a burglar. At my house."

Mimi almost popped her emerald green contact lenses.

"My God! Are you serious? Are you crazy? You could've been killed."

Robin sat down at one of the tables.

"It worked out all right. Turns out he wasn't a burglar at all."

"What was he?"

"A handy person."

Suddenly, Mimi had the uneasy feeling she'd just fallen into one of Robin's traps.

"You're kidding, right?"

"No. He'd come about the job."

"But how did he find out where you live?"

"He said it was no problem. He'd been a spy."

"Robin, now really."

"For the CIA," she added.

Mimi stared at Robin to see what kind of morbid joke she was playing. But, for the life of her, Mimi couldn't find the least bit of deception in Robin's bland expression.

"His name's Manfred. He's German. He moves in today," Robin said, "I gave him the keys."

That was all Mimi needed to hear: spies, CIA, German.

"Absolutely not! I forbid it!" Mimi admonished. "You need some money, fine, you just got a bonus. You let me know much you need and—"

Robin took Mimi's hands in hers.

"It's all right. Maybe you did the right thing for me. I'm going to give it a try."

"But what if this man ... this Manfred ..."

Mimi couldn't bring herself to mention any of the awful fates that could be visited upon Robin by a stranger living in her house. She hadn't thought of that when she'd placed the ad. For her part, Robin wasn't worried. Not about her safety, anyway. If Manfred had been a nutbag, he'd had all the opportunity he'd ever needed yesterday. That was when he could have run her through a meat grinder and nobody would ever have known who did it.

"Mimi, I'll be okay."

"But if anything happened to you, I'd feel ..."

Mimi couldn't complete that thought, either.

So Robin helped her.

"Eaten with guilt 'til your dying day," she said with a wicked grin. "As of course you should, getting me into this fix."

Mimi gave her a sour look.

"There is something you could do to make amends, or at least start to," Robin said.

"What?" Mimi asked warily.

"Switch jobs with me today? You take the counter, let me sit at the register?"

Mimi had never let anyone else handle the deli's cash. That was why she never worried about any of her employees stealing from her; nobody ever had the chance. She knew this was Robin's way of getting back at her for trying to give her back that buyout check. But more than that it was Robin's way of asking if she was still Mimi's partner, somebody she could trust completely.

And what could Mimi say to that?

"Well," she said, grudgingly, "I suppose it'd be better for you to rest your ankle."

"Thank you, Mimi."

Mimi melted. She loved the way Robin could say her name, when she wanted, so it sounded just like Mama. At least to her ears.

"Of course," Mimi added, remembering her place in the universe, "I know how much we take in on Wednesdays to the last penny. And if the total's not right..."

Continuing her theme of the morning, Mimi let that thought dangle, too.

Robin replied, "Heck, Mimi, I know that any good crook has got to establish trust before she makes her move."

She said it with a smile. But then she wondered if that was what Manfred "The Giant" Welk was doing. Gaining her trust. Before he made his move.

She couldn't help but have her suspicions. Life had taught her not to trust men.

David Solomonovich, however, was still a boy. And one that Robin thought she might be able to use.

"What're you doing over here?" David asked, bringing his carryout sandwich to the register.

Robin extended her gimpy leg.

Everybody had been surprised to see Robin behind the register. They weren't sure if the move was a promotion, a demotion or a flanking maneuver to attack them from a new angle. Robin had told everyone she'd injured herself and shown them her ankle without going into all of the details.

More than one wit had opined that it was a good thing the injury was just a sprain and not a break or Mimi would have had to call a vet to put her down. Robin had parried with thrusts to her patrons' intellects, physiques, grooming or ancestry, as appropriate.

David, however, responded only with concern, which made Robin reconsider the wisdom of what she was about to ask of him.

The young genius asked, "Have you had an MRI? They're expensive, but it's really the only way to go when diagnosing a soft-tissue injury." He slapped his forehead. "What am I thinking? Do you even have health insurance? Most foodservice places don't provide it for their workers."

For the very first time, Mimi gave David a dirty look.

Robin noticed. David didn't.

He plowed right on. "Look, my family has connections with the U of C hospitals. Let me call a cab and we'll get right over..."

Robin shushed him before Mimi decided to ban the kid.

"David, it's just a sprain. But if it makes you happy, I'll go see my family doctor."

He started to insist that what she needed was an orthopedic specialist. Which was when Robin finally stopped him cold. "I'd like to ask you a favor," she said.

The implied intimacy of her words made David grin like an idiot not a genius.

"Sure. What? Anything."

Robin made sure that no one was about to approach the register and then motioned David forward. The moment was so delicious for the boy that he shivered. What a *femme fatale* she was, Robin thought sarcastically.

"David," Robin said softly, "forgive me if I'm indulging in an unpardonable stereotype, but is it true most of you smart young guys are computer whizzes?"

"Us nerds, you mean?" He said it with a grin, not offended, just getting in his shot.

"Yeah, you nerds," Robin said, playing along.

David nodded. "It's true. We like to go around bragging, 'My hard disk's bigger than yours.' "

Robin laughed, which made David glow.

"So," Robin asked, dropping her voice even lower, "do you ever do any of that illegal hacking stuff?"

David almost took a step backward, until Robin put a hand on his arm.

"That's the favor," David whispered, incredulous, "you want me to commit a crime?"

"Just listen to what I have to tell you, then decide if you can help me."

Robin took her hand off his arm. David put it back on.

"I'm listening," he said.

"A man is moving into my building. His name is Manfred Welk. He told me he was a political prisoner until last year in East Germany. He said he was a spy. He said he worked for the CIA."

David took Robin's hand off his arm, his eyes narrowing with suspicion. But he kept his voice low. "This is a trick, right? You're setting me up for something."

Robin just shook her head.

"It's true. At least, that's what the man told me. And he is moving into my basement apartment today. He might be there already. I'd like you to verify what he told me."

David goggled.

"You want me to break into the CIA's computer system?"

Robin said, "If you and your hard disk are up to it."

Shameless, Robin thought, just shameless. Using a precocious child this way. Not that she was about to stop. But it made her admit, to herself anyway, that women could be just as rotten as men.

David, of course, rose to the bait.

"Sure, I could do it."

"Will you?"

"Yes ... if you'll give me something."

Robin felt her stomach turn over. She knew David wasn't going to ask for a free cookie, and as much as she wanted to find out if Manfred's story was legit, she wasn't about to commit statutory rape to do it.

"What?" she asked, trying not to wince.

David leaned in close. "A kiss, a real kiss."

Bad enough, but at least it wasn't criminal. What continued to boggle Robin's mind — and frighten her — was that she couldn't understand why David would want to kiss her. She looked at him, trying to fathom the incredible mind behind those wire-rim glasses. Was he a twisted genius, or what?

"Okay," she said, finally, "but no tongue."

A bit of disappointment registered in his eyes, but the boy still nodded.

"Deal," he said, and shook Robin's hand.

She paid for David's sandwich out of her own pocket, but that didn't make Robin feel much better. She'd sent a boy out to commit a crime that would land him in some sort of serious trouble if he got caught. And there he went, almost bouncing out the door he felt so giddy. Smart enough, maybe, to pull it off and dumb enough, no, young enough, not to know how badly he was being used.

Because while Robin would deliver if David did, she wouldn't give him his kiss until he was eighteen ... and then only if he still wanted it.

Mimi came over to Robin at the register.

"That was quite a little conversation you two had."

Mimi was still a little ticked at David, and clearly she wanted to know what had been said.

But Robin only nodded.

Then she said, "I used to think men were awful."

"And now you don't?" Mimi asked, surprised.

"Of course, I do. It's just that now I think maybe we're even worse. Me, anyway."

Robin knew.

Before she ever got home, while she was still three houses down the block, she knew that Manfred had arrived, was in fact present at this very moment. The thought struck her that her home had been changed forever and a chill passed through her. On top of everything else, she smelled something peculiar. Maybe that was how she knew. It wasn't a foul odor, just something unusual. A scent that was not her own.

Wintergreen oil?

Sniffing like a hound — there was a pleasant image, she thought — she followed her nose to the backyard. She was getting close to the source. It wasn't coming from her house, it was coming from the garage. Robin stepped cautiously over that way and peeked through the garage's rear window.

Her eyes bugged out at what she saw.

A roar that would shame a lion drove her away from the window.

She backpedaled quickly and stumbled on her bum ankle as a huge, clanking jolt shook the ground. Robin fell on her can.

She was seated there, dumbfounded, when Manfred appeared in the doorway of the garage and unnerved her even more. Looking up at him, starting at his ankles and tracking upward, she had never seen so much flesh, so much ... so much ... man. He was clothed, if you could call it that, in some kind of spandex unitard with an enormous leather belt around a waist that had the circumference of a beer barrel. He also wore work boots, and a bright yellow headband was stretched around his massive head. But his legs, his arms, his shoulders, his neck, his face, they were all so huge and pink, everything bulging and pulsing...

Robin felt her head begin to spin.

She awoke seated on the sofa in her living room. She awoke because her right foot was freezing. She pulled it out of a bucket of ice that had been tilted on its side and held in place by a pair of folded bath towels. When her mind cleared and she remembered what had happened, Robin looked around quickly. She saw that she was alone. More importantly, she felt that she was alone.

Manfred wasn't here.

But he must've brought her here. He had to have carried her up the stairs. He had to fill the bucket with ice and put her foot in it. So he had been in her apartment. The phone rang. The portable. He'd left it on the sofa next to her.

She pressed the answer button but said nothing.

"Manfred Welk here. You are all right?" he asked.

"Yes, I think so."

"I checked your eyes. Your pupils were equal and reacted to light."

"Thank you."

"Your ankle needed the ice, but I didn't want the frostbite for you, so I called."

"Thank you."

"I am a power lifter. The weights, *ja?*"

Robin almost said "*ja*" in reply, but she caught herself.

"I understand that now," she answered.

"I was on the national team. On my way to L.A. Olympics, but Russians said *nyet*."

Robin wanted to crack wise, but she somehow lacked the will.

"That's too bad," she said.

Manfred asked, "Would you like me to come up and rewrap your ankle?"

"No," she said quickly, still edgy, "that won't be necessary."

"*Ja*, that is what I thought. I left a first-aid pamphlet for you on your kitchen table. Red Cross instructions. They will show you how the ankle should be wrapped."

"Okay."

"Perhaps, from now on, I wear sweat clothes when I lift."

"That would be a good idea."

"Oh ... I bought part needed to complete the furnace repair. I have installed it. You have no more problems with furnace."

"I'm happy to hear that."

"*Ja*," Manfred said. "I left bill for part. Also on kitchen table."

Business concluded for the moment, he rang off.

Robin slumped back on the sofa and stuck her throbbing ankle back into the ice bucket.

The part Manfred had bought for the furnace had cost $47, tax included. It was a rebuilt part, but Robin had Manfred's stamp of approval that it was as good as new. A note he'd left said that he'd checked it thoroughly before buying it.

Robin had smiled to herself.

She had no doubt that Manfred had examined the part closely, and she couldn't conceive of a retail clerk in the world who'd dare try to pull a fast one on him. She'd also found the instructions he'd left on how to wrap her ankle. She'd been pleased that she'd been able to follow them closely and had done pretty much as good a job as he had at binding the injury.

After she'd done that and popped an analgesic, the throb had been barely perceptible. She'd been able to fix herself some dinner and stare at the TV from her bed, even though she had no idea of what she'd watched.

Now, as she turned the set off and the lights out, Robin lay in bed and tried to enjoy the warmth of her gloriously heated home ... but she couldn't keep her mind from drifting downward. He was down there in her basement. That huge pink German. What was he doing right now? He'd been unfailingly polite and even considerate, but she kept wondering whether she was a fool to put any trust in him. He was so big and so strong. It was like taking King Kong in as a pet.

She smiled again.

Her neighborhood, like any enclave for yuppies and their toys, was a target for burglars. And her building, unique on the block, had neither an alarm system nor a sign out front that warned of guard dogs or private cops. But now, Robin thought, she could plant a sign that warned of Manfred.

Premises protected by German powerlifter.

With a silhouette of him in his spandex and boots.

And the legend, "Ve haff vays of making you sorry."

That ought to scare off the creeps, she thought and giggled to herself.

The thing was, she had to get over being frightened of him herself. She was ashamed to admit it but she'd swooned out there in the backyard. Her. Round Robin Phinney. If anyone at the deli ever found out, she'd be finished. Laughed right out of the joint.

And she hadn't even gone down to the park tonight, not because she didn't want to try the stairs on her sore ankle, but because she hadn't wanted to be so close to him, have only one floor separating them. Which was ridiculous. She'd let the guy into her house in the first place to save the park. Now, she wasn't going to let him keep her out of it. She'd go down there tomorrow right after work, no two ways about it.

Having resolved that issue, Robin closed her eyes to go to sleep … and that was when she heard it. The sound. A deep, sharp buzzing roar, like a hundred-foot pine tree going through a sawmill. She tried to place the noise and came up with the only possible interpretation. Manfred was snoring.

So loudly she could hear it two floors away.

God!

Maybe the guy's wife had ratted him out to the Commies just to get away from that.

Robin put a pillow over her head and began drifting into unconsciousness on a tide of mixed emotions, asking herself over and over what she had done, who she'd let into her home, her life, her...

Sleep claimed Robin before she could find any answers.

CHAPTER 7

Tone Morello returned to Screaming Mimi's on the third day following his cheerleader fiasco. This time he brought a cameraman with him. Tone wore a look of grim determination on his face. There was no way he was going to lose this time. No way he could lose.

Because if he did he might have to shoot himself.

After what had happened with the girls, word had gotten out. Two women who had claimed to have personal knowledge of his manhood had gone on record as saying he had a party frank between his legs. The story hadn't made things easy for him when he'd had to do a locker room interview after the following night's basketball game. The home team had won with a buzzer-beater from thirty-five feet; there'd been two fights and five ejections. The second brawl had spilled over so far into the stands that the commissioner had his soft drink spilled on his lap. But as soon as Tone had opened his mouth in the locker room, all the drama and anger of the game had been forgotten. Everybody had looked at him and started smirking. Especially those pencil-pushing creeps from the newspapers. One SOB had even said they were doing amazing new things with silicone implants these days. Tone hadn't been able to get a straight answer to any of his questions. So he'd had his crew shoot the answers to the other assholes' questions and then shoot him asking the proper questions back at the studio and then edit the whole mess together.

Which was when Tone had thought of his latest idea. He'd take his cameraman to Mimi's and have him shoot Tone ripping Robin to pieces. If she got him back, well, that would end up on the old cutting room floor. Then he'd use the tape in one of his sports segments and a million people would see it. He'd be redeemed.

If the people who were in the deli tried to tell a different story, so what? They couldn't hope to compete with the power of television. In fact, it might be better if they contradicted the tape. That way Tone could spread the word that all the other things people had heard about him were lies, too.

Tone had greased his cameraman a grand to back his version of events and make sure that technically there'd be no way anyone could tell the tape had been edited. The guy swore with the new Japanese equipment he had the tape would look cherry.

Tone had also hinted darkly that if the cameraman knew what was good for him—and his family—he'd stay bought. And never even think of blackmail. Tone didn't actually know any leg-breakers, his dad was a roofer, but it didn't hurt to have an Italian name.

So, as he entered Mimi's, Tone was feeling pretty sure there was no way he could lose this one. When the camera's lights came on and blinded just about everybody in the joint he felt even better. Everyone was squinting and shielding their eyes and whining, generally acting like the no-talent, off-camera doofuses they were. He was sure that Robin was going to photograph like a beached whale, too.

Except, looking around, he couldn't see that tub of lard anywhere.

And Tone heard his cameraman scream, "Hey, get away!"

He knew what that hysterical, stay-away-from-my-baby cry of distress meant: Somebody was trying to touch his guy's precious camera, probably put a grubby hand over the insanely expensive lens.

He turned to see that the assailant was Mimi herself.

She had, in fact, squirted the camera with brown mustard.

Tone's accomplice was furiously trying to clean his valued piece of equipment and Tone could tell from the look on his face that this attack was going to cost him extra.

Then Mimi was in Tone's face.

"What kind of stunt are you trying to pull here?" she demanded.

"Hey," Tone responded, the picture of innocence, "what's the problem? I thought I'd do a little slice-of-life piece. How we all face competition in our everyday lives. Put your place on the air. Make you famous."

Tone leaned in close. "Where's Robin?"

Mimi hadn't just fallen off the turnip truck. She wasn't sure what this moron was up to, but she knew he had something that wasn't kosher up his sleeve.

"Robin?" she asked.

"Yeah," Tone said with an oily smile. "Miss Piggy's body double."

Tone was glad to see his camera guy had gotten that one. He'd paid a kid at Second City fifty bucks to write that line for him. He had a half dozen more in his pocket.

Mimi just gave him a hard stare.

"Ah-ah," Tone said. "That's against the rules."

He pointed to the anti-Travis Bickle injunction on the register.

"Maybe I should write a rule against those things," Mimi said, jerking her thumb at the cameraman, who reflexively leaped a yard backward.

"What?" Tone asked. "Every time I come in with somebody, you're going to write a rule against it? Keep that up and nobody's going to have much fun around here anymore."

Mimi looked around and saw that Tone had actually scored a point with her customers. She couldn't just keeping changing the rules. She'd come across as too high-handed. Afraid to get in there and trade punches. But to let this idiot back her into a corner—she wanted to spit.

Finally, Mimi said, "Robin's not here today."

"What?"

Tone seemed genuinely distressed. Then he thought he smelled a rat.

"She's in the kitchen, right? Camera shy. Afraid to face me for the record."

Tone felt a deep satisfaction that all his accusations were being captured on Memorex.

"She hurt her ankle," Mimi said. "She's at the doctor and then she's going home."

"You're kidding?"

Mimi said she wasn't, and a guy eating a Reuben backed her up. Goof didn't even know enough to stop chewing while he was being taped. The guy'd make a good insert shot. Laugh's on you, dummy.

Still, Tone was seriously disappointed that fate had gummed up his plans. Now, the stories about his ... shortcomings ... would keep eating away at his reputation, threaten his position in the local TV scene. The only thing he could do was to fall back on one of his most important tools. The sports cliche.

"Okay," he said sternly, "but you tell Robin Phinney I'll be back." Then Tone turned to look straight into the camera. "She can run but she can't hide."

Tone drew a finger across his throat to tell the cameraman to stop taping, and he stomped out of the deli.

Dan Phinney hadn't been able to find a single guy who owed him a favor, still lived in town, and was someone he'd trust to work in his daughter's house. The older guys, who knew their stuff and how to behave themselves, had all retired and moved to Florida or Arizona. The younger guys were still around, on the job, but Dan didn't think much of their work ethic, their competence or their manners. You never knew how young guys today would treat a woman. They didn't seem to have the same upbringing his generation had. He was uneasy that one of these young guys might make a crack about Robin's appearance or something, hurt her feelings.

Which, he had to admit, didn't seem too likely if you ever saw the way she fielded the brickbats thrown her way at Mimi's. But that was different. That was her job, and Dan was sure that it was an act. It was how Robin protected herself from people ... and from her memories.

But Dan knew different.

Robin was his little girl. He remembered her when she'd been young and lovely—before she'd been hurt—and she'd always be his angel. He took out his wallet and looked at the picture of Robin he kept there. She'd been eighteen when it was taken, a month after her graduation from high school. The image just about stopped his heart every time he looked at it, she'd been so lovely.

Of course, given his medical history, stopping his heart wasn't such a good idea. He folded up his wallet and stuck it back in his pocket.

Dan Phinney still blamed himself for letting his little girl get hurt. He didn't know how the hell he could have prevented it, it all happened so fast. But he should have been there for Robin, stopped that sonofabitch from ever getting close to his daughter. That's what fathers were for, and it ate at him every day that he'd failed her.

So, now he wouldn't consider calling on anyone who would say so much as an unkind word to his daughter.

What he'd do, since he had a key to her house, was go over to Robin's place while she was at work, fix the furnace before she knew it, look around and see what else he could do and be back home before she could say a word about it.

Dan Phinney had no idea as he left his house and got into his shiny new Camaro that Robin had hired a handy person.

Manfred Welk sat on the toilet in his new apartment, never the most comfortable of experiences for a man of his size. He always felt as if he were trying to drop a five-hundred-pound bomb into a thimble.

Still, things had improved since he'd had to take care of his business in front of Billy Tuxton in their cell in East Berlin. Billy had been decent about it, being as discreet as he could, affording whatever sense of privacy was possible, but one time the little Brit had been unable to bite his tongue and had offered the opinion that Manfred could supply the cannonade for the bloody "1812 Overture." That and the smell of death on the battlefield.

It was true. Manfred didn't actually know how bad his snoring was because he slept through it, but he was aware that he could be very loud in other ways. He wasn't always the most fragrant of fellows, either. But what could anyone expect? He was very big. He was an athlete. He worked hard, he sweated, he ate a lot and he kept his bowels moving. A healthy life, but not always a decorous one.

Which was why he was glad that his new abode was so nicely tucked away from anyone else. Down here he shouldn't be a bother to his new landlady. Now, there was a strange one. Not a bad sort really. But hiding something. Not nearly so tough as she acted. What she'd reminded him of was the *Wizard of Oz*. (A movie he'd had smuggled to him in the GDR while he was still a teenager.) Not the wicked witch, but the wizard himself. A small person hiding behind a curtain and an amplified voice.

He wondered who she was behind her facade, and then decided that, no, it was really none of his business. After all, he felt sure she would never snoop on him.

Manfred finished his business and wrinkled his nose. Sometimes he was a little too much even for himself. He'd have to install a vent in this bathroom if his plan succeeded. That and buy some air-freshener, he decided.

Manfred flushed the toilet … and heard a pipe burst.

Robin was riding the bus home, and was in far from the best of moods. She'd just left her family doctor. The same quack her father saw. He'd told her that her sprain wasn't serious but that she should keep her weight off her ankle as much as possible for the next two weeks. He'd given her a pair of aluminum crutches to help accomplish that goal—and the damn chintzy things had started to creak and bend the moment she'd put any weight on them.

Her doctor had given her a look and asked her to step onto his scale. Robin had refused. Knowing he couldn't very well force her to comply, he'd given her another look, and a lecture. One that she felt certain he'd been dying to give her for many a year. About obesity and the increased risk of heart disease, cancer and diabetes. He'd told her that if she wasn't careful and started losing weight soon she could develop a host of very serious problems and shorten her life expectancy significantly.

She'd replied that the way she lived was her choice to make.

Then the crusty old croak had rolled out his heavy artillery. He'd leaned in close, smelling aptly of some medicinal-scented soap, and told her that she could have a fatal heart attack in the not too distant future, and the way her father felt about her that might be enough to do him in, too.

He'd slapped some weight-loss brochures in her hand and left to dispense brimstone to some other unfortunate soul. Then, to rub salt in the wound, the miserable little turd had his nurse give Robin a new, heavier set of metal crutches. Stamped NFL-approved.

Robin wanted to hit someone. Or scream. Do something to get even. But for the moment all she could manage was a volcanic glare that drove away anyone even thinking of taking the seat next to her at the back of the bus. Taking a deep breath, she told herself to hang on. She'd be home soon. She could sit in her park, watch the fish, look at her beautiful plants, and...

She remembered that her home was no longer her own.

That overstuffed sausage was lurking in her basement.

A savage grin crossed Robin's face: payback time.

The kraut was out.

Kaput.

It might not be fair, but so-the-hell what? When had life ever been fair to her? She'd write him a check for fixing the furnace and tell him to hit the bricks. He didn't have a lease. If he gave her any trouble, she'd call the cops. Tell them to bring a crane if Sluggo got balky.

Robin looked up and saw a guy angling toward the empty seat next to her, looking elsewhere to avoid the daggers she was staring at him, but definitely headed her way. Having no other choice, Robin, *oops,* accidentally cracked him a good one across the shin with her crutches.

"Oh, I am sorry," she said.

The guy was hopping up and down on one leg, and Robin had a hard time not laughing.

"Yeah, well, watch out with those things," he said harshly.

But he went to stand in the front half of the bus.

Now that she'd decided to evict Manfred, Robin couldn't wait to get home.

Dan Phinney walked toward the rear of his daughter's house with his toolbox in his hand. At first, he thought he heard the sound of someone taking a whiz against the back of Robin's building. He was about to dig a wrench out of his box and apply it to the head of whatever lowlife thought he could pee on someone's private property when he realized the volume of water he heard was far too great for human plumbing. He bent over and looked in a window at the side of Robin's basement.

A pipe had burst.

Water was gushing everywhere.

And a giant was standing in the middle of the deluge looking like he was trying to squeeze two ends of a pipe shut with his bare hands, all the while cursing loudly in German.

Dan hustled around the corner of the building and ran down the stairs to the basement door. He took a monkey wrench out of his toolbox, brandishing it as a weapon just in case, and opened the door with his key. A wave flowed out that reached his calves. Then a hand grabbed the head of the wrench and jerked him into the basement as easily as he might have plucked a dandelion from his lawn.

Suddenly, Dan found himself standing next to the giant, who politely said, *"Bitte,"* and relieved him of his monkey wrench.

The man turned and was looking for something. Even with the door open the water was a good six inches deep. Then Dan realized what the giant wanted. He rushed over to help him.

"You've got to get the shut-off valve," he said.

"Ja, I tried. It broke off in my hand."

Dan quickly showed him where it was, reaching under the water.

"Here, put the wrench here."

He nimbly stepped aside, giving the German room to fit the wrench to the valve and with great strength and equal control turn it clockwise to shut off the water. The giant turned to look at Dan as he worked.

"Must be careful. These pipes are very old, very brittle."

But, inch by careful inch, Dan watched the guy get the job done. The wrench turned, the water slowed and finally stopped. Dan couldn't get over the size of this guy, the way he could see all those immense muscles at work right through his wet shirt. He stared at the ends of the pipe he'd seen the guy squeezing. They weren't watertight, but they sure weren't circular anymore either. They looked as slitted as a cat's eyes in sunlight.

Dan felt a large finger tap his shoulder and he turned.

"Your wrench, *Mein Herr. Danke."*

Dan took the wrench, knowing it wouldn't be a bit of help if things came to a fight, and asked, "Who the heck are you, anyway?"

Manfred gave a small bow and introduced himself.

"I live here now," he added.

Dan Phinney scratched his head in wonder.

Manfred asked if he might have the pleasure of knowing who'd come to his assistance.

"I'm Robin's father, Dan Phinney."

Relieved of the torrent, the floor drain was disposing of the standing water.

Dan looked at the compressed piping again. Manfred followed his gaze and shrugged modestly.

"I had to do what I could. It needed to be replaced anyway."

"I know a hardware store that can send over what we need," Dan said. "In the meantime, why don't you and I get acquainted?"

Robin sailed through the front door of her building under a full head of steam, moving as fast as she could crutch along. She had her checkbook with her. She didn't even need to go upstairs. She'd just bang on Manfred's door, pay him and tell him to vacate the premises immediately.

Just as she drew her fist back to deliver the first emphatic knock, however, she heard laughter coming from the basement apartment. Manfred. The guy even laughed with an accent. But there was someone else, too. Another man. A friend of Manfred's? Someone just as big? Another weight-lifting hulk? The thought of two such specimens was daunting.

What if she made them angry? They could do her in, cut her into little-bitty pieces and she'd never be seen again. Robin sagged on her crutches. She'd had to be a fool to let this guy into her home in the first place. She was so angry and frustrated she wanted to cry.

Until she saw the cop car pull up directly across the street from her house. There was a fire hydrant over there, but in a neighborhood like this, where street parking was impossible at best, people routinely parked in front of the hydrant, and the cops routinely ticketed the offenders. If the car was still there an hour later it got towed. This little drama was good for at least one matinee and two evening performances daily.

So here they were right outside her door, Chicago's Finest. No matter how big the brutes in her basement were, Robin was sure that she could get the cops attention with a bloodcurdling scream. Now was her opportunity to get Manfred and friend out of her house, out of her life.

Robin banged her fist on Manfred's door, hit it three good shots.

She heard footsteps coming her way, but didn't feel the ground shaking beneath her feet. That had to mean the friend was answering the door, and that he couldn't be as big as *Der Monster*. Good. Maybe he'd be small enough that Robin could just yank him right out of there, make Manfred come to the door and give him the fast brush off, too. Bing, bang. She'd be done with it. Robin shifted her crutches to left hand and got ready to make her move.

The door opened and she grabbed ... her father?

Standing there in his underwear holding a bottle of beer?

"Robin, sweetie," he said with a smile, seeming not to notice that she had a fistful of his undershirt. He gave her a peck on the cheek and she let him go. "Come on in, I'll tell you about our adventure."

Adventure?

Robin hobbled down the stairs after him and saw...

Manfred sitting on the sofa holding a beer ... also in his underwear.

And by the looks of him very surprised to see her.

He was far more covered than he'd been in his workout suit — his boxer shorts were so old-fashioned they seemed to come down to his knees — but both Manfred and Robin realized a serious line of propriety had been crossed here and both blushed furiously. Manfred quickly brought his knees together and put his beer bottle in his lap ... until he looked down and realized the unintended symbolism. So he crossed his arms. That hid the bottle but it made his enormous chest bulge even further. As if he were preening.

Robin stared, hypnotized.

Manfred stood up, taking care that his fly didn't gape.

"Excuse, please," he said to Robin. Turning to Dan, he added, "Herr Phinney, you will please let me know when my clothes are dry?"

Dan Phinney's eyes filled with glee.

But all he said was, "You bet."

Manfred marched off to his bedroom and firmly closed the door behind him. Then the bolt lock was thrown. Manfred was plainly taking no further chances with his privacy.

Robin turned to her father.

"Daddy, what in the world is going on here?"

Dan told her what had happened with her plumbing.

"So when we finally got the water shut off we were both soaked to the gills and the poor guy didn't have any clothes clean, so we stripped down to our skivvies and threw our clothes in your laundry machines."

Robin nodded as if it all made perfect sense.

"We had to throw some of your clothes in, too, since Manfred used a load you'd left down here to seal off the back door to the apartment. Did a real good job, too. Hardly got a drop in here, and there was plenty of water in back, believe me."

Robin's mind was suddenly elsewhere.

"Daddy, you're washing everybody's clothes together?"

"Sure, but don't worry. I didn't overload the machines. Everything should be dry in a few minutes. We can sort it all out and when the new pipe is delivered, Manfred and I can fix the plumbing. And don't concern yourself about me, I'll let him do the hard parts."

Dan was worried that his daughter was going to ask him what he'd been doing over here in the first place or scold him for trying to help with the plumbing. But she didn't say a word.

"I hope you don't mind, but I paid him for that part he put in the furnace. I checked it. He did a real good job."

Robin just nodded.

"We were just sitting around having a beer waiting until we could get back to work. That's why you caught us with our pants down."

"Uh-huh."

Dan didn't know what was going on with his daughter. She looked like she'd gone into a trance ever since he mentioned the thing about doing her laundry. He didn't understand it.

"You okay, honey?"

"Yes, Daddy."

"Good. Because I think this Manfred is a real find. Your furnace is fixed, and we'll get your plumbing done. You keep him around, this place will be as good as new." Dan Phinney laughed and held up his bottle. "He even serves German beer. You can't beat that with a stick."

"No, you sure can't. I'm going up to my park now, Daddy."

Her father said something in reply, but Robin didn't catch it. She just kept gimping her way up the stairs. Manfred had saved the day. Again. Her father liked him. He was clearly here to stay.

That was hard enough to think about, but the thing that most unnerved her was the image of what was happening right now inside of her dryer. The load of laundry Robin had left in the basement had been full of her undies ... and all she could picture were her unmentionables locked in a heated, swirling, tumbling dance with those ... those humongous garments of Manfred's.

Her father would never understand it in a hundred years, but Robin felt he had just sealed her fate.

CHAPTER 8

David Solomonovich thought Robin was a frog. Not in the sense that she was an amphibian. Or ugly as a toad. Rather, he saw her as the kind of frog who would turn into a princess when he kissed her. David had cast himself as Prince Charming.

Further testimony to the suppleness of his mind.

He sat at his drafting table in the offices of his father's research laboratory and doodled sketches of Robin the way he imagined she had looked before she had fallen under whatever evil spell afflicted her — and he was sure there was one. His drawing showed a natural gift for draftsmanship and a fair amount of sensitivity for someone so young.

If he had allowed anyone to see his sketches of Robin — he hadn't — he would have had to confess an adolescent crush on an older woman. No easy feat under any circumstances, especially hard when you were fourteen and working on your doctorate. He'd also have to concede that his mother, who'd seen other signs of his talents, had a point when she said he could be as great an artist — her preference — as a scientist — David and his father's choice.

His mother had acquiesced, with one stipulation. She said she wanted David to paint her portrait while she was still young and beautiful. It was the idea of doing that painting — and how people could change over the course of their lives — that had made him take his first good look at Robin.

When his father had allowed David to start working in the lab, he'd made his son go to Screaming Mimi's and pick up lunch for all the senior scientists and engineers. This was his father's way of showing everyone that David wasn't a privileged character. It was also a way to give David some sense of having to start at the bottom and work his way to the top. Not that anyone expected the climb to take very long.

As ever, though, the first step had been the hardest. Upon setting foot in Mimi's, he'd felt a compelling urge to turn and run. The place had terrified him. The crowd, the jostling, the shouting, the insults — Robin presiding over it all like the chief demon of one of the lower circles of hell — had been just too much to take.

But take the step he had, despite having his toes stepped on, his ribs poked and even being knocked down once. David was small but he was not without grit. And after a while his footwork got better, his reflexes sharpened, his field of vision widened so he didn't get blind-sided so often. He learned to anticipate where holes in the crowd would occur. And when his physical survival seemed assured, he started to listen to what was going on around him.

A lot of these people were funny. Which meant they were also smart. Wry, caustic, blunt or subtle, the put-downs and comebacks racketed around the room like machine gun fire. And the fastest gun of all was Robin.

She never even seemed to have to think of what she'd say next, like she had Oscar Wilde whispering in her ear. Except Oscar probably wouldn't be that sharp if you made him serve sandwiches, too.

David had heard the word for such lightning-fast intellectual activity almost from birth. It was usually applied to him.

Genius.

In her own special way, in Mimi's deli, it applied to Robin, too.

It made him want to get to know her, to test himself against her. Which would help him understand the boundaries of his own mind. So, after he'd proved himself a worthwhile addition to his father's lab and been released from his errand-boy duties, David had started to take a later lunch when the crowd had thinned and he could pit himself against Robin one-on-one.

She clobbered him. Time and again.

That made for some frustrating moments. But it was also exhilarating because going up against Robin was one of the rare occasions in his life when he felt challenged. He was bound and determined that someday he would best her.

Besides that attraction, she made him laugh, even if it was usually at his own expense. That was okay, too. Everywhere he went, with precious few exceptions, people kowtowed to him. The boy wonder. The big brain. Nobody treated him like a person. Except Robin.

She whanged him just like everybody else — and he loved her for it.

Not that he expressed it. Not openly. Not in so many words. But one day when the lunch hour crush had run long for some reason David had been doodling sketches of his mother for the portrait he'd agreed to do. Looking up for a moment, he saw Robin. He wondered if anyone had ever done a portrait of her. He wondered if she'd ever been beautiful.

He tried to look past the excess weight and see who she was underneath.

While he observed her, his hand went to work on the sketchpad.

When he looked at what he'd drawn he gasped.

Robin had been beautiful. Or had he just drawn her that way? He looked back up to see if he was only kidding himself. No, he was sure the image he had drawn was an accurate representation of the way this woman had once looked.

To prove it to himself, he started adding lines and tone to the sketch he'd just drawn, additions that would make it look the way Robin did now. With each stroke that brought the image closer to the present reality, David felt pain and sorrow. He realized that something awful must have happened to this woman — to go from who she'd been to who she was now — and the pain he felt must have been nothing compared to hers.

David kept this insight strictly to himself. He felt sure Robin would throw him out on his ear and never let him return if he tried to talk to her about it. But from that day on he resolved to help her find the beautiful young woman she'd been and to become her once again.

Even so, David wasn't going to go to jail and wreck his life for Robin.

There'd be no attempt on his part to crack the CIA's computer system.

David locked his sketchpad into his filing cabinet and logged onto his computer. What was the point of trying to break into one closely guarded agency of the government, he asked himself, when another left its doors wide open. He accessed the Internet, a network of data bases originally conceived for the Defense Department but now, in 1990, used by a growing number of academic institutions. There was talk that in a few years, say the mid-90s, even the general public would be online, but David thought that he might possibly be the first person to use the Internet to do private investigation.

He accessed the Library of Congress and began looking for the name Manfred Welk.

Robin's father tapped at the door to the park before he left. He called out that the plumbing repair had been made and that her laundry had been folded and left in a basket on top of her dryer. She thanked him, grateful that he hadn't opened the door.

She watched him depart through the leaves of a ficus plant next to one of the park's front windows. Dan Phinney waved to his daughter even though he couldn't really see her. Robin had arranged the plantings so she could peer out but would be shielded by a canopy of greenery from anyone trying to see inside. Nevertheless, she gave her father a small, forlorn wave.

When he was gone, she watched her fish swim back and forth.

She wondered if they ever got frustrated, if they ever felt insanity creeping up on them, being confined in such a small pool. She didn't think so. They swam too smoothly. Their overall behavior was too fluid. There was no sense of desperation about them. They got along well with each other. And why shouldn't they? Their water was clear and warm. They had all the food they needed. Their world was free from predators. Life was perfect.

Thanks to her, their keeper.

Maybe living things weren't meant to be kept, though.

Robin felt she was coming to have a keeper of her own.

And just when she was about to cry, Robin heard a soundtrack for her tears. Someone started playing a blues harmonica. Manfred? At first, she thought he'd put on a record, but when no other instruments joined in, when no vocalist sang along, she realized it was just him down there playing the instrument. Playing it very well, too. The music made her feel sadder and better all at the same time.

Now, where would a guy like that have learned to play the blues? Then she thought: Where else? Prison. Maybe learning to play the blues was a correspondence course you could take wherever you were locked up in the world.

Maybe she should learn it herself.

She listened some more and lost herself in the healing melancholy of the music. After a while, she recognized the song. Billie Holiday. *God Bless the Child*. Was Manfred mocking her? No. The only way he could know about her demons was if her father had told him, and Daddy would never do that.

Robin sat there and hoped he'd play all night, but he didn't.

Because a man strolled up the street and turned onto her walkway. She watched him as he approached her front door. The man was average height, just under six feet. He had a slim build, neatly cut brown hair, brown eyes, no eyeglasses, no facial hair. He wore a navy blue windbreaker, faded jeans and plain white sneakers. He had pleasant enough features, but Robin was sure that if he ever came into Mimi's she'd forget what he looked like five minutes after serving him.

Just before he got to the front door, the man startled her by smiling — nice even teeth, but not the blinding white of someone who smiled for a living — and she thought for a moment he'd seen her and was smiling at her. But then she realized that the man was looking down. He was smiling at Manfred, looking at him through a basement window.

And the music stopped.

Robin heard the outer door open and then the door to Manfred's apartment.

Then it all clicked for her. The guy who'd just come calling, he was the spy. The real thing. Someone who could blend into any crowd. Manfred's contact ... unless he was another musician come to play the blues. True, she didn't see him bring an instrument, but one could be down there waiting for him. Or he could have a harmonica in his pocket. Maybe Manfred was out to reinvent the Harmonicats.

Robin listened.

She didn't hear music. She heard voices. Indistinct voices.

Then, with the music gone and pulled from her self-absorption, she smelled sauerkraut. Industrial strength. Commie-prison sauerkraut, for God's sake.

She hadn't thought to ask old Manfred what kind of cooking he did, had she? Now she knew. Robin had wanted to stay in the park a while longer, maybe see if she could eavesdrop as long as she was there, but within minutes the smell of cooking, pickled cabbage drove her upstairs.

Warner Lisle was a CIA agent.

Blessed with pleasantly nondescript features, he could have been the recruiting poster boy for the Company, had it gone in for such things. The son of a fetching Berliner who'd married a GI serving in the Occupation Forces, Warner spoke perfect German. The recipient of a National Defense (i.e. CIA) Scholarship, he learned to speak perfect Russian.

Warner was bright enough to have had a double major in college. His other area of interest — besides Russian language and culture — was aeronautical engineering. But when his three-year hitch with the Agency was up and his college debt repaid, the aerospace industry was in one of its cyclical slumps. No jobs available. So he stayed a spook.

Not cold-blooded enough, by any means, to take on any of the really nasty jobs, he was nonetheless infiltrated into East Germany and told to see what he could see. Look for targets of opportunity. Soak up the gestalt of a front-line Communist state.

That vague assignment lasted until someone got tired of seeing the East Germans take home truckloads of Olympic gold medals. At that point, Warner was assigned to find out just how they did it. At minimum, exposing Commie cheaters would be good propaganda. And you never knew, maybe something useful would be uncovered. Say a chemical compound that could be quietly added to the seasoning of U.S. Army food to build up the troops.

So Warner was assigned to become the first CIA jock-sniffer and ordered to look for some disaffected Marxist mesomorph who would be willing to spill the beans on his comrades.

Warner found Manfred.

He felt personally responsible for Manfred's imprisonment.

And he was determined to redeem himself before he left the Company in the not too distant future. Warner hadn't found a job in aerospace at long last. Rather he would soon be making a number of very interesting models of flying machines for a special effects house in Hollywood.

But he had to pay Manfred back first.

Warner looked cautiously around the basement apartment before turning his attention to his expectant friend. He couldn't imagine why anyone would bug this place, but old habits died hard.

"Clean environment?" he asked.

Manfred nodded.

That was good enough for Warner. You had to trust that somebody who'd lost five years of his life due to casual treachery would be very careful these days.

"We're making progress," Warner said.

"You know where she is?"

The big guy tried to keep his face impassive, but Warner could see the hope in his eyes.

"Not yet. But we've learned your wife has gone back to using her maiden name. She's using it for your little girl, too."

"Hannelore Krump?" Manfred asked.

Warner shook his head.

"No, your ex changed your daughter's first name, too. It's Bianca now."

"Bianca? What kind of name is that?"

"It's the one Mick Jagger's ex has."

"Bianca Krump?" Manfred shuddered.

"We've got the two of them hooked up with a guy named Horst Muehlmann, a/k/a The Bear."

"Muehlmann," Manfred snorted. "A third-rate shotputter who'd be fourth-rate without his daily fistful of steroids."

Warner said quietly, "Horst doesn't have any athletic standing these days except maybe in the smash-and-grab. He was suspected of doing a number of muggings in Magdeburg, but that was quite some time ago and when the victims wouldn't testify all three of them moved on."

"My daughter," Manfred said regretfully, "my little Hannelore, given a ridiculous name by a vindictive mother and living off money stolen by an incompetent clod of a shotputter."

Warner felt worse than Manfred looked. He also blamed himself for the little girl's misfortunes. If he'd kept Manfred out of prison ... Well, he didn't see any point in adding that the former Mrs. Welk had been fined for working as an unlicensed prostitute.

"We'll find them," Warner said. "It won't be long now. We'll get your daughter back."

Manfred nodded his massive head solemnly.

"*Ja*, please do."

Up in her own apartment, a short while later, Robin heard the blues harmonica resume. More wonderfully sweet and sad than ever, the music drifted up through the heating vents. Along with the warm air that Manfred had also supplied. She ought to be grateful to the guy, Robin thought. So what if he had spies dropping in? All spies did was whisper furtively. They didn't throw loud parties and wreck your night's sleep.

Unfortunately, the scent of the sauerkraut wafted upward, too. But it wasn't as strong up here, and Robin thought of a hint she could drop to Manfred about his cooking. It was just mean enough to make her grin. After all, she didn't want to go all mushy about the guy.

But, she thought, he sure must have some soul inside of all that bulk to play the harmonica that way.

This time the music was interrupted by her phone. Robin picked it up, annoyed.

"Hello," she said abruptly.

"What? Someone calls to find out how you are, and you bite her ear off?"

It was Mimi.

"I'm sorry," Robin said. "I was just listening to music."

"So start the record over, dear."

Robin didn't feel like explaining.

She said, "I'm doing okay, Mimi. The doctor said just take it easy ... and lose sixty or seventy pounds."

"He didn't!"

"He did."

"But you're not —"

"Fat. Yes, I am."

"Not like some people."

"No, I'm fat like me."

"I would have said hefty."

"Mimi, can we talk about something else?"

"That was one of the reasons I called. To tell you what that Tone Morello is up to."

Robin was incredulous.

"You called to talk about Ant-knee? What, the idiot was in today?"

"Yes, and looking for you."

"The guy never learns."

"He had a cameraman with him, Robin. He said he wanted to put you on TV."

"Are you kidding?"

"No. Now, why would he want to do that? He can't have anything good in mind."

"Maybe he wants me to do some grunts for his highlight films."

"Robin, don't you dare."

"Come on, Mimi. I was kidding."

"Well, he made a nasty crack about you right into the camera."

Robin's gloom was lifting. There was a challenge here. She was getting intrigued, wondering what that goof Ant-knee was up to this time.

"What'd he say?"

Mimi hesitated and then told her.

Robin laughed, even if the crack stung a little too, coming on the heels of her doctor visit.

"Miss Piggy's body double? That's pretty good. Too good for Ant-knee. He's got somebody thinking up lines for him."

"I might get some grief for it," Mimi said, "but I think I'm going to ban him."

"Don't you dare," Robin replied.

"But he's up to something."

"Yes, he is," Robin said, feeling tough now, feeling much better really, "and whatever it is, I'll be ready for it."

By the time Robin got off the phone with Mimi, she felt buoyant enough to tiptoe, if you could call it that when you got about on crutches, down to Manfred's front door. Without making a sound, she left a can of air-freshener and a note for him.

The note said: Try adding this to all of your recipes.

CHAPTER 9

Robin woke the next morning with a plan for Tone in mind and a delicious odor in her nose. Somebody had been baking. And the results had been delivered to her front door. She knew who the delivery man had to be: Daddy.

He'd seen that she'd been troubled yesterday, so he'd gone out to a bakery first thing this morning, just when they were taking everything out of the oven, and then he'd let himself into the building and left the package on her doorstep for her to find when she woke up.

What a sweetheart.

Robin crutched over to her front door in her pajamas, opened it and almost got jolted off her feet again.

Daddy hadn't been there, Manfred had.

There was a plate of something redolent of apples and cinnamon and quite possibly God's grace sitting just outside her door. Steam seeped out from the edges of the crisp white dish-towel that covered the plate. It must have been dropped off not more than a minute ago. Whatever it was, it smelled good enough to drop to the floor and eat right there.

Except...

Next to the plate lay the can of air freshener she'd left for

Manfred last night. It was as crumpled as a discarded Dixie cup. Under the can was a note. Leaning against the door frame, Robin carefully bent over and picked up the note.

In a crabbed European-looking hand, it read: *Took your advice. Squeezed every last drop into strudel. Let me know how it tastes.*

As with Robin's note, a signature had not been added or necessary.

Robin looked at the plate. And the can. Was he kidding her? Or trying to poison her for being smartass with him?

The safest thing to do with the stuff would be to just put it down her recently repaired garbage disposal. But it smelled *sooo* good. Then Robin smiled as she thought of an answer to the problem, one that fit in neatly with her other plan. What she needed was a food–taster ... and she knew just who it would be.

"Hello, Nancy," Robin said into the phone.

"Well, isn't this a surprise?" her sister asked. "Would you like to speak with Charlie, maybe ask him for a little favor?"

Robin shook her head. That noodge Charlie. He hadn't been able to keep her plea for help with the furnace from Nancy. But that would only make what Robin planned to do even sweeter.

"Actually, I was wondering if I might ask you a favor, if you can spare a little time this morning and maybe later on today."

Nancy was properly suspicious, but curious, too.

"What do you want?"

"Well, I'm on crutches these days—I sprained my ankle—and I hate to bother Dad all the time, so I was wondering if you might give me a lift to work."

Nancy was silent a moment as she explored that idea for booby-traps.

"I usually have a few extra minutes," she finally said. "I suppose I could do that." Then she probed further. "Anything else?"

"Could I borrow your videocam?" Robin asked.

"What for?" Nancy asked, the mistrust clear in her voice now.

Robin told her sister about Tone and his cameraman, and outlined their previous skirmishes.

"I want to have my own record of any interview Ant-knee does with me," Robin said. "It occurred to me that tapes might be edited."

In fact, she knew this because Nancy was the only person she'd ever heard of who edited her home videos. Just as she put only the *creme de la creme* of still photos in her family albums.

"So you want me to shoot this confrontation for you?" Nancy asked.

"And edit it, if necessary."

Nancy considered the idea for a moment.

"Okay. I'll do it."

"Great. The way we'll do it is, I'll excuse myself to use the ladies' room as soon as Ant-Knee shows up. I'll give you a call from the kitchen and reappear when Mimi tells me you've arrived."

Nancy laughed, "Sounds good." Then she regained her focus. "Robin, why are you letting me help you?"

"You're my sister."

"What's the real reason?"

"You're so suspicious, Nancy. I even baked a plate of fresh, warm strudel to share with you for all your help. But maybe I should just eat it myself and take a cab to work."

Nancy didn't have many weaknesses when it came to food. She could take or leave most things. Mostly she left them. But her Achilles's heel, the one temptation she really had to battle was freshly baked pastry. Especially the first thing in the morning.

"Don't you dare eat it yourself," Nancy said. "I'll be right over."

Nancy came, she ate, she defeated Robin utterly. That damn self-control of hers, the piece of strudel she cut for herself wasn't big enough to bait a mousetrap. Hardly a useful sampling to see if it was poisoned. Still, Nancy seemed to get as much enjoyment out of the tiny crumb as if she'd gobbled the whole plate. Robin half-expected her to start rolling on the floor in ecstasy.

For the first time, Robin got an insight into the success of her sister's marriage. If Nancy could get so much out of so little, she must have made Charlie feel like a god every time they hit the sack.

"Robin, that was wonderful," Nancy said. "I didn't know you were such an incredible baker. You call me any time you make that strudel."

"Yeah, I'll do that. Bake you a plate, it'll last all year."

Nancy smiled and turned in profile.

"Well, I do have to watch my figure."

It was a dig, but Robin let it go. She was depending on Nancy for help today.

"You know what you ought to do?" Nancy asked.

"What?"

"Take that strudel to work. You could sell it at the deli, I'm not kidding."

Robin hated to admit it, but the notion struck her as a good idea. She'd wait and see if Nancy got sick on the drive over. If she didn't, Robin could cut the pastry into little free samples and see how the public tolerated it. Then if there were something wrong with the stuff, maybe Ant-knee would eat a slice and get diarrhea or something.

Wouldn't that be fun to capture on videotape?

"You know," Robin said, "I think you've got something there."

Nancy nodded and smiled and licked her lips.

"Maybe if I do an extra twenty minutes on the Stairmaster today you could save me another little piece?"

"Be happy to," Robin said.

Nancy took Robin to work, and she didn't start heaving or show any other signs of distress. Since Tone and his lensman weren't laying in wait when they arrived, Nancy left, saying she'd be at her office until Robin called.

Feeling just a little uneasy, Robin put out the strudel on the counter next to the cash register. She'd cut the pastry into small squares and made a sign: *Free samples. Take just one.* Even having cooled on the way over to the deli, the stuff still smelled wonderful.

"What's this?" Mimi asked, walking over.

"Just a little something I brought in. Homemade strudel. Nancy thought maybe we could sell it here."

"Nancy, huh?"

Mimi knew Nancy's opinion of the deli's food and calibrated her opinion of Robin's sister accordingly. Even so, Mimi had caught a whiff of the strudel.

"May I?" she asked.

What could Robin say?

"Just one," she said.

"Oh, sure."

With predatory speed, Mimi unerringly seized the largest slice, easily three times the size of the amount Nancy had consumed.

Robin watched her chew ... saw the smile form on her lips ... saw the gleam enter her eyes ... saw the shiver run through her. Head-to-toe. Mimi looked so blissful and relaxed ... well, Robin couldn't help but think that Mimi had just had an orgasm.

Then the thought hit her: What if Manfred hadn't put air freshener in the strudel, but had put something else? Who knew what kind of chemicals somebody who'd worked for the CIA might have on hand? She'd read that the nation's intelligence agencies had experimented with LSD. How was she to know they didn't have some kind of aphrodisiac in their medicine chest?

Mimi reached for another piece but Robin grabbed her wrist. She shook her finger. "One's all you get."

Mimi didn't say a word, just looked woeful until Robin let her go. Then, looking over Robin's shoulder, Mimi's eyes grew large and round with amazement. Robin quickly turned to look, but there was nothing there. The door was still locked. They weren't even open for business yet.

Robin knew before she turned back that she'd been had. Mimi was ten feet away with a slice of strudel in each hand.

"Ha-ha," Mimi said. "There's still a trick or two I can teach you."

Then Mimi headed off to the kitchen savoring each bite of her stolen strudel, "Mmmm-ing" all the way.

Robin muttered, "Hope your insurance is paid up."

In the event of food poisoning, Robin had intended to dispose of Manfred's note and the can of air freshener and lay the blame for the whole thing on him. Until her recent moment of paranoia, she hadn't actually thought he'd put anything into the strudel that would rise above the level of a prank, say adding Ex-Lax to fudge cake.

But the strudel was the hit of the breakfast rush. Nobody got sick and everybody enjoyed the heck out of it. Robin couldn't remember how many hands she'd had to slap when people came back for seconds. Including Mimi, who'd come back several times for fourths.

Knowing she was tempting fate, Robin ate the last piece herself.

It was the best damn strudel she'd ever tasted — every bit as good as it smelled — and she could have had the whole plate for herself!

Worse, she had to admit that sauerkraut-slurping golem had put one over on her good.

Mimi came over one last time and when she saw that the strudel was gone her face fell so far it was comic. But then her jaw firmed quickly and a look of diamond-hard determination glistened in her eyes.

"Robin, I want four trays of this strudel every morning."

"And how many for the deli?" Robin asked.

"Okay, six trays then."

"I'd like to help, Mimi, but I didn't bake it."

"But you said you did."

"I said it was homemade."

It took Mimi a second.

"Your new German?"

Robin nodded.

"I don't care," Mimi said. "You tell him I've got a business proposition for him."

In the lull between breakfast and lunch, Robin told Mimi how she intended to deal with Tone and his cameraman. The taste of the strudel lingering in her memory and on her taste buds, Mimi wanted to stay in Robin's good graces. So she offered some suggestions as to how the plan might be improved. Instead of waiting for Tone to arrive before calling Nancy, Mimi would have one of her oldest customers, who also worked at Tone's TV station, give the deli a call the moment Tone and his accomplice walked out the door. That'd give them the jump on the idiot.

"What's the other idea?" Robin asked.

Mimi said, "You may be too young to remember but a very historic event once happened not more than a few blocks from here. Maybe we can recreate it. As far as the flop-sweat goes, anyway."

"Mimi," Robin asked, "what are you talking about?"

"The Kennedy-Nixon debate," she said with a smile.

Warner Lisle leaned against the door of the weight room at St. Malachy High School. Inside the room, Manfred was coaching some young but already startlingly big student-athletes in the proper way to lift weights. As large as the kids were, they looked malnourished next to Manfred, and the barbells that they burst blood vessels to budge he manipulated as though they were broomsticks, pausing at various points in the range-of-motion to explain technique and calling for questions.

When Warner had first placed Manfred at St. Malachy's his original position was as the building's custodian. A couple of weeks later, Manfred secured the permission of the headmaster, Brother Damian, to use the weight room. After the canny brother happened to see Manfred bench-pressing several hundred pounds without apparent effort, he had an idea. He asked Manfred how he'd like to split his time between his custodial duties and coaching those athletes who maintained a superior grade point average. In short order, Manfred became the school's full-time strength coach, and both the academic and athletic standings of the school soared.

Every boy at St. Malachy's wanted Manfred's instruction and cracked the books to get it.

Manfred saw Warner standing in the doorway and knew something was up, but as a measure of his professionalism he finished his class before leading the spy to his tiny cubicle off the weight room.

"You have news," he said.

"Once we got the names, things went fast," Warner said. "We've pinned them."

"Where are they?"

"Your old home town, Dresden."

"Muehlmann is still stealing for a living?"

"No, he's moved up in the world. He's the bouncer at a bordello that he and your ex are fronting for the Russian Mafia. Ulrike's the madam."

"And Hannelore?"

"She has a room down the hall from where the ladies ply their trade."

Manfred's face grew grim.

"This is no place for a little girl. What will become of her living there?"

Warner didn't tell him that little "Bianca" seemed to like her digs just fine, according to the agent who'd paid his ex a visit. In fact, she was the whores' pet and seemed to revel in the role.

"Our man talked to Ulrike," he said "And just as you suspected, she's perfectly willing to sell your daughter back to you."

Manfred was not pleased with the accuracy of his prediction. The idea of having to buy his daughter back galled him.

"Could you kidnap her for me?"

Warner shook his head.

"The GDR and the Cold War are both finished. Germany's united and an allied nation. I'd never get permission for that."

"I helped you quite a bit," Manfred pointed out.

"And we'll help you all we can. But no kidnapping."

"How much does she want?"

"One hundred thousand dollars."

Manfred sagged under a weight far greater than any barbell he'd ever lifted. When he'd been freed from prison, the CIA had brought him to America, got him his job, set him up for eventual citizenship and given him fifty thousand dollars to start his new life. Manfred had not spent a penny of that money, knowing he would likely have to ransom his daughter someday. He'd worked at his job, lived as cheaply as he could in a tiny room at a YMCA and added to his savings. He now had sixty thousand dollars to his name. He could save even more now that he was living rent-free, but he couldn't stand to wait any longer.

"I don't have enough," he said.

Warner nodded.

"We're friends, right?" The question was rhetorical. "And you know how I feel about you winding up in prison. So I'm going to give you some of my own money, a little something I've put aside, and you're not going to argue about it."

Manfred didn't.

"How much?" he asked.

"Twenty-five thousand."

"That's still not enough."

"It's close enough to bargain."

Manfred nodded, and a look came into his eyes that would have scared the hell out of Warner if it had been directed at him.

"*Ja*, bargain. And tell Ulrike and Horst that if they don't accept the bargain, I will visit them ... and they won't be happy to see me again."

Tone Morello was not happy. The moment he set foot in Mimi's and saw what was waiting for him, he was not a happy chappy at all. He'd have backed right out, and even tried to, except he bumped into his idiot cameraman who was practically stepping on his heels. From that point on, people were shaking his hand, practically pulling him into the room. Everybody was smiling at him, but the smiles were the kind that the big bad wolf had saved for the three little pigs when he was handing out eviction notices.

At the far end of the room Tone saw two lecterns made of stacked cardboard cartons. Somebody had drawn an emblem on each lectern. He had seen enough tapes of sports teams at the White House to recognize the Presidential Seal, but that only confused him further. As he continued to be urged forward, a storm cloud of questions formed in his mind.

What was going on here? Why were all the customers facing this grade school stage set like they were some kind of audience? Why was Robin waiting for him behind one of the lecterns instead of behind the counter where she belonged? And who the hell was the little blonde with the second videocam?

It took a final shove from Mimi to get Tone into position next to Robin. He looked out at the crowd and the two cameras and he started to sweat. He worked in a TV studio, not before a live audience. He wiped his brow. With the cuff of his shirt. Which both cameras caught.

Tone gave a sickly smile.

A thought popped into his head that suddenly made him queasy. He darted a glance at Robin and breathed fractionally easier. She didn't have her carving knife. Thank God for that. She was sitting on a stool and there was a pair of crutches leaning on the wall behind her.

Then he looked back at the cameras, and he knew they'd seen him peeking at Robin. And he knew that it must've made him look as sneaky and nervous as hell.

Off to a helluva start, Tone-boy, he thought. Why prolong the agony? Why not just unzip, hang your schlong out in front of the world and end your life as you know it? Then with a grimace that he hoped he'd kept off his face he thought he probably couldn't even do that. The way he felt right now, his dick was probably shriveled up so tight it was hiding between his lungs.

The best thing to do, he decided, was to hang tight. Tone

might have remained semi-comatose indefinitely had not Mimi addressed the crowd.

"Ladies and gentlemen," she said. "As you know, we usually don't usually go in for formal debate around here; we ad-lib things. But then we usually don't record our goings-on for television, either. However, Mr. Morello recently said that he'd like to do an interview with Robin for his sportscast, something about the competition we all face in our everyday lives. When I informed Robin of this, she said she had a few questions for Mr. Morello, too, and would like to have her own camera person on hand so she could see if there was a market for the unedited tape at any other TV station in town."

Other TV stations, Tone thought aghast. Unedited tape. He'd be the laughingstock of the whole town.

He went ash gray under his sheen of sweat, looking not dissimilar to one of those statues — though hardly the Virgin Mary — that miraculously produce tears and other forms of bodily moisture.

Mimi continued, "Since we don't care much about manners around here, but we do believe in home-field advantage, Robin, you can go first."

Robin got to her feet and turned to her opponent, and waited until he finally glanced her way. Tone looked like a condemned man wondering why it was taking so long for the axe to fall.

Robin shook her head sadly.

"Ant-knee, Ant-knee, Ant-knee," she said, "I really have to ask … Why can't you ever play fair?"

The question took Tone by surprise, hit him just the right way to get him mad, light a fire under his backside, make him forget his fear. His shaking knees suddenly firmed up. A healthy flush of red anger swept the death mask from his face. He straightened his spine so he could look down on Robin.

"What kind of a crap question is that?" Tone asked, repeating in a mocking tone. "Why can't I play fair?" This time Tone shook his head at Robin. "I play to *win*. Same as every other man."

"Anything goes? Ends justify the means?" Robin asked.

"Bet your fat—" Tone caught himself when he saw Mimi staring at him like a network censor. "—rear end."

Robin nodded her head.

"And I suppose this attitude applies to all parts of your life?"

"Like Lombardi said, 'Winning isn't everything, it's the only thing.' "

"So, it's okay to waltz in here one day with your own private cheering section?"

"Right," Tone said, trying to tough out a memory that still stung.

"And it's okay to try to nail me with an ambush interview?"

"*Sixty Minutes* does it all the time."

Tone knew he was on solid professional ground here.

"All's fair on your job, too, I bet."

"TV's dog eat dog. Everybody knows that."

"How about women?"

Now, Tone smiled. Gleefully.

"We're finally getting to it, aren't we?" he asked.

"Yeah, we are," Robin said.

Tone nodded.

"That's the whole thing between you 'n me. You can't stand it that I'd never give you the time of time of day ...that ... " He stopped to think; he wanted to get these lines right. "... That I think you're never fully dressed without your flea collar ... That you don't have a waistline, you have an equator."

Tone was rolling now, remembering the lines he'd had written for him.

People were laughing. With him. At Robin.

It felt great.

He would have kept going except he saw Robin making check marks on an index card she had in front of her.

"Hey, what're you doing?" Tone asked.

Robin slipped the card into a pocket, looked at the crowd and said, "In case any of you happened to miss it, Ant-knee here said the other day that I was Miss Piggy's body double."

The line got a good laugh, even from those who'd heard it before.

"Now, today, he's come up with a couple more nice zingers, but the problem is, he doesn't do his own material. He can't have many darts left. Two, if my information is correct."

Robin looked at Tone. "You want to say them, Ant-knee, or should I?"

If looks could kill, Tone's cameraman would have keeled over on the spot. A true professional, however, the cameraman kept his tape rolling.

"You told, you rat!" Tone accused.

"No, he didn't," Robin said.

The crowd watched, mesmerized, as Tone turned his glare on her.

"Then you found that fink kid writer I hired."

It took Tone a second to realize that he'd just confessed: He didn't come up with his own putdowns. In Mimi's, that was worse than admitting you had the hots for your mom.

Robin rubbed salt in the wound.

"I didn't find anyone."

She took the index card out of her pocket, held it up for the cameras and then showed it to Tone. All it had on it were check marks, nothing else.

"I was bluffing, Ant-knee. Nobody had to tell me anything. I knew you couldn't come up with lines like that by yourself. You wouldn't be the star pupil in a school of fish. No way you got so glib so fast. And why pay for more than the few lines you could memorize? My thinking was, you wouldn't have more lines than you could count on the fingers of one of your tiny hands."

Tone couldn't stand it. It was like this damn broad was inside his head, knew his every move before he made it. He started trembling. Not out of fear or with embarrassment but from rage.

"You gave yourself away, Ant-knee," Robin needled merrily.

Tone clenched his fists.

Stan Prozanski, sitting in the front row, noticed, and slipped out his billy-club.

Tone saw Mimi's pet cop, and he knew as bad as things were, they'd be infinitely worse if he got his nose spread out all over his face.

Robin turned toward the cameras and the crowd.

"Now, on occasion, I've mentioned that Ant-knee has a teeny wienie. Not subtle, but with a guy like him obvious is the way to go. Today, I'd like to say that Ant-knee's penis is the size of a redwood compared to his sliver of a conscience. Why do I say that? Well, look at him. He's a handsome man, I have to admit. And he has a glamorous job that pays him a small fortune. With all that going for him, you'd think he'd be the last guy in the world to be insecure. But I've watched him the past few years, since he started coming in here ... and he preys on women."

"Wait a goddamn minute!" Tone shouted.

He started to make a move, until Stan slapped his billy-club across his palm.

Robin gave Tone a dismissive glance and continued, "You've all seen it. He hits on women in here all the time, and has a lot of success. Now, he's not doing anything illegal or anything a lot of guys wouldn't do if they could. Ant-knee just charms the ladies. And some of them are tough enough or indifferent enough that they continue coming in here after he humps them and dumps them. They don't let it bother them when they see him handing the same load of bull he used on them to someone new ... and ignores them like they're snot-soaked Kleenex."

Tears welled in the eyes of more than a few women present; they knew just who Robin was talking about.

"But these women are the survivors. They've managed to hang in there. But over the past few years I've counted maybe a dozen bright, spunky young women who used to come in here and give as good as they got ... and who just disappeared when this man was through with them. They couldn't bring themselves to come back here and show their faces."

Robin turned to look at Tone.

"What did you do to them, Ant-knee? What did you promise them? What lies did you make them believe? Where are they now?"

Tone had no answer. He'd gone inside himself to the only depths he had: self-pity.

Robin looked back at the crowd.

And smiled.

"All of you know what Ant-knee says about me. I'm fat. Well, I am. And I'm loud. And I'll chew your backside off if you give me half-a-reason. Fat, loud and biting ... that's me. And I'm proud of it. Because I'll never have to worry about an SOB like him humiliating me and breaking my heart."

And when she turned to pick up her crutches, with her face away from the cameras, and in a voice too soft for anyone to hear, Robin added, "Ever again."

Nancy took Robin home early.

"You want the tape?" she asked.

"No."

"Didn't turn out the way you planned, did it?"

"No."

"It was supposed to be more fun."

"Yeah, I was just going to disembowel him, not castrate him."

"Sounds like he deserved it, though."

"So many do."

"Not all of them. There are good men, Robin."

"Yeah, but you married the last one."

Nancy put a hand on Robin's leg.

"I know what you're going to say," Robin said, "but let's not get into it, huh?"

"Sorry, I've got to."

Robin resigned herself. The perfect end to the perfect day. She turned to look at her sister as Nancy pulled to the curb in front of Robin's house.

"Go ahead."

"Okay ... Where's that piece of strudel you promised me?"

Robin couldn't believe it, and then she couldn't help but laugh. She hugged Nancy and because Robin loved her sister so much she burst into tears.

Crutching away from the car as fast as she could, Robin promised to ask Manfred to bake Nancy a whole plate of strudel.

Nancy pulled her car door closed and wondered: Manfred? Who the hell was *Manfred?*

CHAPTER 10

The first thing Robin noticed when she entered the vestibule of her building was that Manfred had added his name to the mailbox. Right there, under the box for the mail, just above the button for the doorbell to the basement apartment, was his name. M. Welk. In some kind of Gothic typeface. Maybe the guy had learned calligraphy in prison, too.

Robin just stared at the intrusion. Stunned.

There'd never been any name but hers on her home before and she was having a hard time getting over it. She knew this was silly. The man had to identify himself to the Postal Service. He couldn't just have his mail left under a brick out back ... No, as much as she'd like that idea, the authorities would never go for it.

Robin was casting about for other possibilities when she noticed that the mailbox itself had been polished. The brass shone brightly enough that Robin could see her reflection in it. That was a heck of a tough job, polishing a mailbox like that. It took a lot of rubbing. Plenty of elbow grease. She knew because she'd done it shortly after she'd bought the building—but not since.

Then she smelled the fresh paint, and noticed that the entry hall had been painted, too. It was the same shade of eggshell white she'd chosen, but it was clean and new. This was getting eerie. What the heck did this guy think he was doing? Taking her back in time, gaslighting her? Robin looked around, half-expecting Rod Serling to step out of the shadows.

Except there were no shadows.

Manfred had changed the light bulbs in the fixture, replacing the old ones with higher wattage substitutes that dispelled the late afternoon shadows and gave off a kind of pleasing pink tone that made the fresh paint look warm and the polished brass sparkle.

Wait a minute!

The guy was changing Robin's home without even asking her permission. Who the hell did he think he was? Robin rang the doorbell for M. Welk's apartment. It had never worked before, but she wasn't surprised that it did now.

But the agreeable three-toned bell brought no response.

He was probably out in the garage lifting his damn weights, Robin thought. Well, she was going to tell him a thing or two.

Robin crutched out of the vestibule and turned the corner of her building under a full head of steam.

She didn't find him in the garage; she didn't have to go that far. She saw him on the backstairs. He was almost done painting the stairs and the landings in a fresh coat of gray. Robin was struck speechless, thinking maybe this was some kind of a German thing, this mania for home improvement. Maybe he'd tuckpoint the masonry next.

Manfred sensed someone was watching him. He turned and saw Robin.

With a bucket of paint in one hand and a paintbrush in the other, he asked, "Did you like the strudel?"

"It was delicious," she said.

Robin couldn't understand herself. She wanted to tell this oaf off, and here she was complimenting him.

Manfred nodded and transferred the brush to the hand with the bucket.

"It's the air freshener that makes all the difference."

He kissed his fingertips in a gesture of gustatory delight.

Robin bristled. This Teutonic moose was mocking her. Well, great. This was just what she needed to—

But before she could tear into him, Manfred said, "We need to talk."

"You bet we do," Robin agreed.

He served her tea and cookies — homemade no doubt — in his apartment.

They had to go somewhere. This wasn't a neighborhood where you held a shouting match in your backyard, and Robin certainly wasn't going to have him up to her place. No way.

So she sat across his kitchen table from him while he poured tea for her and asked if she preferred lemon or milk with it. She muttered lemon between her teeth and wondered how this man could be such a mountain of contradictions. He was as big and strong as a gorilla but he could have the manners of a Junior League debutante when he wanted. It was maddening trying to get a handle on him.

But Robin wasn't going to let her anger go, not this time.

After sipping the tea, and refusing to tell him how good it was, she said, "Just what do you think you're doing, messing with my building?"

"Messing?" Manfred asked puzzled, familiar with the word but not her usage.

"Painting, polishing, changing the damn light bulbs."

"Is that not my job, how I earn my keep?"

"Your job is to fix things."

Manfred shrugged.

"I didn't think it would hurt. You don't like things to look nice?"

"Yes, I like things to look nice, and I like to make them look nice. Myself."

"But I—"

"But nothing. This is my house. The next time you improve it without my permission, you're out."

"Improvements are a bad thing?"

He wasn't that dumb, to ask a question like that. And Robin was far too savvy to fall into such an obvious trap. Then she got it ... she finally understood what he'd been up to, and why he wanted to talk with her. He wasn't sprucing up the place for her, he had somebody else he wanted to impress. Somebody he wanted to move in with him.

Robin told him so directly.

"You want me to let somebody else move in here with you."

Manfred nodded his massive head.

"*Ja.*"

"Well, you can forget it. No girlfriend. No aunts and uncles. No—"

Manfred held up a baby picture and it hammered Robin's heart like a twelve-pound sledge. A little pink angel with downy brown hair and huge blue eyes. She looked to be about three months old. Robin felt the echo of a pain that was decades old and with her every day of her life.

"My daughter," Manfred said. "I live for her. For her, I survived the years in prison."

He extended the picture to Robin, but she refused to take it. She shook her head.

"I'm sorry ... I can't, I just can't."

"I am buying her back from her mother."

Robin's jaw dropped.

"What? Who could sell that child?"

"My ex-wife. I am paying her $85,000."

"No, no ... nobody could sell that baby, not for all the money in the world."

Tears welled up in Robin's eyes.

"My daughter is living in a bordello now. Her mother is the madam. My daughter is learning how to live her life from whores."

Robin took the picture, looked at it with tears streaming down her face.

Then she asked Manfred, "You'd do anything for her, wouldn't you?"

"*Ja.*"

So she had him, Robin thought. All she had to do was tell him tough luck, your kid can't stay here, and he was gone. Out of her life. She'd have gotten her furnace and plumbing fixed on the cheap. With a couple of nice paint jobs thrown into the bargain.

She looked at him and knew he wouldn't argue, either. That big square face was as stoic as if it grew out of the ground on Easter Island. He wasn't going to plead, no matter how dainty a tea party he put on.

All she had to do was say the word and she'd have her old life back.

Robin handed the picture back to Manfred and got up on her crutches.

"Just your daughter," she said. "Nobody else. Ever."

"*Danke.*"

When Robin got to the door, she turned to look back at him.

"And short of putting out a fire, don't you dare do another thing to my home without asking me first."

Manfred didn't say a word, just gave his little nod and clicked his heels under the kitchen table.

A minute later, Manfred was washing the teacups when he heard Robin enter the park above him. There was a moment when the rush of water from the tap was the only sound, and then his ears were filled with the most heart-wrenching sob he'd ever heard. It was all he could do to restrain himself from running up there, ripping the door off its hinges and vowing to do anything, including taking the world onto his shoulders, to ease her pain.

But he knew she would only reject him.

Would have good reason to throw him out.

And he didn't want that, not when he was making a home here for Hannelore.

Manfred dried the cups and saucers with a clean white towel and put them in the cupboard. Looking at the ceiling above his head and nodding once more, he made a promise to himself that someday he would help this woman, would set things right for her.

Whatever the cost.

CHAPTER 11

The next morning, Robin overslept.

When she finally pulled her head off the pillow, wondering why she hadn't heard the alarm, she saw it was 9:30. She'd already missed the breakfast rush! She couldn't believe it. Until last week, she'd never missed a breakfast or lunch at Mimi's. Now, she'd missed two.

She grabbed the alarm clock and shook it, tried to wring from it the reason for its treachery. Then she saw the clock wasn't at fault. She hadn't set the alarm. That oversight appalled her more than anything else.

Until the phone rang.

Robin swung her legs out of bed and picked up the phone.

"Mimi," she said, "I'm sorry. I'm so sorry. I'll never do it again. I'll be right down."

It hadn't entered Robin's mind that the call might be from anyone else, and she was right. But, much to her surprise, Mimi wasn't angry. Wasn't even sarcastic.

"Robin, honey, it's all right," she said. "It works out better this way."

A chill passed through Robin.

"What works out better?"

"I was thinking about yesterday and I want you to take some time off."

"But I don't want—"

"You need to, Robin. If nothing else, you've got to rest your ankle, let it get better. And I don't like being away from my cash register so much."

That was only part of the reason, Robin knew. She waited to see if Mimi was going to tell her the whole truth. After a long pause, Mimi continued.

"Robin, what happened yesterday was my fault. I never should've set things up the way I did. Staging some cockamamie debate. Who am I, Hal Prince? I'm going to start producing musicals next? I should've told that bozo, Morello, to keep his lousy camera out of my place. If he wanted a go at you, he'd have to do it like anybody else, ordering his food on one side of the counter with you on the other. But I made a mistake. I gotta watch myself."

"You think I went too far, don't you, Mimi?"

Mimi's voice was sad and carried a plea for understanding.

"Honey, you know how it is. People come into Screaming Mimi's, they know they're liable to get sliced up faster than the cold cuts, but there has to be ... what ... the feeling that the pieces will fit back together when they walk out the door. There has to be a sense a fun to it. There has to be a possibility that they'll look back at themselves and laugh. I don't think Tone Morello's going to be laughing at anything real soon."

"He got what he deserved," Robin said stiffly.

"Yes, he did, but he didn't have to get it at my place. And that's why I blame myself for letting the whole thing happen. Helping it happen."

"Mimi, I want to come to work."

"Take a week off, Robin. You need it."

Mimi's voice was soft, but Robin knew there was no way she'd change Mimi's mind.

"I love you, honey," Mimi added.

Then she hung up.

Robin watched television, every channel that was on, even the foreign-language stations, none for more than five minutes at a time. She read both newspapers, the *Trib* and the *Sun-Times,* cover-to-cover. She did the same with the *Reader's Digest* and *Newsweek.* She tried listening to talk-radio, but even after all her years at Mimi's, the level of discourse on the airwaves made her gag in the first thirty seconds. All poison, no panache.

When she couldn't make any further attempts at distraction, she sat in her park and thought. About her life. About her tenant. And about the child who would soon appear — for whom she'd have to make a place in her life, if only on the periphery.

Three days passed, and the best Robin could say for them was that after repeated icing and very little weight bearing, her ankle was feeling much better, a working part of her body again, no longer a bloated sausage casing filled with shooting pains.

Robin was sitting in the park on the fourth morning, having just dropped a coin in her wishing well, asking for forgiveness as she did daily, when a note was slipped under the door. It had to be from Manfred. She'd spoken on the phone to both her dad and Nancy, and had told them she was going to spend her time off sorting herself out — Ha! — so give her some time alone. That meant they wouldn't be mousing around sliding notes under her door. Which left only one possibility. *Der Grosse Kraut.*

As she walked over to pick up the note, Robin was pleased at how pain-free her stride was. Time to give the crutches to the Salvation Army. She bent over and grabbed the piece of paper, curious about what Manfred had to say.

He'd given her a list.

He wanted to know which of the following home improvements would be permissible:

— Repainting the window trim
— Replacing the walkway alongside the house
— Weather-stripping all entrances
— Putting new gutters on the garage...

The list covered twenty-two items and went on to the back of the page. It was almost enough to make Robin think the guy was telling her that her house was a dump, almost enough to get her mad at the implication.

Until she remembered that he was asking her permission first, as she'd demanded. The note requested that she check those jobs to which she was agreeable, and it said that they would, of course, discuss the cost of materials before any work began.

She grinned as she imagined how earnest Manfred's face must have looked as he composed the list; and she thought he'd really been considerate the past few days to make himself virtually invisible; and she thought he wanted to have the nicest place possible for the little girl who was currently living in a whorehouse.

Manfred had written she could slip the note back under his door. He'd read it when he got home from school that afternoon. School? No ... no way he could be a student. So was he a teacher? Or a custodian? She'd never actually asked him what he did for a living. She leaned more toward the custodial job: that would explain his Mr. Fix-it skills.

Then Robin thought she better not sell him short. The guy was full of surprises. He might be the school principal, and he lived rent-free in a basement apartment because — well, he had to pay $85,000 dollars to buy his daughter out of bondage.

Who knew what he did?

But whatever it was, she'd bet he was good at it.

She had a pen in her pocket. She wrote on his note: "I think I can scrape up five hundred dollars for materials. Do whatever you can with that."

That ought to buy some more paint and polish, Robin thought. The big stuff would have to wait until later.

Then she added a postscript that she knew someone who had a business proposition for him, and if he had any time to spare, he could see her about it.

When she left the park, Robin didn't slip her message under Manfred's door, she left it sticking out of his mailbox.

Robin spent the rest of the morning cleaning her apartment. She was normally a tidy housekeeper without getting obsessive about it. However, the past few days, involuntarily removed from her routine by Mimi's edict, and the necessity of resting her ankle, Robin had let things slide. Now, she vacuumed, she mopped and she dusted. She rinsed all the things in the sink and stuck them in the dishwasher. She scoured the kitchen and the bathroom.

Then she showered, put on her last pair of clean slacks and a sweatshirt that said: "I love my bad attitude." The latter item a gift from Nancy.

She loaded up all her laundry into two plastic baskets and headed down the backstairs to the basement. There was a nip in the air, and with her hair still damp, she shivered. Maybe she ought to have Manfred put in a laundry chute for her, she thought. See if he'd like to pick up a few extra bucks cleaning and pressing her clothes, too.

Robin opened the back door to the basement, stepped into the laundry area and stopped dead in her tracks. Hanging from a clothesline — that she hadn't put up — were three of the most colossal pairs of underwear she had ever seen in her life. Stripes, polka dots and little zeppelins respectively, she could imagine entire Third World villages taking shelter under them.

She had, of course, seen Manfred in his underwear, but that had been only one fleeting, blushing glance, and having her father there in his boxer shorts had been a further distraction. Now, these great yards of intimate cloth confronted her directly, flaunted themselves and dared her to behold their stature.

So what kind of man...

Robin put her laundry down and looking around to make sure she was truly alone she inched toward the clothesline. Oh, sure, there were other things hanging from the line, old-fashioned ribbed T-shirts and such, but it was those incredible drawers that drew Robin to them hypnotically. Having a man, other than her dad, anywhere in her life was new and strange and sometimes frightening, but this, this gargantuan display of male underwear, brought out feelings in her — well, they were just sick.

Looking around once more and being reassured that she was alone, Robin took a peek up the leg of the polka-dotted pair.

"Woo-woo," Robin said to herself, giggled and then blushed.

She realized just how silly she was being, snorted with disgust, shook herself, gathered up her laundry and started to load the washer...

But she couldn't keep from looking over her shoulder.

They were just so huge. They weren't decent. Why couldn't the man wear white briefs? Probably because he couldn't find them in his size. Well, she'd just have to tell him he couldn't hang those things in here.

Except if she did, he wouldn't.

Robin lowered the lid on her first load of wash and, oh so casually, strolled over to the clothesline. Her hands were a blur as she plucked the zeppelins out of the air. She unfolded the underwear in front of her at eye level. The sight made her swallow hard. Next she held them up to her own waist. It was the first time in conscious memory that a piece of clothing made her feel petite. She swayed back and forth, humming tunelessly, with the underwear billowing out to her sides.

"Well," came a voice from behind her, "now I'll know what to get you for your next birthday."

Nancy!

Robin froze. She felt enough heat in her face to roast a turkey. Taking a deep breath she carefully hung the underpants back on the line and waited for the blood to drain from her face before she turned around.

When she did turn, she asked, "Don't you believe in knocking?"

"The door was open."

"You could knock anyway."

"I guess I better learn," Nancy agreed with a grin.

Nancy had come over to see if Robin needed anything from the grocery store. When she hadn't gotten a response to the doorbell, she'd come around back. Now, the two sisters were on their way to the supermarket in Nancy's car.

"So, you going to tell me about Manfred?" Nancy asked directly.

"There's nothing to tell," Robin said.

"Dad says he's a nice guy."

Robin had no doubt that Nancy had pumped their father for all the information he had.

"I suppose," Robin allowed.

"And handy, too."

"He knows how to fix things."

"I noticed he re-did your vestibule."

Nancy would, of course, notice something like that.

"Yes, he did," Robin said.

"Looks very nice. He painted the backstairs and porches, too, huh?"

"Yes."

Robin was still seriously embarrassed about what Nancy had seen and didn't want to give her anything with which to embroider a relationship that didn't exist.

They rode in silence until Nancy stopped for a red light.

Then Nancy said, "I used to get turned on by Charlie's underwear."

Robin blushed furiously. She didn't want to hear this.

"Sometimes I even put them on. For him."

"Nancy!"

Robin was mortified ... and, okay, a little fascinated, too. Nancy the control freak letting Robin see a little of what she had hidden behind her curtain, admitting that she had a kinky side.

Nancy looked at Robin with a bland, challenging expression.

"What?" Nancy asked, daring Robin to crack wise.

"The light's green," Robin replied, still uncertain she wanted to hear more.

Nancy didn't give her a choice. She continued her story as she stepped on the gas.

"Charlie wears boxer shorts, too. The first time he saw me in them, he said, 'So, you want to fight, huh? See who wears the pants around here.'"

Robin was surprised there was any question that it wasn't Nancy.

"The next day," Nancy said, "when we were getting ready for bed, Charlie threw a pair of his underwear at me. Once I got them on, he brought out these absolutely enormous boxing gloves. It was like wearing a big pillow on each hand. He said we should go three rounds."

Unable to restrain herself, Robin asked, "What did you use for a ring?"

"What do you think?" Nancy smirked. "Our bed."

She pulled into the supermarket parking lot.

"We had a little trouble tearing each other's shorts off wearing those ridiculous gloves, but we managed." As they got out of the car, she added. "Went all three rounds, too."

Robin snorted.

"You were young in those days."

Nancy snorted right back.

"Why do you think Charlie and I work out so often?"

Robin didn't feel it necessary to answer that one.

As they walked toward the store, Nancy said, "Robin, let me tell you something."

"What?"

"It's time you saw a penis again."

"Nancy!"

"A big, hard one wearing a smile."

"Stop it," Robin hissed, looking around to see who might be overhearing them.

Undeterred, Nancy said as they entered the store, "Listen, men's underwear is fun, but what's inside is even better."

After they'd shopped and were on their way back to Robin's house, Nancy dropped the bomb.

"Dad came into the office today."

"So?"

Their father often stopped in at the real estate agency to see Nancy.

"He spent half-an-hour talking to Mom alone in her office."

"What?"

Robin was shocked. Their parents hadn't spent a cumulative thirty minutes talking to each other in all the years they'd been separated. For the first five years, when they'd happened to be in the same place, they'd walk right past one another without batting an eye. Even now, all these years later, "Hello, how are you?" was about as far as it went, and that was on a good day.

"What did they talk about?" Robin asked.

"I don't know."

"You couldn't worm it out of either of them?"

Unlike Robin, Nancy still talked with their mother.

"No, and I tried, believe me."

"I'll ask Daddy."

"Let me know if you find out anything."

"Sure."

Robin got out of Nancy's car in front of her house, pleased that she was able to carry two bags of groceries without difficulty.

"Thanks for the help," Robin said.

"I'm always here for you, kiddo. You remember that."

Robin nodded and then she said, "I have to ask you something."

"What?"

"How can an erection wear a smile?"

Nancy grinned, answering as she drove away.

"That's the part you provide."

CHAPTER 12

David Solomonovich, boy genius, finally cornered the wily international desperado, Manfred Welk, in the pages of *Sports Illustrated*. He'd found a dated copy of the magazine in the on-line archives of the Library of Congress that told Welk's tale. The story intimated that Welk had, indeed, been spying for the CIA. While the details of the former champion power-lifter's trial had been kept secret, it was thought that he had been turning over the training secrets of the East German athletic juggernaut to the Americans. This information, it was said, would be useful in detecting drug-doping by the German Communists, would threaten that nation's future as an athletic powerhouse and would be an altogether crushing propaganda defeat for the GDR.

The story concluded that as punishment for his acts Welk had been given an indeterminate prison sentence, and might never again be a free man. Without saying so directly, the story made clear that Welk, the only East Bloc weight lifter believed to train drug-free, was a genuine hero.

The accompanying photos of Welk in competition showed that he was of heroic proportions, too. The kind of figure, David thought, who might slay thousands on the battlefield before the Valkyries carried him off to Valhalla.

The thought of this guy living in Robin's house made David intensely jealous. David might be too smart to take on the CIA but, with his teenage hormones raging, he was going to find a way to keep this Kraut away from his Robin.

Robin had put her groceries away and eaten a light lunch. She'd been thinking about her damn doctor's admonition to lose weight and now she was peeking through the foliage to look out the park's front windows and see if Manfred might be arriving home from school. She noticed the car parked out front next to the fire hydrant.

The car was a Porsche 911, nondescript gray and in need of a wash. In Robin's neighborhood, it blended in as easily as if it were a Chevy. Actually, on her block, it would be the domestic car that stuck out like a sore thumb. There was a man sitting in the driver's seat, not doing anything in particular. Robin thought he might even have been sleeping, but she couldn't see if his eyes were closed.

In their eternal search for wrongdoers and parking fine revenue, a patrol unit of the Chicago Police Department soon pulled up next to the Porsche. The cop got out and tapped on the driver side window of the Porsche. The guy had been sleeping and woke with a start. He lowered his window and smiled at the cop. Robin could see from where she was that the guy had nice teeth.

He took something out of his pocket and showed it to the cop. The cop reached for whatever the guy was showing him, but the guy shook his head and put the object back in his pocket. Playing keep-away from a Chicago cop is not a course of action taught in Driver's Ed. So Robin was surprised that the cop didn't yank the guy out of his car and throw him in the back of the patrol unit.

Instead, the cop got on his radio, all the while staring at the guy in the Porsche, who was still smiling pleasantly. A moment later the cop apparently got some news he didn't like because he flipped off the guy in the Porsche and drove away at high speed.

All without giving the guy a parking ticket.

This was a bit of street drama that Robin had never seen before.

The next thing she knew the guy got out of the Porsche and was walking right toward her building. He was a nice looking guy, average appearance, neatly groomed and wore a good suit. He could have fit into the neighborhood as easily as his car. Better, actually, since he didn't need a wash. He shocked Robin by waving at her as he entered her front hall.

Robin backed away, not knowing how he could have seen her through the foliage.

She retreated further toward the rear of the park when the doorbell rang.

How had he known she was here?

She decided to wait him out, not answer the bell. Even when it rang the second time. But on the third try, the guy rang "Shave-and-a-haircut-two-bits." Something about that told her that the guy had a sense of humor, that he was probably all right, and maybe she should at least listen through the outer door to what he had to say.

Robin opened the front door to the park.

The guy looked at her through the panes of glass in the outer door and smiled at her. He really was good looking, like the boy-next-door all grown up and making his way in the world quite nicely, thank you.

"What do you want?" Robin asked brusquely.

"A good German beer," the guy said, still grinning, though up close Robin could see deep circles of fatigue under his eyes. "I'm reliably informed I can find some in your basement."

How did he know that, Robin wondered in amazement. That Manfred lived here and that he drank German beer.

For that matter, how had he known she'd been in the park? Robin asked.

"Your camouflage is pretty good," the guy said, "but I saw your breath condensing on the window pane."

Somebody'd notice something like that?

"Who the hell are you?" Robin asked.

The guy reached into the same pocket he'd used for the cop. He brought out a little ID folder and flipped it open.

"Warner Lisle. CIA. I've been flying most of the past 24 hours. I'm here to see Manfred. Now, may I please come in and have a beer before I pass out?"

"Now, I remember," Robin said. "You were here before, but you were wearing different clothes. I didn't recognize you."

"Thank you," said Warner Lisle.

Robin let him into Manfred's apartment. True to his word, Warner found the fridge, pulled out a beer, opened it and plopped down on the living room sofa. He took a long drink, sighed contentedly and renewed his smile in Robin's direction.

"You're not my idea of a spy," Robin told him from where she stood near the front door—the better to make her escape, should it prove necessary.

"Thanks again. That's just the way we like it."

"Why?"

"Think about it. What you want in a spy is someone who's easy to accept and hard to remember. That's me. You'll have a hard time describing me an hour from now. And tomorrow, forget about it. Still, I looked agreeable enough that you let me in here."

That last bit made Robin uneasy again.

"Why're you telling me all this? Why did you even admit you're a spy at all?"

Was he going to kill her?

It didn't appear likely when he put his bottle of beer on the floor, stretched out on the sofa, and closed his eyes.

"It doesn't matter who knows I'm a spy anymore because I'm about to retire."

That would never have occurred to Robin, that spies could retire like anyone else.

"So what're you going to do, write your memoirs?"

"I signed an agreement not to do that."

"Then what?"

Warner turned his head toward Robin and opened his eyes.

"I'm going to Hollywood. I'm going to design special effects like you wouldn't believe."

The CIA agent smiled and closed his eyes again.

"Are you here to tell Manfred about his daughter?"

"Can't give away all my secrets," Warner said drowsily.

"I've agreed to let her move in here with him."

"Then brace yourself."

And with that the semi-secretive agent fell asleep and started snoring softly.

Manfred noticed Warner's car as he drove down the block in his old Mercedes. He knew that his friend must have some word for him about how the negotiations with Ulrike had gone. A wave of anxiety swelled in his chest; he had to hear the news ... but he couldn't find a parking space anywhere on the block.

Since he'd moved in, he'd had extraordinarily good luck finding parking. He'd had to park more than a block away only two times, and since he liked to walk he hadn't minded. But now he had to find a parking place immediately and he knew only one sure way to do that. He pulled into the alley behind Robin's house.

He'd park in her garage. True, he'd bargained for only half of the space there and his weights and equipment occupied that area, but Robin didn't have a car and he knew the other half of the garage would be available. So just this once...

Manfred slowed down as he approached the garage. He tapped the button on the remote control to open the garage door. He'd installed a new opener last week but Robin hadn't noticed. He was about to roll inside when a skinny kid wearing glasses rode up on a bicycle and stopped directly in front of the car. Manfred slammed on the brakes, missing the kid by a whisker.

It didn't seem to faze the kid. He pointed a bony finger at Manfred.

"I know who you are," David Solomonovich told Manfred, "and I'll be watching."

Then the kid rode away leaving Manfred utterly baffled.

But he didn't have time for mysteries now. He pulled into the garage, lowered the door and raced toward the building to find out what Warner had to tell him about Hannelore.

Robin had just opened the door to her apartment when she heard Manfred storm in on the first floor.

"Is that you?" Robin called.

Who else could it be, the building was shaking.

"Ja," came the voice from below, somewhat impatiently she thought.

"I let a friend of yours into your apartment, says he's with the CIA."

"Danke."

That was it. She heard the door to the basement apartment open and slam shut. Robin had been hoping the remark about the CIA would call for some explanation on his part, but apparently not. Well, she'd find out soon enough anyway.

What surprised Robin was how eager she was to know what was happening.

Manfred called her on the phone an hour later.

"I was rude earlier. Please forgive me."

Robin couldn't remember the last time a man had apologized to her for a breach of manners. Possibly it had never happened. But she liked it.

"Okay," she said. "Just don't let it happen again."

"I have also read your reply to my note. You are very generous."

Now, he was complimenting her. It was a heady feeling.

"You do what you can," Robin said modestly.

"I would like to make dinner for you tonight," Manfred told her.

Robin gulped, thought it was a good thing she was fat or he'd hear her knees knocking.

"I ... I don't think so."

"My daughter is coming," he said "It has been arranged."

A long silence ensued.

"*Bitte,*" he said softly.

The word was quiet, but the plea it contained was a shout. He had wonderful news and he was dying to share it. Robin also heard a note of anxiety. Her moat monster was afraid. He'd wished long and hard to get his daughter back, and now that it was about to happen it scared him. His fear, more than anything else, was what persuaded her to accept.

"I hope it's come as you are," she said.

CHAPTER 13

Robin came as she was. By conscious choice, she didn't change her clothes, comb her hair or even tuck in her shirttails. Make-up and perfume were out of the question: She didn't own any. She did brush her teeth, considering fresh breath to be only good hygiene and common courtesy. She arrived exactly when he said dinner would be ready, to avoid any prolonged small talk, and she slapped Manfred's hand away when he tried to hold her chair for her.

He seemed to take that as a clue, let her seat herself and hustled off to the kitchen to fetch the food. Two place settings, a bottle of red wine, a loaf of sliced French bread and butter were already on the old, small dining room table which she had carted down the basement years ago, and which Manfred had covered with a rose-colored tablecloth.

Robin had been expecting something German in the way of food: schnitzel, noodles, cabbage, whatever. But Manfred arrived with a huge steak, homemade fries and a green salad. He cut the meat in two equal portions at the table and gave half to Robin. He poured her a glass of red, toasted her health and, after giving her his little trademark nod, dug in.

The way he ate helped her to lose her self-consciousness. From his first forkful, she could have been sitting there naked with an orchid between her teeth and he wouldn't have noticed. It was consistent with what she knew of him, though; this man focused on the job at hand. Relieved of the need to do anything but follow his lead, Robin began to eat, too.

The meal was delicious. The man was as good a cook as he was a baker. That thought made Robin wonder if she should hope that he'd made something for desert. Which, in turn, and with great perversity, made her put her fork down. All this food was a giant fat-and-cholesterol bomb. Her damn doctor's warning made all those wonderful flavors turn to ash in her mouth. And, if she were honest, she'd have to admit to still feeling uneasy eating the way she liked to eat — gobble, gobble, gobble — in front of someone she hardly knew, and a man at that.

Robin was surprised when Manfred actually looked up from his plate. He saw that she'd stopped eating. He stared at her for a second, took a drink of wine and wiped his lips with his napkin.

"The food is not to your taste? I thought an American meal would please you."

"It's delicious," Robin said.

"But you are not eating."

"My doctor..." Robin started and then descended into a mutter.

"*Bitte?*"

"I have to lose weight!"

Manfred looked at her some more, obviously checking that idea against what he saw. Robin tried not to squirm — or blow her top — under the pressure of this blatant appraisal. Manfred ate another forkful of beef, took another drink of wine.

"Why?" he asked as soon as he'd swallowed.

"Don't you think I'm fat? Just a little?" Robin asked acidly.

"*Ja.* So lose fat." Manfred grabbed a piece of bread and buttered it. "Not weight."

"And what's that supposed to mean?"

"You are big and that is good. But you need to replace your fat with muscle. I could show you. Work you out."

Robin narrowed her eyes, tried to decide if there was any

subtext here.

"Okay, buster, explain that one."

"I am strength coach. At my school. I make students strong. I can make you strong."

Oh ... Well, at least now she knew what he did for a living, and she had the idea that he was being his usual straight-arrow helpful self, but she wanted to get one thing absolutely clear.

"You don't think I'm too big, too round, too heavy, too gross?"

"I like the way you look," Manfred said, devouring the piece of bread. "You look like me."

Robin didn't know whether to laugh or cry.

Instead of doing either, she ate.

Manfred let her look at the baby picture of his daughter again while he did the dishes. He insisted that he had to do them immediately. The idea of leaving dirty dishes in the sink ... well, that was one weight he couldn't bear.

When he joined her in the living room, he took care not to join her on the sofa but sat in an overstuffed chair across from her. He'd brought with him from the kitchen a box of chocolates and offered her one. What the hell, Robin thought, no point in holding back after that meal. She took a piece of candy and he put the box on the coffee table in front of her.

"Thank you," Robin said. She handed the picture back to Manfred. "Your daughter is very beautiful."

He nodded his head and rubbed a knuckle against an eye that was in danger of forming a tear. Then a look of bemusement crossed his face.

"Warner tells me I must call her Bianca now ... Bianca Krump."

Robin made sure her face didn't register any value judgment about this name.

"That is how she knows herself," Manfred continued, "even though in my heart I have always thought of her with the name she was given at birth, Hannelore Welk."

Robin nodded politely when he looked up from the picture.

"Do I bore you?"

"What? No ... no, I'm not bored ... It's just I..." Robin shrugged, tried to express her feelings with a series of gestures, failed and let her hands fall into her lap. "My social graces ... I really don't have any anymore. I'd like to know more about you and your daughter."

Admitting that much was very hard for Robin, telling him the rest was like passing a kidney stone.

"My memory still works. I know if you want to hear about someone else, you're also supposed to tell them about you. I don't tell anybody about me. Someone ever got nosy about me, I'd probably tear their arm off and club them with it."

"I think my arm would not be so easy to remove," Manfred said matter-of-factly. "You may ask me anything; I will ask you nothing."

Robin considered. It was an unfair proposition, but unfair in her favor. She took it, though she started innocently enough.

"Have you always been big?"

"*Ja.* I don't know why. My parents were not large, and even though they always told me I ate all the food we had, I remember always being hungry when I was young. So I searched for ways to earn money to buy food even at a very early age. When I was five I invented a game I could play that would make money for me. For a *pffennig,* I would let any child on the street hit me as hard as he wanted, to see if he could hurt me."

"You're kidding."

"No. Boys had to hit me in the stomach or chest. Girls could hit me in the face, too."

Robin put a hand over her mouth to hide her grin. Manfred spotted it, anyway.

He went on with a smile, "It became a very popular sport, to see who could be the first to make me cry. Children came from blocks away to take up the challenge. Me, I was happy with all the money I was making and the treats I bought with it."

"So you found your niche being a punching bag?"

"*Ja* ... it was a good life while it lasted."

"Then some big kid came along, made you cry and stole your money."

"*Nein*, a girl who was training to be a gymnast broke her hand on my jaw. When her coach found out, he came to see me. He took me from my parents and put me in a state sports school. This was a great honor, and my parents were happy to have the government pay for my food. After only a year of testing, at age six, the state decided that I would advance the glories of Socialism by becoming a power-lifter."

"Not a body-builder, huh?" Robin asked slyly.

Manfred grinned.

"I am too pretty already. "

He told her that he'd gotten into trouble as a teenager. He'd refused to take the "strength-building compounds" that his coaches had given him. He'd been no fool. He'd known they were steroids and were outlawed by his sport's international governing body. On top of that, he'd seen what the steroids had done to the older boys: the psychoses, the prognathous jaws, the pimpled skin, the shriveled nuts. That had not been for him, *nein danke*.

Besides, he'd been good enough to compete and win without the chemicals.

But that hadn't been the point. He'd committed the grave sin of fighting the system.

"I was the worst thing one of my people could be, a disobedient German."

On top of that, he'd shown a worrisome taste for Western music, clothes and comic books. He'd been told to conform or face expulsion. He hadn't given the school authorities the chance. He'd become the first person to voluntarily leave the prestigious sports academy, forsaking the pampered future of the hero-athlete. By this rash deed, he'd identified himself as a thoroughly dangerous sort.

Manfred had returned home to parents who'd been horrified to have him back. They'd been sure they couldn't afford to feed this teenage monster, and loathed the political risk they took if they gave him shelter. So they'd harped on him to return to the school and do what he was told.

He hadn't. He'd found a place in an industrial training program. He'd lasted a year and then had been dismissed without explanation. He'd become an apprentice baker for six months before losing that position. He'd spent the next two years bouncing around every vocational training program the state had to offer, and had been allowed to complete none of them.

Robin was intrigued, and now she understood how Manfred had come to possess such an array of skills and talents.

"Did you go back to the academy?" she asked.

"*Ja*, but not quite the way the state had hoped."

"What's that mean?"

He explained that the GDR's junior power-lifting team had been on its way to a competition in Italy when the train it had been riding went off the tracks outside of Turin. All of the team had either perished or been crippled.

"That's horrible."

Manfred nodded.

"Many obedient young boys met bad ends that day. The ironic thing was that the train had been sabotaged by the Red Brigades. The Communists had killed their own."

"And then they needed you, and brought you back."

"I came back on my own terms. No steroids. Music, clothes and comic books of my own choosing." Manfred grinned ruefully. "They did extract their price, though. Since I was the one drug-free competitor they had, they made me pee for everyone else's doping tests."

Robin moved on to a much more personal subject; he'd said she could ask him anything.

"Did you ever love your wife?"

Manfred looked inward, trying to recall, or decide, or both.

"Ulrike was a heptathlete, good but not great. I think she attached herself to me because I was one of the more promising stars of the time. I ... I loved her body."

"Did it look like mine?" Robin asked, not hiding the sarcasm.

"*Nein*," Manfred shrugged, unruffled. "I was younger then. My idea of women was Betty and Veronica from the comic books or the Playboy playmates."

Robin sneered.

"When Ulrike got tired of competing — when she was in danger of losing her place on the team — we got married. That way she had continued access to all the special privileges of the athletic community."

"What went wrong? Between the two of you."

"Ulrike got pregnant with Hannelore."

"That was a problem for you?" Robin asked with a sudden edge to her voice.

"For her. For me, too, in the end. I was tiring of Ulrike, there really wasn't much between us to make a marriage. Sex can take you only so far. I saw a future that was nothing more than an endless argument, but when she told me she was pregnant, I was immediately captivated. I'd never thought of having children, but instantly I wanted that child. I saw an image of myself as a great bear rearing up to protect its cub ... "

Robin didn't have any problem seeing that picture.

" ... But the only reason Ulrike had told me she was pregnant was to complain about the shoddiness of the Russian contraceptives she'd had to use when the chemist had been out of her usual French brand. She intended to abort the baby."

Robin stood up, suddenly very uncomfortable.

"This is really too personal. I shouldn't be hearing this."

"I forbade her to have the abortion."

Robin sat back down.

"How did you do that?"

"I told her I would divorce her if she did. She'd be out on the street. The luxury flat, the Mercedes, the French lingerie, the foreign travel: Poof, gone."

"Ulrike tolerated the baby, but she hated me for making her have Han—Bianca. She claimed I'd ruined her figure, that she was now an ugly cow. The truth was, she was far more beautiful than she had been, but she couldn't stand it that I'd made her conform to my will."

There was a faraway look in Robin's eyes and she nodded imperceptibly.

Manfred was too immersed in his own memories to notice.

"I was in Bonn, competing and demonstrating the superiority of the Marxist path, when Warner recruited me for the CIA."

"What on earth did they want with you?"

"They wanted to know all about the GDR's training methods: how such a small nation could achieve such astounding results in the field of athletic competition." Manfred told Robin that he'd always suspected the ultimate aim of the spy agency was to find a military application for the information he'd provided, a way to build gold-medal soldiers.

"What did Warner offer in return?"

"Good conversation, unfiltered news of the world, the latest rock albums ... and guaranteed asylum in the U.S. He told me it wasn't such a bad thing to be a disobedient German in America."

"How did you wind up in Chicago?"

"Milwaukee was taken."

Robin laughed.

"Warner chose it for me. He said it was a good place to learn to be an American. He said it was my kind of town."

"That's a joke, too."

"I know, but I don't understand it. Perhaps you can help me see the humor someday."

"Ulrike had long since stopped having sex with me, but she was jealous, certain that I was sleeping with someone else, that I would divorce her even though she'd given me my daughter. She was determined to find out who my lover was and drive her off."

"And she spotted Warner?" Robin couldn't believe that.

"No. Warner is brilliant. His mother was a German national, a war bride, so he speaks the language like a native. And he always wore the right clothes. And as you probably noticed he is both pleasant and elusive, without being sneaky about it."

It was true; Robin couldn't quite picture the man now, even though she'd met him for the second time only that afternoon.

"Unfortunately, Warner broke his leg skiing in Bavaria, and his superiors, over Warner's objections, thought that having him contact me wearing a cast and walking with crutches would make him far too obvious. They replaced him with a woman. She also had agreeably plain features and spoke perfect German, but she was new and had yet to obtain a local wardrobe. Ulrike spotted her for an American immediately. She jumped to the hasty, yet entirely correct, conclusion that the woman was a spy and I was working with the Americans. The irony, of course, was the woman was not my lover; in fact that was the only time I ever saw her."

"Still, Ulrike turned you in."

"*Ja,* and divorced me and vowed publicly that I would never see my daughter again."

"You must have felt awful."

Manfred shook his head.

"Determined. I told all of them, Ulrike, the Stasi, the judges, that I would last longer than they would, and I did."

"So what are you afraid of?" Robin asked.

"Afraid?"

The question seemed to strike Manfred as odd. Robin thought that he probably had his courage questioned about as often as she got wolf-whistles.

"Yeah," she said. "Scared."

Manfred looked as if he might try to run a bluff, then he sighed and shrugged his massive shoulders.

"My daughter. I am afraid she won't love me. She was only ten months old the last time I saw her. She can have no memory of me, and I am sure if Ulrike told her of me at all it was only that her father was a traitor and is a monster."

Manfred rubbed a hand across his face.

"I have always liked who I am; I enjoy being big and strong ... but just this once ... when I first meet my daughter again, I would like to be small and unthreatening. Like Warner."

Robin immediately thought of the innumerable times when she was growing up that she'd wished she'd looked like Nancy.

Now, she wished she could find some words of comfort for him, but she didn't know any. It had been too many years since she'd felt sorry for anyone but herself.

Manfred's rueful smile returned.

"This is why I fix up everything. If I can't be what I want, I make a home for Ha—for Bianca that is warm and cozy and beautiful. Someplace where she can come to see her Vati must not be such an ogre after all."

Robin nodded, glad that she had acceded to Manfred's list of requests.

He then explained to her that the deal Warner had negotiated with Ulrike had left him with a reserve of five thousand dollars. Manfred wanted to know if he could add that to Robin's five hundred for the building's rehabilitation.

Robin immediately felt a childish surge of anger. Here he was trying to take over again, but she stifled it. The man had just bared his soul to her. He was just trying to do the only thing he could think of to make sure his daughter would love him.

She said, "You might want to hang on to that money for other things. From everything I hear, kids are one unexpected expense after another."

He started to object, but she told him about Mimi's business proposition. He could make some extra money that way, and if he wanted to put that money into the building ... well, that would be his business.

"I have very much enjoyed our evening," Manfred said, as he stood with Robin at his front door. "Thank you for joining me."

Then, before she knew what he was doing, Manfred took her hand and kissed it.

Robin used her other hand to brace herself against the door-jamb so she didn't fall over; being hit with a feather would have done the trick. Okay, he'd just kissed her hand, but at that point she'd been trying to decide if they should shake hands.

"I've got to go," Robin said quickly.

Manfred gave her his little nod.

But before Robin could flee, Manfred brought up one more thing.

"Oh, I almost forgot. Do you know a young, thin boy with glasses who lives around here?"

Robin had no idea what he was talking about.

Manfred explained.

"I nearly ran him over in the alley. He stopped his bicycle directly in front of my car."

"That's very strange."

"*Ja.* And he said he knew who I was and he would be watching me."

Robin's stomach suddenly felt queasy.

"What did he look like?"

"Just a boy. Except for his eyes. They were wise far beyond his years."

David Solomonovich, no question. He'd followed through on Robin's request, found out something about Manfred, and was acting out some pubescent Galahad fantasy ... Oh, God. David was going to demand a kiss from her.

Manfred said, "It's probably nothing, a case of mistaken identity. But with my history, I think I will ask Warner to investigate this boy."

Robin's mind went tilt. She'd sent David to snoop on the CIA, and now Manfred was sending the CIA to snoop on David. What was she going to do now?

Run.

"I've got to go," Robin said.

But before she did, without conscious thought, she grabbed Manfred's hand, perhaps to shake it as she'd originally intended, but to her acute horror, unable to stop herself, she watched as some impulse from hell made her bring his hand to her mouth and kiss it.

She'd kissed his hand!

Robin couldn't believe it.

Manfred stood there nonplussed himself.

Robin turned crimson, let his hand go, and finally ran upstairs.

Not seeing the broad smile that formed on Manfred's face.

That and his little nod.

CHAPTER 14

Robin wanted to die.

The embarrassment had lasted the whole restless night through and, if anything, was worse when she rose bleary-eyed the next morning. She couldn't remember ever having done anything so mortifying even when she'd been a teenager. An hour ago, she'd pulled the covers over her head when she'd thought she'd heard Manfred's footsteps on the landing outside her front door. She would have died if he'd rung the bell, but he hadn't. Then she'd wondered if he'd left some baked goodies for her. But when she hadn't smelled anything, she'd wondered if she hadn't fantasized the whole idea that he had come to call on her.

That depressed her enough to finally permit an hour of sleep.

Still, when she got out of bed, she tiptoed over to her front door and opened it a crack ... just to check on the state of her mental health.

Manfred had been there.

He'd left a large gray sweatshirt, matching sweatpants, and a note.

The note gave directions to his school and told her that if she wanted to stop by at lunchtime he could show her how to stop being fat and start being strong.

Robin could think of only one person to call for advice.

"He's offering to be your personal trainer?" Nancy said from her office at the real estate agency. "Woo-woo, hubba-hubba!"

Robin ground her teeth.

"I'm asking for some help here, some serious advice. Can you manage that or not?"

"Robin, you're almost forty. Don't you think you can work this out for yourself?"

Robin hung up.

Nancy called back.

"Okay, let's take this one step at a time. Are you sorry you let Manfred move in?"

"Only occasionally now," Robin said.

"Oh, brother," Nancy said, but she continued before Robin could hang up again. "Let's put it this way then: Is your life better since he moved in?"

"My house is much better maintained."

"Always the romantic, that's you. What about your discovery that you possess an entertaining new underwear fetish?"

"Will you please not mention that?"

In the hour that she'd slept that morning, Robin had had a most disturbing dream, a nightmare really. She'd gone down to her basement to do some laundry and the moment she'd stepped through the door she'd been surrounded by clotheslines hung with giant pairs of underwear. Each pair was covered with a pattern of erections, and each erection ended in a little smiley face. Damn Nancy for putting that image in her head. Then the erections leaped off the underwear and started doing an elaborate dance number — like they'd all been choreographed by Busby Berkely — and Robin suddenly had a silver top hat and cane in her hands and started high-kicking at the center of a long chorus line of giant smiling phalluses. It was all too—

"Are you still there?" Nancy asked loudly, making Robin realize that her sister had been talking to her while she'd been out in the ozone.

"Yes, I'm here."

"Good. So, what's your answer?"

"To what?"

"Do you think this guy is interested in anything more than being friendly?"

"I ... I don't know." Then Robin remembered something Manfred had said. "He said he liked the way I look." She didn't add that he also thought she looked like him.

This time the silence was on the other end of the line.

"You think he was sincere?"

"What's that mean?" Robin snapped. "I'm ugly or he has an ulterior motive? Like maybe he wants a reduction in his free rent? Yes, he was sincere. He's honest — to a fault."

Nancy chuckled.

"What's so funny?" Robin demanded.

"You're defending him, kiddo."

"I am not."

"You've got feelings for him, even if you won't admit it."

"I do not."

"Mom thinks it's great you've got a boyfriend."

That stopped Robin as if she'd been pole-axed.

"Mom?" Robin asked after a long silence.

"Sure. I tell her about you. She's interested in what you're doing."

"I didn't know she was interested in whether I'm still alive."

"Life is full of surprises. Look, I've got to get back to work. If the guy just wants to help you get fit, that's great. You could use it. If he's interested in more, that's great, too. You deserve it. But if you're not interested in his offer, give him my number, will you? I think I'm ready for a personal trainer."

That notion galvanized Robin. Nancy horning in on Manfred. Well, his offer to train her, she meant. What gall!

"Thank you, Nancy. But I'm going to accept the offer."

As Robin hung up, she pretended that she didn't hear Nancy chuckle again.

Robin called David Solomonovich's work number from a pay phone outside a nearby Walgreen's drugstore. She was taking no chances that the CIA would be able to trace the call back to her house. She hoped to get a number from David's office where she could reach him at the University of Chicago, since he attended classes during the morning hours. But she got lucky because he was on some kind of quarterly break or something and she was put right through to the boy wonder himself.

"Hi, it's me," Robin said, not giving her name.

Because he was a genius, David immediately drew the proper inference from the fact that Robin hadn't identified herself by name: He wasn't to use her name or his own; they'd talk between the lines.

"Hi," David said, "nice to hear from you again."

Tell me what the heck's going on.

"Did you stop by yesterday but not come in?"

What in God's name did you think you were doing?

"I happened to be in the neighborhood, but didn't want to bother you."

Okay, you caught me, but I was only doing what you asked.

"Did you happen to bump into a friend of mine in passing?"

Are you crazy or what, giving warnings to someone five times your size?

"Friend, was that a friend of yours?"

Hey, this monster was the guy you were worried about, remember? I was just trying to help.

"You made quite an impression. He's going to ask his friend from Washington to see if you have any mutual acquaintances."

He's putting the CIA on your tail, you idiot.

"I doubt there's anyone to find, and it's a shame but I happen to be going out of town since I'm off of school for a while."

I didn't leave any tracks, and I'm blowing this pop stand.

"Well, have a nice time then."

"I will. And I'll look forward to collecting on my IOU when I get back."

The subtext of that line was painfully obvious. Robin hung up. She looked down at herself standing there in her new gray sweatclothes. What did David see in her? For that matter, what did Manfred? He did see something, didn't he?

With great trepidation, Robin headed off to stop being fat and start being strong.

Robin never would have made it through the front doors of St. Malachy's if the gray-haired man in the black suit hadn't been there to meet her. It was lunchtime and any number of teenage boys idled about the grounds of the school. They were remarkably well behaved for specimens of their kind, but even so they couldn't help but notice — check out — someone new approaching their turf. As she passed various knots of students, Robin heard the raw, raucous laughter that came from those first torrents of testosterone, and she was sure that at least some of it was at her expense. She felt absolutely elephantine in her gray sweats, and would have walked right on past the school except the man in the black suit stepped forward and intercepted her, extending his hand.

Robin made good and sure she only shook it.

The man said, "You must be Ms. Phinney. Coach Welk said we might have the pleasure of your company. I thought I might welcome you."

"Thank you, Father."

"Brother."

"Pardon?"

"I'm Brother Damian, Order of Christian Brothers, headmaster of St. Malachy's."

"Oh, I see."

"I come out here at lunchtime to keep an eye on things and catch a smoke."

Brother Damian put the index finger and thumb of his left hand to his lips and inhaled deeply ... but he wasn't holding a cigarette. He saw the look Robin gave him and smiled.

"My confessor and I got into a debate last year as to whether smoking is a sin, since everyone knows that it's suicide on the installment plan. Our argument proved inconclusive, but the lack of a clear-cut victory was enough to make me reconsider my wicked habit. So, I gave up smoking in fact and continue to smoke symbolically. I hope that will please both God and my doctor, but I'm afraid it amuses the students no end. I don't see why, as so many of them play the air-guitar — but you may have noticed some of them laughing at me."

With that, of course, he eliminated any possibility that anyone had been laughing at Robin.

"Allow me to show you to our gymnasium," Brother Damian said, and gestured to a nearby door.

Robin thanked him again, and walking at his side, nobody laughed at either of them.

The gym was sparkling clean and there was a hint of some perfumed disinfectant in the air, but beneath it all was the smell of sweat, of generations of boys who had used this space for their games, hurling their bodies into one another, yelling and cheering and cursing. Well, no, not cursing, not as long the likes of Brother Damian had been around. Still, it was an environment that made Robin feel powerfully out of place.

"I'll leave you here," Brother Damian said. "Coach Welk will be with you momentarily. I've noticed him sticking his head out of his office at ten second intervals." Robin didn't doubt the school's headmaster noticed everything that went on in his domain. "Oh, look, here he is now. A pleasure to have met you, Ms. Phinney. Feel free to visit us any time."

Brother Damian waved to Manfred and left the gym.

Manfred walked over to her and Robin was sure he was sizing her up every step of the way, as if she were some underachieving student he was going to have to work hard to whip into shape. Which reassured her no end. Busting a gut she could handle; hanky-panky, especially with Brother Damian lurking like an all-seeing God, no way.

Manfred gave her his little nod.

"You came. *Gut.*"

Robin noticed that his German accent was much thicker in this place.

The better to scare you with, she thought.

He gestured for her to come along and she followed him to the weight room.

They started with stretches. Robin was amazed at how supple Manfred was; he bent, folded and twisted his massive body with a plasticity that would have done credit to an Indian yogi. She was appalled at her own rigidity; she had all the flexibility of a two-by-four. Next came rope jumping. She seemed to remember being able to jump rope for hours at a time as a girl. Now, she lasted thirty seconds with four misses, three of which nearly sent her sprawling on her face. Robin glared at Manfred to make sure he wasn't laughing at her clumsiness, her total red-faced, air-gulping lack of aerobic fitness.

But he remained deadpan.

"You will get better," he said.

More of an order than a prediction, Robin thought.

Finally, they moved to the weights themselves. Manfred told her that there were over six hundred muscles in the human body and he could show her how to exercise all of the ones that worked voluntarily. But they would start with the two main strength-builders: squats for the lower body; bench-presses for the upper body.

He bent to step under a barbell that was set on a rack a foot or so lower than his shoulder height. The bar itself weighed forty-five pounds, Manfred explained, and each of the four plates at either end of the bar also weighed forty-five pounds, for a total weight of four hundred and five pounds. Manfred straightened under the load without noticeable effort, taking the bar behind his head on his shoulders.

If he'd had the slightest smirk on his face, Robin would have thought he was showing off. But he spoke in the same no-nonsense, pay-attention tone that he'd been using throughout. He instructed her that you kept your back straight and, inhaling, bent your legs only until your thighs were parallel to the floor. Then, exhaling, you straightened your legs, but did not lock your knees. Then you repeated the motion. Ten repetitions were required.

Manfred did his ten. Without the least bit of difficulty, Robin thought. He went up and down like he was on springs. Didn't break a sweat, didn't even have to breathe deeply. But that apparent ease wasn't something that was reflected in his face. There, Robin saw a look of determination so fierce it almost scared her. This man was willing himself to be strong, so strong she could imagine leaving now and coming back in a week only to find him doing the same perfect, rhythmic repetitions.

But after ten reps Manfred set the bar back on the rack, in a lower slot, and looked at her.

"Your turn."

"I can't do all that weight," Robin said.

"Not yet," he agreed.

Manfred stripped off the eight forty-five pound plates, leaving the bar bare.

That looked easy.

"Sure, I can do that," Robin said.

He guided her under the bar, showed her where to put her hands and told her to use her legs to lift it off the rack. Robin did, and staggered under the load. Manfred was there, behind her, to help support the weight, letting Robin regain her balance.

"*Ein*," he barked out, not giving her any time for second thoughts.

She bent her legs, her knees sounding like bowls of Rice Krispies under the first splash of milk. His fingertips under her elbows kept her from bending her crackling knees too far. Then, somehow, she found the strength to straighten her legs and carry the weight back to a standing position. Robin felt this was a major triumph.

But Manfred roared, "Do not lock your knees ... *zwei*."

Somehow, sweating, shaking, heart thumping, blood roaring

in her ears and loathing Manfred with every aching fiber in her being, Robin made all *zehn*.

The bench presses proved even worse. Again, Manfred demonstrated the proper form with eight plates on the bar. Again, Robin couldn't believe how pathetically weak she was; she couldn't lift the unburdened bar off her chest until Manfred aided her with the index finger of each of his hands. It was infuriating. The man could do with two fingers what she couldn't manage with all the strength in her body. She hated him. The only reason she didn't evict him then and there was she was afraid he might leave her pinned to the bench for eternity, that and the fact that he didn't let the least bit of condescension seep through to his expressionless mug.

When they finished he gave her a nod and said, "You will come to my office, please."

His office was barely big enough for the both of them. Robin watched with mounting anger as he blandly pulled a form out of his desk, put her name in large letters at the top and then started making crabbed notes that she couldn't decipher. A muscle started twitching in Robin's back, her sweatpants were stuck up the crack in her butt and she'd just about had it with all this muscle crap when Manfred looked up and gave her a beaming smile.

"Of all the students I have worked with at this school, only two members of the basketball team and one from the football team show more potential than you."

"Oh, goody," Robin said.

"You are frustrated now, but soon you will see progress that will astound you."

"Sure. I'll be a regular Terminator."

"Who?"

"Never mind. Listen, I appreciate what you tried to do here, but I really don't think —"

"You have more natural talent, a deeper reservoir of strength, than Ulrike. If you had trained from childhood, you could have made the American Olympic team in a number of sports."

That was the most outrageous compliment that Robin had

ever received in her life. And the fact that Manfred had compared her favorably to his ex-wife hadn't escaped her notice either. All in all, he had her thoroughly off-balance. Insults, jibes and digs she could handle no problem; compliments, flattery and praise made her nervous, scared her. She'd told Nancy that he'd been sincere when he'd had kind words for her before, but at the back of her mind doubt had lingered. Self-esteem of any sort had been missing from her life for so long ... but looking at him now she couldn't see the least hint of deceit.

And what possible reason could he have to BS her?

"You will come three times per week," Manfred said, dismissing her unfinished objection. "That is how you will see the most progress."

"But I can't come at this time of day. I'll be going back to work soon."

"Before work then."

"I start at seven."

"Then we will start at five."

Two hours later Robin lay on her living room sofa entirely sure that she would never move again. Every muscle in her body was so sore, so inflamed with pain, that she was certain she'd have to linger in a horizontal position for the rest of her life, being fed through one set of tubes and drained through another.

She couldn't even get up when there was a knock at her door. She could only think, Oh God, not Manfred, anybody but Manfred. He'd see her, make her get up and do a hundred jumping jacks, with wrist and ankle weights.

When a key turned in the lock, she sighed with relief — and even that hurt — knowing it had to be either Nancy or—

"Hi, Sweetie. How's my girl?"

Her father.

"Hi, Daddy."

"So how'd the workout go?" he asked.

Robin was momentarily taken aback. She hadn't intended to

tell him what she'd been doing. She still felt uneasy admitting anything about Manfred. Of course, it was obvious that blabbermouth Nancy had spilled the beans. Her father sat down opposite her.

"It was hard."

Her father leaned over and patted her on the shoulder and Robin bit back a cry of pain.

"Sore, huh?"

"The way I feel makes me think of one of those old Westerns where the guy gets dragged behind the horse. I feel like that, only I was dragged over railroad ties — and then run over by a fast freight."

"No train, no gain?" her father asked brightly.

"No brain, all pain," Robin replied miserably.

Her father reached out to comfort her, but he withdrew his hand when he saw Robin wince at his very approach.

"You'll feel better. You're a strong girl. When you were just a baby — oh, about six months old, I guess — you used to grab onto my fingers, support your weight with your arms and we'd walk all over the living room. I swear, you were so strong there were times I thought you were going to do chin-ups. And before you were nine months you smacked my hands out of the way and insisted on walking all by yourself. That's about three months younger than most kids. I stayed close by, of course, in case you lost your balance. But pretty soon you'd start looking over your shoulder, and if I was too close, like I didn't trust you to walk on your own, you'd give me a dirty look and start screeching at me."

"A charmer right from the start, huh?" Robin asked wryly.

"The light of my life from the first moment I held you."

Robin reached out to her father and ignored the pain when he squeezed her hand.

"I have something to tell you, Honey."

A mortal chill passed through Robin. She sat up, certain that her father would tell her he was dying. The news he gave her was only slightly less stunning.

"Your mother and I are getting divorced."

"But you, you're okay?"

Dan Phinney smiled and thumped himself on the chest with both hands.

"Me? I'm fine. Why? Oh, you thought ... "

Robin lay back down, once again aware of her every shrieking nerve ending.

Her father continued, "I've been talking to your mother. You know I've wanted a divorce for some years now, and your mother wouldn't give me one because the Catholic Church forbids it. I never really pushed the matter before this because ... well, I thought there might be some value to it if we were all still a family in name if not in fact. I ... I thought that might make it easier for your mother and you to reconcile someday."

"You never told me that, Daddy. Not that it would have helped. Nancy says otherwise, but I think I'm pretty much dead in Mom's eyes, and that's okay by me."

"That may have been true for your mother once, but not anymore. She asked me to give this to you."

Dan Phinney held out an envelope, the kind that holds a greeting card, with Robin's name on it. Even after twenty years, she still recognized her mother's handwriting. But she refused to take it. Dan put the envelope down on an end table.

He said, "The other reason I didn't push as hard for the divorce as I might have is I didn't want you to ever have the idea that somehow I might be leaving you, too. I'll never do that, Robin. Only God will take me from you. But I think you're changing lately. I think you're stronger now."

Robin snorted derisively.

Her father ignored the self-deprecation.

"I think that when my time does come, you'll even be strong enough to accept that."

Robin blinked away a tear. Then she turned and looked at her father.

"Why did Mom agree this time? After all these years, why did she finally consent to a divorce?"

"She said it was time we stopped hurting each other. She said that she was sorry for her part in causing all the pain. She said she'd prove that even if meant going against her church."

Dan Phinney got up, bent over and kissed his daughter's cheek.

"Don't throw away your mother's card, Sweetie. See what she has to say."

Then he left.

CHAPTER 15

The next day, Robin got a call from a masseuse. No, the woman corrected her, a certified massage therapist. Her stern tone and German accent left no doubt as to the legitimacy of her work. She'd been given Robin's name by Herr Welk. As a courtesy, she offered a free introductory massage to members of the Chicago sports community.

Was Robin interested?

Robin was still bemused at the notion that she was part of any sports community when Frau Berger told her she had an opening at eleven that morning. But she'd have to decide now because Frau Berger was a busy woman and her openings never lasted very long.

Normally, the question of whether she wanted to be rubbed down, worked over and generally kneaded like dough by another woman would have been an easy one for Robin to answer. No, thank you. But she knew this was not a normal time in her life, not by any stretch of the imagination. She had a man in her house, his child was on the way and she still felt as if she'd been hung up and beaten like a rug.

If she were going to continue with this strength program madness, what harm could there be in getting a free massage?

Robin said okay.

Robin shrieked in agony.

Then she begged Frau Berger to continue, not that the massage therapist had slackened in her efforts for even a second. The woman's disregard for Robin's cries of pain was absolute. But then her general demeanor might have inspired George C. Scott's take on General Patton.

When Robin had arrived, Frau Berger had ordered her to go into the changing room, strip and wrap herself in the body towel she would find there. If her feet were dirty or smelly, she would wash them in the sink she would find there. A separate towel was provided for the drying of feet. If she used it, she would deposit it in the hamper she would find there. She had two minutes to do all this and present herself to Frau Berger in the therapy room. Any tardiness would be deducted from the time for her massage.

Robin obeyed.

Not even thinking of cracking wise.

This woman was as big as Robin was and, Robin knew instinctively, a helluva lot stronger. Robin would not antagonize her. Not without an exceedingly good reason.

The pain Robin felt when Frau Berger first laid hands on her almost passed for such a reason. The sensation was incredible. As Frau Berger's iron-hard fingers dug into her flesh, the story of St. Stephen being transfixed by arrows flashed into her mind; she knew how he must have felt.

But at the tail end of every screaming synapse came a groan of relief. A binary code of pain and pleasure flashed across Robin's brain. She'd much rather have had the pleasure alone, but she was certain that nature didn't give you one without the other, and more than certain that Frau Berger wouldn't have had it any other way.

"You have good muscles," Frau Berger said, adding her voice to the massage for the first time as she worked Robin's shoulders.

"Thank you," Robin replied.

"Good muscles in very bad condition," the massage therapist added. "Like mush."

Robin bit her tongue, as a matter of self-preservation.

"Herr Welk will fix that, I'm sure," Frau Berger predicted.

"Sure," Robin said, unable to restrain herself any longer, "that Herr Welk, he's a real fixer."

Frau Berger must have caught the note of sarcasm, and disapproved, because Robin gasped in pain and felt certain that the woman had just punctured one of her lungs.

After she'd showered, tipped Frau Berger ten dollars and, much to her surprise, made an appointment for the following week, Robin stepped out onto the street feeling decidedly odd. She started walking to the corner where she would catch the bus to go back home, and with each step she took she had to restrain herself from bouncing. For the first time in more years than she could remember she felt a spring in her step. Boy, she'd like to show that Manfred how she could jump some rope now. Even do those lousy squats. Maybe push that bar off her chest by herself a time or two.

The pain she'd been feeling was gone. Frau Berger had squeezed it out of her. The therapist had explained as she'd finished the massage that vigorous exercise built up concentrations of lactic acid in the muscles and that was what made them sore. A proper massage dispersed the lactic acid and increased the circulation of blood to the muscles, resulting in a feeling of relief.

Robin felt more than relief; she felt rejuvenated. Just like a kid again, doing what she did again. Skipping toward the bus stop. Robin laughed at herself but didn't stop. Instead, she started humming. She tried for the overture from the Olympics, but somehow wound up with the theme from the movie Rocky. "Gonna Fly Now." Close enough to suit her mood. Man, she thought, if this is what exercise and massage therapy could do for you they could blow recreational drugs out of the water.

An old woman sitting on the bench at the bus stop saw a bouncing, grinning Robin closing in on her fast and recoiled in horror.

Robin stopped and said, "Don't be a grump, get pumped!"

She struck a body building pose, the incredible Hulkette.

The old woman protectively pulled her shopping bag up to her chest and retreated to the far end of the bench. She was genuinely frightened.

Robin hadn't wanted to scare the woman. So she sat down and kept quiet.

Maybe she'd been overdoing it.

Manfred was home early that day installing a floodlight for the backyard — couldn't be too careful in America, he was constantly told — when Dan Phinney spotted him.

"Hey, Manfred," he called, walking toward the rear of Robin's house.

Manfred nodded politely from his perch on the stepladder.

"A pleasure to see you again, Herr Phinney."

"Come on, we settled all that. My name is Dan. I came by to take Robin to lunch, but since she's not here I'll let you buy me a beer."

Manfred had more work to do but, after all, this man was his landlady's father ... and he thought of something he'd like to talk with Dan about.

"*Ja*, let's have a beer."

"Has Robin told you about me?" Manfred asked.

Manfred and Dan sat at the kitchen table. Dan put his stein of beer down and wiped the mustache of foam off his upper lip.

"What do you mean? You haven't done something awful, have you?"

"That would depend on whom you asked."

Manfred filled Dan in on his history; his respect for Robin was increased by the fact that she hadn't passed along what he'd told her. When he'd heard Manfred's story, Dan Phinney slapped his leg, smiled and drank some more beer.

"You were an athlete and a spy for the CIA? That's great!"

"The part that concerns me is my daughter."

"What's the problem? You're getting her back, aren't you?"

Manfred drained his own beer.

"I am afraid she will reject me," he said. "The closer the time comes to her arrival, the more certain I am of it. I need help. I need advice. You are the father of a daughter —"

"Two daughters."

"Two, then. Please. Tell me what I must do ... how I must behave to keep from losing my daughter again."

Dan saw that Manfred was keeping a straight face, but his eyes gave him away. There was genuine fear in them, terror even. And finding such vulnerability in a man who was so big and strong was both surprising and touching.

Dan Phinney patted Manfred's hand as if he was a little boy.

"You remember how you felt the first time you saw your daughter?"

Manfred nodded.

"It was the only time I felt a..." Manfred lost his English. ".... *Frolichkeit* ... a joy so great that I could not contain it. I wept as though I were the infant."

Dan smiled.

"Sure, even you were overwhelmed. I was the same way with both my girls. There's something special about daughters. You have a son, you've got to figure he'll be a chip off the old block. You just take it for granted that if you give a boy a decent start, he'll stand tall, and with his wits or his mitts he'll make his way, he'll do all right. But with a girl you always worry. This world is too damn mean for little girls, they oughta have a better place. So you do your best to protect them. You do your best."

Manfred saw that Dan Phinney had set foot in a painful memory. He took the two empty bottles from the table and returned with full ones. Dan poured the beer into his stein and sipped. He sighed deeply as though exorcising this particular demon for this particular moment.

"But you can't always be there for them. Sometimes, as hard as you try, they get hurt anyway. So what you have to do is two things: You love them, and then you love them some more. When you do that, when you keep that in mind, you won't have any trouble deciding about anything else. You have a choice to make about how to behave with your daughter, you just ask, am I doing this out of love for her or something else for me? Choose love, Manfred. Choose it every time. Your daughter won't reject you. Not for long, anyway. And once she sees how you feel, you'll never lose her. She'll always know she has you to turn to."

"I'll never lose her?" Manfred asked hopefully.

Dan Phinney shook his head.

"Oh, she may move away someday. In fact, you can pretty much count on it. But she'll always have a place for you in her heart, and no father could ever ask for more."

Mimi called Saturday night.

Robin had spent that morning not doing her laundry, unsure if she wanted to bump into Manfred or his underwear. That afternoon, she'd talked for hours on the phone with Nancy about their parents' upcoming divorce, agreeing that it was probably a good thing, but both of them admitting that they felt strange about it. That evening Robin had gone out for an early-bird special dinner with her dad, both of them taking it easy on the cholesterol, and she'd just returned in time to hear the phone ring.

"What?" Robin asked Mimi. "You were so sure I'd be home, that I wouldn't have I date?"

"I've missed you, too, sweetheart. How's the ankle? You ready to come back to work on Monday?"

"Work? What's that? Did I mention I won the lottery?"

"No, you didn't. Did I mention that Manfred's strudel is a big hit?"

"What?"

"Yes, so far it's sold out within an hour of opening every day. The breakfast rush must be up ten percent. He says he does some very nice cherry tarts, too. We're going to try those next week."

Robin felt aggrieved. Sure, she'd been the one who told Manfred about Mimi's business proposition, and she knew how good his strudel was — even though he hadn't offered to bake her any lately — but the idea that he'd gone ahead and followed through on her lead without even telling her, that he was becoming important at the place where she had always been the star, it just plain put her nose out of joint. Strudel, indeed.

She'd show him who mattered at Mimi's.

"I'll see you Monday, Mimi. My ankle's fine."

"I'm happy to hear it."

"But, Mimi?"

"Yes?"

"If that idiot, Ant-knee, tries to get back at me, I won't cut him any slack."

There was a significant pause at the other end of the line.

"Haven't you heard, Robin?" Mimi asked.

"Heard what?"

"Tone Morello lost his job, he was fired. I don't think he'll be back."

"Oh," Robin said.

Well, she wasn't going to blame herself for Ant-knee's problems. The smug jerk had probably ticked off the wrong person at his television station with his stupid, macho, win-at-all-costs attitude. She hadn't gotten him fired.

And why should she care if, for some bizarre reason, she had? After the way he'd treated all those women, it'd serve him right if he wound up in a soup kitchen. Hell, it'd serve him right if he wound up in a soup pot — and if any of those other jerks who came into Mimi's thought she was going to take it easy on them...

Robin worked herself up into such a fine lather that it took her several moments to realize that someone was knocking — banging by now — on her door.

She yanked it open to find Manfred.

"What?" she said testily.

"Bianca is coming," he said, trying to keep the anxiety out of his voice. "Her airplane will arrive in one hour. Please. You will come with me to the airport."

In her current mood, Robin thought: Why the hell should I?

But for reasons she was unable to articulate, she said through a humorless rictus, "Sure, why not? We can talk about cherry tarts on the way."

Manfred wasn't in the mood for conversation. He was intent on getting to the airport. He found his way to the Kennedy Expressway and got on going in the right direction, but would have missed the feeder road for O'Hare if Robin hadn't elbowed him out of whatever reverie was showing at the cineplex behind his eyes.

"*Danke*," he said.

"Yeah, yeah," Robin muttered.

A plane roared overhead, coming in for a landing. Manfred leaned forward, his head over the steering wheel, turning sideways, trying to see into the aircraft's windows.

"Keep your eyes on the road, will you?" Robin said. "You don't know that's her plane, you can't see anything anyway, and you don't even know what she looks like these days."

Manfred turned a face to Robin that made her think: You really don't want to get King Kong p.o.'ed at you. He might grab you with one hand, climb the control tower and fight off the Air National Guard.

"I will recognize my daughter," Manfred said stiffly.

But he didn't try to spot anymore in-bound aircraft. And he followed Robin's directions to the proper parking structure and to the international terminal. Manfred had a whispered word with a Customs official, who checked a note on his clipboard and let them cross the barrier which held all the non-CIA-affiliated hoi polloi at bay. They stood side by side at the arrival gate not saying a word to each other.

What a pair, Robin thought. Just what a little kid dragged away to a foreign country wants to see. The troll twins in a snit. They were enough to make a brothel look homey.

After several minutes of waiting, Manfred trying not to fidget,

Robin wondering, the way people did when their car was about to go off a cliff, what am I doing here, a plane taxied up to the gate. As the jetway goosenecked out to the plane, Manfred turned to Robin. His expression was different this time.

"I am sorry for my rude behavior," he said. He gave his little nod to make it official. "I am very nervous, and I am not good at being nervous. I have not had much practice. You are doing a favor for me, and I should not be cross with you. You were right: I have no idea what my daughter will look like."

For a moment, his face sagged. Then, as if he were lifting a barbell, he gathered himself and pushed his features back up into an approximately neutral position. A second effort raised them a millimeter higher, so Robin could see a flicker of hope in his eyes and the hint of an expectant smile on his lips.

"She'll love you," Robin said. "If she doesn't, she's nuts."

Manfred looked at her with such pathetic gratitude Robin was almost sorry she'd opened her mouth.

At that moment, the door to the jetway slammed open and a high, keening voice filled the terminal with curses that you didn't have to be a linguist to translate. The raw venom in every shout and shriek was an idiom familiar to everyone. Robin and Manfred turned to see the source of the commotion. The point of origin was a thrashing dervish of a child being held and only partially restrained by CIA agent Warner Lisle.

Warner's face, while not cut to ribbons, was bleeding in several places, including a point on his chin where the damage looked as if it had been inflicted by teeth. Spotting Manfred, Warner immediately thrust the child into his arms.

"Your daughter," he said to Manfred. "She's all yours."

Warner took out a handkerchief and began blotting his wounds.

The girl looked at Manfred, to see who her new captor was, and for a moment she was quiet. She had blue eyes, which nicely matched her spiky blue hair. She had a long straight nose and lips full and wide enough to put her on the cover of Vogue. She had a gold safety pin through the lobe of her left ear. She was long and slender in her steel-toed boots, torn jeans, "Eat Me" t-shirt and black leather jacket, but overwhelming the whole punk ensemble was a sense of malice so strong that Robin hadn't seen anything like it since that kid in *The Exorcist.*

If her head did a three-sixty, Robin was out of there.

Having given Manfred the once over, she rendered her opinion of him by screaming in his face. She tried to claw him, too, but he was made of sterner stuff than her last warder. One arm pinned both of hers to her sides and the other restrained her legs. That left her mouth. She opened it to flash a set of pointy little white teeth, but Manfred quickly raised his right hand. He didn't strike her, he crooked his thick index finger and let her bite it. Which she did, to the point of drawing blood that flowed from the finger and out the corners of her mouth.

"Now, why didn't I think of that?" Warner asked.

Manfred didn't make a sound, didn't even give a disapproving look. Just waited stoically, and until the end of time if necessary. The little girl saw that she was getting nowhere, her jaws were starting to ache and she realized that any further attempt at a physical assault against this monster would be futile.

When she removed her teeth from his flesh, Manfred said, "I am your father and I love you." He repeated the sentiment in German.

Bianca stared at him a moment, then turned away, her eyes sullen and downcast. Manfred wiped his blood off her chin with his wounded finger.

Warner took a long envelope out of a coat pocket and handed it to Manfred.

"Here you go, buddy. Bianca Krump. All the necessary paperwork. Legal entry into the United States. Resident alien status, eligible for citizenship. Signed, sealed and delivered."

Manfred stuffed the envelope in his jacket pocket.

"She has a bag?" Manfred asked.

Warner shook his head.

"She comes as is ... and one more thing," Warner added. "We're even now."

Robin drove home.

Manfred and Bianca sat in the back of the old Mercedes. Robin listened to the kid. She wasn't screaming anymore, she was talking, a non-stop snarl of German about everything that passed in front of her eyes. The disparaging tone made it plain that nothing she saw was as good as the place she used to know.

Bianca noticed Robin sneaking peeks at her in the rear view mirror.

"*Fett und scheusslich,*" Bianca judged Robin.

Robin drove a mile trying to figure that one out. When she thought she had it, she asked Manfred, "Fat and ugly, right? The kid said I'm fat and ugly?"

Manfred shook his head.

"Fat and hideous."

He saw Robin's jaw set, and knew she was making an effort to restrain herself.

"Please don't take offense," he said. "She says much worse about me."

By a stroke of divine grace, Robin found a parking space just one house down from her place. She zipped into it, turned off the engine and the lights and flipped the keys back to Manfred. She intended to make a fast getaway and barricade herself in her apartment, putting a safe distance between herself and the wretched refuse that had washed up on her shore.

But that was when the kid decided to pitch her latest fit.

She went into hysterics. Not acting out anger this time, but fear and longing. She was crying for her mother. Robin didn't know the words this pathetic child was sobbing, but the meaning was crystal clear. She felt she was about to enter a place from which she would never escape ... and she was pleading for her mother.

Robin knew that Manfred wouldn't have any physical difficulty carrying his daughter down into his apartment, despite the fact that the kid was clinging to the car's upholstery with all her might, but she thought the least she might do would be to hold the doors for him. She closed the rear door of the Mercedes after he gently tugged the forlorn girl out of the car. She opened the outer door of her house and allowed them to enter. One more door, she thought, and that would be the end of it for her. At least for tonight.

But Manfred asked, "May I show Bianca the park? I think it might help."

The request took Robin by surprise. And it wasn't one she was inclined to grant — but she made the mistake of looking into Bianca's eyes. The child was so lost, so frightened, so doomed.

"Just for a minute," Robin said grudgingly.

She unlocked the inside hall door and made her way up to the first floor landing. After a moment's hesitation, she inserted the key into the deadbolt lock and opened the door to the park. There were Gro-Lights on inside, working off their timer, and it gave the place the aspect of some magical jungle. The effect on Bianca was instantaneous: she fell silent and her eyes went round.

She pulled away from Manfred's arms and he let her go. Bianca stepped cautiously over to the wishing well and the fish pond which were always lit at night. She dipped her hand in the water. The piscine inhabitants fled from her intrusion, but she didn't pursue them. She didn't try to filch any of the coins, either, as Robin thought she might. She just rubbed the water she'd collected on her fingers all around her face. Then she turned to look at the rest of this fantastical environment.

She stepped gingerly into the park as if strange creatures might lurk beyond the nearest clump of leaves and fronds. She carefully poked her nose around a curve in the plantings. Robin and Manfred watched with interest. With a sudden burst, Bianca ran toward the rear of the park. Robin thought she was trying to escape, find a back way out, but she dove under a thick schefflera. A little hand parted the leaves and the child's eyes peered out at the grownups.

She said something to Manfred in German.

"Bianca has decided she will live here," he translated. When he saw the alarm in Robin's eyes, he shook his head. "You have been most patient. I will take Bianca downstairs now. Will you please turn on the overhead lights?"

Robin did, but the lights were a big mistake. The kid knew the game was over, and her rage flared up once again. She bounced to her feet and started shredding the schefflera leaves. Before the destruction could go too far, Robin was past Manfred and upon the kid in a heartbeat.

"Stop it!" she roared. "Don't you dare hurt my plants!"

Robin couldn't have been more ferocious if Bianca had been attacking a child of hers.

Bianca didn't need any translation, either. She fled to her father's arms and babbled at him while pointing at Robin, obviously urging Manfred to crush her. Robin wasn't amused.

She grimly said to Manfred, "You tell her ... tell her that if she ever tries anything like that again — if I ever let her in here again — you're both out."

Bianca had been listening to Robin. Now she turned to her newfound father to see whose side he would take. When she heard what he had to say, she tried to attack him again, with the same lack of success. Bianca burst into bitter tears, until Manfred whispered into her ear. She stopped crying immediately. She looked at Manfred with wary, calculating eyes. Hopeful, but not daring to trust.

Robin wondered if he'd given the kid her message.

"She understands?" Robin asked. "You understand?"

Manfred nodded.

"She will behave. I have just promised her that if she is good, and if she so wishes, she may return to her mother in six months."

CHAPTER 16

Robin heard the sound of the harmonica coming through the heating vent just as she slipped into bed. The music was slow and simple and so full of heartbreak that she thought she would cry, and then she did and felt better for it. As the tears rolled down her cheeks, she tried to identify the song, but she couldn't. She wondered if Manfred's repertoire was simply larger than her knowledge of the blues, or if the song was something he'd written to console himself during his stretch in prison ... and was now putting to use for his daughter.

Not knowing the music, having no sense of where it might be going, made it more elemental as it rode up the current of warm air that also arrived courtesy of the man in her basement. He was a considerable assault on any number of her preconceptions. Here was a man who'd gone to extraordinary lengths to reclaim his child, and yet shortly after getting her back said he would relinquish her.

Robin didn't think for a minute that it was just a ploy on Manfred's part just to get the kid to shut up — although the fact that she had closed her yap was a definite plus.

She didn't think it was a matter of cold feet, either. A guy who'd let a kid bite his finger down to the bone without making a peep wasn't a quitter.

No, he'd made his promise because the kid's happiness meant more to him than his own. He'd given his word because he loved that little girl more than anyone. The harmonica moved into a particularly melancholy passage and Robin wondered why men couldn't love their women as much as they loved their daughters.

She hoped that his playing eased Bianca's pain and fear as much as it did hers, but with a mild sense of shame, Robin had to admit that it wouldn't break her heart if the little plant-shredding snot soon fled back to the Fatherland.

To escape the guilt that followed on the heels of such an uncharitable sentiment, Robin fell asleep.

Robin smelled the pastry before she heard the knock at her door. It wasn't strudel, though. It was ... sniff ... cherry tarts? Then came the knock. A small knock from a small hand.

The picture immediately formed in her mind: father and daughter had come calling on Sunday morning with a plate of fresh-from-the-oven, melt-in-your-mouth pastry. The day was sunny and pleasantly crisp in its autumnal fashion. Robin had just showered, put on clean clothes and brushed her hair. What a perfect setting for inviting her considerate tenants in to share breakfast with her.

Yeah, right.

She wondered if they'd heard her moving around, or if she could pretend she was still asleep. Robin suddenly felt crowded and wasn't at all sure she wanted company. The little knock came again, and then she thought she heard Manfred whisper something about *schlafen langer* or something like that, recognizing the German word for sleep. So maybe she'd had them fooled after all.

Bianca said something that Robin didn't understand, but her tone was clear. *We tried, she's not interested, let's beat it, okay?* Out of sheer perversity, Robin went to the door. Of course, that wasn't what she told herself. No, she'd just decided that she had to check out this new pastry she might soon be serving to her customers.

She opened the door just as Manfred was bending over to

leave the plate of pastry on her doorstep. He looked up, saw her, straightened and gave her his nod.

"Good morning," he said.

He handed the plate to Bianca and gave her a gentle nudge.

"*Gut morgen,*" the girl said, handing the plate to Robin, and giving her father a look over her shoulder.

"Cherry tarts," Manfred said.

Robin had known that before she'd opened the door; drawing close the smell had become unmistakable. Now, though, she was more interested in what Manfred had done with the kid. The black leather jacket was gone, as was the gold safety pin from her ear. The holes in the knees of her jeans were neatly stitched and the "Eat Me" t-shirt had been laundered and turned inside out. The kid's hair was still blue but it had been thoroughly shampooed and combed flat and back with a part on the left side. Just like a boy's, Robin thought. Manfred must have missed hairdressing school. She noticed that Bianca's roots, chestnut brown, were starting to grow out.

Manfred's index finger was neatly bandaged.

"Good morning," Robin said. "Thank you for the tarts."

An awkward silence ensued as they all stood there for the next several moments trying to decide who should say what to whom. Then Manfred took Bianca's hand, gave Robin another nod and started to leave.

Again, out of perversity, or for some other reason she couldn't fathom, Robin took the initiative. "Have you had breakfast?"

"No," Manfred said, "we are just now —"

"Come on in," Robin suggested. "I'll cook. You've done enough for one morning."

Bianca didn't exactly skip inside. But she didn't complain aloud, either. She was a model prisoner quietly serving her time, giving the warden no excuse to extend her sentence. She sat at the kitchen table between her father's place and Robin's and awaited the French toast she'd chosen from the list of possibilities Robin had offered. Manfred preferred scrambled eggs, as many as Robin cared to fix, crisp bacon and a toasted English muffin with raspberry preserves. When he saw that Robin intended only one soft-boiled egg for herself, he told her to eat more if she wanted, he would help her turn her food into healthy muscle.

It struck her as oddly threatening that a man would tell her to eat as much as she liked. She'd used her size, her obesity, as a barrier against unwanted male attention. Yet, here was a man who brushed aside one of her main lines of defense as if it were a cobweb.

Still, Robin loved to eat a hearty breakfast and so she seized the opportunity, adding more eggs to the bowl to be scrambled.

She wasn't a fancy cook, but with almost two decades in food service, Robin knew how to make what she liked, and prepare it well and efficiently. She had everything on the table in appropriately short order. It looked good, it smelled better, it was all hot and everyone was ready to eat at the same time.

Except Manfred had something to say.

"Do you offer thanks?" he asked.

"For the food?"

Bianca watched the exchange, interested.

"Ja."

"No."

"Would you mind if we did?"

"You're religious?"

He shrugged.

"I started praying at school meals to annoy the Communists. In prison, I became sincere. Prayer helped me there. I would like my daughter to learn. Even if it means nothing to her now, someday, perhaps, she will become sincere, too."

"If that's what you want," Robin said, "this is a free country."

Manfred took Bianca's hand and bowed his head. Robin was about to reach for her fork, and dig into her rapidly cooling eggs, when Bianca startled her by taking her hand and joining them all together.

But the kid wasn't being pious. There was a smirk on her face. The look said: *If I'm stuck with this mumbo-jumbo, so are you.*

Manfred was pleased with the food, complimenting Robin, and disappointed that she wouldn't let him do the dishes as a gesture of gratitude. For a moment, she wondered if this was some kind of elaborate con. She'd never heard of a man offering to do someone else's dishes. Even her dad didn't do that.

While she mulled the issue, Bianca spoke to her father.

Manfred listened, gave her a strange look and then turned to Robin.

"May Bianca watch your television? She says while she was being torn from her mother's embrace, she consoled herself with the thought that at least she'd get to watch American TV."

"Sure," Robin said. "The set is in the living room."

"What is a good channel? Nothing with the violence."

"Try PBS. Channel 11."

Manfred went with Bianca to introduce her to the joys of television. Robin started rinsing off the breakfast dishes. The three of them hadn't exchanged more than a dozen words during the meal. Manfred's focus on eating was, if anything, more absolute than his concentration on weightlifting. The kid had really dug in, too, eaten all the French toast and started to lick the syrup off the plate before her father had given her a frown. Then she'd checked Robin out to see if she'd been laughing at her. When she'd found Robin's face suitably neutral she'd asked if she could have orange juice, like she was asking for gold, and had been astounded that Robin actually had a carton, and had swallowed the whole eight-ounce glass in three gulps. Then she'd used the back of her hand as a napkin, which had drawn another frown but not a word of reproach.

Robin was halfway through rinsing the dishes when Manfred returned.

"You are sure I cannot help?"

"Okay, okay," Robin relented. "I'll rinse, you stack things in the dishwasher."

She pulled open the front of the machine. Manfred took a second to study the arrangement of the racks and quickly transferred the contents of the dish-drain into the washer. He caught up with Robin so she could hand the remaining plates, pans, glasses and flatware directly to him.

Robin was impressed at how adept he was. She had the feeling he'd never seen a dishwasher before. But he loaded the racks as quickly and neatly as she could have done. The natural hand-eye coordination of a world-class athlete, she guessed.

He knew he was doing it right, too. He gave her a smile and waggled his eyebrows when he neatly tucked the fry pan into a tight spot. Robin laughed at his clowning.

Then a chill passed through her. This scene was the height of domesticity. Disposing of the Sunday morning dishes while the kiddy watched cartoons in the other room. Who was this man who'd penetrated her armor so completely in such a short time? She started to look ahead, worrying and wondering where this madness might lead, when she slammed on the brakes. Told herself to get a grip. Washing dishes was about as mundane an activity as any in which a human being could engage, even if there was someone helping out — even if that someone was still smiling at her and would probably make her laugh again any second now.

It was no big deal.

Manfred said, "May I ask you a favor?"

And just like that her paranoia roared back to life.

What?

What did he want?

What would he ask?

"Bianca needs new clothes. Proper clothes for a young girl. I know more about the dark side of the moon than such things. Please. Will you help me?"

Not please, you will help me. The way he'd probably have said it before.

He was making the effort to learn better manners. Or better grammar, anyway. Prompted by what? She didn't want to think about it.

But she said okay.

She'd go shopping with him and the kid.

They stood at the door, ready to go, and Robin asked Manfred what kind of clothes he wanted for the kid.

"First class," he said.

"Okay," she said, "you want to be Daddy Warbucks, it's your bank account."

"Daddy who?" Manfred asked, puzzled.

"Never mind," Robin said. "I just meant that first class in this town costs a lot of money."

Manfred pulled a wad of bills out of his jacket pocket appropriate to his size and line of work; you'd have to be a weight lifter to pick it up. Bianca spotted the roll immediately, gawking with great interest at the money. Robin noticed the avarice in the kid's eyes. Maybe life with Daddy won't be so bad after all, huh kid, she thought.

So, they piled into Manfred's old Mercedes and Robin led them to North Michigan Avenue, the Magnificent Mile.

Robin decided that this was what brought people to America as she saw her two immigrants hit one of the country's most glittering retail streets: They came to shop. The ambitious ones stayed so they could keep on shopping.

Robin had intended simply to take them to Water Tower Place, a gilded vertical mall, where any normal person could satisfy any consumer need that wouldn't draw the attention of the police. But that plan soon went out the window. Just as soon, in fact, as father and daughter saw the endless shops lining both sides of the street.

Taking in the sights, Manfred craned his neck to look up at the one hundred stories of the John Hancock Center.

"*Wunderbar,*" he opined.

The guy probably didn't know from architecture, but Robin could see how someone who pumped iron for a living would like a building that was all black steel, giant X-shaped braces and soared halfway to the moon.

"Yeah, it great," Robin said. "There's an observation deck on the 95th floor, too. Best of all, it's right next door to where we're going to shop."

That was her best shot at heading off the shopping safari, but it was doomed to fail. The kid yammered something in German and they were off. Up one side of the street to the river and back down the other. If there was a thing that the kid asked for and didn't get, Robin didn't see it. And not just clothes: toys, games, stuffed animals and electronics. By the time they got up to the 95th floor of the Hancock, even Manfred had trouble carrying everything, and Robin had sore feet.

Robin sat down at a table and sipped a ginger ale, the only thing she'd allowed Manfred to buy for her. She looked at the big man with his tiny daughter. He was looking out a window with her and pointing at the lake. Robin tracked the gesture but all she saw was water, not even a boat or ship in sight.

Manfred joined her at the table and ordered a beer when the waiter came over.

"Bianca asked which direction she should look to see Germany. I told her, but explained she wouldn't be able to see it. She is trying anyway; she said we are high enough. She wants to see her mother."

Manfred shrugged.

Robin did, too. She was under the distinct impression that the kid's affection for her old man had grown with each passing purchase.

"I have another problem," Manfred said.

"Don't we all?" Robin responded, rubbing one of her aching feet.

"Tomorrow I must work."

"Me, too."

"But I must have someone to care for Bianca. I cannot leave her alone."

"What about school? Didn't the CIA wire that for you, too?"

"There are always things that you don't think about. To be honest, I dared not get my hopes so high as to think about school. And I think Bianca needs to adjust to me, to America."

"Then what you need is a daycare center."

When she saw his puzzled look Robin explained what she meant.

"I would prefer personal care for Bianca," he said.

"You mean a nanny?"

"*Ja.* Someone good and kind and experienced." Manfred turned to glance at his daughter for a moment. "Someone firm."

Robin was about to crack that he didn't want too much, did he, when an idea hit her. An idea that made her smile.

"I've got just who you want," she said.

"Nancy," Robin said into the phone. "You've got to try some of Manfred's cherry tarts ... Better than the strudel ... You'll be right over? ... Good."

Robin put her phone down. The shoppers had returned home.

"Who is Nancy?" Manfred asked.

"My sister."

"She has children of her own?"

"Two grown boys."

Manfred looked at Bianca who sat playing among her new possessions like a kid at Christmas.

"She is firm, your sister?"

"Oh, yeah. She works at it every day. You'll like her."

Manfred did like Nancy. She seemed to take to him, too. And she had a hard time not swooning after her first bite of cherry tart. Which damn near made Manfred blush with pleasure. It was almost too much for Robin to take.

The only thing that cheered her was the kid's reaction. She sat like some little miser amidst her pile of gold, worried that someone might filch a small coin from her. That someone being Nancy. Robin was eager to see how her ever-competent sister would handle this one.

Robin explained the kind of help Manfred needed.

"Hey, I go to work everyday, too, you know," Nancy said.

"Yeah, but you're the boss at your place," Robin said.

"Office manager," Nancy replied.

"Okay, you don't own the place, but who runs it?"

Nancy looked at Robin, then Manfred, then Bianca.

The kid was staring intently back at the adults.

"I do."

"And there isn't something you could work out?"

"I will pay, of course," Manfred said.

Nancy didn't need the money. With Charlie's business income, she worked because she enjoyed it. She liked to bring order to things. If she could have put up with all the handshaking and backslapping, she would have run for mayor.

"I will bake for you, too," Manfred added, when he saw that the money angle wasn't playing.

That was tempting ... but Nancy didn't know what she'd do with the kid around the office all morning. There was no way that she'd give up her job to become a nursemaid.

"Let me talk to the kid."

The three adults advanced upon the child who protectively gathered up as many of her purchases in her arms as she could. Bianca looked at Nancy and said something in German.

Manfred frowned, big time.

"What'd she say?" Nancy asked.

Manfred looked for a way to phrase his response; Robin filled the gap.

"The kid said I was fat and hideous," Robin told Nancy.

"So what did she say about me?" Nancy repeated.

Manfred shrugged in resignation and told her.

"She said you looked like a prostitute ... one of the women in the brothel where she lived."

Nancy gave Bianca a look that would have made Dracula whimper.

Bianca quickly directed a flurry of words to her father. Not exactly a cry for help, but a hurried explanation. Manfred provided simultaneous translation as the child continued.

"This woman — the one Bianca says you resemble — she says that she is the highest priced prostitute in the house ... the prettiest one."

Manfred stopped, clearly embarrassed, shocked by his daughter.

Bianca repeated herself.

"What? What was that last part?" Nancy asked.

Through his deepest frown yet and clenched teeth, Manfred said, "The most skilled in the bedroom."

Bianca looked at Nancy, hopeful that she'd appeased her.

Robin had a hard time keeping a straight face.

Manfred sighed, let his face drop and said, "I am sorry my daughter has insulted you. Please forgive her. Her circumstances have not been the best. I will look for someone else to watch over her."

Nancy shook her head, a tight smile on her face that a drill instructor would have envied.

"No, no," she said. "This little girl and I are going to get along just fine."

Manfred was surprised.

Robin wasn't, not really.

"You are sure?" Manfred asked.

"Oh, yeah. First, we'll have to teach her English, and —"

"I speak English," Bianca said. She looked at her father and Robin, whose mouth hung open. "When I want to."

Her accent wasn't half as thick as Manfred's.

"Good," Nancy said. "Then tomorrow you can come to work with me and start learning real estate."

CHAPTER 17

The next morning, Robin was awakened by someone banging on her door. Not just knocking, banging. Loud, hard, and fast. It scared her silly. She looked at the clock and saw it was five a.m. The banging continued unabated. Robin ran to the door in her pajamas, wondering what the emergency could be. It had to be an emergency. What other explanation could there be? Was her house on fire? Had her father had another heart attack? Had—

She flung the door open heedless of who might be on the other side.

It was Manfred.

"What?" she gasped. "What's wrong? Is it you? The kid? What?"

"It is five a.m.," he said blandly. "Time for your workout. Please dress and meet me in the garage in five minutes."

Robin hit him. That might have been unacceptable behavior at Mimi's, but when some cretin scared her witless out of a sound sleep in her own home, it was entirely appropriate. Entirely futile as well. She hadn't been able to reach his head and her fist glanced off his enormous chest like a powder puff off granite.

Manfred wasn't the least bit perturbed. He merely nodded as if she had only confirmed his suspicions. "We will work on your upper body strength this morning."

Then he turned on his heel and repeated that she should present herself in five minutes.

Robin looked at his retreating bulk and screamed.

The scream woke Bianca. It didn't alarm her, though. Where she'd lived screams were a common enough occurrence. In fact, not a night went by without them. After all, a cry of feigned delight was a harlot's stock-in-trade. All of her girlfriends at the brothel had told her that. They said she should never worry about their screams; they were only what the customers had paid for and expected. In no time at all, Bianca had become adept at recognizing these sounds. In fact, when she was alone, she even practiced her own screams so that they would be right when her turn came to entertain the customers.

Of course, there was that one time when the screams got entirely too real. A customer had gone too far with Greta and hurt her, and then it was the customer's turn to scream when the Bear came into the room and twisted his head almost all the way around. Those screams were horrible.

But the scream that had woken her, that was more like the ones that Mama and Horst, a.k.a the Bear, exchanged when they were arguing. Bianca looked out through her bedroom doorway. The sofa-bed where the giant slept — she still didn't believe he was her father, even if he had bought her all those presents — was folded away and all the cushions had been replaced.

Where was he?

Arguing with *der hexe.* The hag.

Bianca got up to investigate.

Robin got dressed. The morning was pitch black and from the way the windows were frosted she knew it was cold outside. She wore leggings and a long-sleeved t-shirt under her sweat-clothes. She laced up her sneakers over heavy white socks. Oh, she was going to work out, all right. And at just the right moment she was bound and determined that, oops, a weight would be just too heavy for her to hold and she'd manage to drop it squarely on fat-head's toes.

She stormed down the back stairs and out to the garage, ready to do battle.

Bianca tiptoed through the apartment. The giant wasn't there. She poked her head out the front door, but there were no sounds in the hallway. She listened for footsteps from above in the Magical Garden — she very much wanted to get back in there, but not at the expense of kissing the *hag's* hem — but no sound came from above. With no other choice left, she opened the rear door of the apartment.

The giant had shown her this was where the building's laundry and other utilities were located. He had shown her that there was nothing to be afraid of back here, but Bianca was sure that a huge red rat lived in this place. It was the giant's pet. And if she ever made the giant truly angry, Bianca knew he would give her to the rat and the rat would eat her.

This was very similar to the warning her mother had given her about what would happen to Bianca if she ever caught her sneaking into the brothel's money room. But there had been a time or two when Bianca had slipped in and taken a few marks, and no one had noticed, and the rat hadn't gotten her.

So now she took her chances with the giant's rat. She looked all around and when she was sure that the rat was either sleeping or out eating other children, she scurried over to the rear window of the basement. She repositioned a cardboard box so she could climb up on it and look out. She saw another building that the giant had told her was the house's garage.

And now, across the distance of the small backyard, she could hear more screams ... and moans. Her keen, educated ear told her that strenuous physical exertions lay behind the sounds ... and the sounds were genuine, not pretend.

The giant was *shtupping* the *hag* — and she was enjoying it!

Bianca was revolted. She looked around once more to make

sure the rat hadn't snuck up on her and then she scurried back into her apartment, slamming the door to the rat's lair behind her. She ran back into her room, jumped in bed and pulled the covers over her head.

A terrible fear ran through her.

What if the giant really was her father?

What if her mother refused to take her back, even if the giant permitted it?

Would the *hag* then become her new mother?

Bianca would not have it. She'd feed herself to the rat first. Or she could turn the giant against the *hag,* make him see that he would be much better off with the hooker who looked like Geli. She at least would be a presentable choice.

And the hooker was coming to pick up Bianca for the day.

So she could start working on her right away.

Robin took the bus to work.

Manfred had offered to drive her; he had to drop off the cherry tarts at Mimi's anyway. But Robin declined. Firmly. The idea of riding with Manfred and the kid, who'd get dropped off at Nancy's, was too ... too ... too much like they were a family. The whole thing gave Robin the feeling that some malign force had set her at the top of a ski jump with a strong wind at her back. If she didn't fight it with all her might it'd be, eeek, down the slippery slope where she'd finish not with a graceful jump, but pitching head over heels.

No, scratch that. She wasn't doing anything head over heels.

In fact, she was still angry that she hadn't been able to drop the weights on Manfred's toes. She'd tried, twice. But he'd skipped neatly out of the way both times. The man's reaction time and agility were not to be believed. At that point, Robin had abandoned the idea. A third time would have been too obvious, and undoubtedly as unsuccessful as the others.

And by that time he had her so involved in the workout she'd had to concentrate solely on what she was doing. She'd had to put so much effort into each movement that she'd had to grunt and shout just to complete it ... and it had felt so good to succeed she hadn't even minded how loudly or rudely she'd been bellowing.

Now, she was sore again — but not as sore as the first time. This pain felt kind of good, strangely enough. It made her aware of herself in ways that she'd long since forgotten, since she'd been a kid racing around a playground anyway. She could feel actual muscles tightening and toughening under her suet. It was invigorating.

Made her feel really ready to go back to work and kick some tail.

Manfred had come and gone, leaving his tarts behind him, so she didn't have to deal with him when she arrived at Mimi's. Didn't have to worry about him putting her off her game.

Good thing, too, because all her regulars were glad to see her back. Gave her a warm Screaming Mimi's welcome. They lined up to take their shots.

"Well, look who's back. Our charm school drop-out."

"High praise from a med school lab rat," Robin replied.

"Where'd you go, Robin? A mushroom farm to work on your pallor?"

"Sure, saw you there feeding the crops, fertilizer-for-brains."

"It wasn't the same without you; it was like a day without a headache."

"Now you know how your wife feels when you're gone for the night."

"Love your hair, dear. Amazing what you can do with Johnson's Glo-Coat."

"Thanks, sweetie, it'd probably bleach out that little mustache of yours, too."

After the breakfast rush ended, Mimi came over and gave Robin a quick peck on the cheek.

"It's so good to have you back where you belong, Robin. Just like old times."

Robin waited for the zinger, but there wasn't one.

Mimi, and everyone else, really was glad to see her. Robin had been a little worried that people might tread gently around her after what she'd done to Ant-knee. But inside Mimi's, at least, all was right with the world.

That pumped her up even more than her workout had.

"You got your ass kicked," said Iggy Gross, boy shock-jock.
"Well ... "
"You did. You got it kicked."
"Okay. I did."
"I heard there's a tape. Vid-e-o."
"There's no tape."
"I'd pay you big bucks for that tape."
"There is no tape!"
"But there was, wasn't there?"

Tone Morello said nothing. He was enduring his twenty-third interview since he'd been fired from his job. He'd been to every TV station in town. He'd been to all the radio stations. He'd even been to the newspapers, including the neighborhood papers and one supermarket advertiser, to which he'd pitched his idea for a sports column. The electronic media had told him no thanks, to which the pencil press had added maliciously that everybody knew he didn't write his own material. Basically, Tone had fallen off a cliff, had gone from being a six-figure-a-year celebrity to an unemployable nobody. And had done it in breathtakingly quick time.

All because of Robin.

Not so much that she'd kicked his keister in that damned debate of theirs. Tone didn't know anybody in Chicago journalism who'd go up against Robin one-on-one of their own accord. And he had made sure that the tape his cameraman had shot of the nightmare had long since been reduced to slag. There was another tape, of course, the one that little broad had shot for Robin, but it hadn't surfaced or one of his old buddies would have added to his humiliation by making it public. But that story Robin had laid on him, making him seem like Jack-the-freaking-Ripper instead of just a guy who got around, brother, had that done a job on him.

The cause for Tone's dismissal had been moral turpitude, a reason that made him gag to this day. There were no morals in TV or journalism, and if everybody in the business who slept around got the axe for it, people would be getting their news from a town crier.

But him, he had become the poster boy for reckless, predatory sex — the bull's-eye for the new puritanism. All because of Robin. They'd bought that tub of lard's story lock, stock and barrel. So what if it was true? The thing that surprised Tone, though, when he stopped to examine that painful memory, was how personal Robin had made everything. There was more to it than just slugging it out with him. There was ... what? Something ... no, someone. That was it. Robin was getting even for someone else who had hurt her.

Insight wasn't an everyday occurrence for Tone, and he was greatly pleased with this one. Now, he had something that maybe he could use to get even one day. He might have explored the idea of revenge further but he was distracted by someone yelling at him.

"Hey, you listening to me?" Iggy Gross shouted.

"Yeah, sure," Tone said.

"What'd I just say?"

"I don't know."

Tone decided he'd better try to pay attention. Iggy Gross had actually called him and asked him to come in and talk. And the idiot — whose act consisted of pimple-faced, obnoxious, teenage, toilet humor — had a coast-to-coast radio audience of millions. He'd also said he might have a job for Tone.

"Okay," Gross said, "we'll forget about the tape for the time being. Now, here's my angle: You're a broken man. An evil, vicious, ball-busting man-hater has emasculated you and trashed your life? That's right, right?"

Tone forced himself to nod.

"Good," Gross smiled. "So what I want to do, on the air, of course, is give you a big, hairy ball transplant. Radio testosterone."

"What?" Tone said, seizing the front of the skinny radio geek's shirt.

"Balls," Gross said without flinching. "I'll give you balls and a hundred K for the first year."

At the mention of money, even though it was less than a third of what he had been making, Tone let the shock-jock go. Gross continued unperturbed.

"You'll do the sports reports for my show. We'll start you out real meek, half-fag. You'll try to do some of your sports grunts and they'll come out like a squeeze toy. In fact, we'll do an audio mix of your voice and a plastic squeaker to get the effect right. Then after time, exposure to me and my coaching, little by little, you start to get your balls back. The public gets to follow your progress. By the time I'm done with you you'll be roaring like a friggin' lion. All thanks to me. Whaddya say?"

At that moment, Tone experienced his second insight of the day.

"You've got something more in mind, don't you?"

Gross sat back and looked at Tone, surprised that the guy wasn't as stupid as he'd been told.

"Yeah. When I say the time is right, you have to fight a rematch with this diesel dyke who cracked your nuts in the first place."

Tone wondered if he was suddenly getting smarter, or if he just seemed that way compared to Iggy Gross. Because he knew the jerk still hadn't given him the whole story. This guy wanted him to go up against Robin again, get slaughtered again, and then Gross would do Robin in himself on his show.

Tone smiled.

"You in?" Gross asked.

"You bet," Tone replied.

What the hell, it was a job ... and it'd be fun to see what Robin would do to this idiot. Meanwhile he'd work out a plan that'd really nail her.

"Who's the kid?" Patty Phinney asked her daughter Nancy.

Nancy and Bianca had arrived at the offices of Gold Coast Realty.

Patty was sixty-two and looked ten years younger. She didn't work out as hard as her daughter did, but she ate sensibly, walked three miles a day, had her blonde hair touched up every week and dressed to the nines: the upscale real estate diva.

Bianca had her face scrubbed, her blue hair combed straight back and a dead-end-kid-on- her-best-behavior expression on her kisser. She wore a bright red parka, a cornflower blue cotton sweater, blue jeans and blindingly white sneakers.

"Are you the madam?" Bianca asked Patty.

Nancy gave her a look.

"I beg your pardon," Patty said, and then turned to her daughter for enlightenment.

"The kid was raised in a brothel."

Patty added two plus two and turned red.

"And she thinks I'm—"

"She asked if I was a hooker. She likes to get a rise out of people."

"Well, what are you doing with her?"

"She's the kid who's staying at Robin's."

"And the reason you brought her here?"

"I thought we'd break a few child-labor laws together."

Patty gave Nancy a mighty frown, not that it did the least bit of good.

"Well, just keep her away from the clients."

"Sure. You think I could borrow your hair dryer, Patty?"

Nancy never called her mother "Mom" at work; Patty kept a hair dryer on hand at all times because you never knew when you might get caught in the rain or snow and have to do quick repairs.

"Of course," Patty said. Since her daughter's hair was perfect, she knew Nancy wanted it for the child. "Just clean it before you give it back."

Nancy fixed Bianca's hairstyle in the ladies room. Spritzed it with water from the tap, dried it and fluffed it. Got it to come out looking reasonably close to a pixie cut rather than the Slickback

Sam special it had been. The kid didn't think much of it, but after Nancy told the kid to smile — or else — Nancy approved of the job she'd done. Even the blue hair didn't bother her too much.

She took Bianca back to her office.

"Do you know how to read?"

"Yes."

"Do you know how to count?"

"Of course."

"Good. Then I can put you to work."

"How much will I be paid?"

Nancy considered. The kid had spirit, and she liked that.

"Two dollars an hour."

"Is that a fair amount?"

"You have anybody else offering you more?"

Bianca considered. She hadn't expected to be paid at all; she'd just asked the question as a basis for lodging future complaints. But this woman — not a hooker, she had to admit — was going to pay her. They might actually get along.

"No."

"Then we'll start by having you put these files in alphabetical order."

Nancy pulled a chair over to one end of her desk, plunked down a stack of files and explained in detail what she wanted. Bianca looked up as Nancy leaned over her.

"You are much prettier than the *hag*. I think my father should *shtup* you instead of her."

Nancy stood up and fixed Bianca with a stare hard enough to cut diamonds.

"*Hag?* Did you just call my sister Robin a *hag?*"

Determined to stick to her plan, Bianca nodded.

Nancy pointed her right index finger squarely at the kid's nose. Then she shook it. Then she started to speak several times but bit her tongue. She couldn't remember the last time she'd come so close to flying off the handle — but Nancy did not believe in flying off the handle. Not ever. She leaned in toward the kid, one hand on the back of the kid's chair, the other on her desk. Nose to nose with Bianca.

"You are never to speak of Robin like that again. She gave your father a place to stay, which meant he could give you a place to stay. It cost her a lot to do that. If you were my kid, I'd give you a punishment you'd never forget for being so unkind. If you do it again, I'll turn you back over to your father and tell him to give you a punishment you'll never forget. Do you understand?"

Bianca thought of the red rat.

"I understand."

The child knew she'd have to find another approach — if she still wanted this *hure* in her life.

"Good," Nancy said, standing up.

She kept a hard look on her face as Bianca bent to the task she'd been set, but Nancy had a hard time not smiling.

If the kid had it right, Robin was finally getting laid.

David Solomonovich sneaked up on Robin while she was wiping off some tables after the lunchtime rush and stole a kiss. He'd had to time it just right, and stand on tiptoes, but he got her just as she turned from one table to the next. It wasn't just a little peck on the cheek, either. He threw his bony adolescent arms around her and kissed her full on the mouth.

Then he stepped back and hyperventilated through an idiot's grin at his boldness.

There were no other customers in the place at the moment to witness this stunning event, but Mimi, Manny and Judy all looked on slack-jawed.

David was just about to say something when Robin clobbered him with a right-handed head-slap that sounded like a rifle shot. The same blow that had bounced off of Manfred knocked David right off his feet and sent his glasses flying, in a two-cushion shot, into a tray of egg-salad. Robin looked down at the dazed and fallen Romeo and saw that tears were forming in his myopic eyes.

"Don't!" Robin commanded. "Don't you dare cry!"

David wasn't a woman scorned, but a hellacious tide of fury flooded his face. He scrambled to his feet and tried to flee but, relying on his shortsighted vision, he misjudged the doorway and ran smack into the jamb. Robin caught him on the rebound, grabbed the back of his collar and slapped a napkin over his bleeding nose.

While David was still seeing stars, Robin marched him off to the rear of the deli.

"Mimi," she said, "I need to use your office a few minutes."

Mimi mutely nodded her assent and handed Robin the boy's cholesterol encrusted glasses.

Robin sat behind Mimi's desk grimly wiping David's glasses clean with a tissue. David sat in the guest chair still holding the napkin to his nose. He could have made a break, but David learned very quickly from his mistakes. Running through the deli's kitchen without his glasses, he might pitch headfirst into the soup *du jour.* He stayed put, awaiting his fate.

After letting him sweat a while, Robin said, "There's no excuse for what you did, I don't care how young you are."

"We had a deal," David replied in a small voice. He wasn't entirely sure that Robin wasn't going to hit him again, but he had a point to make. "You owed me a kiss."

Robin put his glasses down on the desk in front of him. She waited until he put them on; she wanted him to see her.

"Is that what you thought that was? A kiss? A kiss is something that's given not taken. That wasn't a kiss; it was an assault. You follow through on what you did, it's rape."

The idea that he would rape anyone, much less Robin, jolted David to his soul ... but he couldn't deny characterizing what he'd done as a sneak attack. He'd consciously planned to take Robin by surprise, he'd grabbed her and he'd kissed her.

David began to cry, and this time Robin didn't stop him.

She handed him a tissue.

Robin was still angry, but her feelings were only slightly less jumbled than David's. She just didn't understand what he saw in her, but she knew she had to put an end to the infatuation once and for all. She had to get through to this boy wonder that in some respects he had to act his age not his IQ.

Then she had an idea.

When David stopped crying he said, "I won't bother you again. I won't come back here anymore."

"Oh, yes you will," Robin said.

"No, I won't," he insisted. "How can I show my face after what happened?"

"Showing your face is part of your ..." Robin was going to say punishment, but she changed her choice of words at the last moment. "... penance."

David wasn't Catholic, but Robin saw immediately that casting his act in moral terms was the right way to go. He still parried, but his heart wasn't in it.

"How can you make me?"

"You want your father to know what you did?"

"That's blackmail."

"Exactly."

There was no doubt in David's mind that Robin would tell on him, and he did not want his father or mother to find out how he'd behaved. For all his intellect, he could not imagine how they would react — except of course to be deeply hurt.

"What else do I have to do?"

"You have to apologize to me, and mean it."

David hung his head. He wanted to tell Robin that he loved her, that he'd been jealous of that big German jerk, that he'd been stupid like he couldn't believe, but he'd forfeited the right to tell her any of that. Excuses at this point would sound pathetic. As if lifting the weight of the world, David raised his head and looked at Robin.

"I'm sorry," he said.

Robin nodded.

"Okay, there's one more thing you have to do."

"What?"

"Manfred."

Just the mention of the guy's name made David nervous.

"Yeah?"

"He's now one of Mimi's suppliers, makes pastry for her. Since the two of you will be in here and your paths could cross, I'm going to introduce you. I'll tell him you were just kidding him the other day, so don't worry about that."

Actually, Robin getting him off the hook for that dumb move made David feel a lot better.

"Thanks," he said. "You going to tell him not to put the CIA on me, too?"

"Yeah."

"I appreciate it."

David got up to go.

"We're not done here," Robin said.

David sat back down. Uneasily. Now knowing the worst was yet to come.

"Manfred has a daughter. Bianca. She's new in this country. She needs someone to show her the ropes."

David was agog. Was Robin setting him up with a girl?

"How old is she?"

"Eight."

"Eight?"

"That's not a problem, is it? She's closer to your age than you are to mine."

What could he say to that?

"No, it's not a problem," David said tightly.

He realized then that Robin was too wily for him. He didn't care how smart he was, how smart he'd ever be, she'd always be able to lay out traps for him that he'd walk right into. She was teaching him a lesson and, given her threat of blackmail, he had no choice but to learn it.

Robin kept any hint of glee off her face, but she thought the idea was terrific. She'd sell Manfred on what a great kid David was and let him take some of the weight for caring for the little blue-haired imp off of Nancy. It'd be good for David to see a May-December relationship from the other side of the coin. The more she thought about it, the more she was sure David and Bianca deserved each other.

Who knew, maybe something good would even come of it.

"One thing, David. Manfred is very protective of his daughter. Fathers are like that. Your behavior with her will have to be impeccable."

More than just a shot, Robin was making a point that David would have to remember when he finally started dating girls of his own age.

Cure him of that stolen-kiss crap right now.

The snow started an hour before closing time. Within minutes, it was coming down so hard you couldn't see the other side of the street from the deli. Two minutes after that, you couldn't see past the curb on the near side of the street. Snow had not been predicted that day.

But that was winter in Chicago. What were you going to do?

Mimi decided that what she'd do was close early.

There was only one customer in the place. He'd intended to eat there, but Mimi bagged his sandwich, slice of carrot cake and cup of coffee, told him it was on the house and sent him on his way. The staff had the place cleaned in fifteen minutes, Stan Prozanksi got there early to escort Mimi to the bank, and they were all out the door.

And into the blizzard.

Stan offered Robin a ride home in his patrol unit, but there was no room in front with him and Mimi, and she knew what the back of a cop car smelled like from a once-in-a-lifetime juvenile misadventure. She declined and said she'd brave the storm.

Which basically meant she'd have to mush home through the snow drifts on foot. Everybody else in town had gotten off early, too. The CTA buses were packed, everyone jammed in cheek-to-jowl, smelling each other's breath and wet clothing, pressed together so intimately in a crowd of strangers that if it hadn't been for all those damp layers of nylon, wool and cotton it would have been one huge cluster —

The subway trains were even worse.

So Robin mushed. Head bowed. Snow sticking to her hair and eyelashes and shoulders. Trusting to some primitive part of her brain that it would lead her home without conscious awareness, like a saddle horse or a homing pigeon. Her one consolation was that her labored march proceeded at a pace faster than that of the cars, trucks and buses stuck in the doomsday traffic jam that seemed to grip the whole city.

Leaving her body to make its way home on autopilot, Robin thought about how hard she'd hit David. Hard enough to make her hand sting. She hadn't regretted it at the time; she still thought she'd had the right to do what she'd done, but upon reflection she knew she hadn't had to put as much muscle behind the blow. She thought about banging that wonderful brain around inside its skull and she cringed. She felt even worse when she thought about hitting Manfred, too. She was lashing out at people, literally striking them. That wasn't her. She hated bullies. What was happening to her?

Sure, her circumstance had changed. She had less privacy — but she had more company. And, as much as she hated to admit it, that wasn't such a bad thing. Then there was her house, it was in better shape than it had been for years. And after only a couple of workouts, she was in better shape than she'd been in years. She was back on the job. She was continuing her buyout plan with Mimi. Everything was going pretty well.

So why did she feel as if a piano was going to fall on her head, instead of just half of the snow in creation?

Robin heard a car horn honk. Of course, she'd been hearing horns all along; that's what people did when they got stuck in traffic. They vented their feelings with the palms of their hands, or, if they were reckless, with their middle fingers. But this horn seemed to be directed specifically at her. She wondered how people could distinguish that "Hey, you!" quality when someone wanted to get their particular attention.

She looked up and pierced the curtain of white crystals to see Manfred's old Mercedes. The kid was with him. Robin realized that she'd already walked halfway home. Manfred popped open the back door of the car on the driver's side for her. The car was in traffic, but traffic continued at a crawl so Robin had no problem stepping right into it.

Manfred said hello. The kid just gave Robin a look.

"Thanks," Robin said.

"*Es steht Ihnen frei, zu,*" he said. Then he shook his head with a smile. "Ah, I am sorry, Bianca and I were speaking German. It is our pleasure to give you a ride."

The kid didn't look like it pleased her any, Robin thought.

Manfred didn't appear to notice.

"I have not seen snow like this since I visited the Alps," he said.

"Yeah, that's winter in Chicago for you. The Alps without the mountains."

Manfred gave her a puzzled look in the rear-view mirror. Then he got the joke and laughed. "*Sehr gut,*" he said.

When they got to Menominee Street it was predictably parked in, and the way the snow kept coming it looked like all those cars would be snowed in, too, until the spring thaw. Manfred offered to drop off Robin and Bianca in front while he found parking, but Robin knew he'd probably have to drive to St. Louis to find an open spot.

"Just put it in the garage," she said. "Save yourself some trouble."

"*Danke.*"

He steered the heavy car into the alley. The snow here was even deeper because there had been no traffic to compress it. Manfred kept the car moving, but as they approached the garage, Robin saw an odd look cross his face, almost as if he were embarrassed.

"I hope you will not mind, but I have installed an automatic opener. I fear if I stop to open the door manually the car will become stuck."

"You don't think you could push it free?"

"*Ja,* of course, I could. I only mean..."

Manfred got this joke, too. He used the automatic opener.

Even though it still rankled her a little to have him trifling with her house, Robin told herself not to be such a hard-ass. And when Manfred grinned at her she grinned back.

Bianca was the only one not smiling as the Mercedes entered the garage and escaped the storm.

Manfred was not one to let a continuing blizzard keep him from shoveling the walkways around the house. Indeed, with Teutonic precision, he had a plan to lay out for Robin's consideration as they all stood in the shelter of the garage.

"I will shovel, *ja?* You will follow behind with the broom and sweep the concrete bare. And Bianca will spread the salt to keep the snow from accumulating again."

Since they had all the necessary personnel, equipment and salt, it seemed a reasonable plan even in the face of nature's ongoing assault — except one member of the team wasn't on the same page in the playbook.

"I do not wish to help," Bianca said. "This is laborer's work."

Manfred frowned. Bit back an impulse to use the parental imperative. Looked for a way to reason with his daughter.

"We need your help," he said. "Without you, the snow will just pile up even higher."

"Let it," Bianca said stubbornly.

"Please," Manfred said, framing his plea with a bit of iron.

A shrewd look came into Bianca's eyes.

"How much will you pay me?"

"I will pay you a warm home, good food, and a snug bed."

There was no room for bargaining in his tone, but Bianca blithely ignored it.

"I make two dollars an hour at my new job," she said. "Can you do better?"

Negotiations got serious at that point because Manfred

switched to his native tongue. Robin decided it was time for her to slip away, but Manfred spotted her, held up a hand and asked her to please stay.

She did, with great reluctance. The kid was shooting daggers at her, obviously preferring that there'd be no witness to whatever was to follow.

Manfred went down on one knee in front of his daughter. Continuing in German, he seemed to Robin to be giving the little brat a quiet but firm lecture on the necessities of meeting one's responsibilities.

Bianca sneered.

Robin caught the word "television" as the kid launched into a tirade, also in German, and then pointed first to Robin and then to the weight bench that sat not ten feet from where they all stood. Whatever the kid said, it made Manfred blush. Set him back on his heels.

Then Robin realized that she'd heard a word, a cognate, that she understood.

Shtup.

And now the kid was doing a burlesque turn on a series of moans and groans. Sexual sounds. Obscene sounds coming from such a young girl.

The light dawned on Robin. The kid had heard them out here this morning ... and she'd thought Robin's exertions had been —

"Oh, my God," she said.

Manfred saw that she understood. He rose and started to apologize, but Bianca reclaimed his attention, still speaking their mother tongue.

She craned her neck to look up at her huge father and gave him a searing earful.

And got more of a reaction than she'd ever bargained for.

Manfred seized her with one hand as easily as if he'd picked a grape off a vine. He held the dangling, wide-eyed child even with his face and drew his free hand back as if to strike her. Robin was horrified. Even a slap from this man would kill the girl, snap her neck like the thinnest of reeds.

"Stop!" Robin screamed.

She leaped at Manfred, grabbed his arm and hung on it, but even her weight didn't drag it down an inch. She realized immediately that if Manfred wanted to hit Bianca, she wouldn't be able to stop him. But Robin's intervention shattered the moment, shifted his focus, made him think about what he'd intended to do. A violent shudder surged through the man.

He set Bianca down, and Robin released his arm. Manfred took a step back and looked at each of them. He seemed as if he might break down and cry. Then he grabbed a snow shovel off its hook on the wall and plunged out into the snow.

Robin and Bianca looked at each other ... and listened to the harsh clang of the metal shovel striking the pavement beneath the snow as Manfred fought the storm.

Robin took Bianca into the park.

The little girl immediately ran and hid behind a palm. Robin thought she'd just leave her there. Let her work it all out for herself. But she reconsidered.

She said, "I don't know what you said to your father, but it must've been truly awful ... because you made him do something he'll probably regret the rest of his life. And I'd bet my life no one has ever treated you better than he has."

The kid didn't say a word.

Robin could have told her she wasn't having sex with Manfred, but she didn't. Why the hell should she have to explain herself?

She left Bianca where she was.

She peeked out the front window. Manfred was out there clearing the sidewalk, huge and white in his overcoat of snow, looking like he was determined to shovel out the whole town. For the first time since she'd known him, Robin felt sorry for the man.

She left a note on his door, explaining where his daughter was.

Just before she was about to go to bed, a reply was slipped under her door.

Robin gave Manfred a minute to withdraw in peace before she picked it up and opened it. He apologized for his behavior. It was monstrous, he said. It would never be repeated. He was profoundly grateful that she'd brought him to his senses. He owed her a debt he would never be able to repay. Nevertheless, he would make every effort to do so.

He didn't tell Robin what had set him off.

He also apologized that he wasn't able to keep the snow off the sidewalk all by himself.

CHAPTER 18

"I am very sorry," Bianca said. "My behavior yesterday was..."

She frowned as if she couldn't find the right word and looked up at her father.

Manfred had appeared at Robin's door again that morning — not in the pre-dawn darkness, thank God — with Bianca in tow. Robin hardly recognized the kid. She was in a denim jumper over a white turtleneck sweater and matching white tights. Either her hair grew with phenomenal speed or Manfred had succeeded in scrubbing some of the blue dye out of it, because the brunette roots had made dramatic progress in overtaking the punk blue. She even had a barrette in her hair.

Bianca listened to her father's whispered instruction.

"My behavior was atrocious. I am very sorry."

The performance was obviously rehearsed, but Robin was quietly amazed that Manfred had been able to direct his temperamental little leading lady at all. Must be some kind of Otto Preminger gene in Germans, she guessed.

As if to confirm her suspicion, Manfred gave his daughter a gentle but prompting nudge.

"And thank you," Bianca said, "for letting me visit your Magic Garden ... I really like it there."

That, the last bit, was spontaneous and sincere.

Bianca looked up at Manfred to see if she was finished and how she'd done.

He raised his eyebrow, making Robin think that all he needed was a monocle, but the little girl took her cue. She turned to Robin and curtsied.

Robin kept a straight face, knowing that it must have cost the kid a lot of her pride to show respect to someone she really didn't like. Robin couldn't imagine what had gone on between the kid and her father last night to produce such a startling turnaround, but she knew it wouldn't do to laugh or even smile at the kid's efforts.

"Your apology is accepted," Robin said, "and such a lovely young lady as I see this morning is always welcome to visit my park."

Bianca looked up at Robin, and they both knew her message was crystal clear. Play ball, you get special privileges; be a jerk, forget about it.

"Thank you," Bianca said.

Manfred took his daughter's hand. He gave Robin his nod and was about to leave when she stopped him.

"In all the excitement yesterday, I didn't have a chance to mention that there's someone I'd like Bianca to meet."

Both father and daughter looked at her with curiosity, and some small measure of suspicion.

"A young man. An absolutely brilliant student. Attends the University of Chicago even though he's only fourteen. He'd be delighted to show Bianca the sights of the city."

"What sort of sights?" Manfred asked guardedly.

"Museums, libraries, children's symphonies, the zoo, maybe a boat ride on the lake in the spring."

Manfred found himself nodding at Robin's list of activities.

"Is he a good boy?" Manfred asked.

"Is he good looking?" Bianca asked. "Does he have lots of money?"

Manfred gave Bianca a frown, and she reverted to her coached demeanor.

"You've already met him," Robin told Manfred. "If you feel like giving me a ride to work today, I'll tell you all about him."

Manfred nodded, and Bianca silently determined that she would listen closely to every word *Der Hexe* had to say.

Bianca presented herself to Nancy for her second day of work at the real estate office. Reprising that morning's performance, Bianca curtsied to Nancy and everyone else in sight.

Unlike Robin, Nancy smiled.

Smirked even.

"Quite the little actress, aren't you?"

For just a second, Bianca was about to snarl a reply. But she stayed in character and played the innocent.

"I do not understand," she said.

"You understand," Nancy said.

Heure, Bianca thought.

If I don't have you fooled now, I will soon enough.

By the time the giant had come for her last night, Bianca had mastered her terror. She'd made her plans. They were quite simple really. First and foremost, she would do nothing, absolutely nothing, as long as that nothing was not too vile, to infuriate the giant again. Bianca was sure that he'd been about to kill her — she still couldn't understand why the *hag* had saved her — and that had been the worst fright of her life. Far worse than when Horst used to fight with Mama and shove Bianca aside if she tried to get in his way. No, this time a man was directing his anger at her. And she intended for that never to happen again.

So, she would do what all of her friends at the bordello had done. She would pretend that she was enjoying what was happening to her. She would pretend to everyone. They would love her for it. And soon she would return to Mama, as the giant had promised — and she would spit on them all.

Meanwhile, she would gain excellent practice at feigning

enjoyment. It would serve her well when the time came for her to join the girls at the bordello. She would be the star and make more money than any other prostitute in the house. Just look how she'd fooled the giant last night.

Grosse dummkopf, thinking that all his talking with her had made her act the way he wanted.

Still, this one, this American witch who looked so much like Geli, standing there in front of her, would be harder to deceive. But Bianca would manage it. She would fool them all.

"Please," Bianca said. "How may I help you today?"

Iggy Gross played the opening line of "Help" by the Beatles on his radio show that morning.

"We've got somebody new on the show today, a new guy to help us do the sports ... a new guy who needs our help."

Iggy grinned nastily at Tone to let him know his moment was coming. Tone, completely comfortable with studio work, kept his face impassive. Sure, he'd have to take a load of crap from this radio geek, but no way could it be worse than what had happened to him already. His name was mud right now, so he had nowhere to go but up.

And he was determined that with the first step he took on his comeback trail he'd leave a footprint right on Iggy's head.

"This is a guy all you slobs out there know and love ... Toooone Mo-rel-lo. Say hello, Tone."

"Hello, Tone."

The joke hadn't been funny since Burns and Allen had done it, but Tone's part of the show was tightly scripted to say the least, and Iggy brayed like a jackass.

"Now, as many of you already know, and the rest of you are about to learn," Iggy continued, "poor old Tone got his butt fired from that high-paying TV job he had. Why was that, Tone?"

"Moral turpitude, Iggy."

"Moral turp-i-tude?" Iggy asked incredulously. "Geez, you get caught playing with your piccolo in the newsroom or something?"

"No, it wasn't that."

"Well, listen, even if it wasn't, you feel like pounding off here, go right ahead. Just do it when we play a song, and keep the beat, okay?"

"Thanks, Iggy. I appreciate —"

"I mean, don't worry. We got no stinkin' morals around here, and there isn't a dipstick in the building who can even spell turpitude."

"I'm sure you're — "

"Damn right, I'm right. So what'd you do, anyway, to lose your job and have to come work for me?"

"I guess I dated too many ladies and got called on it."

"Dated?" Iggy giggled. "Took'em to the Tastee Freeze or what?"

"Well, it wasn't just that. I had sex with them."

"Sex! S-E-X?"

"Yeah."

"Can you imagine that? A man having sex with women. Who knows where that kind of thing might lead? You know what your mistake was, Tone?"

"No, what was it, Iggy?"

"Your mistake, you big gorilla, was being born straight. You'da hit the sack with a couple dozen guys, who'd dare to criticize you for that? I mean, some people these days, you just can't object to any little thing they do, much less where they stick their wienies ... but unfortunately for you, Tone, you're one of us poor white male clucks who like broads, and we can't do anything right. Am I right?"

"Well, I'm certainly poorer than I used to be."

Iggy shot Tone an evil look. There was no room to ad-lib on his show, and chumps like Tone damn sure didn't get the laugh lines.

"But maybe not as poor as you could be. Anyway, who was it ratted you out for putting your thing where God intended it to go?"

"A woman named Robin Phinney."

"Robin Phinney. Yeah, I heard of her. Fat broad. Supposed to have some mouth on her. Works in a deli not far from our studios. Heard she fills in pullin' the Bud beer wagon, too, whenever one of the Clydesdales is sick."

Not a bad line, Tone thought, but then Iggy didn't do his own writing, either.

The radio was on in the kitchen at Screaming Mimi's. The dishwashers liked to listen to Iggy Gross. That morning, they were joined by Mimi and Robin. Mimi had been tipped about Tone's debut by one of her media friends.

"Yeah, that's her," Tone said.

"So this fat, nasty broad cost you your job for doing what every red-blooded male dreams about doing: getting laid as far, wide and often as he can."

"That's it."

"Must've hurt you some."

"It did."

"No, I mean it must've hurt you bad right where it hurts the most."

"I'm not sure — "

"You know what I mean, Tone. I brought you on my show because I always liked your sports-grunts. Man, you sounded like Hercules with a hard-on. You still sound that way?"

"Well, I ... "

"Quick, Tone. Jordan scored forty-five last night."

Back at the studio, his eyes filled with glee as he looked at Tone, Iggy hit a sound-effects button.

"Squeek," said millions of radio speakers, including the one at Mimi's.

As planned, the predominant sound came from a rubber duck, but there was just enough underlay of Tone's voice to leave no doubt as to its source.

"Oh, God," Iggy said oozing sympathy, "this vicious broad, this Robin Phinney, she neutered you!"

Tone, as scripted, didn't reply. Rather, an artfully done tape of a man softly sobbing was played.

"Don't you worry, buddy. You stick with Iggy. We're gonna grow you the biggest, hairiest set of *cojones* this city has ever seen ... Next to mine, of course."

Everybody in the kitchen looked at Robin, waiting for a comment.

"The things people will do for money," she said, shaking her head.

"He should be ashamed," Mimi put in.

Robin didn't correct Mimi, but she'd been thinking of herself.

Then, knowing she had no alternative, she went out front to open the deli and do it some more.

Manfred and Bianca showed up at Mimi's at 2:30 that afternoon. Mimi gave her new favorite baker a hug and, charmed by Bianca's curtsy, gave the little girl a cookie. Robin spotted them the minute they walked in, of course, even though she was unusually busy for that time of day. Robin didn't miss anything that went on at work.

One of the year's bigger conventions was in town — the Holy Roller Hardware Dealers Association or somesuch — and the lunchtime rush just kept going and going.

Robin was getting tired and cranky.

And your conventioneer–tourist type was not her favorite customer.

"Ma'am," one corpulent, deep-fried, self-important gomer said, "I heard about you all the way down home. And your picture in the brochure, it just don't do you justice. Why you don't have no curly little tail at all."

The gomer looked over his shoulder at a group of lesser trolls and they all guffawed.

There was, in fact, a brochure put out by the North Michigan Avenue Chamber of Commerce that mentioned Screaming Mimi's, its modus operandi, and showed a picture of Robin holding her knife and fork, arms folded across her chest. All comers were invited to screw up their courage and try their luck against her.

Manfred didn't know about the brochure. He didn't find the gomer amusing and got up from the table where he and Bianca had seated themselves.

Robin sat him back down with a single deadly look.

The gomer's pals saw the look, too, and turned pale.

But by the time the gomer turned around to face her again, Robin had stepped forward into the in-your-face space and was smiling.

"That's pretty funny, Clem," she said, handing the man his turkey sandwich.

"My name ain't Clem."

"Okay, Jethro then."

Southern guys were pushovers, Robin knew. Sitting ducks. All you had to do was get them going about their names, their heritage, their twang.

The gomer's response was perfect. He pushed his overcoat back to reveal a "Hi, I'm..." name tag on his lapel. Made a big deal of it, like he was the chief of police flashing his badge.

"See what it says, see right there?"

Robin's smile widened. These guys were so easy.

"Cletus," Robin said. "Cletus Bob?"

The gomer's eyes narrowed.

"Cletus Raymond Urbanville-Duplessy, Regional General Manager," the gomer said through clenched teeth, grabbing his sandwich.

Bianca watched raptly. As did Manfred.

For a moment, Robin was unable to speak. She just stood there shaking with repressed laughter. She had to put a hand on the counter to steady herself.

"What's so damn funny?" the gomer asked.

Robin wiped tears of mirth from her eyes.

"Your initials, C-R-U-D." Robin could restrain herself no longer. She laughed in the gomer's face. "Your parents must have known what was coming."

The gomer turned purple.

Robin looked at the gomer's tag-alongs.

"That what you boys call your regional general manager when he isn't around, CRUD? You get home after a long day, you have to wash the CRUD off?"

The gomer whirled on his underlings, and more than one guilty face looked back at him and turned red at Robin's dead-on reading.

Robin wasn't done yet.

While the gomer still had his back to her, she said, "You print up your business cards that way? CRUD, a real down-to-earth kinda guy?"

Murder flashed in the gomer's eyes — but then he noticed the look someone was giving him, saw just how big that someone was, big enough that he should have been continued on the next two or three guys. Cletus Raymond Urbanville-Duplessy decided to live to fight another day. Back home. Where the odds were decidedly more to his liking.

Squishing the turkey sandwich he held in his hand, he stormed out.

Without paying.

Mimi's cop-on-duty went after him.

Well, the brochure did mention that visitors tried their luck with Robin at their own risk.

David Solomonovich came in at three o'clock, after the fun was over and the crowd had finally thinned. He was anxious but not eager. He walked like a man being prodded up the steps to the gallows.

Robin, who'd been expecting David, met him just inside the door, took his hand, squeezed it hard enough to let him know there would be no escape and led him to the table where Manfred and Bianca sat.

"Manfred, Bianca, I'd like you to meet my friend David Solomonovich. David, this is Manfred Welk and his daughter

Bianca Krump."

David tugged his hand free, but he didn't run. He bowed politely, and Robin noted with some amazement his bow was an exact duplicate of Manfred's.

"Herr Welk, Fraülein Krump, *guten tag.*"

"You speak German?" Robin asked, surprised.

David nodded. "Of course, it's one of the great languages of Western intellectual thought. I speak German and French."

Manfred watched the exchange closely, wondering if this was a set piece rehearsed for his benefit. He rattled off a string of German at the boy.

Robin didn't understand a word of it, but at the end of Manfred's little speech she saw David stiffen.

"Yes," David said in English. "I am a Jew."

Christ, Robin thought, please don't tell me Manfred's a bigot.

Manfred smiled and resumed in English. "I ask because I once thought of converting to Judaism."

"What?" David asked.

What, Robin wondered.

"Yes, I studied your religion quite seriously for almost a year."

"Did ... did you convert?"

Manfred shook his head.

"No. In the end, I discovered that my motivation was an act of rebellion and not of faith. But I came to admire what I'd learned of a people who'd persevered in their faith despite thousands of years of relentless persecution. I have the greatest respect for such fortitude."

Manfred stood and gave David a perfect bow.

The boy was greatly ashamed that he'd ever considered Manfred nothing but a brainless hulk, and, though it hurt him to concede the fact, he could see already that Manfred would be perfect for Robin. He also knew that he'd do whatever he could to see that they got together.

Manfred turned sideways and gestured to his daughter.

"I'm told you would like to introduce my daughter to the sights and culture of your city."

David looked at Bianca. She was kind of cute, even with the goofy blue hair, but she was just a kid. Practically a baby.

But he couldn't forget that Robin was right, she was closer in age to him than he was to Robin — the woman he'd been fantasizing about. So maybe a spell of babysitting was just what he deserved.

"It would be my pleasure," David said.

"Bianca?"

Bianca didn't look at her father, only nodded.

She couldn't take her eyes off of David.

Geeky, bespectacled, brilliant David.

Suddenly, the teenaged man of an eight-year-old's dreams.

Bianca had fallen in love.

Which Robin recognized immediately, making her uneasy that she'd started something that might end up very badly.

CHAPTER 19

Despite Robin's fears, the next several weeks passed quietly. Winter had arrived in earnest four weeks before the calendar said it was due. But after the town had been hit by its initial blizzard no one was really surprised. To Robin, it looked like it would be an in-law winter: the kind that arrived on your doorstep unexpectedly and lingered far longer than anyone wanted. Still, the coming of the cold and the snow seemed to bring a comfortable routine to Robin's house, one that, like winter, would last for the foreseeable future.

Robin went to work everyday, sliced and diced anyone who challenged her, and continued her buyout plan with Mimi. The gomer who'd been sent home with his tail between his legs had written a letter of complaint about her that the *Trib* had published. Iggy Gross had picked up on it briefly, commenting that he soon might have to open a hospice for all of Robin's victims. Tone was still on the air with the radio idiot, and had managed to get his grunts down into the alto range. Judy Kuykendahl and a group of feminists took umbrage at the Iggy-and-Tone act and offered to come to Robin's aid with a publicity counter-offensive. Robin declined, making more enemies.

Manfred continued coaching, baking, and being the best dad

he knew how. He also managed to persuade Bianca to help with snow removal and other household maintenance. He kept improving the building, painting the entire front stairwell and re-carpeting the stairs. He also bought Bianca a harmonica and was teaching her how to play the blues.

Robin saw much of what he did, and asked him if he ever slept.

Manfred said that five years of enforced idleness in prison had left him with a great hunger to be active. In fact, he liked to work more than he liked to eat. Robin said she thought he liked the two equally.

Bianca became a curtsying fool. She curtsied to everyone for every reason imaginable. Manfred beamed every time he saw her do it. After a while, though, seeing Bianca curtsy had become so commonplace to Robin that she no longer noticed ... except every once in a while the kid would give her this sneaky look and make this funny little groan, like she was constipated or something. Bianca continued working with Nancy, and did a heck of a job filing and bringing the Realtors their coffee and tea. The only hitch had come when one busybody do-gooder client had reported Bianca to the Department of Children and Family Services, saying that the kid should be in school and not on the job. A quick, discreet intervention by the CIA secured Bianca's place in the workforce.

The kid was more smitten than ever with David, and as far as Robin could see he liked her, too — in an entirely appropriate way, of course. He'd taken Bianca to the Adler Planetarium, the Shedd Aquarium, the Art Institute, several other museums, and to the CSO's performance of Tchaikovsky's *Peter and the Wolf*. It was a program of acculturation of which Manfred entirely approved and encouraged.

Even Robin's trepidation eased when she saw the two of them come into Mimi's in the afternoons and jabber away in German while they ate. Many times, when Robin was scorching somebody good, the kid would watch her closely and then question David about the nuances of what she'd just seen. Robin thought the kid had come to respect her more, having seen her work. She didn't like Robin any better, curtsies or no, but there was more respect, and for Robin that was enough.

Other times, Robin would look over and see David seeming to hang on Bianca's every word. She figured that he was just being very polite, a really good listener, because, after all, what could an eight-year-old tell a genius who had more information stuffed into his head than you could find in the Encyclopedia Britannica.

Robin had forgotten, or maybe it never occurred to her, that Bianca could tell David what it was like to live in a brothel. She could tell him many a strange tale about what went on among the denizens of those nether precincts. She could tell him what the girls really enjoyed, and what made them laugh at the customers behind their backs. She could and she did.

At first, David had resisted. To hear such things from such a young girl seemed depraved. But after he made it clear that there would be no hanky-panky between them — and not just because he'd be mortally afraid of her father — and after Bianca had insisted on telling him her stories anyway, he found the idea of this personal tutorial irresistible.

David knew that with Robin lost to him he would start wanting to see girls his own age soon — in the next few years anyway — and knowing at least some of the things he should never attempt with them would be useful. He'd have to make allowances for cultural and moral relativities, of course, but he felt Bianca was giving him a course in sex education unlikely to be offered at any university, and that was far more than he ever bargained for in this relationship.

Bianca knew that she wouldn't have physical sex with David — not until she was a teenager. But she knew that he was brilliant and that someday he would be a wealthy and powerful man, and her mother had always told her that women must be on the lookout for such men. Taking control of them was how a woman made her way in the world. Bianca thought that David would be tiring of his first wife just about the time she came into full flower.

Besides all her calculations, Bianca honestly thought David was cute. Someday she would make him hers. In the meantime, she did what she could. She talked dirty to him.

And everybody who saw the two of them chatter together thought they were so cute.

Except Nancy.

Nancy knew kids and she knew human nature. At Thanksgiving, Nancy invited Manfred, Bianca and David, along with Robin and Dan Phinney, to come to her house for dinner. As the two youngest, Bianca and David sat at the foot of the table, speaking softly in German and laughing at regular intervals.

"I'd sure like to know what those two are talking about," Nancy said.

She quietly asked Manfred if he could hear their conversation. Manfred said it would not be polite to eavesdrop, and for him that was the end of the subject. Still, Nancy might have pursued it further if Dan Phinney hadn't grabbed everyone's attention by making a comment that maybe it was time he and Manfred went out and started looking for some girls together.

Patty Phinney was not at the table to pass judgment on this idea as she was following her tradition of giving thanks in Cozumel while working on her winter tan.

Dan had spent the past several Sunday afternoons down in Manfred's apartment drinking beer and introducing the immigrant to the joys of watching the Chicago Bears. When Dan had explained the size and the objectives of the opposing linemen, Manfred did, in fact, become interested in the game, appreciating runs and passes in the context of blocks and tackles performed by men who were approximately his own size. Seized by Dan's enthusiasm, he soon became a fan of the home team.

Dan and Manfred had become buddies.

Now Robin's father was suggesting they carouse together.

Robin's heart did a flip-flop ... and to her great surprise she was more concerned that Manfred would find a girlfriend than her father would. This was surprising because, after all, neither of them had a claim on the other. They were friends, and that was certainly more than Robin had ever expected. Well, they did also work out together. Robin was getting strong, and she appreciated that. So that did give another dimension to the relationship. But, really, there was nothing remotely romantic going on between them. So why should she...

Feel so relieved when Manfred blushed at the table and said he was much too busy for that sort of thing. And...

Feel so grateful later when she overheard Nancy read her father a whispered riot act about daring to think of anyone but Robin for Manfred.

Robin didn't know why she should feel either of these things ... but she did.

And life rolled on toward Christmas.

CHAPTER 20

The second week in December, Tone Morello went to hire a private investigator.

By now, Tone was a well-established and popular feature on the Iggy Gross show. He got his own fan mail, some days, much to Iggy's fear and loathing, more than the shock-jock did. Tone didn't overplay his hand, though. He never made a big deal about the mail, and he didn't tell Iggy that the station manager of a local TV network affiliate had asked him out for drinks two nights ago. Nothing had been offered directly to Tone at that meeting, but the man had spent much of the evening talking about his pending divorce, how much his wife would be taking him for, and how castrating some women could be; he was sure Tone could sympathize. Showing unusual restraint, Tone had limited himself to a polite nod. Then the guy had brought up the other big problem in his life, how the jerk he had doing his sports was the weak link in a broadcast that would otherwise be number one in its time slot, and how, even though the jerk's contract was up next spring, he didn't know who was around to replace the guy. Again, Tone refused to jump at the bait. He just sipped his drink and shrugged.

This same yutz had refused to take Tone's calls six weeks earlier.

Humiliation had made Tone humble, or at least more so than he'd ever been, and if humility hadn't actually made him smarter it had let him see things more clearly than before. As a result of this new clarity, Tone was learning some new moves. Being patient for one. He was sure he'd be free of Iggy and back on TV in a few months. No need to rush, no need to force it, no need to pass up enjoying someone else's discomfort.

And in the meantime, he had some business to attend to.

Tone entered the IBM building where the private investigator had his offices. No gumshoe above a storefront for him. He rode the elevator up to a suite of offices that might have belonged to a law firm. Several copies of the Wall Street Journal were neatly arranged on a coffee table in the reception area. The reception-ist was a knockout, but she was dressed so conservatively and groomed so severely that no one would ever think of hitting on her. Especially not Tone. Restraint with women — okay, fear of women — was another of his new moves.

He announced himself and was taken directly back to the corner office of Aubrey Tannis, president of the company and chief of investigations. Tone shook Tannis' hand and declined the offer of coffee. When the receptionist left, Tone got down to business.

"Do you know who I am?" Tone asked.

The investigator gave a perfunctory smile. His teeth were like the rest of him: small, tidily arranged and immaculately kept.

He said, "I know of you, somewhat. You're a media personality, formerly on television, presently on radio."

A fancy computer sat on the return of Tannis' desk. To Tone, the investigator looked and talked like the kind of guy who did all of his work right there. Digging dirt with his keyboard, never ruin-ing his manicure or putting a hair out of place. Tone wondered if he and the receptionist were getting it on, phoning in the sex over the intercom.

Tannis was supposed to be the best, but maybe he wasn't the kind of guy who could sympathize with Tone's problem.

"I'd like you to check out a woman for me."

"Regarding?"

"Regarding whether she has it in for me personally."

"You're speaking of Ms. Robin Phinney?"

Tone wasn't too surprised that the investigator had learned of his ignominy.

"You checked me out?"

"Whenever a prospective client comes to us we do a light background check before the initial appointment. It gives us something to talk about ... and insulates the company against any unpleasant surprises or unwanted legal proceedings."

"Then you know what happened?"

"The popular press intimated that Ms. Phinney may have been indirectly involved in your recent career change."

"She gutted me," Tone said. "She did it in public, and she cost me a three hundred and fifty grand paycheck!"

Tone lost it there for a second as the heat of the memory came back in a rush. Then he got a grip on himself and calmed down before Tannis started looking at him funny.

"What I want to know is, did she do it because of something personal. She kept my picture over her bed and was pining away for me? Or is she some kind of sadist that ruins guys on a regular basis? I want to know anything and everything that makes her tick. You think you can do that for me?"

"To what use would you put such information?"

Tone was ready for that one.

He couldn't come right out and say what he wanted to do, he knew that.

"I want to know if there's any point suing her."

"A woman who works in a delicatessen isn't likely to have many recoverable assets."

"I want my day in court, if I can get one, that's all. I want my good name back."

Tannis cupped his chin in his right hand and looked at Tone.

Tone kept his face straight, but he knew all the way down to his bone marrow that this neat little creep didn't believe a word he'd said. The guy was just trying to decide if Tone had given him enough cover in case Robin were to come back at him.

Tannis reached his decision and folded his hands in front of him, like a parochial school kid getting ready for morning prayers.

"Very well, Mr. Morello, I'll find out everything there is to know about Ms. Phinney for you. Everything relevant to your request."

"Everything, period."

For a moment, Tone thought that demand would be the deal-breaker ... but then Tannis nodded and smiled again.

And told Tone how much the job would cost.

David had caught a cold, so instead of taking Bianca to a cartoon festival at Columbia College he brought her home early. Bianca said she would be fine alone in her apartment for the forty-five minutes until her father got home from school. David insisted he would wait with her until Manfred arrived, and then he'd go home and drown himself in his mother's chicken soup. When they stepped through the outer door of Robin's house, Bianca gasped.

"What?" David asked, alarmed. "What is it?"

Bianca pointed.

David looked through the glass panes of the inner door and up to the first floor landing. The door to the apartment there was ajar.

Bianca said, "The door to the Magic Garden is open, and it is never left open."

"Magic Garden?"

"You haven't seen it?" Bianca asked.

"No."

"Oh, you must see it. It is wonderful."

"You have a key to this door?" David tried the inner door, it was locked.

"Manfred does," Bianca said with an impish grin.

She let herself into her apartment, for which she did have a key. She hurried to the kitchen and pulled a ring of keys out of a drawer. Then she ran back to David and handed the keys to him.

He said with more than a little uncertainty, "You really think Robin would want us to do this?"

Bianca played him like a fiddle.

"That door is never left open ... something could be wrong ... terribly wrong ... she might be lying there hurt ... in great pain ... perhaps crawling upstairs ... collapsing before she can reach the phone."

"All right, all right," David said. A life-long city dweller, he was highly suggestible to images of urban violence.

He looked at the brand name on the lock, found the appropriate key and let the two of them in. Bianca shot past him like a streak. David followed more cautiously, softly calling Robin's name.

He got no answer. Checking, he saw that Robin was not lying unconscious on the stairs and that the door to her apartment was tightly shut. When he stepped into the park, he saw no immediate sign that Robin was there either. Bianca was sitting on the edge of a fish-pond, trailing her hand in the water.

She smiled at David.

"Isn't this the most wonderful Magic Garden? I shall have one just like it someday."

"I can't find Robin anywhere," David said.

That was the least of Bianca's concerns. The only thing better than having the Magic Garden to herself was sharing it with David. She wanted the moment to last.

"Don't worry. She'll turn up. She always does."

Bianca's grasp of colloquial English had grown by leaps and bounds since she'd become a regular at Mimi's, especially with David there to fill in the gaps.

David was not comforted by Bianca's blithe reassurance. He walked slowly to the back of the park, looking under thick clumps of plantings, half-fearing he'd find Robin lying in a pool of blood, done in by some vicious home-invader. With increasing trepidation, he made his way to the rear of the space — and almost jumped out of his skin when someone tapped him from behind.

He whirled to find that Bianca had stolen up behind him.

"Don't worry," she said in German, "who could hurt such a *hag* as her?"

Then she scurried to a nearby park bench and patted the space next to her for David to take, which he did.

"Isn't this a beautiful place," Bianca asked looking around, still speaking her native tongue.

David replied in the same language, but not to the question she'd asked.

"You think Robin is a *hag*?"

Bianca heard the note of disapproval in his voice and grew defensive.

"Do you think she is beautiful?"

"Well, yes ... yes, I do. I always have."

"Then you need new glasses," Bianca said dismissively.

She had learned there were times when you simply had to let a man feel your scorn.

David frowned.

He had his book bag with him, as he always did on school days. In the bag was his sketchpad. On one of its pages was one of his "princess" drawings of Robin. He was still convinced that it was an accurate representation of how Robin had appeared at one time. He was tempted to show the drawing to Bianca.

The problem was that since Bianca had begun telling him stories of life in the *demi-monde* he'd been illustrating the images those stories had conjured up in his mind. That was why he no longer felt safe leaving his sketchpad locked up in his desk at work, and took it with him everywhere he went. The last thing he wanted was for Bianca to see those drawings.

"Actually," Bianca said, continuing her theme, "I sometimes think *hag* is too kind a word for her. Witch comes closer, I think."

That did it for David. This smug little brat was insufferable. He dug into his book bag and pulled out his sketchpad. Taking great care to reveal only the drawing he desired, he thrust the page at Bianca's nose.

"This, this is what Robin once looked like! This is what she looks like inside, and if *you* could see better, you would know it."

Bianca instinctively pulled her head back from the object thrust at her. She was about to glare at David when the image he'd drawn captured her attention. Yes, this woman was beautiful, and if you looked very closely you could see some resemb—

"Hey, who's there?" a voice called out.

"Robin?" David asked.

He snapped the sketchpad shut and quickly jammed it back into his book bag. He stood up just as Robin came into sight.

She saw the two of them, David and the kid ... and the kid was staring at her, like she'd never seen Robin before and was trying to, what, look right through her or something.

Well, the kid was weird. Robin knew that, and she wasn't going to let it bother her.

"What are you two doing here?"

David sneezed, sniffled and blew his nose.

"I brought Bianca home early, and we saw the door to this ... this place was open. Bianca said it was never open so we came in to see if everything was all right."

Robin gave the explanation a two-bit analysis to see if it rang true, and in the end she bought it.

"I knocked off work early to go to a doctor's check-up with my dad," she said. Then she added with a pleased tone, "We're both doing better. Then I was in here when a FedEx guy came to the door, and before I could come back in, the phone upstairs rang. That's why the door was open."

"This is a great place, Robin," David said.

"Thanks."

The kid was still staring at her. What the hell was she trying to see?

Robin said, "I was kind of surprised when I came out of my place and heard voices speaking German down here."

"We were just chatting," David said.

"Yeah. Well, with all the German chat going on around me these days, I thought I better do something about it."

"What do you mean?" Bianca asked, suddenly jarred out of her inspection of Robin's face.

"What I mean is, this is what the FedEx guy brought."

She held a book up for them both to see: an English-German primer.

Nancy had suggested the idea to her.

The two young people left her then, David with a wave, Bianca with a curtsy.

Robin sat in her park and set about becoming fluent in a new language.

The Christmas season was a relatively slow time at Screaming Mimi's. People made their annual stab at peace on earth, good-will toward men. In that frame of mind, they weren't inclined to come into a place where hurling insults was the order of the day. Still, there were a few determined grinches who kept the spirit of invective alive.

One sharp-eyed wiseguy noticed the increasing musculature of Robin's upper body and asked if she intended to have "Mother" tattooed on her bicep.

Her mother being a touchy subject with Robin, she made a determined effort to keep both her voice and visage mild. She did however pick up her whetstone, and with smooth, hissing strokes began to put a surgical edge on her carving knife.

"Funny thing about weight training," she told the wise guy. "The stronger a woman gets — stronger like a guy, you know — the more she can sometimes find herself thinking like a guy. You know what I mean, don't you?"

Robin kept the knife sliding over the stone with a serpentine sibilance.

The wise guy was hypnotized watching it.

"You say to yourself," Robin said, "I don't have to take any crap offa anybody."

Robin smiled vaguely at the wise guy, her eyes just a little crazy.

"Of course, maybe that's just the effects of all those steroids. 'Roid rage, you know. They say it can make you psychotic. Affect your memory, too. Like right now, what was it you just asked me?"

Robin stopped sharpening the knife and held it point up.

The wise guy had visions of being carved like a Christmas turkey.

"Uh ... nothing. I just remembered some shopping I gotta do. I'll eat later. Merry Christmas."

He had a hard time not running out of the deli.

Mimi came over wearing a frown.

She said, "If not the letter, that violated the spirit of the Robert DeNiro rule."

"People shouldn't talk about other people's mothers," Robin replied.

The thing that most bothered Robin about her mother was that this year she was taking her father away from her. Every Christmas, Patty Phinney invited Nancy and her family out to dinner at some fancy restaurant, and since Charlie's parents had passed away and they had nowhere else to go, they always accepted. Dan Phinney and Robin had never been invited to this annual feast and that had always been fine with them. They always ate Christmas dinner at Robin's.

Except that this year, Patty had invited Dan — and he had accepted!

With their divorce only a few weeks from becoming final Robin's parents were ending decades of marriage and years of estrangement with a blossoming new friendship.

Robin didn't know if she could stand it.

CHAPTER 21

Robin and Nancy exchanged their Christmas gifts late on the afternoon of the twenty-fourth in the living room of Robin's house.

Robin gave Nancy a midnight blue cashmere sweater. With Nancy's hair and eyes and figure, the sweater would look gorgeous on her. Robin didn't even mind that it cost five times more than she ever would have spent on herself. Nancy was always there for her, she'd come through for Robin again this year when she'd needed her ... and Robin still got a vicarious thrill out of seeing how good her "big" sister looked when she wore beautiful clothes.

Nancy knew how Robin felt.

She gave her a hug and a kiss.

"My turn," Nancy said. She took two packages out of a shopping bag and handed the smaller to Robin. "This one first."

Robin carefully undid the wrapping paper and looked at the name on the box.

"Cartier? Are you kidding me? Are we getting engaged, or something?"

"Just open the box, Robin."

She did, and found a necklace with a diamond big enough to make her eyes pop.

"Nancy! It's beautiful, but what the heck am I supposed to do with it? This is something you should wear. Here, you keep it."

Nancy took the necklace, without offense, and then deftly slipped it around Robin's neck and hooked it in place. Robin put her hand over it, gently examined the big stone with her fingertips.

"It does feel nice," she said, "so cool and smooth and—"

"Just what you deserve. Go look at yourself."

Robin got up from the living room sofa where they sat and walked into the bathroom. Nancy watched her examine herself in the vanity mirror. Robin turned toward her sister.

"Goes well with gray flannel," she said.

Robin was wearing a Chicago Bulls sweatshirt, practical for work or workouts.

"Yeah, well, why don't you come over here and see what else I got you?"

Robin returned to the sofa, warily eyeing the box Nancy held on her lap.

"I hope it's not a mink. I wouldn't want the animal rights people after me."

"Said the woman who serves cold cuts all day long. Just open the box, will you?"

Robin did, as if it was booby-trapped. Which metaphorically it was.

"Victoria's Secret? You got me a lingerie catalogue?"

"There's a five hundred dollar gift certificate inside."

A sour smile formed on Robin's face.

"You really think they make French silk bikini drawers in my size? Sears, that's where I shop. That's who sells underwear for the likes of me."

Nancy regarded her sister coolly.

"If you haven't shopped lately, I'll bet your underwear is loose on you."

"What?" Robin said, wondering how Nancy knew that.

"I've been watching you. Your workouts are working. Your backside is tighter and so is your tummy."

Robin was agog.

"You've been looking at my ass?"

"And your bust-line is higher, too. More pectoral support."

"I can't believe this."

"Believe it. You're changing, and for the better. You can find some nice things in that catalogue right now. Things that would go very nicely with your new necklace."

"Yeah, sure, I'll just parade around in my undies and diamonds for all my boy—" Then the realization of what Nancy intended hit Robin like a clap of thunder. "You ... you think ... Manfred ... and me ... we're ... "

"Well, aren't you?"

"No!" Robin shook her head. "No, no, no!"

"That wasn't the impression I got from someone who should know."

"Who?"

The light dawned. "That little brat."

"So, it's true?"

"No, it isn't."

With more than a little mortification, Robin explained that Bianca had misinterpreted the grunts and groans of one of Robin's workouts as something else. Now, Robin wished that she'd denied that she'd been having sex with Manfred to the little imp before the kid had blabbed her misconception to everyone in town.

"Well, that's a pity," Nancy said. "But there's still hope."

"For what?"

"That you will have sex with Manfred. The two of you are perfect for each other."

Robin sat mute.

"What, no ringing denial?" Nancy smirked, before she continued in a mock baritone. "Your honor, the defendant is implicated by her silence."

"Go suck an eggnog," Robin said.

She got up and walked off to the kitchen. Nancy followed.

"Robin, there's nothing wrong with liking a man. Especially one who's good and strong and kind. As you pointed out to me one time, there aren't many like that around. So when you've got one living right under your own roof, hey, put on your baubles and bangles and make your move. Because if you don't, you never know when he might be on his way."

Robin looked away from Nancy.

Nancy moved closer and took her hand.

"Robin, you're stronger now. A *lot* stronger. You don't have to worry about being hurt again, and Manfred's not the type to hurt you, anyway."

Without turning toward Nancy, Robin said, "I might ... I might, except ... "

"Except what?"

"I don't like that kid. And she's everything to him." Robin turned toward her sister. "Isn't she?"

Nancy shook her head.

"She's a lot to him, more than most kids are to their parents. But take it from me, because I've been watching him, too, the part that the kid isn't, you are."

Robin walked back into the living room and stared sightlessly at the lights twinkling on her Christmas tree. Nancy was right behind her.

Robin said, "It's ironic, isn't it, a damn laugh riot, that a kid should come between me and a man?"

Nancy shook her head.

"It's ironic only if you let it be. Work it out. She's a kid. How hard can it be?"

"You see her all the time, too. You tell me how hard."

"Okay, it won't be easy. But tell me anything worthwhile that ever is."

Nancy kissed Robin's cheek and walked over to a shopping bag that Robin had placed by the front door. In it were several gift-wrapped boxes.

"These are for Charlie and the boys?"

"And Dad," Robin said. "They all have name tags on them."

"Robin, don't spend Christmas alone. Admit it, at least to

yourself, that you'd like to share your life with Manfred. Start tonight. You'll find a way to work things out."

Robin didn't have to go to Manfred. He came to her apartment just after dusk wearing a beautifully cut blue suit. He was groomed like *GQ* and *Muscle and Fitness* were doing a combined holiday issue and he was the cover boy. He came bearing gifts, and the only thing Robin had in her hand was the doorknob. She managed to find the grace to invite him in, and poked her head out into the hallway, wondering where the kid was.

Manfred knew who she was looking for.

"Bianca is downstairs. She is getting dressed for Christmas mass tonight."

Robin smiled briefly.

"Going to church, that's nice."

Manfred set his packages down on the dining room table.

"Brother Damian asked me to extend his invitation for you to join us. He said God always likes a full house for his Son's birthday."

Robin smiled again, but shook her head.

"Thanks but it's not for me."

"We have reserved, front-row seats."

"Sorry," Robin said.

Manfred took a deep breath and spent a moment contemplating the shine on his shoes. When he looked up all the air of light banter had left him and he appeared as somber as Robin had ever seen him.

"*Bitte.* It would mean a great deal to me if you joined us tonight ... this may be the only chance I ever have for such a moment."

"What's that mean?"

"It has to do with my Christmas gift to Bianca," Manfred said cryptically.

Robin didn't know how to respond to that, and apparently she remained mute for too long.

Manfred said, "I am sorry. I should not try to impose. Here are your gifts." He gestured to the packages on the table. "I will leave you now so you may open them at your leisure."

He bowed and left.

Robin watched him close the door softly behind him and then she looked at the gifts. She opened the larger one first. It was a chocolate torte. Homemade. Beautiful. Mouth watering. She opened the smaller package next, hoping to find neither jewelry nor lingerie. She didn't. She found a pair of leather workout gloves. The tag that came with them said they were of Olympic quality. The same kind the last three gold medalists in power lifting wore when they trained.

Robin was waiting in the vestibule when Manfred and Bianca stepped out of their apartment. She was wearing the only dress she had, a summer weight cotton frock that had been hanging in her closet since she'd worn it to her father's retirement party. It was ridiculously skimpy to wear on a night when the temperature already had fallen to ten degrees and was far from hitting bottom, but at least it was green to go with the season. So was the ski parka that Robin wore over it to keep from freezing to death entirely. On her feet she had the black Reebok cross-trainers that she wore to work, the dressiest shoes she owned.

Her hair was washed and combed, but it hadn't been professionally cut since the Carter administration, so there wasn't much she could do there. Her face was scrubbed, but she didn't have any make-up to apply to it. She wore no ring or watch or bracelet...

But around her neck, in a brilliant rebuke to the rest of her slapdash ensemble, Robin wore her new diamond necklace.

Not that it was enough to keep Bianca from rolling her eyes at the sight of Robin.

Manfred's reaction was just the opposite: his eyes sparkled like the diamond he beheld. Then he asked Robin if he might take her jacket off. She didn't know where he was going with that, but she allowed it. He tossed the parka down into his apartment, and then he took off the beautiful black wool overcoat he had on and draped it around Robin's shoulders. The effect was magical, transforming.

The huge, elegant coat covered her like a cape from shoulder to toe, gaping dramatically at the throat to reveal her necklace.

Robin had never felt so warm, secure, or lovely in her life.

Manfred beamed at her.

Bianca ground her teeth, as no one was presently looking her way.

Manfred said, "If you ladies will please wait here, I will bring the car around."

Without his coat, Manfred stepped out into a blast of cold air that he never felt.

Robin turned and looked at the kid.

Bianca, too, had been transformed from what she'd been only two months earlier. Her hair had grown out to its natural chestnut brown, and Nancy had taken her to have it styled in a pixie cut. She was still lean, but her father's cooking had taken away the stick-figure angularity she'd once possessed. The clothes she wore would have suited a little princess not a punk rocker. She didn't seem as feral as she had at first, but there was still cunning behind those big blue eyes.

Bianca, as if acknowledging this assessment, smiled at Robin. And curtsied.

Robin sat next to Brother Damian at Mass; Bianca made sure that she had her father between her and Robin. Having asked and found out that Robin wasn't a Catholic, Brother Damian kept up a running, whispered narration as to the significance of each step of the service. He did so without being the least bit preachy. On the contrary, his spiel had a good deal of humor and even self-mocking irreverence. Robin enjoyed his performance, thinking of him as a cross between Robin Williams and Alistair Cooke.

Robin was only glad that he didn't try to probe further into her beliefs, like did she believe in God at all?

Bianca started to nod off in the car on the way home, but rather than let her sleep Manfred began to sing carols in German. Robin almost shushed him, thinking that if the kid had to be around at all let her sleep, but she got the feeling that Manfred had something special in mind so she held her tongue and lost herself in the satiny folds of his coat.

When they got home there was no longer any question that something was up. Warner Lisle was waiting on Robin's doorstep. Some people got a visit from Santa Claus on Christmas, others got a call from the CIA. It was apparent from the look on Bianca's face that she remembered vividly the last time she'd seen this man.

Manfred evidently was expecting him and greeted him warmly.

"I knew you would come," he smiled, "but I didn't expect you until morning."

"I thought the least you could do was offer me a cup of cheer," the agent said dryly. "Something with a little anti-freeze in it. The temperature was about a hundred degrees warmer when I got on the plane in L.A."

Lisle nodded to Robin and looked at Bianca.

"Some job you've done with the kid. I almost didn't recognize her. Now, can we please go inside before I crystallize?"

Manfred sat on the sofa next to his daughter. Robin and Warner Lisle looked on from facing easy chairs, the former agent nursing a glass of schnapps. Manfred has asked them both to stay. He took his daughter's hands in his, but Bianca had a hard time keeping her eyes off the ex-CIA man. Finally, Manfred crooked a finger under her chin and gently tugged her head around until Bianca's eyes met his.

He spoke in English for Robin's benefit.

"I love you, Bianca, and I hope in the time we've spent together you've come to see that. I hope that you will love me, too, if not now then perhaps later. For Christmas, I wanted to give you the best gift in the world. Something that would show you how much I love you. I thought and I thought ... I looked and I looked ... I planned and I planned. But it was all a game. I knew from the start there was only one thing I could give you that you truly wanted ...

your freedom."

Robin's breath caught in her throat, but nobody seemed to notice. Manfred and Bianca had eyes only for each other, and Warner Lisle calmly sipped his schnapps.

Manfred took a Lufthansa folder from the inside pocket of his suit coat.

Tears formed at the corners of his eyes.

"This is your ticket home," he said, and handed the packet to his daughter. "Warner will take you back to your mother in the morning."

Bianca examined the tickets, wanting to know if some awful trick was being played on her, but the tickets read Chicago to Frankfurt with continuing service to Dresden. It was true. The giant was letting her go. Far sooner than she'd expected or hoped.

Far sooner than she'd planned.

What would she do about David? How would she stay in touch? He was far too big a prize to lose now, after all the work she'd put into him. If she left suddenly, in a matter of hours, she would be nothing more to him than the quickly fading memory of a strange little girl.

"Bianca?" Manfred asked. "Do you want to go?"

She wasn't entirely certain, but her head nodded of its own accord.

"I understand. But there's something you should know." Slowly, so she wouldn't think he was taking them back, Manfred reached out and fanned the tickets. "If you change your mind, if you ever want to come back here, you have a return ticket that you can use at any time. Warner will have it kept in a safe place for you, and he will give you a number to call anytime you want to pick it up. And if you do want to come back, tell your mother she better not try to stop you. I won't pay for you again ... I'll come fetch you."

The threat to Ulrike was implicit but unmistakable. This, however, wasn't what caught Bianca's attention.

"You paid for me?"

Manfred nodded.

"How much?"

He told her.

Bianca started to curse in German under her breath — until she noticed everyone looking at her. Oh, yes, she wanted to get home now. She would have a long talk with her mother about just how much of the giant's fortune was rightly hers. Then she noticed that the tears that had welled up in the giant's eyes were now rolling down his cheeks.

Much to her own surprise, she started to cry as well. She threw her arms around the giant ... and thought that it really wasn't fair that every time she left someplace she wound up missing someone.

And she wondered if the giant might not have another fortune hidden away somewhere.

Manfred didn't ask Robin to come to the airport with him this time. He simply came to her door Christmas morning and told her that Bianca wished to say goodbye. Robin strongly doubted that the kid was making the gesture on her own initiative, but this was hardly the time to be openly skeptical. Still, Robin was surprised when Bianca grabbed her sleeves and tugged her down for a kiss on each cheek.

Then Bianca gave Robin a long, penetrating stare as if trying to see all the way down to her very soul. It gave Robin the creeps. She was just about to say something when Bianca picked up on her mood and curtsied.

"*Auf wiedersehen,*" Bianca said. Until we meet again.

"*Wiederkommen,*" Robin replied. Come again.

To her credit, the kid grinned, and Robin smiled back ... neither expressing sentiment, just the respect of worthy adversaries.

Then Bianca turned on her heel and led her father off.

Manfred came back alone. He stopped up to Robin's apartment in response to the note she'd left on his door. She'd offered him a cup of coffee. It was the best she could do in the way of a

Christmas offering.

She served the coffee with the torte he'd made.

"Bianca get off okay?" Robin asked.

They sat across the kitchen table from each other.

"*Ja,*" Manfred said absently. He forked some torte into his mouth.

"Warner will take good care of her."

"*Ja.*"

"Care for a little arsenic in your coffee?"

"*Ja...*"

As the question and his response registered in his mind, Manfred looked up at Robin.

"You are always so considerate."

"That's what everybody says."

For the next few minutes they dedicated themselves to eating and drinking. Through the doorway to the living room, the lights on the Christmas tree blinked on and off, oblivious to the lack of holiday cheer around them.

When they finished, Robin collected the dishes and took them to the sink to rinse. She still had the water running when Manfred spoke. Robin didn't catch what he said. She turned the water off and dried her hands on a dishtowel.

"What'd you say?" she asked.

"I asked if you remember the day I almost struck Bianca."

Robin nodded.

"There was no excuse for what I did ... but I never told you what caused my anger."

Robin shook her head.

"Bianca was offended that she wouldn't be paid, and paid well, to shovel the snow."

Manfred paused to collect himself; the burden of the memory was still a difficult one for him. He took a deep breath and continued. "She said that as soon as she was old enough — fourteen she thought — she would sell herself in the brothel her mother manages. She would become the star of the house, and any man who wanted to have her would pay dearly for the privilege — far more than it was costing me to keep her."

Great, Robin thought, the kid likens her father, unfavorably, to a string of future johns. She could see where he'd want to haul off and belt her.

The problem was, Robin couldn't exactly tell him the kid hadn't meant it. The little brat had meant every single word. At that moment, Robin didn't know what she could tell Manfred that would comfort him. She didn't think "good riddance" would exactly cheer him up.

"She's come so far since that night." Manfred continued.

Robin kept her doubts to herself.

"And what have I done? I've sent her right back to the person and the place that had twisted her so. Because I love her. Because I could think of no better way to show her I love her."

Robin started to speak, but Manfred was not finished.

"I am going away," he said.

"What?"

"For a week. A retreat in Wisconsin. Brother Damian has arranged it for me."

Robin sighed in relief, and realized she'd grabbed onto the fridge to keep her rubbery knees from giving way entirely. She saw that Manfred hadn't noticed the effect his words had on her. She quickly gathered herself to stand straight.

"When are you leaving?"

Manfred looked at her and stood up.

"Now."

He smiled grimly.

"The place I am going, it is a monastery. I will use the same accommodations the monks do. I will not have a room, I will have a cell. Somehow, today, I find that an entirely fitting place to be once again."

Manfred gave Robin a solemn bow and left.

She followed him to the living room and stared at the door after he'd closed it behind him. The heat from her wonderfully functional furnace poured out of the wall vents and kept her warm. The plumbing awaited her every need in perfect working order. The wiring kept her Christmas lights blinking merrily. Her house was immaculate and perfectly maintained. And it was all hers.

Robin was alone again.

CHAPTER 22

Tone Morello knew he was going to miss his plane, he just knew it.

More to the point, that geek Iggy Gross knew it, too, and he was toying with Tone, keeping him cooling his heels in Iggy's office while Iggy would be "just a few minutes with this important long-distance call." The little jerk knew that you couldn't find an open seat to St. Maarten in the Netherlands Antilles the day after Christmas; you blew your flight, just kiss your winter vacation goodbye.

Not that Iggy cared. Even though the show was in reruns for the holidays, he didn't take a vacation like any normal person. He stayed in his office and kept searching the nation's freak shows and tabloids for ever weirder and more grotesque people to put on the show when broadcasts resumed.

And who was he talking to now? Some yahoo who had the notion of providing topless caddies at a golf course he'd bought in Texas. The idea had been tried before, of course, and had been brought to a screeching halt by the vehement objections of nearby property owners and others who believed that bare–breasted sports should be kept indoors. This idiot, however, was looking to get around that problem by scheduling his first tee-time at dusk and letting his duffers play by starlight. He said playing in the dark would certainly make the game more challenging, but nobody had to worry because his caddies were guaranteed to find your balls.

Tone knew all this because Iggy had the yutz on his speakerphone.

The Texas twit said he already had three chartered jumbo jets of eager golfers coming in from Japan. But he was looking to drum up the domestic side of the business so he was offering Iggy a free round, and he could tape all eighteen holes for his show if he wanted ... and heck, if he had a mind to, he could have a different caddy for each hole.

Iggy had a pertinent question.

"What about the cops?"

"Well, hell," the Texan said, "this is a private club. Po-lice ain't got no business here messin' with consenting golfers."

"You saying the cops are greased?"

Tone ground his teeth. He had his own little plan for amorous adventure. One with just a bit more style than getting your fiddle diddled in a sand trap. He wanted to go down to the Caribbean, find a nice blue-eyed Dutch girl working on her all-over tan, someone who didn't know from American sports, who thought Chicago was where Al Capone still lived, and who wouldn't mind a week of abandon with a good-looking American guy who had money to spend. They'd have lots of great sex, say goodbye without regret and, best of all, Robin Phinney would never, ever hear about it.

Tone thought it was a reasonable plan for a man who hadn't had sex in nine weeks, but he saw it crumbling before his eyes.

The Texan twanged on.

"Let's just say the po-lice 'round here got more on their minds than somebody's caddy sizing up his putts."

Iggy laughed, started to buy into this idiocy. Tone could see he'd have to act fast.

"What about the caddies?" he asked.

"Who's that?"

"Nobody," Iggy said. "Shut up, Tone."

Tone remained undeterred.

"No, I'm serious," he said. "I'm sure some of these caddies you're hiring have, shall we say, professional management. The kind that drives rhinestone Cadillacs. What if those gentlemen think to themselves, hmm, fat-cat golfers, cash in their pockets, fancy watches on their wrists, are they going to complain if their caddy takes them into the rough and, oops, someone's waiting there to rob them? Are they going to tell the cops or their wives where and how they got ripped off?"

"Well, uh, you answered your question right there," the Texan said, trying to put the best face on it. "Shoot, no, they're not going to tell ... and we're not gonna let it happen in the first damn place. Say, who is this sumbitch anyway, Iggy?"

Iggy started to talk, but Tone held his hand up.

"Here's something else to think about. What if one of your imported guests is some crazed sushi chef who's got his Ginsu knife in his golf bag and would like nothing better than to carve some hardworking American girl into cold cuts and be back in the land of the Rising Sun before all the parts are found? What about that?"

Iggy stared at Tone in awe. He'd never have guessed what a truly lurid imagination Tone had. Maybe he could find some further use for this yo-yo.

But the Texan was not amused.

"You're one sick puppy, mister. All we're tryin' to do here is have some good clean fun."

"Yeah, but you obviously haven't thought it through," Iggy said. "Get back to me when you get the kinks worked out."

Iggy hung up on the guy.

"All right," he said to Tone. "I know you're itching to get outta here. So here's the deal. Starting right after New Year's, we're gonna start a stick-it-to-the-fat-broad contest."

"What's that?"

"We're gonna have all our idiot listeners call in and try out their best put-downs of your fat friend, Robin Phinney. We'll do maybe fifteen minutes a day, three five-minute blocks. Monday through Thursday. On Friday we recap and you pick the week's winner, who I'll pick for you before we go on the air, and we buy them lunch at the deli where they can go face-to-face with the blimp."

"She'll eat them alive."

"That's the whole idea. She creams them. Then when the time comes, you go back there and clean her clock."

Tone was sure that Iggy thought she'd cream him, too, and then Iggy would then be the one to vanquish Robin. He was more sure than ever that had been Iggy's plan all along.

"Mimi won't let you record in her place, and she's got the cops to keep you out."

Iggy smiled.

"I thought of that, and that's the beauty part. I don't want any-body recording inside. That was your mistake, remember? What I'm gonna do is have lip-readers outside, and they'll be miked."

Tone was amazed.

"You really think that'll work?"

Iggy shrugged.

"They'll only be looking for something good. Otherwise, they'll be working from scripts."

Tone laughed. Iggy did, too, thinking Tone appreciated his genius.

But Tone was laughing because the little geek had confirmed his thinking. There was no way Iggy would script anyone but him-self as the ultimate victor. And Iggy thought there was no way he could lose to Robin if he was the one putting the words in her mouth.

Yeah, that was what Iggy was thinking, all right — but all he'd done was make it that much easier for Tone to screw him in the end. The idea of how he'd do it had come to him just now, as soon as Iggy had mentioned his plan.

Tone thought he really must be getting smarter.

He got up to leave without Iggy even saying it was okay, but the little jerk thought they were friends at the moment so he didn't try to pull a power trip.

Iggy just waved and called out, "Hey, Tone. Get some for me."

"Oh, you're gonna get yours," Tone said softly.

Robin sat in her park, dropped a coin in the wishing well, watched the fish ... and tried her best not to go crazy.

She'd been alone in her house for the last three days now and she didn't know what to do with herself. Which was crazy because she'd lived alone for better than nineteen years and had liked it that way. Demanded it be that way. But now, after just two months of having other people under her roof, it drove her to distraction to be alone.

To make matters worse, things were deadly slow at work. More and more people were bagging work the week between Christmas and New Year's Day, and the take at the deli was so small that Mimi had told her today that if they had another bad lunch crowd tomorrow she was going to close until after the holidays; it'd be cheaper to give the staff a paid holiday than keep the doors open.

Which meant Robin would have even more time on her hands that she didn't know what to do with. She'd picked up half a dozen novels at the library yesterday and hadn't been able to get into any of them. She'd even gone to a video rental place for the first time in her life thinking that she'd buy a VCR if she found anything she wanted to watch, but hadn't found a single thing. The closest she'd come was an old bodybuilding flick with that Schwartzenberger guy, or whatever his name was. But she remembered Manfred saying those pretty boys weren't really serious athletes.

She couldn't believe how much she missed Manfred...

How much she hated to admit it, even to herself...

Not that there was anything ... romantic ... about her longing...

Nothing sappy like that...

She'd just come to value his friendship...

His decency...

His damn silly little nod.

So Robin had spent just about every minute she was home,

and not eating or sleeping, in her park. She wanted to hear if he came home early. She wanted to be there when he came home. She tried not think about how he might decide, after a week of monastic reflection, that he should return to Germany so he could be closer to his daughter.

Robin jumped when she heard the knock at the park's front door.

"Man ... " she started, and finished with, "... cy" when she saw her sister enter.

"Mancy?" Nancy asked.

"I thought you were someone else," Robin said tightly, daring Nancy to tease her.

"How're you feeling?" Nancy asked.

Nancy had called on the day after Christmas and Robin had told her about Bianca and Manfred leaving.

"Fine, I'm fine."

"I dropped by to see if you have any excess energy you want to burn up."

"What do you mean?"

"You haven't worked out since Manfred left, have you?"

"No."

"You want to lose your conditioning?"

Robin thought about it a second.

"No."

"So, come with me to my club. Let's get pumped."

Robin had never worked out anyplace where anyone but Manfred could see her. The thought was more than a little daunting. Which was plain for Nancy to see.

"Come on. I guarantee it, you won't be even close to the worst body there."

"You're such a comfort."

"Besides, everyone will be looking at me, anyway."

"Wondering how you got so shy, no doubt."

"And I want to see if you can lift half as much as me yet."

The ploy was transparent but effective.

"You're on," Robin said. "Loser buys dinner."

Nancy was right on both counts. Robin's wasn't the worst body at the club — a temple of chrome, leather and mirrors — and every male eye was on Nancy. With good reason. Lycra and spandex had been invented for bodies like hers. Pushing middle age or not, Nancy had all the right curves in all the right places. She hadn't yielded a millimeter to childbirth, time or gravity.

On top of that, Robin observed, "Your nipples are hard."

Nancy smirked.

"Yours aren't?"

Now that Robin thought about it.

"But I'm wearing a sweatshirt."

"Which you'll probably want to take off shortly."

"No way."

Not even with a t-shirt and her workout bra on underneath.

"Look, Robin. Tom, the manager here, is a bit of a scamp. He keeps the place chilly on purpose. That's why my nipples are hard, but, believe me, all the guys here have seen nipples before. After you start working out a little and your body heats up, you'll appreciate the temperature. You'll also appreciate that if you want to stay warm you have to keep working out. Which means guys don't spend as much time standing around schmoozing, monopolizing the equipment and hitting on the women. Which makes it a pretty nice place to work out, actually. And if somebody gets a quick peek at your goodies, so what? You just take a peek at theirs."

"But you like it, don't you? All this peeking."

"Absolutely. Strength and health are all well and good, but what keeps people coming into places like this is ego reinforcement."

"What if some women were eyeing Charlie the way these guys are eyeing you? How'd you feel about that?"

Nancy put a hand on Robin's shoulder.

"Eyeing and being eyed are permissible," she said. "The occasional flight of fancy is okay, too. It all makes for high self-esteem and a strong heartbeat. And just between you and me, when a man thinks he's hot stuff and he brings it on home to Mama, why, Mama usually has a pretty good time. Especially when she knows she's hot stuff, too."

With that, Nancy whacked Robin on the butt and said it was time to get to work.

Robin out-lifted Nancy in every area. Chest, shoulders, arms and legs.

She out-lifted Nancy in terms of sheer weight, that was. But not by much, given Robin's considerable advantage in size. And when it came to the number of repetitions in each exercise, Nancy did more. For the first time, Robin got to see just how strong her sister actually was, how she kept her body in such fantastic shape, and how she had the iron will to make that last rep that Robin never would have thought she could manage.

At the end, both of them were sweating buckets and the gym felt anything but chilly.

As they showered, Robin caught Nancy looking at her. Until then, Robin had largely lost all sense of being self-conscious. Now, she felt very ... vulnerable. In a way she hadn't felt for many years.

But Nancy just smiled and said, "You're really going to be something."

Business at the deli was slack again the next day and, as promised, Mimi decided to close up shop and send everyone home until January 2. Fortunately for Robin, before she left, Nancy called. When Nancy heard the deli was closing, she took time off work, too. She could afford to; people didn't buy many condos over the holidays, either.

At Nancy's suggestion, they went clothes shopping. Robin agreed to the idea because she realized she couldn't always count on a man donating his overcoat to make her presentable.

As they walked along Michigan Avenue, Robin asked, "Why'd you call Mimi's today? You keeping an eye out for me?"

Nancy laughed.

"Actually, I had a real yen for some of Manfred's strudel. I was hoping there might be a scrap tucked away in a corner of your fridge somewhere."

"Fat chance."

They walked along for a block in companionable silence.

"You know, I actually miss that little snot," Nancy said.

"Who? Bianca?"

"Yeah. She was actually a good little worker. She was cooking up some scam she was going to unload on all of us sooner or later — all that curtsying crap was a dead giveaway — but until then she was a real help around the office. I think I might even have been bringing her along just a little, too ... helping to make a normal kid out of her."

Robin, who hadn't missed Bianca at all, kept quiet.

Nancy looked at her.

"Kids take a lot of work. You can't write them off too quickly."

"I don't think I have to worry about Bianca anymore."

"Not just her, any kid."

This was very sensitive ground for Robin. Nancy was probably the only person in the world who could approach it even obliquely.

"I don't think I'll ever be in the market for maternity clothes, either."

"You never know."

Robin didn't want to discuss the matter — and she didn't want to get into an argument with Nancy after things between them had been going so well lately. So she changed the subject to something that really concerned her, a problem with a lot more here-and-now to it.

"I've got something that's been bothering me," she said.

"What?"

"Well ... you know how I'm buying out Mimi little by little?"

"Yeah."

Robin stared straight ahead.

"I'm not sure I want to anymore."

Nancy stopped dead in her tracks and stared at Robin in

disbelief.

"What?"

"Yeah. When you came over Christmas Eve and made that crack about me serving cold-cuts all day, for just a moment there, I got a real flash that I'd like to be a vegetarian. Never look at another piece of meat in my life."

There was a faint ring of truth in those words, but Nancy's keen ear was still listening for the real reason, the fanfare of trumpets that had yet to sound.

"What else?" she asked.

"Have you heard that Tone Morello is on the radio now?"

Nancy nodded.

"My boys listen to Iggy Gross on the sly ... until I catch them at it and ask them if they'd like to hear someone talking about their mother the way that creep talks about women. That shames them away from him for a few days."

Robin was surprised that Nancy's sons did anything of which she didn't approve, but then her life had been full of surprises lately. But that wasn't what she wanted to talk about now.

"You know what Ant-knee's act is?"

"Unh-uh, I never listen that long."

"He's pretending I've castrated him, metaphorically, and good old Iggy's going to make a man of him again."

Nancy snorted.

"It's sick," Robin said. "I can't imagine how someone could humiliate himself publicly that way ... but I can't help feeling I'm responsible for it."

"You're feeling sorry for Tone Morello?"

"No. I guess I'm feeling sorry for myself. I think I'm getting tired of cracking wise after all these years — maybe in my own way I've damaged as many people as Ant-knee has — but I haven't left myself anywhere else to go."

That, Nancy knew, was the trumpet fanfare.

"You think that could actually happen?" Robin asked. "That I could get tired of cutting people down?"

Nancy shrugged.

"Charlie says that every pitcher loses his fast ball."

Robin looked at her sister bleakly.

"Next time I need advice, I'll try a fortune cookie."

Nancy laughed.

"Good to know you haven't lost your mean streak entirely."

Robin grinned.

"No, but it ain't what it used to be."

"Which is why God gives us comforts like shopping in our declining years. Let's go."

And with that Nancy led Robin off to Neiman-Marcus.

Despite her denials, Robin knew that Nancy had been putting herself out the past week, keeping Robin company in Manfred's absence, keeping her spirits from plummeting into the holiday blues. But on New Year's Eve Nancy had a standing date with Charlie that took priority. Every year, even when their boys were little, the two of them booked a suite at the fanciest hotel they could afford, which by now was the Ritz-Carlton, and they did their best to recreate the excitement of the first night they slept together, which had also been a New Year's Eve.

Nancy had once confided to Robin that this meant they would have sex the same number of times they did when they were eighteen. She never revealed just what that number was, but she told Robin that Charlie took the challenge very seriously, trained for it like a marathon, and so far, even though he was over forty, he hadn't come up short.

Sweetheart that he was, Charlie had asked Robin if she'd like to join them for a drink at the hotel bar before he and Nancy retired to their suite for the night. Robin had declined, thanking him for the offer. She said she would be just fine.

It hadn't even bothered Robin when Nancy had shared the rumor with her that Mom and Dad might be spending the night together somewhere themselves. Robin still found her parents' divorce-cum-reconciliation incomprehensible, but tonight it didn't disturb her.

For some reason she couldn't yet identify, she was beginning to feel at peace with herself. After she'd gone shopping with Nancy, she'd even let her sister persuade her to get her hair professionally styled. Nothing fancy. Just a short simple cut that parted on the left and framed her face nicely.

Robin had drawn the line at a manicure. She didn't see herself with painted nails whatever became of her. She had held out against eye makeup and lipstick, too. She was who she was, and she was coming to appreciate that over the years a certain strength had been etched in her features. She'd never see herself as a beauty, but she suspected that someday she might be handsome.

She did have lovely deep blue eyes, and now they were picked up by the smart indigo track suit that Nancy had picked out to replace her baggy gray sweats. Buttressed by a pair of brilliantly white running shoes, Robin felt the picture of athletic elegance.

Not bad for someone who'd been a confirmed couch potato only two months earlier.

She gave her hair a fluff before the bathroom mirror and admired the way it settled artfully back into place. She grabbed a bottle of champagne, a crystal flute and a boom box loaded with a big-band cassette and headed down to her park to ring in the New Year.

At that moment her doorbell began to ring.
Insistently.

CHAPTER 23

Bianca stood in the outer hallway sobbing hysterically, one thumb pressed firmly against Robin's doorbell and the other against Manfred's. She stopped when she noticed Robin's approach, but it took a moment and several rapid, tear-clearing blinks before Bianca realized who Robin was. Then she began crying again and shrieking in German.

"Der riesig." The giant, she demanded. *"Der riesig!"*

With Bianca was a cabbie, whose taxi was double-parked outside, and whose expression said he had great regrets about the sticky situation in which he found himself.

He pleaded, "Lady, I hope you can help me out here. Please tell me you're this kid's mother. Or at least you know her."

Robin opened the door and Bianca streaked past her. She tried the door to the basement apartment she'd shared with Manfred. It was locked. Bianca turned beseeching eyes to Robin.

"He's gone," she said.

The child looked stricken.

Then she ran up the stairs, tried the park's door, found it unlocked and bolted inside.

Robin turned to look at the cabbie. He held his hands up defensively.

"Don't look at me. I didn't touch her, I swear."

"Tell me what happened," Robin said.

"Yeah, right." The cabbie ran his right hand over his face as he recalled. "I was out at O'Hare. It's a good night, New Year's Eve. You get a lotta happy drunks who tip big."

Robin gave the man a frown.

"Okay, okay. Anyway, I'm waiting at the international terminal hoping to pick up some guy who's been getting loaded the past ten hours crossing the ocean or something and out comes this little girl. I figure, okay, Mom and Pop'll be along any second ... but, no, the kid just shuts the door and gives me an address. I think to myself, 'Wait a minute here.' But she hands me a double-sawbuck and says her father will pay the rest when I get her to the address. I ask where she's been. She says Germany and without batting an eye shows me her passport. I looked at the picture and it was her, all right. So, I think, maybe I don't let my kids fly around the world by themselves, but maybe other people do. And the kid has given me money up front, she knows where she wants to go, she's polite, cute as a button. So where's the harm taking her home to poppa? The guy does live here, doesn't he?"

"What happened," Robin asked. "When did the hysterics start?"

"We're on the Kennedy, right? Heading into town. Everything is peaches and cream. All of sudden the kid shrieks, liked to curdle my blood, almost shot me across the divider into oncoming traffic. Then she starts babbling, in German I guess since that's where she just came from. I get my cab back into just one lane and look over my shoulder. I say, 'Kid, kid, calm down. Tell me what's the matter.' She just babbles on and points to this car behind us."

"What kind of a car?"

"A big black shiny Mercedes, the kind you and me would dream of having, but the kid acts like it's some monster out to gobble her up. Then she looks at me, babbles some more and then, out of the blue, in perfect English, she yells, 'Faster, goddamnit!' I figured at that point a speeding ticket was the least of my worries so I hauled ass. The Mercedes was out of sight, but the kid kept looking back like it was after us or something. But I swear I haven't seen it since I hit the gas. And now we're here..." He took a deep breath. " ...and I still got twenty-three dollars owing on the meter."

Robin went upstairs and got the money to pay the man, including a generous tip.

Then she went into her park.

Knowing that her New Year's Eve wouldn't be as she'd planned it.

Bianca was at the back of the park, hiding behind a clump of ferns and schefflera. As she heard Robin approach, she carefully parted the leaves, revealing one eye like she was a World War II coast-watcher.

Robin decided on a hands-off approach.

She sat on the nearest park bench and waited.

The kid let the leaves fall back into place and effectively disappeared.

After ten minutes, Robin said, "There are three deadbolt locks between you and whatever you're afraid of."

After another few minutes, the kid said something softly in German, and the only thing Robin caught was that word *riesig* that the kid had used before, and she didn't know what it meant.

"Sorry," Robin replied. "You'll have to speak English."

"The giant," Bianca said, the disapproval clear in her tone that Robin hadn't mastered the German language in the week she'd been away.

"Your father?"

After several seconds a soft yes issued from behind the plant.

"He's on a retreat at a monastery in Wisconsin."

All of which meant nothing to Bianca.

"Is that bad?" she asked.

"Only if he doesn't come back."

"He's not coming back?" she asked with alarm.

Robin knew she better be careful; the kid was still on the edge of hysterics.

"He'll be back. Probably in a day or two."

Though, for a fact, Robin didn't know that it might not be for another week.

The leaves parted and the kid peered out at her again. For quite a while.

"You look more *weiblich*."

"Yeah," Robin said. "*Weiblich* is the look I was going for."

The kid came out from around the clump of greenery and took a seat at the far end of the bench. She kept staring at Robin, but didn't say anything.

"You want to tell me about it?" Robin asked.

The kid shook her head.

"Are we safe here?" she asked.

Robin nodded.

Then Robin said, "Of course, if I knew what we needed to be safe from, I might take some extra precautions."

Bianca considered that.

She informed Robin, "I have run away from my mother."

Robin nodded again.

"Who did you think was in the black Mercedes?"

The kid started to bolt for her hidey-hole, but on impulse Robin caught her wrist and pulled her close.

She looked down at Bianca and said, "Nobody, and I mean nobody, is going to get to you without going through me ... and we *hags* are a tough bunch."

Despite her troubles, Bianca blushed.

Robin kept a straight face.

"I may not speak German yet, but I heard *hexe* enough to look it up in my new dictionary."

Bianca looked away and said, "You do not look like so much of a hag now."

"Kind of you to say."

Robin released Bianca's wrist, half-expecting her to run, but she stayed where she was. Robin looked at her. She hadn't come back with blue hair again, but the clothes she wore looked foreign and cheap. Since Warner was nowhere to be seen, and hadn't figured in the cabbie's story, she had to assume that the kid had somehow managed to take an international flight by herself. That spoke to Robin not only of incredible moxy but also of extreme desperation.

If the kid didn't come across with an explanation soon, she was going to have to call Brother Damian and see if there wasn't some way Manfred could be reached.

The thought had barely crossed Robin's mind when Bianca began to speak.

"My mother wouldn't give me any of the gi ... any of my father's money," she said softly. "He had paid that money for me, and I was back so at least some of it should have been mine."

"Was that what mattered to you, the money?" Robin asked.

"How can a woman live without money?" Bianca asked harshly.

"Wasn't your mother happy to see you?"

A long silence was followed by a small shake of the young girl's head.

"She had given my room away. The house was making money from that space now. I had to sleep on the pantry floor. I told my mother I would find my own apartment if she gave me my money. I kept asking for it, which made her very angry. Then two nights ago she said I could have my room back. A lot of the girls giggled when she said that."

A feeling of dread came over Robin.

"What happened?" she asked.

"My mother brought a man to my room. A disgusting old man. She said he was Herr Rausch. He was very wealthy, Mama said. He owned a dozen black Mercedes, four houses and two castles."

Bianca's voice had grown small and very far away.

"Did he hurt you?" Robin asked.

"My mother said he wanted to love me. He wanted to take me away in his Mercedes and I would live with him in one of his castles forever ... but first ... first I had to learn some tricks to please him. Herr Rausch would explain the tricks to me, and if

I didn't understand, one of the girls would come in and show me what he wanted."

Robin felt an urge to kill. That any mother could do this to her child made her blood boil and her mind reel.

"Did you have to do these tricks for him?"

Bianca looked directly at Robin and with tears streaming from her eyes shook her head.

"I did a trick to him. One that Geli showed me when I was five. I punched him in his *Geschlechtsteile*. And when he doubled over, I kicked him there. He was in great pain, just the way Geli said a man would be when you do that. But even when he was lying on the floor he looked up at me and said he would make me pay — he would lock me up forever and make me pay every day of my life."

Robin hugged Bianca close to her.

"And that's who you thought you saw tonight, in the black Mercedes?"

Robin felt Bianca nod.

"Honey, there are lots of black Mercedes in this town. That wasn't the bastard you thought it was."

And Robin quickly reassured herself that it wasn't. It couldn't have been the German pervert or the Mercedes would have chased after the taxi.

Still, the story was horrific enough that even after Robin took Bianca upstairs and tucked the kid into her bed, she sat up, on guard, in her living room facing the front door.

With a carving knife in hand and the will to use it firmly in mind.

A carload of singing, shouting drunks roared by at three a.m. and woke Robin from her sleep. She jumped out of her chair and only half-conscious swiveled her head back and forth looking for the source of the threat. It was a moment later that she remembered the knife she held in her hand. Gathering her faculties, she heard the sounds of the drunks diminish as the car moved on down the street. She looked around her apartment and saw that everything was quiet and peaceful.

She walked softly to her bedroom, wondering if the jerks in the car had wakened the kid. Just in case they had, she lowered the knife and hid it behind her leg. It wouldn't do to have the kid see her enter the room with the knife held high. She'd probably jump right out the window. After all, if her own mother could betray her, who was Robin to be trusted?

But she saw that Bianca had slept right through the uproar.

Robin had left the light on in her closet with the door opened just a crack, and in that sliver of radiance she beheld the face of an angel.

It broke her heart.

She'd dreamed of a face like that for almost twenty years. Dreamed of it but knew she'd never see it. Guaranteed she'd never see it through one blind, tragic, damning act of stupidity ... and, yet, here it was ... the face of an angel.

Tears fell from Robin's eyes.

Suddenly, the angel's face was replaced by that of a frightened child. Beneath their closed lids, Bianca's eyes danced helter-skelter through an onrushing nightmare. She whimpered in fright.

"Nein, nein," the little girl whimpered in her sleep.

Robin dropped to one knee and laying the knife aside stroked Bianca's brow.

"Mama," the little girl said with relief, and grabbed Robin's hand.

Then she opened her eyes and saw her mother wasn't there at all. Robin was.

"You were having a nightmare," Robin said, "but everything's okay."

Bianca didn't say a word. She released Robin's hand, rolled away from her and within seconds was fast asleep again.

CHAPTER 24

Robin called Brother Damian at eight a.m. on New Year's Day. Bianca was still asleep, but Brother Damian was up, fresh and chipper. He expressed his wish that the New Year be a joyous one for Robin.

"It'll be off to good start if you can get in touch with Manfred for me," she said.

Brother Damian picked up on her tone immediately.

"What's the problem?" he asked.

"Manfred's daughter is back, and she thinks some very bad people are after her."

"She came back from Germany? Who brought her?"

"No one. As far as I can tell, she made it back alone."

"Good Lord. Then her fears must be credible."

Robin had given that matter further thought. She didn't think that Bianca had seen anyone but an affluent Chicagoan in his fancy car last night, but if the creep the kid had laid low back in the Fatherland was as wealthy and vengeful as described, he could be looking for her. And it wasn't much of a reach to think that dear old Mama Krump knew of Bianca's Chicago address from the kid. You put two and two together and it made for a very uneasy morning for Robin.

"They're real enough for me," she said. "Do you know when Manfred's due home?"

"It should be sometime today. School resumes tomorrow."

Robin sighed in relief.

"You can come over here," Brother Damian said. "I can recruit several of Coach Welk's more strapping students to stand guard."

Robin considered.

"That's very kind of you, but I think Bianca would feel safer here. Me, too, for that matter. We can hold out 'til Manfred gets back."

This time there was a pause at the other end of the line.

"Then would you mind if I dropped by to keep you company?" Brother Damian asked. "I boxed CYO as a lad, was a middleweight champ in fact, and there's still a bit of the Lord's righteous wrath in my hands."

"Thank you, Brother Damian, I'd appreciate that."

Robin also called David Solomonovich. He was up early, too. Men of the cloth and young rocket scientists apparently didn't go in for debauchery on the last night of the year. It pleased Robin more than a little that David agreed to come over immediately.

The two visitors arrived within minutes of each other, and Robin made the introductions. Seconds later, Bianca poked her head out of Robin's room and as soon as she saw David she ran to him and threw her arms around his waist. She started babbling to David in German, apparently recalling for him in much greater detail the ordeal she'd been through.

David patted her gently on the back, like a big brother. He led her over to the sofa where they sat with his hands clasping hers. The narrative of events continued to gush from the little girl. David listened closely and every so often he'd ask a question, seeming to seek clarification on a point he'd found incredible. Bianca would then explain, apparently telling him that his ears had not deceived him.

Robin mentally scolded herself for not having learned more

German. She ought to know what was going on here. After all, it was happening under her roof.

At one point, Bianca began to cry. David looked over to the adults and it was Brother Damian who picked up on the cue.

"Let's give the young man a little room," he told Robin. "This sort of job requires a measure of privacy."

Robin didn't care if he left, but she intended to stay right there.

Until Brother Damian whispered to her, "Purging a soul is a delicate business — and you must have known David would be helpful this way or why would you have called on him?"

"You're good," she quietly told the man in black. "You're very good."

She led him to the kitchen and poured coffee for both of them. Brother Damian took his black and as he sipped he looked over the rim of his cup at Robin.

Putting his coffee down, he asked, "Is there anything you'd care to tell me?"

She almost snapped at him, had the urge to say he wasn't a priest and she wasn't a Catholic ... but she looked into his calm gray eyes and saw nothing but the offer to be of help.

Robin shook her head.

"I'm not one to share my troubles," she said.

Brother Damian only nodded.

An hour later Manfred arrived.

By that time, Bianca was sleeping in Robin's bed again. Her catharsis had exhausted her. Which left David to explain to Manfred what Bianca had told him. This time, no argument in the world was going to keep Robin out of the room, and she insisted that David tell the story in English.

He repeated much of what the kid had told Robin last night in the park, but there was more.

David recounted, "This guy, Rausch, when he was in the room with Bianca he didn't actually touch her ... but as things went along he did ... expose himself to her. While he was doing that, and basically fondling himself, he was showing her a small photo album of other children, boys and girls, that he said lived in his castles ... "

As David told the tale, a bright red band of anger appeared at his brow and rose to his hairline. Manfred remained as still as death and was all the more fearsome for it. Brother Damian clenched his fists. Robin didn't even want to think what her own expression was.

"He said that all his children had every toy they could ever want, they ate all their favorite foods every day and dressed in the nicest clothes. And all they had to do was be nice to Herr Rausch and his gentlemen friends when they visited. He said the children should never try to run away because there were monsters outside his castles that would eat them up. They would be safe only with him and his friends." David took a deep breath, trying to impose a measure of equilibrium on his psyche. "Bianca said that was when he started to get an erection, and she knew she had to do something before that happened, so she hit him and she kicked him. She said a girl from the brothel named Geli helped her get on the airplane to Chicago."

David shook his head.

"Now, she's worried that this animal is after her. Somebody ought to kill that bastard."

"*Ja*," Manfred said. "Somebody should."

He stood up and walked into Robin's bedroom and sat on the floor next to the bed until his daughter awakened that afternoon.

When Bianca saw Manfred there she sat up and threw her arms around his neck.

"*Vati*," she cried. Daddy.

Robin overheard the start of another long conversation in German. David and Brother Damian had gone home. Robin returned to her kitchen to await whatever was going to happen next. Manfred came in forty-five minutes later.

"Would you like something to eat?" Robin asked.

Manfred shook his head and sat at the kitchen table. Robin sat across from him.

"Did she tell you the story again?"

"Yes."

"Anything new this time?"

A thin smile crossed Manfred's face.

"Only that I would have been proud how hard she hit the nasty old man. She's asleep again."

"Probably the best thing. Do you think she should see anyone? A doctor, or a therapist?"

"I don't know. I want to thank you for taking Bianca in last night. She had nowhere else to turn."

"What was I going to do?" Robin asked. "Put her out in the street?"

"No, of course not ... but I know you and Bianca are not *gemachlich* together."

"Yeah, that's pretty obvious, isn't it?"

"That is why I have difficulty asking you what I am about to ask."

"What's that?" Robin asked warily.

"I must ask you to watch Bianca for a few more days, possibly a week."

"Why?"

"I am going to Germany. This man and his friends will never frighten my daughter again."

"You're going to kill him?" Robin asked, incredulous.

"I will do whatever is necessary."

Robin really didn't have a problem with the idea of Manfred killing the guy — except that it might put him right back in a German prison. Which would leave her stuck with the kid for a heckuva lot longer than a week. And she would be stuck, because no way would she send the kid back to Mama again; that bitch would just sell her to some other pervert.

Robin was wondering how she could raise this set of concerns without seeming too cold when the phone rang. She picked up and said hello.

She looked at Manfred and said, "It's for you. Your pal from the CIA."

Manfred took the phone, *"Hier ist Manfred."*

Robin watched as he listened. Manfred said *ja,* gave one emphatic nod and then seemed almost to collapse inward on himself. He softly said thank you and hung up. Then he sat back down at the kitchen table and remained silent.

Robin, still on her feet, waited until she could stand it no more.

"What? What's going on?"

"Warner was calling to make sure Bianca was home safely. He'd been called by his contact in Germany. Bianca and Geli picked up the return ticket that Warner had left for her. The agent who held it was a little surprised that Bianca didn't have her mother with her. Bianca explained that her mother was a former Communist and didn't like Americans. And Geli was her cousin. The agent gave her the ticket, but decided to follow up and see if it was used not cashed in."

"She used it all right," Robin said. "Made it all the way back."

"Ja."

"Um ... about going to Germany. Since you have friends in the CIA and all, don't you think —"

"It will not be necessary to go now."

"Why not?"

"The agent who gave Bianca the ticket made some other inquiries. He discovered a situation that made him nervous, which is why he called Warner. After Rausch recovered from his injury, he went to Ulrike and demanded his money back; he'd paid several thousand marks for Bianca. Ulrike refused to give it to him, saying she'd turned Bianca over to him and if he lost her that was his doing. The argument turned violent. Rausch produced a gun, and Horst Muehlmann, Ulrike's lover, wrestled him for it and ultimately broke the pervert's neck."

"So you don't have to worry about him now?" Robin asked, the relief clear in her voice.

Manfred shook his head.

"No ... but during the struggle, the gun went off." Manfred looked at Robin. "Ulrike was killed. When Bianca wakes up I will have to tell her that her mother is dead."

They waited until Bianca woke up, and then Manfred took her down to their own apartment to break the news.

After they'd left, Robin went into her bedroom and took an envelope from the top drawer of her dresser. It had been lying there unopened for weeks, most of the time covered by her underwear. She looked at her name written on it, the Palmer script as instantly recognizable as ever. Robin sat on the edge of her bed just looking at it, turning it over and over in her hands, as if she hoped to divine the message held inside without having to open the damn thing.

The loudest sound she heard was the pulse in her ears. The light was fading from the first day of the year. Robin knew that if she were ever going to read what her mother had to say to her it would have to be soon. If she got up, it would not be to turn on the light or put the card back in the drawer. It would be to throw the card in the garbage.

A year ago, she might have allowed the choice to be made by default. Let the light fall away and carry with it the final thread of the bond between mother and daughter. But she wasn't the same person she'd been then. Nancy kept telling her she was stronger, and she was right. Maybe even strong enough to stand up to her mother these days.

Strong enough to avoid the final default. Robin slipped her finger under the flap of the envelope and tore it open.

The card she withdrew had a picture of a mother and daughter on the front. The little girl, who looked to be about six years old was walking on top of a stone wall that rose to the height of the mother's waist. To steady the child and keep her from falling, the mother extended her hand to her daughter. The mother's eyes were on her child, but the daughter's eyes were looking ahead to see where her path might lead.

Robin opened the card.

She saw more of her mother's familiar script and the words spoke to her in a voice she had not heard since she was twenty years old.

Dear Robin,

I went out to buy a congratulations card for a colleague, and when I saw this card it seized my soul. The picture on it shows so clearly what a parent should do. Extend a hand, but let your child seek her own way. I not only withdrew my hand from you, I pushed you to the other side of the wall and stacked the stones so high I wouldn't have to see you.

I am grievously sorry.

What you did ... what happened to you ... I'm not so sure how to describe it these days ... is something that still rends my heart. To that sorrow, I must add the shame that I have only recently realized how your pain must have been infinitely greater than mine.

I have always tried to do what I was taught was right, and even now I'm bewildered how I could have gone so far wrong. Perhaps your father can help me to understand. I know I've hurt him deeply, too, but for some reason, and I can only think it is the grace of a very generous God, he has seen fit to forgive me.

I can't expect you to do the same, certainly not now, but if you could accept this message as my attempt to remove just one of the stones in the wall I've built between us, I'd be happier than I could tell you.

I truly love you.
Mom

CHAPTER 25

"You're on the air."

"Yeah, Iggy, I love your show, man."

"You got something to say, dummy, say it."

"Hey, fu—"

Click.

"We're not doing four-letter words now. That's next hour. Next caller ... you're on the air."

"This Robin broad, Iggy?"

"Yeah."

"She'd have to get a makeover before she could go out with Oscar Mayer."

"Not bad. Next caller."

"I saw this Robin what's-her-name in the park once. Couldn't believe the way she could catch a Frisbee in her teeth."

"Woof. Next caller."

"She can't go swimming during whaling season."

"Lame. Next caller."

"Hey, this broad ain't all bad. You go out with her, she'll probably let you borrow her mustache cup."

"Or her jock. Next caller..."

" ... Last guy she took to bed said the Grand Canyon was a

tighter fit."

"Oooh, nasty. But I like it. Next caller"

"That's filthy," Mimi said.

The radio in the deli's kitchen was tuned to the dishwashers' delight, the Iggy Gross Show.

She reached up to turn it off. Robin stopped her.

" ... She couldn't find a date in a holding cell."

"Next caller."

"My girlfriend looked like her, I'd volunteer for a lethal injection."

"Next call... "

"I'm not listening to anymore of this," Mimi said. "This is hateful."

She stormed off toward her office, then turned back to point a finger at her staff.

"That is not what we do around here. We always give a person the chance to hit back."

Undeniably true, Robin thought, but a fine distinction nevertheless.

Still, she'd had about enough of Iggy Gross. She was about to join Mimi in her office for the last ten minutes before the deli opened when Tone Morello came on the air.

"So what do you think, Tone?" Iggy asked. "You're the guy we're trying to help out here. Any of these callers nail your fat friend Robin Phinney?"

Tone was tanned, rested and sated after a very merry Caribbean holiday. He never found his Dutch girl, but over on the French side of the island he met a lissome Canadienne who was everything he'd hoped for, and more. She wanted an encore for next Christmas when her stuffy banker husband and his boring friends would once again be off hunting moose. *La jolie blonde* said she preferred fur trappers.

So Tone was feeling pretty good.

Especially since when he got home there was an offer of a TV job to start next month. Tone's attorney was working out the details right now.

All in all, Tone felt free to ad-lib his response to Iggy's question.

"Well, what I was thinking, Iggy, it's easy to call a radio show and say anything you like. It's like fighting Mike Tyson from the cheap seats: You can throw all the imaginary punches you want. But it takes a little more iron in your diet to actually climb into the ring."

Iggy looked at Tone. He was pissed that Tone wasn't following the script, but he played it cool.

"So, what're you saying here, Tone?"

"I think your callers are fly-weights. They wouldn't last thirty seconds with Robin."

"You're insulting our listeners?"

Iggy was steaming now. Insulting the audience was strictly his prerogative.

"Just following ol' Howard Cosell's advice, and tellin' it like I see it."

"Well, maybe they see you as something that fell outta a chicken's rectum, too."

"Couldn't blame 'em if they did," Tone said. "That's the impression we've been working on here the past month or so ... and I will admit it, Robin Phinney cleaned my clock."

In the kitchen at Screaming Mimi's, everyone looked at Robin and grinned.

She grinned, too. That dummy Ant-knee had actually learned something from her. He was baiting Iggy, and she could practically see that idiot shock-jock putting his foot in the snare.

"Tone, Tone, Tone, grab some testosterone," Iggy said with mock sadness. "I thought we were making some progress here."

"Oh, we are, Iggy."

"Yeah, how's that? You sound like you're content to eat this broad's doo-doo with a spoon."

"Just realizing my limits."

"So where's the progress?"

"Well, you know how you were planning to let some of these numbnuts you got calling in go over to Mimi's and go up against Robin for a few weeks?"

Iggy almost burst a blood vessel. He hadn't yet revealed the scheme to his audience. Now, Tone was giving away the whole plan.

"Hey!" Iggy yelled. But Tone kept right on going.

"Look, Iggy, trust me. None of these guys would stand a chance. It would be such a wipeout it'd be boring. You'd lose ratings."

At that point, a small vein in Iggy's right eye did rupture.

"Now," Tone said, "you've already told everyone a million times how Robin cut my nuts off, so there's no point in my looking for a rematch. No, Iggy, there's really only one way to handle this. There's only one man in town — maybe in the world — who can keep this woman from emasculating us all ... and that's you!"

Iggy lacked a tail, otherwise his resemblance to a trapped rat was dead on.

"Come on, Iggy, whaddya say?" Tone asked. Then he added, "You blockheads out there, you want to see your man Iggy take on big, bad Round Robin Phinney?"

Within seconds the switchboard lit up like a Chinese New Year. At that point, it didn't matter what Iggy wanted. His public had him by the short hairs.

Iggy's producer decided it was a good time to go to commercials.

Tone grinned at Iggy.

"You prick, you're fired," the shock-jock said.

Tone shook his head.

"Too late. I handed in my resignation before we went on the air."

He took off his headset and started for the studio door, but when he got there he stopped and looked back at Iggy.

"Better get in training. You're gonna be fighting way outta your weight class."

Robin realized that rat Ant-knee had snared her, too. Maybe changed her life.

Apparently everyone in town had heard what had transpired on the Iggy Gross Show that morning. As a result, nobody who came into Screaming Mimi's insulted her anymore; they cheered her on, they wished her well. They told her to wipe the floor with Iggy Gross.

Robin had become the home team and her fans were pulling for her to win the championship.

Iggy, of course, was not without his partisans. More than a few teenage boys ran past Mimi's giving everyone inside the finger and raucous jeers. One cretin even stopped on the sidewalk outside the deli and exposed himself, pressing his member against Mimi's window, making her exclaim that she'd just had that window washed. The idiot was trying to zip back up when Stan Prozanski cuffed him and threw him in the back of a paddy wagon that soon arrived.

The media appeared by lunchtime. Mimi promptly laid down the law. One video camera for pool coverage only, and everybody who came in had to order something.

Undeterred by these conditions, the press asked Robin if she thought she could handle Iggy Gross. Had she ever confronted a celebrity before? Where would the match take place, Mimi's or Iggy's studio? And did she really hate men?

Robin said that she hadn't started the whole mess; Ant-knee Morello was the instigator. They all knew what she'd done to him, and they could decide for themselves if he was a celebrity. The only place she worked and traded barbs with people was Mimi's; and with one exception — not Iggy Gross — she didn't hate anyone.

A reporter asked who the exception was.

Robin told the guy, "Come here, and I'll whisper it in your ear. Of course, after I do, I'll have to slice your ear off."

As Robin held her carving knife and serving fork in her hands, the reporter declined amidst a round of nervous laughter. The question was not repeated.

But the newsies still wanted to know if she thought she could handle Iggy.

For just a second, Robin thought she should end all this lunacy by simply saying no. Iggy was too much for her. That would let all the air out of the balloon. Of course, it would effectively end her job, as she knew it, at the deli, too. You couldn't be a wimp and hold court at Mimi's. The thing was, after all this time, she thought that might not be such a bad idea, either.

There had to be more to life than what she'd been doing with hers.

She almost came out and said it: No, she didn't think could take Iggy. But right then one of the shock-jock's twisted little acolytes appeared outside the deli. He looked like he couldn't be any older than David Solomonovich, but from the insipid leer on his face it was plain that he didn't have the intelligence of David's toenail clippings. The kid was holding a large piece of cardboard that seemed to be hinged on one side with a strip of duct tape. He opened the cardboard like it was a centerfold, and inside was a crude drawing of a naked woman with her legs spread. The figure's genitals had been replaced by a photo of the Grand Canyon.

Guess who.

The kid had the nerve to rap on the window to attract everyone's attention. Once he got his moment of glory, he laughed, folded his show and took off running.

Okay, Robin thought, maybe she'd have to reconsider. Somebody who motivated such contempt for women did not deserve to prosper or maybe even draw breath.

When the media returned their focus to her, Robin looked right into the videocam.

"Can I handle Iggy Gross? Yeah. Like Hank Aaron handled a hanging curve."

***

Slugger Phinney Says She'll Hammer Iggy Out of the Park.

Dan Phinney showed her the headline that appeared in the early edition of the next day's paper when he picked up Robin after work. The story made the front page below the fold, along with a picture of Robin to which a baseball bat had been added.

"A friend of mine at the *Trib* gave me this," Dan said with glee. "It won't even hit the streets for another hour or so."

Robin looked at her father, as he sat behind the wheel of his Camaro, taking her home. He was as excited as a little kid, or a parent whose child had just won a gold medal.

"This is great," her dad enthused.

Despite his excitement, Robin thought her father looked a little peaked.

"Are you okay, Dad?"

"I'm great. I haven't had so much fun since... " He paused as another thought caught up with him. "Well, I did just have a pretty terrific New Year's Eve ... but before that, I can't remember when I was so tickled."

"But you're feeling okay?

"First rate. Why, don't I look it?"

"Sure you do," Robin lied. "Just checking."

There was something about his color she just didn't like.

"I can't wait until you tear into this creep honey. You're gonna—"

Dan Phinney stopped when saw the look on his daughter's face.

"You're not worried, are you?"

"About Iggy Gross?" Robin rolled her eyes.

"Then what?"

Since Robin didn't want to say anything about him not looking right, she told her father the other thing that was on her mind.

"I can't help feeling that Ant-knee's sitting out there some-where lapping all this up. That, behind it all, he's got some other scheme. Something he's going to unload on me. It's almost like the jerk went out and grew a working brain, and that's a very scary thought."

Dan snorted.

"You worry too much. Listen, how about I drop in and say hello to Manfred? Haven't seen him for a while, and I wouldn't mind wetting my whistle with one of those brews of his."

Robin had awakened that morning with the firm intention of pushing the troubles of Herr Welk and Fraulein Krump aside for the day. With the rush of events, she had succeeded completely in meeting that goal. Now, she gave her father a quick summary on why a social call wouldn't be such a good idea at the moment.

"That's terrible," Dan said. "Poor kid."

"Yeah."

Robin was tempted to tell her father that she'd read her mother's card ... but she couldn't quite get it out.

"Well, say hello to him for me, anyway, okay? Give the kid my condolences."

Dan pulled to the curb in front of Robin's house.

He kissed his daughter's cheek.

Then he stared off through the windshield and shook his head.

"Life is just too damn short." He looked at Robin. "You gotta make the most of it."

CHAPTER 26

Manfred had taken the day off of work.

He let Bianca sleep late. He was in no hurry to have to tell her the bad news. She'd been through enough as it was. He was still undecided as to whether he should lie about the circumstances of Ulrike's death. The last thing he wanted was for Bianca to think that she had been responsible for her mother's shooting death.

Having lived under the thumb of Communist tyranny, Manfred had always hated the way the Party would revise history to suit its purposes. But now he was thinking that possibly a tram had run over Ulrike. Perhaps, as with most lies, the deception would not last forever, but it should serve long enough to spare Bianca's feelings while she was still a child.

When Bianca did awaken, it was with a scream.

Manfred ran to the bedroom at the same time that Bianca flung the door open and burst out of the room. The little girl bounced off her father's massive legs and landed on her bottom. She was looking up at him with her head spinning when he scooped her up into his arms. He held her head to his shoulder and crooned to her in their native tongue.

"*Es ganz recht, alles recht.*" It's all right, everything's all right

Bianca's breathing, which had been rapid, calmed down. The

comforting weight of Manfred's huge arms enfolded her from shoulders to knees. He rocked her back and forth until he thought she'd fallen back to sleep, but then she lifted her head from his shoulders and spoke to him — in English.

"Put me down, please."

Manfred looked her in the eye. She was no longer afraid, so he put her down.

She walked to the sofa and sat. Then she extended her hand to him. He sat next to her and took it. They regarded one another.

"Are you really my father?"

"Yes," Manfred said, not *ja*.

"Were you really a traitor to the state?"

"Yes."

"Was that a bad thing?"

"No, it was a bad state."

"Then why did Mama send you to jail?"

"She was angry with me. She thought I was seeing another woman."

"Were you?"

"No. I was seeing a spy."

"Is that worse?"

"Sometimes it is enough to send you to prison."

"I will stay away from spies then."

Manfred nodded.

Bianca bit her lip, seemed to think deeply and frowned.

"I was not seeing anyone else, not even a spy, but Mama tried to send me away with that terrible man. I do not understand why she was so angry with me." The little girl's chin began to tremble. "All I wanted was the money that should have been mine, and Mama was the one who taught me how important money is, so why did she want to send me away?"

Bianca's tears began to flow, but she cried silently.

Manfred put his arm around Bianca and drew her close.

She said, "I will stay with you forever, Father. I will never go back to Mama again. I wish she was dead."

Manfred moved off the sofa, knelt before his child and took both of her hands in his.

"Bianca, you must never blame yourself for what I am about to tell you, and you must remember that for most of your life your mother tried in her own way to care for you."

Manfred took a deep breath and found the strength he needed to continue.

"Bianca, your mama *is* dead."

Bianca looked at her father and made a leap of intuition. Any hope of disinformation on Manfred's part was kaput.

"That nasty man killed her, didn't he? He was so angry. And when he couldn't find me, he killed Mama."

Manfred nodded.

"Will he come after me now? Will you let him?"

"He is dead, too. Horst killed him."

"The Bear?"

"Yes."

"Am I safe then?"

"Yes."

Bianca looked at Manfred a long time before asking her next question.

"Will you ... will you ever send me away?"

"Never."

"Will anyone ever take you away from me? Send you to prison again?"

Manfred stroked her cheek, loving his child so much he thought his heart would break. He used virtually the same words of reassurance that Dan Phinney had given to his daughter two floors up in the same building.

"Only God will take me from you."

"Will he do it soon?" Bianca asked with a sniffle.

"I pray every day that He will not."

"I will learn to pray, too. I will pray that we will always be together."

Manfred took his daughter in his arms so she would not see

him weep.

"*Vati?*"

"What?"

"May I ask you something?"

"Anything."

"Could we... "

"Could we what?"

"Could we find a new place to live?" Bianca asked. "I do not like it here."

Manfred brooded for two days. He brooded as only a German can. His barometric pressure dropped so low it was only a matter of time before storm clouds gathered around his head. *Sturm und Drang* was the forecast for his soul.

How could he fail to do anything within his powers to make his daughter happy?

Yet ... he didn't want to go.

He didn't think it was because he actually loved Robin. No, he was sure he didn't love her, but he found her ... worthy. Of him. And of much more than she would ever allow herself to be without his help. She was strong in many ways, but he could help her understand that strength was more than simply lashing out. It was also the ability to absorb the worst blows the world could deal out to you and not let that punishment change who you were inside Not let it disfigure your character.

As he ruminated, a ray of levity momentarily penetrated his gloom. This Robin had humor. True, her wit often had the bite of a fresh radish, but he enjoyed radishes. A crisp radish and a good strong beer — as he might consider himself — made a wonderful combination. Moreover, she was a passable cook. And with her improving physique and new hairstyle, she was becoming very *ansehnlich*.

Achh! Who was he kidding?

Of course, he loved Robin.

And one of the most important reasons to stay was he had to

prove himself worthy of her.

But how could he persuade Bianca to stay? And how ... how could her convince her that Robin should be her new mother?

For that matter, how could he win over Robin to the idea of making Bianca her own child?

These were weighty problems to say the least. Fortunately for Manfred, he was one of the world's great power lifters. He racked the three-hundred-pound barbell he'd been bench-pressing for the past quarter-hour and went to his office to start making phone calls.

That afternoon the group gathered, at David Solomonovich's suggestion, at the Lincoln Park Conservatory. Outside it was eighteen degrees and a powdery snow was falling. Inside the huge glass structure of the flower house, the heat and humidity of the tropics prevailed. The scents of dozens of exotic blooms filled the air.

Manfred, Bianca, David, Nancy and Dan Phinney gathered at a bench next to a wishing pond that was carpeted with coins. Bianca ran her fingers through the water, then she turned and looked at the adults who surrounded her. Her father and Mr. Phinney stood on either side of her. David and Nancy stood in front of her.

Bianca knew instinctively they were forming a united front — against her.

"This is a beautiful place you have brought me to," she told them. "What have I done?"

Manfred took her hand and sat with her on a nearby bench.

"It is beautiful here. Does it remind you of any other place?"

Bianca had no intention of playing coy.

"The Magic Garden."

Manfred nodded.

He asked, "Why would anyone build her own Magic Garden when this beautiful place is only a few kilometers away?"

"I don't know," Bianca said. "Why?"

Manfred didn't know either, but he was betting that Nancy or Dan Phinney did and that one of them would see where he was going and would help him out. He looked at Nancy and then at Dan.

They looked at each other.

Uneasily.

Then Nancy sucked it up and went down on one knee in front of Bianca.

"When Robin was young, she was very beautiful, and very gentle, and very giving. Unfortunately, she was also far too trusting. Even when she was twenty years old, she probably didn't know as much about who to trust as you do now."

Nancy glanced over at her father, wanting to know that she was about to do the right thing.

He nodded his assent.

"Robin wound up trusting the wrong person. He turned out to be a monster, and he hurt her terribly."

Perhaps because she'd so recently been through her own monstrous encounter, Bianca was able to empathize, and was curious.

"Is that why she built her Magic Garden? To hide in it?"

Nancy nodded.

"What did the monster do to her?"

"He ... stole something from her."

Things were moving onto very delicate ground, and Nancy knew she couldn't even look to her father for help now. Whatever she said from this point on would have to be her responsibility. And from the way both Manfred and David had inclined themselves toward her, Nancy knew that the kid wasn't the only one who was interested in this story.

"What?" Bianca asked. "What did the monster steal?"

Nancy needed a minute to decide how to answer.

"He stole Robin's ability to ever like herself. Or forgive herself. He might as well have cast an evil spell on her."

David drew a sharp breath, and everyone looked at him.

Not that he had ever said a word about it, not that he ever

could, but Nancy's words made him think of his idea that some evil sonofabitch had turned Robin into a frog. Now, Robin's own sister was telling him that he'd been right.

Only what could he say to the four people who were staring at him?

Bianca took him off the hook. Sort of.

She said, "David made a drawing of Robin. He says it's how she looks inside. Maybe it's how she looked before the monster cast his spell."

Everyone returned their attention to the boy.

The drawing was in his art pad that was in his backpack which was on his back. Of course, the other drawings were there, too. The erotic ones he wasn't going to let anyone see.

"Just a minute," David said.

He moved a few steps away, and obscured by a screen of green leaves he was out of sight for several seconds. When he returned, hoping with all his heart that he wasn't blushing, he held the drawing of Robin in his hand. He'd torn it out of the art pad.

He handed it to Bianca and the others crowded around for a look.

Nancy and Dan Phinney looked at the image and then, in wonder, at the boy who had rendered it.

"The drawing is pretty," Bianca said, "but maybe David just made it the way he wanted it to look. He has a crush on Robin."

At that, David did blush.

But nobody noticed because, without a word, Danny Phinney took his wallet out of his hip pocket and opened it to the photo he'd carried for decades. Robin's high school graduation picture. He held it up next to the drawing David had done.

David leaned in to look at the photo and now it was his turn to be astounded.

The images were all but identical.

Manfred pulled Bianca up onto his lap.

He asked, "Do you know what I was going to do before I heard that Horst had ... made sure that you never had to worry about that terrible man who frightened you?"

"What?" Bianca asked.

"I was going to go back to Germany to see him myself."

"To kill him?"

"To make sure that he never frightened you, or any other child, ever again. To do that, I had to ask Robin if she would care for you while I was gone — just as she cared for you when you came to her door so sure that man was chasing you."

Bianca beetled her brow and stared at the hands she folded on her lap. She didn't want to look at her father.

"Do you think it is right that as soon as you are safe we should leave someone else who needs help?"

"No," Bianca said in a tiny, grudging voice.

"Should we stay and help her?"

Bianca considered. Thoughts raced through her mind as she weighed not just what was right but what would be acceptable to her father and the others. Her expressions betrayed the great struggle being waged within. Finally, her face settled and she looked at Manfred.

"If we stay, will you bring me here whenever I want, so this can be my Magic Garden?"

Manfred nodded.

"Very well," Bianca conceded. "We can stay. For a little while anyway."

Manfred hugged his daughter. He kissed her cheek and whispered in her ear how proud he was of her. Then he looked at Nancy.

"It is time Robin confronted her monster, no?"

Nancy nodded. "Yes."

"Dan?" Manfred asked.

"High time," Dan Phinney said.

"Does my vote count?" David asked.

"Of course," said Bianca.

"Then I say Robin will never be free until she does."

"Very well then," Manfred said. "I will find him."

CHAPTER 27

"I've found something," Aubrey Tannis said when he called Tone.

"For the money you're charging me," Tone told his high-rent gumshoe, "you better find the Titanic if that's I want. So whattya got?"

"The Titanic has been found."

"Hey," Tone snapped into the phone. "I'm paying you to tell me I'm a dummy?"

"I doubt you'd need to pay anyone for that."

Tone couldn't believe it. Here he'd shafted Iggy Gross, just signed a three-year deal at a half-mil a year to be senior sports editor at a network affiliate, was even getting unexpected, and completely personalized, filthy French postcards from Montreal, and this dipstick was busting his chops?

He didn't need it.

"You want to crack wise, send me a refund."

Aubrey Tannis cleared his throat.

"What I've found is an anomaly."

"A what? Is that like making it with animals or something?"

Sometimes Tone worried that he only seemed smart when he had Iggy Gross around to look completely stupid.

"An anomaly is something that's out of the ordinary."

Okay, so now Tone knew. And he liked the way the guy had been polite about explaining, not snotty. The creep remembered who held the whip hand.

"And that's a big deal? That's all you have to tell me?"

"I think it's where I'll find what you're looking for. You see, the anomaly occurred when Ms. Phinney was nineteen and twenty years of age. Shortly before that time, she was described as a likable, conscientious college student. Afterwards, she began her present line of work, which, as you well know, calls for a considerably more abrasive personality."

There was a little shot in there, but Tone let it slide.

"So what are you saying?" he asked.

"I'm saying that at a very volatile time of life Ms. Phinney seems to have been jolted off one track in life and onto another. I've narrowed down the time-period to perhaps six months. During that time, I think it's safe to say, the event occurred that made her the woman she is today. Now, do you understand why I called you?"

"Okay, you've got a point."

"Two, actually. That's the first. The second, just as salient, is that the fee you've paid so far has been expended. If you wish me to continue, you'll have to remit another check. Of course, if you find my services disagreeable, you can find someone new and start over."

The SOB was hitting back, Tone knew, but at this point, so freaking what?

"We're close, that's what you're saying, right?"

"We're close," Aubrey Tannis agreed.

"Okay, all right. No hard feelings then."

"And the check?"

"Don't worry. You'll get your money."

What the hell, Tone had plenty of dough now.

And he could practically taste it — he was going to give Robin a shafting she'd never turn around on him.

Maybe it was fear of Robin, or maybe he just had a cold in his nose, but something knocked Iggy Gross off the air that morning. Well, it knocked his live show off the air, anyway. In its place was a rerun of the program where Iggy had invited listeners over eighteen years of age to drop by the station, examine through his studio window the bare derrieres of three professional strippers and then comment on the relative merits of each and what made the perfect female backside. That particular show was a perennial favorite and always got good ratings.

Even so, the buzz around town was that Iggy was already running scared, especially since Robin had made it clear that the only venue for the contest would be Screaming Mimi's, her home turf. By lunchtime, the media picked up a rumor that Iggy'd had a nervous breakdown. A reporter and photographer, looking for comments and art, arrived at Mimi's just in time to see a group of regulars present Robin with a satin robe that bore the legend Heavyweight Champ.

Always knowing the value of psyching out the opposition, Robin even put the thing on for the photographer and held up her fists, although more in the fashion of John L. Sullivan than a modern-day pugilist.

All day long, the patrons and staff at Mimi's complimented Robin, predicted a glorious victory, and expressed the fervent hope that somewhere they'd be able to find fools simple-minded enough to put their money on Iggy.

Being the object of public adoration was something completely unprecedented in Robin's life ... but she thought she could get used to it.

The close of her day was also out of the ordinary. Her father didn't come to pick her up, Nancy did.

"Where's Dad?" Robin asked as Nancy drove her home.

"He said he was feeling a little tired today. He asked me to come get you. I'm glad, because I think I would have come anyway."

"Why?"

Because Nancy didn't believe in letting secrets clutter up her mind anymore that she believed in leaving dirty dishes in her sink. In either case, you left crap like that lying around, it started to stink.

Nancy glanced at Robin.

"Let me ask you straight out: How much does Manfred mean to you?"

Robin was glad that Nancy had put her eyes back on the road after she'd asked the question.

"You know how I feel," Robin said.

"I've got an idea how you feel, but why don't you tell me in your own words?"

"He means a lot to me."

"You love him?"

Robin didn't answer.

"Okay," Nancy said, "let's take small steps first. You want to keep him around?"

"Yes."

"You know there's a price for everything?"

"Better than most."

"You know that I love you and want what's best for you?"

"Yes."

Robin meant it. Nancy did love her. Maybe even more than her dad, because Nancy had to take a lot of guff from Robin that her father never did, and she was still there every time Robin needed her.

Even so, that last question made Robin distinctly uneasy.

Nancy double-parked in front of Robin's house and turned her emergency blinkers on.

She turned and looked directly at Robin.

"I told," Nancy said.

"You told what? To who?"

"I told Manfred and Bianca that there had been someone in your life once who'd hurt you very badly. I called the guy a monster. I did it because Bianca wanted to leave your house, and

Manfred was looking for any reason he could find to persuade her to stay. You might not know if you love him, but I can tell you for a fact he loves you."

Robin's face was a blank as a mannequin's.

"Did you tell him everything?"

"No ... but you should."

Robin popped her seatbelt off and pushed open the car door. She got out and looked like she was going to close the door, but she leaned back in the car.

"You had no right," Robin said, her chin quivering with anger. "You had no right to say a single word!"

"Sometimes you do things anyway," Nancy replied.

Robin had no way to respond to that except to slam the door on her sister.

Nancy lowered the window and called to Robin.

"There's something else I have to tell you."

But Robin didn't turn back, she just kept walking and went into her house.

All right, Nancy thought, I tried.

When Manfred found Phil Leeds — the sonofabitch Robin had hated all these years — and dropped him into her lap she would just have to deal with it.

At school that day, Manfred shifted his schedule around so he could have the afternoon off, and he left Bianca in the care of Dan and Patty Phinney who would watch her until he came to pick her up. Freed from his other concerns, Manfred went hunting.

He'd been given two names by Nancy. Phil Leeds was the man he was looking for, and Jeri Whitman, a former friend of Robin's, was a woman who might point him in the right direction. Nancy had also given Manfred a twenty-year-old phone number for Jeri Whitman's parents, and that was where he started.

An elderly woman answered the phone.

"Is this Mrs. Whitman?" Manfred asked.

He tried as hard as possible to diminish his accent and sound harmless, thinking this was how a professional like Warner would do it.

"Yes."

"Is Jeri at home, please?"

"She hasn't been at home since I used to go out dancing on Saturday nights, and that was before I got arthritis in both my ankles and my husband died. Which was fifteen years ago. Which oughta give you some idea of how long it's been since Jeri's been at home." After a pause, she added, "She still drops the baby off once in a while, though."

"Would you know where I could reach her?"

"Why?"

"An old friend of hers asked me to look her up."

"Not one of those bums who never gave her a penny of child support, I bet."

Manfred instinctively felt the need to leaven his act with a grain of truth.

"The friend's name is Robin Phinney."

"Oh, sweet Jesus! Poor Robin. How is that girl?"

"She could be better."

"I don't doubt that, but I can't imagine why she'd want to say one single word to Jeri — even after all these years."

He sensed the old woman withdrawing from him. Whatever had happened to Robin had also caused Mrs. Whitman pain. He knew that if he lost her he would have a much harder time finding the woman's daughter. He quickly thought of another approach, and tried to ignore the shame the idea made him feel.

"Mrs. Whitman? Perhaps I might make a small offering, to help the children you mentioned with some food or clothing."

He could feel the mood of the conversation shift immediately.

"How small an offering?"

"Perhaps a hundred dollars."

"How about two hundred?"

Manfred said he could come right over with the money, and while he was there perhaps she could give him Jeri's current address.

For two hundred dollars, Mrs. Whitman gave Manfred detailed directions on how to reach her daughter.

Manfred drove out to a small blue-collar town south of the city, just across the Indiana line. The house he found turned out to be not much more than a run-down cottage at the back of a large unkempt lot. An old American car of a make unfamiliar to him sat parked on the sparse, frost-covered lawn directly in front of the cottage. He pulled his Mercedes up behind it.

As he stepped out of the car, a spotted mongrel came racing up at him from behind the house, barking for all it was worth. The dog came to an abrupt halt three feet from Manfred. Arching its neck, looking up at him, it seemed to realize that should it bite this stranger there might be a lot more to him than it could chew. It retreated a step, and then two more, but maintained its dignity by continuing to bark as it gave ground.

Manfred squatted and extended the back of his left hand for the dog to sniff. The mutt inched forward cautiously as if suspecting a trick. But it came close enough to sniff the stranger's scent and when it seemed satisfied allowed itself to be scratched behind its ears.

"What do you want?"

Both Manfred and the dog looked up.

A doughy woman with graying blonde hair stood in the front door of the cottage. She wore only a thin housedress, and that was opened at the neck to allow the infant in her arms to suckle her exposed breast. Neither the mother nor child seemed to mind the January cold.

The dog had resumed barking, but this time it was strictly for show.

"Are you Jeri Whitman?" Manfred asked, standing up.

"I asked what you want."

"I've come to talk about Robin Phinney."

The woman drew her head back sharply, as if she'd just been

slapped. The sudden motion or the continuing exposure to the sub-freezing temperature, made the baby pull away from her and begin to cry. The woman covered her breast and stroked the baby's head while giving Manfred a long, hard look.

"Come on in," she said. "I gotta put Gracie here to bed."

Manfred sat with Jeri Whitman in a small front room furnished with tattered odds and ends that wouldn't have made the grade at a Salvation Army store.

"Robin Phinney. Dear God, I can't tell you how hard I've tried to forget her. In fact, I haven't thought about her the past few years, not with all the hell I've had in my life. Now you waltz in out of the blue and smack me right between the eyes with her name."

She looked pointedly at Manfred's hands.

"No ring, so I guess you're not her husband. That make you a boyfriend?"

"Just someone who is trying to help her."

"Yeah," Jeri smiled thinly, "and why would you want to do that?"

"She gave me a place to stay when I needed one."

"And you're grateful? A grateful man? Jesus, mister, you oughta be front-page news."

Manfred had seen that the baby's crib was in a small cramped room with two other children's beds. Posters and toys that lay scattered about suggested that the children were of school age, and would probably be home soon. He'd seen no sign that there was a man living in the house. This woman was undoubtedly the sole support of her children.

He didn't want to bring any distress to the children when they returned. He wanted to be gone by then.

"I would like to help you," Manfred said. "I don't have much cash with me, but I could write you a check."

He took out his checkbook and the woman laughed.

"Sure," she said, "a check. Just sign it and leave it blank, huh?"

"I will make it out for two hundred dollars." Equity with the woman's mother. "It is a perfectly good check."

Manfred made out the check, tore it out of the book and handed it to Jeri Whitman. She looked at it and then at him.

"What do you want? You don't want to just hear about Robin and me and old times."

"I want to find Phil Leeds."

She laughed harshly.

"That's easy. Just look for the biggest pile of shit drawing the most flies."

Manfred remained stoically silent.

"You know what he did, that bastard? After what he did to Robin and me, he knocked me up again, then left me for an *older* woman. The sonofabitch. You want to kill him?"

Manfred shook his head.

"Just find him."

Jeri took another look at the check and then told Manfred everything she knew about Phil Leeds. He'd been married two more times locally after he left her. But she'd heard he'd been out to California and down to New Orleans over the years, too. So he'd undoubtedly left more damn-fool women in his wake, ones she didn't even know about. But he seemed to come back home on a regular basis, no matter where he'd been. Not that he'd ever stopped in to see how she was doing or if their kids were all right.

"How do you know he comes back then?"

For a fleeting moment, Jeri Whitman almost seemed ashamed. Then a look of defiance formed on her worn face.

"We like to drink in the same places."

The statement was no sooner out of her mouth than the light of fear entered her eyes.

"Don't you worry, though. This check, I'm spending it on the kids. You don't have to worry about that and stop payment or anything. You know what else? I think I got that prick's Social Security number around here somewhere. That'd help you find him, wouldn't it?"

Without waiting for an answer, she disappeared into the back of the house. When she returned, Manfred's check was no longer in her hands. She'd made sure he wasn't going to take it back from her without a fight. But true to her word she'd returned with a decrepit Social Security card. She handed it to Manfred.

"Why I kept that I'll never know, but it's your lucky day, huh? If the bastard's still alive and able to hold down a job."

Her attempt at being ingratiating was more than Manfred could take. He politely inquired where she liked to drink, in the event Leeds was in town, and then thanked her for her help and headed for the door.

"Hey," Jerri said, stopping him.

"Yes?"

"You see Robin, you tell her from me that I ... I ... I probably deserve everything that's happened to me. I'm sorry, too ... and I really will spend that money you gave me on the kids. Most of it, anyway."

"Good."

"And I hope you find Phil, whatever it is you want to do to him, but that creep's so slippery you know who you'd really need to catch him?"

"Who?"

"The friggin' CIA."

Manfred smiled — and gave her his trademark bow.

Jeri Whitman had her two school-age kids home when she saw another fancy car pull up into her front yard. First it was that big old boy in his nice old Benz. This time it was a little prissy-looking dude in some megabuck rice-burner. A Lexus or Acura, one of those.

Jeri sent her two kids into the kitchen with instructions to the older girl to make a snack and take care of the baby if she woke up; otherwise stay put and be quiet. Her kids knew better than to cross Mama when she got that hard look in her eyes. Luckily, the mutt was off chasing squirrels or something and didn't scare the visitor away.

She met the prissy dude at the door before he had a chance to knock.

"You here about Robin?" she asked straight out.

Aubrey Tannis nodded neutrally.

"Come in then."

This one didn't care a fig about Phil Leeds. Not directly anyway. He wanted to know about what had happened to Robin. And since she got him to pay her five hundred dollars — cash in advance — she told him.

Jeri knew this was yet another betrayal of her one-time best friend, but she needed the money. And once you were damned anyway, what else did you have to worry about?

CHAPTER 28

Manfred called Warner Lisle from Dan Phinney's house, where Robin's parents had been watching Bianca for him. The former intelligence agent, now living in Venice, California, took Phil Leed's Social Security number from Manfred. Then he told him this would really be the last favor he'd be able to do for him. He was phasing out his own contacts with the Company and getting on with his new career as a special effects designer and consultant.

Manfred assured Warner that he would bother him no more, just help him find this one man. Warner sighed and said he'd do what he could.

They both knew if the guy was upright and drawing breath Warner would nail him.

Dan Phinney was taking a nap when Manfred had arrived and so the big man thanked Patty for taking care of Bianca and asked her to thank Dan also when he woke up.

When Manfred and Bianca got into their car to go home, she stared fixedly at him.

"Yes?" he asked mildly as he pulled into traffic.

"I am looking at you."

"I noticed. Have you found what you are looking for?"

"I want to see if I look like you or if ... if I look like Mama."

Manfred stopped for a red light and looked back at his daughter, giving her his full face to examine. The light turned green and she had to make do with his right profile again.

"More of your mother," Manfred said. "Fortunately for you."

"I have your nose."

"Well, give it back."

He spared a glance to see how his joke had been received. Bianca rolled her eyes, and then looked down. Manfred directed his gaze at the road ahead.

"What?"

"I miss Mama. I want her back."

Even after she sold you to a pervert, Manfred thought with an inward sigh. He reached out and found his daughter's hand, engulfed it with his own and held on gently.

"Your mother was never a happy person. Sometimes there were moments when she thought she was, but they never lasted."

"Why wasn't Mama happy? She was beautiful."

Manfred furrowed his brow and tried to think of a way to explain. Ulrike was a subject to which he had given much thought during his years of confinement. He'd come to his own conclusions about her, but he hadn't considered how to convey them to Bianca.

He thought a moment longer and then released her hand and held up his thumb and index finger an inch apart.

"Your mother thought she was this close to being beautiful. She thought she was this close to being a great athlete. At times, she thought she was this close to being rich and important. But no matter what she did, or how hard she tried, or what successes she had, her goals always seemed to be this far away. Do you know why she felt that way?"

"No."

Manfred took Bianca's hand again.

"Because she was right. The things we tell ourselves we want never look quite the way we expect when we finally get them." Manfred pulled over to the side of the street and parked. He turned to face his daughter. "When you were little, growing up with your mother while I was in prison, did you ever wish you had a father?"

"I thought the Bear was my father."

Manfred nodded, sadly.

"But when I learned he wasn't, I wished I had one."

Relieved, Manfred again held up his thumb and finger an inch apart.

"Am I this close to looking like what you wanted your father to be?"

Bianca shook her head. She held her hands out at arms' length.

Then she smiled, and Manfred smiled back.

"I'm not so bad, am I?"

Bianca shook her head.

"Maybe you've even come to love me, just a little?"

Bianca nodded.

"*Liebchin*, this is what we all must learn. Take happiness where you find it, not where you expect it to be." He held up his thumb and forefinger once more. "That is why your mother could never get closer than this."

Bianca's face gathered around a thoughtful expression.

"Have you found happiness with..." Bianca almost said *Der Hexe* just to be mean, but her father's face was so kind and gentle she couldn't do it. "Have you found happiness with Robin?"

Manfred nodded.

"Do you think she is happy with you, too?"

"I hope so."

"She is not my mama."

"No."

"It is hard for me, *Vati*."

Manfred nodded. "I will tell you something else."

"What?"

"We are strong, you and me. There is nothing we can't face."

"Really? Nothing?"

"Nothing at all," Manfred said.

"I want you out," Robin said.

She'd been waiting at the door to Manfred and Bianca's apartment when they returned. Her mouth was compressed to a surgical incision and her eyes were chips of indigo ice.

"*Bitte,*" Manfred said, not wanting to believe his ears.

"She said she wants us out," Bianca supplied.

Robin flicked a glance at the kid before returning her attention to Manfred.

"You've been prying into my personal life. That's intolerable. You've involved my family, which is unforgivable. You can stay the night, but I want both of you out in the morning."

Bianca looked up at the adults, expecting her father to laugh off the demand. After all, he'd just told her how strong they were. They could face anything. Surely, this would be no problem ... but Bianca saw the pain in her father's eyes. It was not weakness; she didn't know just what the word was, but she could tell he was going to give in if she didn't do something soon. He was going to let this woman send them away.

She knew this would hurt her father to his heart.

So Bianca plucked the house-keys Manfred held loosely in his hand and turned a defiant face up to Robin.

"We are not leaving!" Bianca said, and stamped her foot for emphasis.

With that she opened the door to her apartment and went inside.

This was the last thing Robin had expected. From what Nancy had told her, she'd thought the kid would be jumping for joy. Okay, so she didn't know exactly what was going on here, but that didn't change her intentions. Not in the slightest.

"You are leaving," Robin said. "In the morning."

Manfred nodded.

"I will have Bianca ready. We will be out first thing."

"The hell you will!"

Neither of them had heard Nancy arrive. Not having told Robin about Phil Leeds earlier had hung like a cobweb on Nancy's frontal lobe. She'd never know peace until it was swept away. So she'd come back to tell Robin whether she wanted to hear it or not. And instead she'd found these two huge idiots about to ruin their best chance for happiness.

Well, Nancy Cassidy would not have it!

"Stay out of this Nancy," Robin said grimly. "It's none of your business."

"We are not going to discuss the matter in your hallway," Nancy replied.

"We're not going to discuss it at all. The matter is settled."

The two sisters glared at each other. Neither blinked.

Manfred didn't know whether to say something or withdraw like a mouse while the two cats faced off. But he found himself unable to retreat; it simply wasn't in his nature. Even so, he kept his mouth shut.

Nancy finally broke the silence, speaking in a whisper filigreed with iron.

"Robin, you're going to invite Manfred and me up to your apartment. You're going to listen to what I have to say to you. You're going to do this ... or I am going to knock your block off."

Robin smirked at her older, smaller sister.

"You and who else?"

She turned quickly to Manfred.

"You stay out of this."

Manfred held his hands up. He was a neutral observer.

"I don't need any help," Nancy said, drawing Robin's attention. "You remember the last time we got into it?"

Robin's cockiness dissolved faster than spring snow as the childhood memory came back to her in a rush. She'd been twelve and Nancy fifteen when Robin had gone uninvited into Nancy's room and helped herself to her sister's makeup and perfume. When Nancy had instructed her not do it again without permission, Robin had boldly proclaimed that since Mom and Dad had paid for all of Nancy's stuff she had as much right to it as Nancy. Robin still couldn't recall how she'd wound up on the floor with

Nancy sitting atop her — especially since their size difference then had been almost as great as it was now — but she could clearly remember how much it hurt when Nancy's hard little fists started tattooing her head like it was a speed bag.

Robin didn't think Nancy could still do that — but she wasn't about to take the chance. Not with Manfred watching. She'd die of embarrassment, if not physical punishment.

And it'd be that much harder tossing Manfred out if he had to pull Nancy off her.

Robin ground her teeth and led them upstairs to her apartment.

"Sit," Nancy said.

Like a pair of slow-to-heel hounds, Robin and Manfred circled each other and found their respective seats, Robin taking an easy chair, Manfred occupying most of a love seat.

Nancy stood between them with her hands on her hips and zero tolerance for any more of this foolishness.

She started with her sister.

"Robin, you've been beating yourself up for twenty years. That's long enough."

"It's my business," Robin said through clenched teeth, "nobody else's."

Nancy shook her head.

"That's where you're wrong. What you did affected everybody in our family. It hurt you the most, but it basically cost Mom and Dad their marriage for the last two decades, and it's meant I have had to see my parents one at a time for the same twenty years. My kids have had to pick which grandparent they want to see any given holiday, too. So don't you dare tell me it's nobody's business but yours."

Manfred squirmed as he witnessed this barrage of dirty laundry being aired.

Nancy wasn't about to cut him any slack either.

"Sit still. You were the one who had the bright idea of bringing everything out in the open, and you were right. So don't act like you've got ants in your pants all of a sudden."

"Maybe he just doesn't feel like it's his place to hear all our family problems. Maybe he's thought better about what he started," Robin said.

Nancy gave the notion a moment's honest consideration. She looked at Manfred.

"Is that right? You're having second thoughts, and I'm standing here making a jackass out of myself for no reason? A little embarrassment is enough to scare you away?"

The gauntlet had been flung.

Manfred drew himself up. He squared his massive shoulders and expanded his enormous chest. The great mason-block that was his head moved a millimeter to either side of the centerline of his flinty stare. He was not going anywhere. He was Gibraltar.

"Okay, then," Nancy said "That's one thing settled."

"Nothing is settled," Robin objected. "This is my life and you can't stage-manage it."

Nancy looked back at her sister.

"You think you're the only one who's ever done something stupid, who's ever had to endure a tragedy?"

"Tell me what you've endured," Robin said.

"Okay," Nancy replied, "okay, I will. This is something I should have told you a long time ago."

She sat down next to Manfred, annoying Robin that she could fit so neatly in such a small space. Nancy looked directly at her sister.

"Only I have to be real careful what I say here and how I say it. I don't want to drag out any more family skeletons you'd rather leave in the closet."

Robin felt a shiver of fear pass through her. Even though she planned to permanently remove Manfred from her life, she didn't want him to leave with the knowledge of what she'd done. She didn't want his last memory of her to be a shameful one.

"Don't say anything," Robin said.

"Oh, no, I have to say it now. I want to say it now."

Robin waited anxiously while Nancy considered her words.

After a moment, she said, "Maybe it's this simple. You know how Dad always blamed himself for not looking out for you better?"

"Yes, and I've told him a million times that's crazy. He couldn't have done anything, he didn't know what was going on."

"But I did," Nancy said.

Robin looked as if she'd been pole-axed.

"What?" she whispered.

"Not all of it, of course. But I found out Jeri was pregnant before you did, and I knew who the father was."

"How?" Robin asked. "How could you know?"

"Charlie and I went to a drive-in one Saturday night, and when I went to the ladies room I found Jeri there crying. I made her tell me what was wrong."

"Why didn't you tell me?" Robin asked, anger starting to build on her face.

"I should have ... I would have ... except Jeri begged me not to. She said she was going to have an abortion."

"Oh, my God," Robin said.

Nancy smiled sadly and nodded her head.

"Yeah, that's been my dirty little secret all these years. I knew. Maybe in time to have helped you. And you know how I hate secrets. Keeping that one just about drove me crazy more times than I can tell you. I think keeping that secret was what made me, maybe, just a touch driven all of my adult life. I want things out in the open and perfect so I can see them and control them. So *nobody* will get hurt."

Nancy opened her arms, inviting understanding if not an actual embrace.

"I'm sorry, Robin," she said. "I can't tell you how sorry I am."

Robin didn't seem inclined to understand or forgive; forget about a hug.

Nancy let her arms fall and got to her feet.

She said, "But, now, I am who I am. A hard-ass, unyielding

perfectionist. So I'm going to put it to you straight. This man," Nancy said, glancing at Manfred, "is someone who can make you happy. He's strong and good and kind. He was willing to cross an ocean to take on the bastard who'd frightened his daughter. With the same courage and generosity, he's been willing to dig up and help you confront the prick who has made you miserable all these years. And, Robin..." Nancy had to draw a deep breath for what came next. "Robin, you say goodbye to him, you say goodbye to me, too."

Robin looked at them, first Nancy and then Manfred, lines of mulish determination still etched in her face, but with tears in her eyes, too. But before she could say anything, before she could decide which way to cast her fate, the phone rang. She took the easy way out and went to the kitchen to answer it. Unfortunately, the call gave her no refuge from personal upheaval.

"Mom?" Robin said. Then she listened, and her face grew ashen.

"What? What is it?" Nancy asked.

Robin wailed, "Oh, God. We'll be right there."

"Tell me," Nancy demanded as Robin hung up.

"Dad's in the hospital," Robin said still reeling from what she'd heard. "He's had another heart attack."

Now, the two sisters fell into each other's arms. But only for a second. Then Manfred took each of them in one hand and led them toward the door.

"I will drive," he said. "You will give me directions, please."

CHAPTER 29

Patti Phinney looked ghastly. Her hair stood on end as if she'd been electrocuted. Her eyes were red and swollen. Her mouth was a puffy, twisted wound.

She embraced both of her daughters the moment they entered the waiting room.

Manfred stood three steps back, Bianca sheltering, silent and trembling under his right arm.

The little girl looked up at her father and whispered nervously in German, "Will God take Herr Phinney from them now?"

Manfred replied softly in the same tongue, "I don't know."

But he understood Bianca's fear perfectly. If Robin's father could be taken, why not hers? "Would you like to say a prayer for Dan?" Manfred asked.

Bianca nodded, tears falling from her eyes.

Manfred stopped a passing orderly and asked if the hospital had a chapel. He was given directions. Manfred caught Robin's eye. He steepled his hands to indicate their intention and led his daughter away.

Patti Phinney began to sob as Robin and Nancy got her seated.

"Mom," Nancy asked, "what happened?"

Patti took the tissue Robin gave her, blotted her eyes and blew her nose.

"Your f-father and Monsignor Wrightman... "

It took several minutes before Patti Phinney could compose herself sufficiently to tell the story. Nancy took one of her hands and, after a second's hesitation, Robin grasped the other.

"After Manfred picked up Bianca, I made a bite to eat for your father," Patti began. "He promised me he'd eat it even though he said he didn't have much of an appetite. I asked him if he wanted me to cancel my dinner plans with the monsignor, but he said no. Then he joked that maybe I should bring Monsignor Wrightman by after dinner in case he needed the last rites."

Patti slipped her hand out of Robin's and covered her face for a moment. She choked off another round of sobbing, and then she took Robin's hand again and squeezed it gently.

"We did stop by. I joked with the monsignor that maybe this was the time I could finally get Dan to convert."

Patti and Monsignor Wrightman had entered the house. Dan Phinney hadn't touched the light dinner his ex-wife had prepared. He was lying on the sofa watching television and received them both with good humor. They were talking for a few minutes when Dan suddenly clutched his chest, looked at Patti, and then his eyes rolled back in his head.

The monsignor moved quickly to Dan's side, felt for a pulse and when he didn't find one told Patti to call 911. Then he began to administer CPR. In between breathing for Dan, while he compressed Dan's chest, the monsignor prayed for the repose of Dan's soul.

The emergency crew arrived and rushed Dan and Patti off to the hospital. Dan was resuscitated en route and was alive when they reached the hospital. He was taken directly into surgery. Monsignor Wrightman arrived at the hospital in his car minutes later. He was trying to comfort Patti when he started having chest pains. He'd been rushed off for tests. Patti couldn't believe all of this was happening. She didn't know what to do.

An hour had passed before she thought to call her daughters.

And now they were all here together.

After all these years.

Each of them hoping desperately that the man they all loved would live.

Bianca lay asleep on Manfred's shoulder as he sat in the front pew of the chapel. They were the only ones left in the room. The eight-year-old child nestled against the great mass of her father, seeming no bigger than an infant. Manfred stared through dim light of electric candles to the altar and the lank figure nailed to the cross wearing his crown of thorns. He was the ultimate survivor, Manfred thought. His humanity, suffering and resurrection were what gave Christianity all of its power.

The lesson was compelling: Believe in me and even death shall have no hold on you.

Dying wouldn't be the end, it would be a doorway.

How could anyone do better than that?

Manfred asked himself if Dan Phinney was on the other side of that threshold right now.

He felt Bianca's heartbeat against his chest and wondered if his faith would hold when the time came for him to leave her.

He felt a soft tap on his arm and turned to see Robin.

"Dad's out of surgery," she said quietly. "He's stable."

"Good."

"They say the first 24 hours are the most critical period. "

"We will stay."

Robin shook her head. "There's no point. He's being moved to the cardiac care unit. Nobody will be allowed to see him until tomorrow, and we'll be called if we're needed. Nancy's taking my mother home." Robin looked at Bianca asleep on her father's shoulder, and thought once again how angelic she could look.

"Are we still to go?" Manfred asked.

Robin knew what he meant.

She said, "When we get home I'll tell you a story. After you hear it, you can decide if you want to stay."

CHAPTER 30

They talked in the basement, in Manfred's apartment, with Bianca tucked snugly away in her bed. They sat in the kitchen. Manfred served coffee since neither of them expected any sleep that night, and when Robin didn't object he began to bake strudel. They could eat what they liked, Manfred said, and he would take the rest to Mimi when the deli opened.

They passed the first hour talking about Dan and encouraging each other that he would be fine, and when she finally was ready Robin got down to it.

She looked at Manfred and asked, "What did Nancy tell you?"

Manfred stopped stretching the dough for the strudel and sat down. He told her what he knew. A man named Phil Leeds had hurt her badly.

Robin shook her head.

"I hurt myself. I used to blame Phil, but it was my doing. Nancy didn't go into detail about what happened?"

Manfred shook his head.

"But she did give me Jeri Whitman's name. I saw her today."

Robin's jaw sagged.

"You saw Jeri?"

"Yes." Manfred repeated the only detail of the visit he thought was important at the moment. "She said to tell you she was sorry."

Robin shook her head.

"Was Phil still with her?"

"No, not for a long time."

Robin hesitated for a moment, then asked, "Was there a child … no, the baby would have to be a young adult by now. Was there a young man or woman living with Jeri, someone about twenty years old?"

Manfred said no. "An infant, and I saw pictures of two other children. One looked to be about Bianca's age, one a bit older."

A look of rue crossed Robin's face and her eyes lost focus.

"She was my best friend. We swore we'd never lose touch with each other, buddies to the end, and now I don't know the first thing about her."

Robin cleared her throat and looked at Manfred.

"Phil Leeds was Jeri's boyfriend. Only I didn't know that. I thought he was just the guy she worked for, the manager of a donut shop. Jeri went to work there after we graduated from high school. I went to college."

For a moment Robin was silent as she had trouble giving voice to her story.

Manfred said, "I am no one to judge you. You do not have to tell me this if you don't want to. My only thought was … when something bothers me I must confront it. I know no other way. But perhaps my way is not your way."

"No, you're right," Robin said. "You're right and Nancy's right — and I don't want to lose either of you."

She bit her lip and then continued.

"I used to go to the donut shop to meet Jeri when she got off of work. She had a car and she had a paycheck and we'd to go out to eat or to a movie, and more often than not she'd pay. Everything was fine until one day she told me that Phil wanted to take me out, and would I do her a favor and go out with him? Well, that was something that never would have occurred to me on my own. I mean, I'd seen Phil and I knew he wasn't my type." Robin laughed.

"And I didn't even know what my type was.

"But Jeri kept harping at me, go out with him, go out with him one time, just one time. So I decided to hold my nose and do it — and Phil surprised me. He was polite and courteous. He dressed nicely and he poked fun at himself instead of others. He had a pretty nice car for a guy in his early twenties, and he brought me flowers. Sounds perfectly lovely, doesn't he?"

Manfred hated him already.

"Well, one date turned into a lot of dates. The only thing I thought was funny at the time was he kept making excuses not to come into my house and meet my family. But that didn't bother me too much because pretty soon I was sure we were going to be married and then, of course, he'd have to meet everyone. In fact, Phil was the one who started to talk about getting married after the fourth or fifth time we went out. Just little teasing jokes at first, but then the discussions turned fairly serious."

"He wanted sex," Manfred said bluntly.

"No, I wanted sex. I was the one. See, Phil didn't touch me for quite a while. I mean, he'd give me a kiss when he dropped me off after a date, but he never tried to paw me. At first, I thought that he was being gentlemanly, that he had great manners. Then I started to wonder if it was me, I didn't turn him on. But he still kept buying me romantic gifts and talking about getting married, so I had a hard time figuring it out.

"Then one night he invited me to his apartment, and I couldn't believe the place. Most of my friends still lived with their parents. And the ones who did have their own apartments had hand-me-down furniture and chipped dishes. But Phil's place looked like a small corner of the Playboy Mansion. You know, leather sofas, chrome and glass coffee table, deep carpeting, framed posters, fantastic stereo system, recessed lighting, for God's sake. I was bowled over. My parents' house wasn't that nice. And Phil said this was just the beginning for us."

"The donut business must have been very good to him," Manfred said dryly.

"Yeah," Robin snorted.

She was about to continue when Bianca cried out softly in her sleep.

"One moment, please," Manfred said, and went off to investigate.

Robin sipped her coffee, not begrudging the interruption, but envying Manfred his opportunity to be a good dad. It was nearly enough to make her weep.

She was under control when he returned a moment later.

"I am sorry," he said. "You were saying."

"That was the night we first had sex. I had no intention of leaving that fantastic apartment until we did. I'd been promised a future and I wanted a down payment on it."

"Of course, that was just what he'd intended."

Robin gave Manfred a baleful look.

"Where were you when I needed you?"

"Striving to build Socialism, I believe."

"Yeah, so you had your problems, too."

Manfred nodded.

"The next month was wonderful. At the time, I couldn't imagine life being any better. I had a wonderful boyfriend. He had a wonderful apartment. And we had wonderful sex there every chance we got. Phil told me that he was just the manager of one donut shop now, but he was learning the business, he had ideas how to improve on it and someday soon he was going to open his own chain of shops and we'd be rich."

Robin seemed to sink under the weight of the old false promises. Then she looked at Manfred, as imposing as Everest, and she drew strength from him.

She went on, "It never occurred to me to think about birth control. So like any dumb bunny I got knocked up. At first, it scared the hell out of me. I didn't tell anyone. I didn't know what I was going to do. Then a great feeling of peace came over me. Why was I worrying? I had a boyfriend who wanted to marry me. He had a good job and great future. We'd have a terrific place to live ...

and I was head-over-heels in love with the baby I was carrying. So when I was two months gone I told Phil."

"He was not pleased," Manfred said knowingly.

"He was terrified. He was livid. He almost foamed at the mouth. The sweet, gentle guy I knew had disappeared and he was replaced by an absolute madman." Robin licked her lips and looked away from Manfred. "For just one moment I was absolutely panic-stricken that he was going to beat me up and cause a miscarriage."

"Did he?" Manfred asked grimly.

Robin looked back at him. She could clearly see that Manfred was angry, very angry, that he would be perfectly willing to visit a terrible retribution upon a man he'd never met for something that had happened twenty years ago.

"No. It was like someone flipped a switch in his head. All the anger, the ranting and raving, the stomping around the room stopped in a flash. He hugged me. He held me. He took me to bed and we made love.

"That was the first time I stayed the whole night with him. In the morning he apologized and said he'd been so upset because he didn't want to jeopardize the plans he had for us. Having a baby would be expensive, it could ruin everything. He just wanted me to think about that. Then he left me there and went off to work."

"And you thought you could make him change his mind."

Robin nodded absently.

"He kept making love to me."

"He kept using you." Knowing the sooner he grew bored, Manfred thought, the better for him.

"He kept talking about our future."

"He kept lying."

"I was sure he'd come to love the baby as much as I did."

"He was incapable of love."

"He'd have to marry me soon because I'd start showing."

"He'd have to make his escape before it was too late."

In a voice devoid of all emotion and inflection, Robin said, "I was almost four months pregnant, I'd been feeling my baby move inside me for weeks, when Phil gave me the ultimatum. Keep the baby or keep him. I couldn't have both. If I chose him, he'd pay for the abortion and he promised we'd have all the kids I wanted when the time was right."

Robin shook her head gravely, still not believing the decision she'd made.

"I won't judge what any other woman does with her life, but I wanted my baby. I loved it. The idea that I could end my baby's life was more horrible than I could imagine. I wanted to ask my parents for help, I wanted to ask Nancy. But how could I when I'd kept everything secret from them? I was too ashamed to go to the people who meant the most to me.

"The people who should have meant the most. But right then I couldn't get past the thought that Phil was going to leave me. He couldn't do that. He couldn't. We loved each other. He was my baby's father. We had to be together. We just had to — but he kept hammering me. 'Make the choice, me or the kid. Me or the kid, make the choice. Choose goddamnit!'"

Tears fell from Robin's eyes.

"I let him take me to an abortion clinic, and he was there with me, and he paid the fee ... and that was the last time I saw him. You talked to Jeri, so you can probably guess the rest."

"He got her pregnant, too," Manfred said.

Robin nodded.

"He was seeing her the whole time he was seeing you."

Robin nodded.

"And he chose her over you."

"Couldn't very well support two families on a donut-shop salary, could he? Not when he had to steal from his employer to support his lifestyle."

"How did he make your friend ask you to go out with him?"

"She was helping him steal. He blackmailed her; she told me the last time I ever talked to her. 'Get me a date with Robin,' he said, 'or I lay the whole thing off on you.' But, at the time, Jeri was very angry with me. She thought the whole thing had been my fault. After all, she'd told me to go out with Phil just one time."

"Then when she became pregnant," Manfred said, "she used the blackmail threat against him. 'Marry me or we'll see who the police believe.'"

Robin nodded once more. Her eyes were glazed with a pain that wouldn't go away.

"So for people like them I killed the baby I loved so much ... and when I finally told my parents I wrecked their marriage because my dad supported me and my mom condemned me. And me, hypocrite that I am, I took my dad's support and accepted my mom's estrangement, but I condemned myself, too."

Drained, Robin wiped the tears away and looked at Manfred.

"So now you know. You still want to stick around?"

"*Ja,*" he said.

Robin called the hospital to ask about her father and Manfred looked in on Bianca again. Both of their loved ones were resting quietly. Robin and Manfred moved to the living room and sat opposite each other. The baking strudel filled the apartment with its heavenly aroma. After a lengthy, contemplative silence, Manfred spoke.

He asked, "Do you have any religion?"

Robin looked at him bleakly.

"I believe in God. For quite a while, I didn't, but then I realized I was making a mistake. I needed God ... if I was going to have someone to punish me after I died."

"I was raised to be an atheist," Manfred said. "That was the official doctrine of any good East German. For most of my life I accepted without question that religion was just a pack of superstitions. That changed in prison. In my second year, I came to ask myself how I knew that I would ever be free again, how I knew that one day I would see my daughter again. And I did know both these things. But how? The only answer I could come up with was faith."

"In yourself?"

He nodded.

"At first. I knew I was strong, stronger than most. But I was not stupid. I knew my physical strength was nothing compared to the bars and walls and guns that confined me. And my sentence was indeterminate; that was part of my punishment. The state could have held me until I died and then kept my bones until they turned to dust. So, faith strictly in myself would have been nothing more than egomania. But I knew I was not mad, either. That meant that, without realizing it at first, I had to believe in some force far greater than any man or woman. Something that transcends the might of nations."

"You found God in a Communist prison?"

"Brother Damian told me you find God when you need Him most. Wherever you are. I concluded that atheism was just another lie that I'd been fed. Because I knew I would be free, I knew I would see my daughter again ... and in due time my faith was rewarded."

"There's no bringing my baby back," Robin said. "No matter how much faith I have."

"No, not here. But if you can believe in punishment after death, why not redemption? Why not reunion?"

The first shading of pre-dawn gray crept in through the ground-level window.

Manfred continued, "If you think God cannot forgive you, why not ask Him? Maybe you are the only one who cannot forgive you."

Robin stared at Manfred a moment and then got up.

"I think I'd like to spend a little time alone now. I'm going up to my park."

Robin sat on a park bench, among her beloved plantings, in the one place that she'd found solace over the years. But now there was no comfort, only fear. Fear that she would be a fool to think that even God could forgive her for what she had done. Fear that she might be struck down for just having the effrontery to ask for forgiveness. But her greatest fear of all was that if she didn't ask, she would be forfeiting the last opportunity she'd ever have to know peace.

Still, she couldn't bring herself to ask for outright forgiveness. Instead, she asked only for a sign that someday she might be shown mercy.

An hour later, because there was nothing else to do, Robin decided to go to work. Because he had the strudel to deliver, Manfred drove her. Because there was nobody else to watch her, Bianca came along, too.

CHAPTER 31

Tone Morello got the goods on Robin early that same morning.

He received a report from Aubrey Tannis that was sent by Special Messenger, a courier service that specialized in making its deliveries regardless of circumstances. In Tone's case, the damn guy had managed to slip past his building's doorman and bang on Tone's door at 5:55 a.m. This was the earliest Tone had to drag himself out of bed since he'd been an altar boy. Half asleep, holding the handgun he kept in his nightstand, he stumbled to the door fantasizing about the coverage he'd get for killing a crazed home-invader.

It never occurred to him that home-invaders rarely knock, and he might have found himself up on a manslaughter charge if the courier hadn't casually disarmed him, smacked him across the kisser, and told him to sign on line fourteen. Tone scratched out his signature. With that accomplished, he was given his gumshoe's report and had his handgun returned, minus its ammunition.

Now, Tone was awake enough to think about filing criminal charges against — and suing — the SOB who'd clipped him. But as soon as he sat down with the report he forgot about all that and focused on what lay before him.

Tannis had left him a note.

The gumshoe had written: *This concludes our business, now and forever.*

Amen, Tone thought. As if he cared. Just so long as the dirt was there. He opened the report and quickly read the low-down on his nemesis, Round Robin Phinney.

It was essentially the same story that Robin had told Manfred, albeit from Jeri Whitman's point of view, which omitted her own penchant for theft and made Robin look like she'd tried to steal her best friend's boyfriend, for which she had paid a lamentably high price.

So now Tone knew why Robin hated men.

She'd been screwed by one, both literally and figuratively.

It was too bad about the kid and all, but who could she blame but herself? A good Catholic, Tone didn't hold with abortion. That's why he was very demanding that all his ladies always show him their birth control pills or pop in their bush-beanies before any action got underway. Of course, the Pope forbade the use of contraceptives, too, but, hey, you could take that church stuff only so far.

The way Tone saw it, if Robin wanted to beat herself up for what she did, fine. If she wanted to take out her gripe on the world at large, that was also okay. But when she came after him, who'd never touched her and never would, well, then she had to expect payback.

And Tone was sure he had enough here to do just that.

The report concluded with a name and a phone number.

That little creep Tannis knew how to follow through, Tone thought, at least you could say that for him.

Tone made the call.

"Yeah," he said, "is this Phil Leeds?"

Tone listened a minute.

"Hey, I'm awake, you could be awake — if you want to make a quick hundred bucks."

Tone smiled.

"That's better. Now, listen. My name's Tone Morello ... Yeah, the sports guy. What do I want? I want you to have breakfast with me."

In an hour, he told Leeds.

At Screaming Mimi's.

Iggy Gross was running on adrenaline so pure that if he could have bottled it nobody would ever bother with cocaine or speed. It had kept him up all night rehearsing in front of a mirror. He knew that nothing less than the future of his career was on the line. He had to get this Phinney broad or he was finished.

The buzz had gone coast to coast. Word was — in every market where his show was syndicated — that he was wussing out, backing down and hiding from some fat chick who sliced cold cuts for a living. The pressure on him to hit back, do it fast, and generally nuke this broad had been excruciating.

So he'd quickly gathered an all-star team of the baddest, nastiest, funniest comedy writers on earth and had them write material for him. Razor sharp put-downs. Crushing slams. Acid-in-your-eyes insults. Then ... then he had them insult him. And when one did, he'd turn to another for a comeback. All this material was recorded and transcribed and Iggy sat down and feverishly committed all the permutations of vituperation to memory.

He practiced, practiced, practiced.

Rehearsed until he would have dropped, had it not been for the million volts of electricity crackling inside him.

Now, he was ready.

And he was going in alone.

He would not make that dumbass Tone Morello's mistake.

Nobody important would be there watching him or recording him if he bombed.

But Iggy felt good.

He felt mean.

He had a stainless steel hard-on.

He slammed out of his penthouse apartment and he had so much juice in him he ran down 30 flights of stairs to the parking garage.

And just in case everything went right ... Iggy had a micro-recorder hidden on him.

David Solomonovich's mentor-session at the university was canceled that morning. The grad student he was tutoring in particle physics couldn't make it; the guy had blown out his knee while cross-country skiing in Grant Park. David would have reamed his twenty-three-year-old protégé if he'd hurt himself doing something dumb like alpine skiing. But cross-country had a benefit-to-risk ratio that even David had to concede was compelling, assuming you didn't catch your ski in a bicycle tire some cretin had abandoned under the snow.

Not one to be at loose ends, he decided to go into his father's lab, where he'd either continue his work on achieving super-conductivity at room temperature — or continue to illustrate what was rapidly becoming a manuscript-length series of erotic drawings inspired by Bianca's tales of bordello bacchanalia.

David realized, of course, that it was perfectly normal for a male his age, caught in that first tsunami of testosterone, to fantasize grandly about women and all their mysteries, and he was doing his usual thorough, cohesive and compelling job of it. He had no doubt that with a little further organization and the addition of a narrative thread he could market his drawings as a book.

He was also sure that he would not. They would never see the light of day. Not while his parents were still alive. Well, maybe when he was older and he found just the right girlfriend he would show them to her. The thought of acting out the scenes he'd drawn made his heart race.

Which was just the problem.

He was letting his adolescent hormones distract him from serious work.

He knew just the person, though, to give him a cold, bracing dose of reality.

Even though he'd have to put up with the hurly-burly of the breakfast crowd, David headed off to Mimi's to see Robin.

CHAPTER 32

"Sweetheart," Mimi asked, "should you even be here?"

Robin had just told Mimi about her father. The deli had yet to open.

"It's where I want to be."

Mimi nodded and squeezed Robin's hands.

"You let me know just as soon as it's okay to visit your father. Stanley and I will be right over to see him. Meanwhile, I'll keep an eye on things today. Make sure it's nice and quiet around here for you. As much as possible, anyway."

Mimi looked over to Manfred sitting at a table with Bianca.

"I want you to keep an eye on Robin."

"I will," he said.

Bianca looked up from the piece of her father's strudel she was working on.

"Me, too."

"You, you munchkin," Mimi said, "sitting there eating all the strudel your daddy made for me, I ought to put you to work."

Bianca had already been told that because of Herr Phinney's illness she would not be working with Nancy today.

So she told Mimi, "I could use a new job."

Everybody laughed.

"I am serious," Bianca said, putting on a very serious face.

Mimi looked at Manfred and raised an eyebrow.

"I could use some help with her today. I have classes later."

Robin said, "Let her work behind the counter. She'll be safe back there with me."

"Would you like that, Bianca?" Mimi asked.

Bianca nodded decisively.

Then she confided to Robin, "I like to watch the way you *herunterputzen* everyone."

"Yeah, I'm good at that," Robin said, knowing just what she meant. "How about you serve the strudel?"

Bianca nodded and smiled.

"But no filching anymore."

The smile faded abruptly.

"Very well. But then I shall want more pay."

Robin looked from Manfred to Mimi.

"I think she's going to fit right in around here."

With a gunfighter's gleam in his eye, Iggy Gross strode through the front door of Screaming Mimi's Deli not ten seconds after it had been opened for business.

There were no other customers present, but Manfred was enjoying a leisurely second cup of coffee before departing for school. He had no idea who Iggy was, but he didn't like the look on his face or the way he marched directly toward Robin. He knew what went on at Mimi's but this was not the time, to his mind, for anyone to be giving Robin grief. He started to rise from his chair. He didn't even get upright before Robin curtly gestured for him to sit back down.

He did, but he didn't like it. He glowered.

Mimi had seen Iggy enter, too, but she'd also seen the by-play between Robin and Manfred, and she knew she wouldn't be allowed to interfere either.

Manny Tavares and Judy Kuykendahl locked on to what they were sure would be an epic encounter. A busboy who spotted Iggy

— and knew just who he was — hissed to the dishwashers in back. They quickly appeared in the doorway from the kitchen, grinning like carrion, sure that one way or another they were about to feast.

Iggy stopped at the counter directly in front of Robin. Man, he was ready. He was jazzed. He was ... not even going to let it bother him that this broad was bigger than him. And what was a kid doing there? Sitting on a stool, just behind and off to one side of the fat broad, sucking a lollipop for God's sake. A lot of Iggy's material was X-rated. If it got around he used that kind of stuff in front of a little kid — a girl no less — it might backfire on him. He started talking about pussy and such, it might get him busted for contributing to the delinquency of a minor or some such crap.

He sure as hell couldn't record what he had to say with a kid present.

He had to think — fast.

The fat broad was staring at him.

Hard.

Had a knife in her hand like she might cut his liver out any minute.

Bianca looked at the man with the darting eyes on the other side of the counter and tried to decide if he more closely resembled a weasel or a rat. It was a tough choice, but she really didn't think that either of those animals could break a sweat on their upper lips as this creature just had. In any case, she didn't like him, and she knew this was one place where she could freely display her disapproval.

Bianca removed the grape Tootsie Roll Pop from her mouth and stuck a purple tongue out at Iggy.

His writers had not prepared Iggy for this, and it showed in his disconcerted look.

Nor was he ready when Robin burst out laughing at him.

She slapped the countertop with her hand, threw back her head and roared. Iggy was finished before he'd gotten his first word out. A surge of volcanic anger turned his face the color of glowing magma.

Suddenly, he forgot all his material, all his preparation, and even the last twenty-six years of his life. He was back in the schoolyard. He was once again the little bug-eyed geek the girls had always laughed at. They hadn't even tried to conceal their ridicule for him; they'd pointed right at him and laughed out loud. Iggy'd never said a word in his own defense back then, but he would now.

"Bitch!" he screamed at Robin.

His feeble invective was blown away by Robin's gale of laughter.

"Whore!" he screamed.

Robin's laughter grew louder, more manic. It had made Bianca nervous at first but now she was swept up in the contagion of it, and she laughed at Iggy, too. And pointed at him.

"Cunt!" Iggy shrieked.

Robin fell silent as suddenly as if she'd been guillotined. Her eyes grew wide, and Bianca's titters trailed off in the wake of a deepening hush. Robin's mouth opened and her jaw began to tremble.

Iggy Gross smiled. This was really rich, he thought. He'd paid big money to some of the top names in the business to give him their best stuff and all he'd needed was a four-letter word that every street monkey in the country knew. Well, he'd didn't care. He'd found this fat broad's weakness and now he'd use it.

He hadn't noticed that all along Robin was looking over his shoulder.

A hand fell heavily on Iggy and spun him around hard enough to give him whiplash.

The hand didn't belong to Manfred, though.

Phil Leeds had just arrived.

"I don't think a lady ought to be talked to like that," Phil told Iggy. "Especially one of my old girlfriends."

Trying to ignore the shooting pain in his neck, Iggy looked at the creep who'd grabbed him. He wasn't any taller than Iggy and he was just as skinny. He had thinning greasy black hair, crooked gray teeth, bloodshot blue eyes and the muscle tone of an overripe banana, all of it stuffed inside of a Salvation Army markdown suit. Iggy could take this guy.

Mimi saw what was coming.

"Hey, hey!" she said. "No fighting allowed, not in here!"

The first knot of the breakfast crowd arrived at that moment, including David, and was riveted by this high and unusual drama — but Mimi's usual centurion from among Chicago's Finest had yet to put in his appearance. She looked to Manfred for help.

But before he could reach his feet, Tone Morello stepped out of the growing cluster of customers and extended his hand to Phil.

"Phil Leeds?" he said, shaking the man's hand with a smile. "You're Phil Leeds, right?"

The sudden appearance of a fellow media-creature, someone who could cause him major public embarrassment, knocked Iggy for a loop. He started to slink away, but Tone let go of Leed's hand and grabbed the shock-jock's arm.

"Where ya goin', Iggy? Stick around. The fun's just starting."

Everybody was watching. The crowd at the door was getting thicker by the second. No way Iggy could slip away now. He'd have to bust through that mob, and that'd look just like what it was, an abject retreat.

Not good at all for his image.

"Yeah, sure, Tone. I'll stick around," Iggy said, now trying to sound nonchalant. "So why don't you tell everyone just what's going on here, anyway?"

"Yeah," added Phil, "I'd like to know myself, and, by the way, where's my money?"

Tone handed him a hundred dollar bill, and that calmed Phil.

Then Tone looked straight at Robin.

"I just felt like playing Cupid, that's all." Tone turned to the growing crowd. "Phil here is Robin's old sweetheart. They were real close once upon a time."

Robin's soul froze. Ant-knee *knew*.

He was standing here with Phil in the place where she worked and he was going to tell the world what she had done. It had taken her twenty years to confide her secret to anyone outside of her family, and now, just hours later, Ant-knee was going to tell the world.

With a gleeful grin on his idiotic face.

And there wasn't a damn thing she could do about it. Except put her knife down.

Because if she didn't she was going to climb right over the counter and slit Ant-knee's throat. Maybe Phil's, too, while she was at it. But she didn't want to do that. Because there were some people here who cared for her, and she wanted to have a life when all this was over.

Robin lay her knife down atop the shelf of the in-your-face space, the blade pointed away from Ant-knee and toward her.

The symbolism of defeat was not lost on Tone.

He gloried in it.

Others were not so ready to yield.

Manfred stayed put, as he'd been directed, but he drew himself up. He narrowed his eyes, squared his jaw and clenched his fists. He caught Robin's eye.

"You are strong," he told her. "Remember how strong you are."

Robin began to cry.

"Don't give in," David pleaded. "Don't let him do this to you. Don't let him win."

Robin began to wail.

"Robin, sweetheart," Mimi called. She held the Heavyweight Champ robe up, urging Robin to win one last fight.

Robin began to shake.

"What, what?" Tone asked with his grin widening. He stepped to the customer side of the in-your-face space. "All I want to do is tell everyone a story of young love ... between Phil here ..." Tone spun the knife to point at Phil, who realized he'd sold out for far too little and was trying to disappear inside his shabby suit. " ... and our own dear Round Robin Phinney."

Tone picked up the knife and pointed the blade at Robin.

"Listen to me," Tone said, "while I tell all of you just how Robin got to be who she is today."

But Tone never got the chance.

A howl — the high, keening shriek of a wildcat — snapped everyone's head around. All eyes locked on the source of that animal outcry. Bianca. The child's face was a feral mask. Her eyes were flat and her teeth were bared.

Now, Manfred rose to his feet.

"Bianca!" he said.

But the child didn't hear her father. She was focused solely on Tone.

"Hey, kid," he said, warily, "take it easy."

Without conscious thought, Tone's hand tightened around the knife handle.

Robin saw this, felt something horrible was about to happen and knew she had to stop it. She couldn't let her damn history be the cause of any more trouble. Her trembling stopped, her legs steadied. She turned toward Bianca.

Who didn't even see her.

The wild-child focused like a death-ray on Tone. She cursed him in German, spittle flying from her mouth. She formed her fingers into claws and gathered her legs under her.

"Bianca, *nein!*" Manfred yelled, bulling people aside.

But he was too late. Bianca leaped at Tone.

Never seeing the knife that would impale her before she reached him.

Never seeing Robin jump in front of her at the last possible second.

Bianca weighed scarcely seventy pounds, but she had leaped with all her might, and with Robin already in motion, the child sent the much larger woman staggering backward.

Impaling her on the knife that Tone held fast in his hand. The blade plunged deeply into Robin's back. Tone looked on in horror. The knife was still in his hand. The blade ran red with Robin's blood.

He had his revenge at last.

CHAPTER 33

Tone released the knife, but otherwise froze.

Everyone around him, however, moved with incredible speed. Already heading in her direction, Manfred vaulted his 300–plus pounds over the counter and caught Robin before she crumpled to the floor. Mimi was on the phone dialing 911 at the same time. She dropped the phone when she saw Stan Prozanski walk through the door. He was quickly turned around.

Stan, Bianca and Mimi piled into the front of the sergeant's patrol unit. Robin, with the knife sticking out of her back, lay across Manfred's legs in the rear. Lights flashing and sirens howling, they headed for nearby Northwestern Memorial Hospital. Stan radioed ahead for help.

Robin was still conscious.

"Mimi," she gasped.

"Yes, sweetie?" Mimi asked, doing her best not to go into hysterics.

"I quit."

"Get it out," Robin growled.

She lay on a table in the emergency room. The ER physician and nurse tried to calm her. Instead of removing the knife, they'd built a dressing around it. A second nurse was putting an IV line into Robin.

"The sedative will help you with the pain," the doctor said. "We've got to do this the right way."

"Get it out, get it out, get it out!" Robin yelled.

"We've called for the trauma team. There's a surgeon on his way right now."

Manfred, Bianca, Mimi and Stan watched, not six feet away. The ER staff had tried to shoo them away, but, clearly, this group would not to be budged. And they were looking increasingly unfriendly.

"Get it out!" Robin shrieked, but this time she seemed to be losing steam.

Manfred caught the physician's wrist. "You will remove the knife or I will."

"Sir, that knife has likely collapsed the lady's right lung. Air and blood are where they don't belong inside her chest cavity. There may be damage to her diaphragm and even her liver. We're trying to — Hey, come back here!"

But Bianca had slipped past the physician and the nurse. Using two hands and one mighty yank, she pulled the knife out of Robin's back. The trauma team, and a crowd of patrons from the deli, arrived just in time to see this.

Knife in hand, Bianca addressed the assembled medical personnel.

"You will fix her! You will fix her *now!*"

And just to let them know she was serious, she repeated herself in German.

"Hurry," Robin added, before she lapsed into unconsciousness.

EPILOGUE

Athens, Summer, 2004

Robin shifted in her seat at Olympic Stadium, trying to find a position that didn't press uncomfortably against the scar on her back.

"Any minute now," Bianca said excitedly as they watched the parade of nations at the Opening Ceremony of the Athens Olympic Games.

Robin nodded, looking at the beautiful young woman sitting in the seat next to her and loving her with all her heart.

Robin had spent nine hours in surgery. Pneumohemothorax and lacerations of the diaphragm and liver were serious business. At one point, she went into shock and her heart stopped. The surgical team was genuinely afraid they were going to lose her. But they didn't.

Later, her survival would be attributed simply to the will to live.

This woman had not yet finished with her life.

The first person Robin saw when she regained consciousness was her father. He sat in a wheelchair next to her bed. As ever, when Robin needed him, he put aside his own troubles and was there for her. Right next to him was her mother. And the sight of them together brought Robin a comfort she thought she'd never know again.

Nancy and Charlie and their boys came.

Mimi and Stan visited daily.

David Solomonovich came and held her hand and kissed her — on the cheek.

Manfred and Bianca became fixtures in the room. A cot was set up for Bianca, and Manfred slept in a chair. The only times they left were when Robin asked for privacy as her doctors attended to her needs.

The last night in the hospital, as Bianca slept, Robin held Manfred's hand and told him simply, "I'm healed."

They both knew what she meant.

Dan and Patti Phinney were remarried by Monsignor Wrightman, whose angina pectoris was being controlled with medication. Robin and Nancy served as co-matrons of honor. Manfred was Dan's best man. Bianca was the ring bearer. Dan and Patti moved to Lahaina, Maui, where Patti got a terrific deal on a darling condo. These days, they watch whales and Hawaiian sunsets and neither of them goes anywhere without the other.

David Solomonovich forsook science for art, which partially explains why room-temperature-superconductivity still hasn't been achieved. The muse that had found its way into David's heart through Bianca's erotic tales refused to yield to any other use of his time. In typical fashion, David had to carry things out as far as he could, and he became not an illustrator or a painter but a sculptor. He quickly gained a reputation for doing the most romantic and classical nudes since Rodin, works of which even his parents were proud. He now works out of both a loft in Chicago and his farm-studio in Galena. There have, of course, been rumors of affairs between the artist and his models, but those who know better understand that David is waiting for a certain young woman to finish medical school at which time her formidable father will allow her to marry.

Tone Morello suffered another career setback that day at Mimi's. His job with the network affiliate disappeared when he was found to be in violation of the public morals clause of his contract. He did beat the rap on the assault with a deadly weapon charge when Robin refused to file a complaint. In due time, Tone regained his place in the scheme of things when he became the sports–scandal reporter for a national tabloid. There was no shortage of material for him to exploit, and he had a flunky who did all of the actual writing. Tone had been scheduled to cover the Athens Games — the Olympics always being a fertile field for sports shenanigans — but the preceding winter while vacationing in the Caribbean he went fishing with a group of Canadian businessmen and fell overboard. His body was never recovered.

Phil Leeds scurried back to the margins of society where he was most comfortable, taking with him that day at Mimi's the wallet he picked from the pocket of the stunned Tone Morello.

For a while, Iggy Gross regained his popularity as a radio loudmouth. He even got a brief bump in his ratings when someone started a rumor — Iggy swore it wasn't him — that what had happened to Robin was an example of what people got if they messed with him. Iggy lost his life when he literally could no longer stomach himself. His digestive system turned on him and refused to absorb any of the food he gave it. Everything he ate slipped right through without providing any nutrition. Some observers felt this was a sure sign that everything Iggy touched turned to shit.

Warner Lisle slipped into the seat next to Robin. She was amazed at how the ex-spy hadn't seemed to age at all. He was still easy to look at, easy to forget, and could still blend into any crowd at will. But Warner's spying days were well behind him. He was a Hollywood special effects legend now. His company was even doing consulting for the laser shows and pyrotechnics being used at the Athens Games.

"Haven't missed anything, have I?" he asked.

Robin smiled and shook her head.

"Any second now," Bianca said, quivering with excitement. "Any second."

"You leave your place in good hands?" he asked Robin.

"The best. Nancy's."

Screaming Mimi's Deli had closed forever the day Robin was stabbed. Mimi never set foot in the place again. She, too, considered herself guilty for what had happened, running a business where people were encouraged to scream at one another. She and Stanley retired to Florida, where he finally made an honest woman of her. She sold her place to Robin as planned, Robin completing the purchase with Manfred's help. The new establishment was reopened as the Continental Cafe, the place with the best baked goods and friendliest service in town. Nancy had changed jobs to manage the cafe's business — and she constantly battled to keep her weight down, having become addicted to Manfred's baking.

Bianca jumped to her feet.

"I see it! I see the flag!"

Robin and Warner rose to their feet, as did the sizable contingent of other Americans in the stadium. Many of them began to chant, "U-S-A, U-S-A..."

The American team stepped proudly from the shadow of the tunnel and into the bright light of the track. At their head, holding the Stars and Stripes, was an enormous man.

The press had been telling his story for days now. Denied the chance to compete for the East German team at the 1984 Los Angeles Olympics because of the Soviet boycott — and his political imprisonment — he now carried the American flag as the honorary team captain, a tribute to the fact that five members of the American weightlifting squad, three wrestlers, a shot–putter, and the power-forward on the basketball team had all been coached by this man in high school.

The crowd roared as Manfred Welk stepped into the stadium.

From the stands, Robin Welk beamed at her husband.

Bianca threw her arms around Robin.

"Oh, Mom," she cried. "I'm so proud, I'm so happy."

Robin nodded as tears ran down her face.

"So am I," she said. " So am I."

ABOUT THE AUTHOR

Joseph Flynn is a Chicagoan, born and raised, currently living in central Illinois with his wife and daughter. He is the author of thirteen novels and a collection of short stories. Flynn has been published by Signet Books, Bantam Books, Variance Publishing and his own imprint, Stray Dog Press, Inc.

You can read a free excerpt of each of his books by visiting: *www.josephflynn.com.*